De.

Retribution

By Michael Patterson and available from
Crescent Books Publishing

Playing at Murder
Deadly Retribution

Deadly Retribution

Michael Patterson

Crescent books
publishing

First published in the United Kingdom in 2012 by
Crescent Books Publishing

ISBN 978-0-9569798-1-0

Produced by
The Choir Press, Gloucester

Acknowledgements

A big 'thank you' to all those friends and family members who provided the support and encouragement for me to continue with my embryonic writing career.

Chapter 1

'Are you looking forward to returning to work tomorrow?' asked Mary, looking directly at Tom. They were sitting at Mary's kitchen table, at her house in Bagshot. They had just returned from their very first holiday, as a couple, and were spending a little more time together before Tom headed back to his own house in Staines.

'Actually, do you know what? I really am,' he replied, before adding, 'I think this must be one of the longest periods I've ever been away from work. I can't remember the last time I took so much time off. Probably back when I was married, just after Paul was born.'

Mary laughed. 'I'm not sure whether I should be pleased about that or not.'

'What do you mean?' asked Tom.

'I'll take it as a compliment that this is one of your longest holidays but I'm also a bit worried that now you can't wait to get back to work. Is that because you've had enough of me?'

'I refuse to answer that as it might incriminate me.' He paused for a while before pulling her towards him and looking into her eyes. 'I think you know the answer to that, Mary Parker.' He kissed her.

'I think I'm going to miss that,' she said, returning his kiss with real passion.

As a Detective Chief Inspector, within the Met Police's West London Region, Tom Stone's professional and personal life had recently taken a dramatic turn for the better. It seemed only like yesterday that his life had been at one of its lowest points.

He had become increasingly depressed at work, even convincing himself that there might be a conspiracy to exclude him from any of the more important operations. He felt that he was being shunted sideways, until the time came when he could be 'persuaded' to take early retirement. He suspected younger, more ambitious colleagues were beginning to patronise him. Worst of all, he felt that colleagues were now starting to pity him.

Deep down he knew that this sense of paranoia, which had taken him into such a downward spiral, seriously eroding his self-esteem, was probably illogical. But despite him knowing this, if anything, these feelings had become even stronger.

Even his health had started to suffer. Although he had never been a good sleeper, during the past few years he had found it even more difficult to get a good night's sleep. He had no problem nodding off whilst watching television. As soon as he went to bed, though, it was a different matter completely and, anyway, he'd got into the habit of waking regularly during the night. This lack of sleep meant he seemed to be continually tired and lacking in any energy.

His doctor was convinced it was all of these factors which had affected his general health, but particularly his stress levels. His blood pressure has risen and he had also developed headaches. Although no one mentioned it to him directly he'd realised himself that, apart from feeling his age, he had suddenly started to look it as well. Although he was still only fifty-three years old he had noticed recently how he had begun to develop a bit of a paunch. It was probably not noticeable to anyone else, but he knew it was there. Of average height he was, by nature, on the slim side and so the extra few pounds he had put on felt, to him at least, like significantly more. Whilst he never subscribed to the theory that today's officers needed to be super fit, he had, nonetheless, always made sure that he was on the positive side when it came to overall fitness levels. But even that had suffered over the past couple of years, in direct proportion to the reduction in his motivation levels.

His hair had started to go grey when he was in his mid-forties but since then had changed again, so now it was more white than grey. Someone had recently mentioned that he looked 'distinguished'. In his experience that was just a polite way of saying old.

His personal life had not helped either. He had been long divorced and, although the marriage had produced a son, it had been many years since he had last seen him. In fact, it quite shocked him to realise that he had only seen Paul once since he and his mum had emigrated to Australia to start a new life with her new partner.

As he had got older, and his career within the Met had stagnated, Tom had started to think more and more about his son and whether or not he should try and make contact with him. But, like most things of late, there were always reasons for simply doing nothing.

He tried to rationalise this on the basis that it wouldn't be fair on Paul. But Paul was now a grown man and, anyway, he suspected that the real reason was that this was a convenient way of not facing up to his own guilt.

But that was then. He still couldn't quite come to terms with how much things had changed during the past few weeks. In a short while he would be fifty-four years old and, under normal circumstances, starting to think about retirement. Not too long ago this had almost obsessed him and, as far as he was concerned, could not come quickly enough. In fact, he'd discussed with his boss, Superintendent Peters, the possibility of retiring early. But that was before a series of events that had changed his personal and professional landscape entirely.

Firstly, he had become involved in a murder inquiry which had been led by another of the Met's Regional Forces. Although, initially, his was only a minor role, it had soon developed faster and further than he could ever have imagined.

It began when he was asked to conduct a routine follow-up interview of the murder victim's ex-wife, who was now living in the West London area. He was under no illusions that he'd only been asked to do this because most of the other senior officers, within West London, were involved at the time in *Operation Torch*. This was a major investigation into one of London's largest and most notorious drug gangs; an operation from which he had been conspicuously excluded.

Of course there was no way of knowing then that this would ultimately lead to him to become deeply involved in one of the UK's most sensational and high-profile multiple murder inquiries. Then there was *Operation Torch* itself. It had proved to be such a complete disaster that the head of the gang, Tommy Fuller, was now almost untouchable and the lead officers involved in the operation were seriously compromised. The reality was that Fuller felt so confident in his position that he had even instigated legal proceedings against the West London force, claiming, amongst other things, continual harassment. To really rub salt into their wounds he, or at least his lawyers, had lodged a complaint claiming that police activities had infringed his human rights!

What strengthened his case was the volume of video evidence Fuller's team had at their disposal. Most of it had been taken at the time of the failed police operation, and clearly showed, at best, very robust policing. Ironically, as it turned out, it had been Tom's good fortune that he had been excluded from this investigation.

On the other hand, perhaps if he had been involved then some of the fundamental mistakes that had been made would not have happened. He would never know. What he did know, however, was that, after the *Operation Torch* fiasco, he had been discreetly approached by his immediate senior officer, Superintendent Peters, and asked to review all of the case files and report back with recommendations as to any procedural or operational changes.

This had then taken a more sinister turn as he looked deeper and deeper into the case. He had become increasingly convinced that the operation had not failed simply due to incompetence or poor leadership – although that had undoubtedly contributed. No, the more shocking conclusion, to which he kept coming back, was that the operation itself had been seriously compromised right from the outset.

He'd reviewed all of the information and then gone back and repeated the process again and again, each time from a different angle. Every time, though, he was left with only one logical conclusion. There was a mole, or moles, working within the West London Regional Force, who was systematically passing operational information to Fuller.

Tom was acutely aware that this was probably the most serious accusation that a serving police officer could make and, if wrong, was definitely a career-ending mistake. He had thought long and hard about how he should voice these concerns and harder still as to whom he should voice them.

In such situations it was probably wise to suspect everyone but he'd decided, ultimately, he would have to trust his own judgement and so had raised his concerns with Superintendent

Peters. He was due to meet Peters tomorrow, on his return to work, to discuss them in more detail.

Then there was Mary. The last couple of months, since they had first met, had probably been the happiest time of his life – in some ways even better than when he had been first married.

He had met Mary when they had been matched via the 'You're Never Too Late For Love' dating agency. Even now he still couldn't quite believe he had actually taken the plunge and signed on. Looking back it seemed so out of character. But it had proved to be the best £200 he had ever spent.

Not that it had started very auspiciously. Far from it. His first date, with Pauline, was such a disaster he'd tried, unsuccessfully, to get his money back from the agency. In his opinion, largely based upon his professional experience, Pauline was borderline neurotic. Despite the fact that his own personal profile had clearly mentioned that he was a current police officer, she still appeared to be genuinely shocked when he mentioned this to her. After that it was almost as though she couldn't wait to get away from him quickly enough. This suited him though, as it was crystal clear to him that they were totally incompatible. As far as he could see he couldn't think of even one thing they might have in common. He did think about running a few checks on her, but at the time thought better of it. It would be better if he just completely forgot about the whole dismal experience.

So, it wasn't with the most positive of attitudes, and even less expectation, that he had reluctantly agreed to go ahead with his second date and meet with Mary. Looking back it would have been so easy to have stopped there and then and put his dating agency experience down to just 'one of those things'. But, thankfully he hadn't. Perhaps fate does have a big role to play in life after all. From the very first time they had met there had been a mutual attraction.

To begin with they just enjoyed each other's company, sharing the same sense of humour. But what particularly appealed to Tom was her strong sense of independence. He liked that in a woman. Then there was the physical side of their relationship. Mary had been widowed for a number of years and, although she'd had a couple of dates since then, none of them had come to much. She had recently admitted to him it was probably because she had always set herself unrealistically high standards. Tom had taken that as a compliment.

So, they had both been surprised when their relationship quickly moved onto a sexual level. They were both in their early/mid-fifties. Not old, of course, but, nonetheless well passed the age when sex was accepted as being such a major driving force in a relationship. But there had been an intensity in their relationship which had both surprised and worried him. Surprised, because he didn't think he could express those feelings any more and worried because he couldn't help thinking that he might wake up one day and realise it had all been a figment of his recently underused imagination.

After the stress of the multiple murder case, Detective Superintendent Peters had insisted Tom should take some time off work. It had been an extremely tiring time, both physically and emotionally, and even Tom, not normally known as a person who admitted to any form of weakness, was glad to take up his offer. He and Mary had spent a wonderful ten days in the Canary Islands.

He had worried that being together for such a length of time might start to reduce the intensity of their relationship. Not so much on his part, but more Mary's. If anything, though, the time spent there just seemed to bring them even closer together and their relationship had become even more intense. But it was this feeling of happiness and contentment that, ironically, was nagging away at him. He had always found it difficult to enjoy the moment. He couldn't help worrying that this was just a temporary situation and there was something lurking around the corner that would change things yet again. He hoped that he was wrong.

When he arrived back home he found himself having to almost step over the mountain of mail that was waiting for him. He placed his case at the bottom of the stairs and picked up his mail. He would go through it in the kitchen after he had made himself a cup of tea. He could immediately see that most of the letters were the usual mixture from utility and insurance companies, no doubt offering him some fantastic deal to switch to them. There were also a large number of leaflets from local food takeaways, advertising special deals on everything from pizzas to exotically named Mexican food.

He put all of these straight into the bin. There was one envelope, however, which stood out. It didn't have any stamp, just his name, hand-written, on it. So he picked it up, opened it and began to read.

It was from Pauline, his very first date.

Dear Tom,
I hope that you dont mind me writting to you. I only just remembed where you lived. Ive been thinking about you a lot since we met for our date. I saw you on the telly and it reminded me to contact you. It would be good if we could meet again. You can tell me all about those murderrs. We could meet at the same place as last time. You have my number. PLEASE ring me.
Love Pauline
XXXX

He put the letter down on the table and took a sip from his cup. He had always thought there was something a little bit strange about her. Even during the brief time they had been together she appeared to be slightly unbalanced, alternating between over-the-top exuberance and an almost moody silence. He suspected it was his recent fame which had prompted her to write the letter. Worryingly, it looked as though she had delivered the letter herself. He suddenly had one of those 'sense of foreboding' feelings as all of his instincts told him that this was very bad news indeed.

Chapter 2

'Good morning, Sir. Welcome back. Did you have a good holiday?' asked Acting Detective Sergeant David Milner. Tom still couldn't quite come to terms with just how cheerful Milner could be.

Although it was less than three months since Milner had been 'reallocated' to work with Tom, a lot had happened during that time. Back then Milner was a lowly Detective Constable, just starting out on his police career. At the time Tom felt that Milner had probably been assigned to him because it was unlikely he would make many mistakes working with him. This was, not least, because Tom had found himself, more and more, being assigned to the more routine policing matters.

The events of the following few months, however, had resulted in Milner's promotion to his current position of Acting Detective Sergeant. Although during that period Tom had begun to appreciate Milner's qualities, he still couldn't quite come to terms with this incessant cheerfulness. Tom was from the old school, where constant cheeriness was interpreted as a fundamental weakness. He believed no one should join the police force to enjoy themselves.

'Yes, very enjoyable. Thank you for asking.' He paused for a while before adding, 'But now we've gone through the usual, back-from-holiday pleasantries, perhaps you can tell me what's been happening since I've been away?'

If Tom had looked more closely he might just have detected the merest hint of a smile on Milner's face. He had been away from work for almost two weeks and, despite Tom's frosty, but not totally unexpected, reply, Milner was still genuinely pleased to see his current boss back at work.

It had taken him a while to get used to DCI Stone's sometimes frosty manner but it had been worth the effort. He did think about mentioning this to him, but, if his time spent working with DCI Stone had taught him anything it was that DCI Stone was economical with any social chit chat. So he would just have to continue to read DCI Stone's mood music quite carefully if they were to work successfully together. He had to admit though, he was still on a high following his involvement in the arrest of the person responsible for the murder of those five people. It was this that had resulted in his rapid and recent promotion.

For a while all of the media, but particularly the press, had run wall-to-wall coverage of every conceivable aspect of events, however tenuous and trivial, that had a link to the murders. Eventually though the feeding frenzy abated, as even the UK media decided they'd had enough of this particular story and, after successfully squeezing out every last drop of sensationalism from it, had now moved on to something else.

Milner was still standing directly in front of DCI Stone. 'For God's sake, Milner, sit down. You look as though you're standing to attention, waiting for someone to inspect you.'

Milner sat down opposite DCI Stone. He then placed all of the files which he had brought with him on the desk immediately in front of him. 'Did you read any of the papers, about the murders, whilst you were away? It was unbelievable the amount of coverage that was generated.'

'Let me give you a bit of advice about the press, when it comes to their reporting of high profile murder cases.' He paused for a while, just long enough to ensure that he had Milner's undivided attention. 'Don't believe half of what is written and then only ten per cent of the rest. That way you might get somewhere close to the truth. Right now it might be tempting to bask in the glory of helping to catch the murderer, but the reality is that five innocent people died. If we had been doing a better job then perhaps some of those five would still be alive today.'

Although he would never admit it to Milner he had, whilst he had been away, indeed read some of the coverage of the murders. Eventually though, he'd come to realise that the more he read about them the more depressed it made him feel. Even though the press were, generally, supportive of his role in finally catching the murderer, there was nonetheless a growing undercurrent of criticism levelled at the police, which was now starting to surface.

Questions were being asked, for example, about the time it took to finally apprehend the killer, as well as why some of the early clues were missed. In truth, Tom could only agree with this criticism but it wasn't only this thought which was worrying him.

The press had also mentioned that there was likely to be a police inquiry. One which would examine all aspects of the case. In his experience this usually meant that, along with the usual procedural change recommendations, it was also likely there would have to be a scapegoat. Of course, it would not be described as that but everyone, at least everyone in the force, knew that's exactly what it was.

He'd really come to like and respect DCI Jack Chapman, the lead officer on the case, and was really concerned he might be the chosen scapegoat. Before going away on holiday he'd spoken with Jack a couple of times and whilst, on the surface at least, he still appeared to be very positive, he wondered how much of this was just an act. Jack had been around long enough to know that the top brass had previous when it came to sacrificing decent, honest coppers on the altar of media opinion.

Although he was in a different regional force to DCI Chapman, there would be many opportunities during the next few months, as the evidence was gathered ahead of the trial, for them to meet up. He had already decided though he would only offer any advice to Jack if, and when, asked.

In the meantime, having returned to work from his recent holiday, he was determined to get back into a normal work routine as quickly as possible.

'I'm starting to see that for myself, Sir,' replied Milner. 'One paper even mentioned that I'd dived into a raging torrent to save the intended victim. As you know it was nothing of the sort. Just a still, fairly shallow river.'

'There you are then. I suggest you always remember that when you're reading about murder cases. It will stand you in good stead,' answered Tom. 'But it was still brave of you to jump in. You didn't know how deep it was at the time.' This was as near as DCI Stone ever came to offering compliments. He continued to watch Milner very closely who, hearing this, had started to redden a little. He resisted the opportunity to reply. Tom liked that. There was a time to speak and a time to keep quiet and, in his opinion, this was a time for continued silence.

So, it was Tom who eventually spoke. 'Right, tell me what's been going on whilst I've been away.'

Milner was relieved he could now look away from DCI Stone and so he quickly opened one of his files. Then, almost as though he had just remembered something important, he looked up and said, 'Have you heard that one of Tommy Fuller's gang was found dead? It looks as though he was murdered.'

This seemingly throwaway line caught Tom's attention. Given the fact that he had been asked to carry out a formal review of the failed *Operation Torch* investigation any mention of Fuller was bound to be of special interest.

'Who was it?' asked Tom, his voice betraying his interest.

'Jimmy Ryan. Apparently he was a drug dealer working for Fuller. He was shot. A single bullet to the head.'

Tom knew Ryan. He had arrested him a couple of times over the years. He had also been one of the reasons why *Operation Torch* had been instigated as, according to the report, he had been DCI Shaw's main informant. This had never sat very comfortably with Tom as he knew Ryan as a very low-level criminal. Right from the start Tom had major doubts concerning the reliability of Ryan's information. And now, coincidentally, he was dead. If there was one thing which always prompted Tom's alarm bells to ring it was a series of coincidences.

'Has there been any progress in catching the killer yet?'

'I don't know,' replied Milner, before adding, almost nervously, 'DCI Shaw is the investigating officer.'

Milner knew that there was history between DCI Stone and DCI Shaw. They had never particularly liked each other. That much was very obvious. In fact, he had personally witnessed outright contempt shown by DCI Shaw towards his boss. As a consequence he had always been wary of even mentioning DCI Shaw's name whenever his boss was nearby.

'So, officially, you don't know. What about unofficially though? I'm sure you've spoken with other officers about it.'

Milner was clearly now uncomfortable. How was he supposed to answer this? In the past DCI Stone had admonished him for listening to station tittle-tattle, yet now he seemed to be encouraging him to do just that.

Tom, sensing Milner's reluctance, decided to help him. 'Don't worry, I won't hold you to whatever you tell me.'

Slightly hesitatingly at first, Milner told Tom what he had heard. 'Well, yes, there are a few theories doing the rounds. The one which they seem to think is the most plausible is that it's a gangland killing. Most likely carried out on the instruction of James O'Driscoll.'

Tom interrupted. 'Isn't O'Driscoll already in custody?'

'He is, Sir. But that wouldn't necessarily prevent him from ordering it to be carried out. If you remember O'Driscoll, and most of his gang, were arrested as a result of *Operation Sunlight*.' This had been an earlier, very successful operation, led by DCI Shaw which had resulted in the removal of another major West London criminal gang.

The implication was clear. O'Driscoll had blamed Ryan for his current incarceration and he had exacted his revenge in classic gangland fashion.

'I suppose that is possible,' replied Tom, although in a way which suggested just the opposite. 'Do you know if DCI Shaw's team have any specific leads yet?'

'I don't Sir. If they do, then they're keeping them close to their chests.'

'Hmm,' replied Tom, before adding gratefully, 'anyway, thank you for updating me on that. If you hear anything else I'd appreciate it if you could let me know. Now, why don't you tell me what you've been working on.'

Milner began to summarise what was in the file. 'We've recently had a spate of metal thefts from public buildings and other places. Two churches in the area have had lead stripped from their roofs. There have also been a few instances where copper cabling has been cut out from railway lines and even manhole covers taken up from roads. We've even had three instances where bronze commemorative plaques had been stolen from some of the war memorials in our area. They were jemmied off the stone memorials. It seems this is now happening all over the country as the thieves take advantage of the rising prices of metal.'

'Anything else?' asked Tom.

'The usual mix of domestics, car thefts and burglaries.

They're all here in the file if you want me to take you through them,' he replied.

'Why don't we do that later,' answered Tom, adding in explanation, 'I'm sure uniform are looking into those. Is that all?'

'There was one other thing. About a week ago we had a report of a missing person. I know we get these all the time but there seemed to be something different about this.'

'And what was that?'

'Nothing specific.' It's just that, well . . .'

'Go on, spit it out,' replied Tom, voicing his impatience.

'You've often said how important it is to trust your instincts,' Milner answered, looking directly at Tom. 'Well, this was one of those occasions for me. There was something about the circumstances that worried me.'

'Why don't you share it with me. I've never really subscribed to the theory about a problem shared being a problem halved. As far as I'm concerned that just means there are now more people worried about the same problem. Even so, I suppose, it's good to have it challenged by another person.'

Milner could never really work out whether or not such advice was meant to encourage him or dissuade him from raising any concerns. But, by raising the subject, he was now committed. He opened his notebook and began to read from it. 'His name is Maciej Sipowicz. He's a Polish national and lives at 15A Challenor Road.' He then looked up and offered further details. 'It's a block of flats just behind the shopping centre. He's lived there with his girlfriend for about six months.' He once again referred to his notes. 'Her name is Anna Nowak. He works at the Community Recycling Centre on Barton Street.'

'The Community Recycling Centre?' repeated Tom. 'Is that the same as the Council tip?'

'I suppose it is, Sir. As a matter of fact I've used that one myself a few times. I have to say it's much better than the old one. Sometimes, depending upon when you go, especially at the weekend, there's a bit of a queue, but generally they're very efficient. The people working there even help you to carry your stuff to the skip.' Milner was now suddenly in full explanatory mode. 'The big thing now, of course, is to recycle as much as possible. So there's separate skips for paper, cardboard – that type of thing – garden refuse, wood and metal. There's even a section specifically for old electrical products, like computers and televisions.'

'Very interesting, Milner. You make it sound like a nice day out. With that glowing recommendation I'm tempted to take my own rubbish there in future just to experience the ambience.' Tom instantly realised that his clumsy attempt to try and make a joke of this might instead have come across as crass sarcasm. He tried to correct this situation as quickly as possible. 'When was the last time he was seen?'

'According to his girlfriend, he hadn't been home for about four days. Uniform checked with the Recycling Centre, who confirmed that he hasn't turned in for work for the same number of days.'

'Isn't it a bit early to be launching a full missing persons investigation? What is it that's worrying you?'

'I spoke with Miss Nowak when she came to the station. All I can say is that she was really worried about his whereabouts.' He hesitated briefly and then said, 'Actually, she was more scared than worried. In all of the time that they had been in the UK he had always come home.'

'Did she have any idea where he might be?'

'None at all. And that was another reason why she was scared. Although his English was okay, she said that, as hers was much better, he tended to rely on her. And anyway, they were still just finding their way around here.'

'Could he have gone back to Poland? Perhaps he was homesick.'

'I asked that,' he answered quickly. 'His passport is still at the flat.'

Tom smiled. 'It looks as though you've asked all of the obvious questions. What do you want to do next?'

'I thought that I'd go and talk to her again. There might be something that she's remembered since our first meeting.'

'That makes sense. I think I'll come along with you if that's okay?'

Milner was momentarily stunned. As far as he could remember this was the very first time DCI Stone had ever asked for his permission to do anything. This was definitely new territory for him. If he was being totally honest it made him feel slightly uncomfortable.

'Err, yes. I'm sure that would be okay,' was all he could think of to say in reply.

'Good. That's settled then. Let's go and see her tomorrow morning. Now tell me about the metal thefts. What's the situation there?'

'The Transport Police are following up on the cable thefts. I was talking with one of their officers recently who told me it's becoming one of their biggest problems. Nationwide it's costing them millions of pounds, and then there's all of the disruption it causes to the travelling public, as well as the safety aspect. He seemed to think it's only a question of time before there's a serious accident. They've had to set up a new crime unit specifically to counter this new type of crime. I also visited one of the Churches, St Augustine's, just a few miles away from here, where the lead was stolen. Whoever took it had left a hole immediately above the altar and, as luck would have it, it just so happened to coincide with a torrential downpour. The result was that the interior of the church was wrecked.'

Milner, once again, seemed to have become quite animated as he described this and when he next spoke there was a hint of uncharacteristic anger in his voice. 'The priest there told me the total cost of repairs, including replacing the lead on the roof, will run into hundreds of thousands of pounds. In the meantime they've had to close parts of the church because of the potential danger to the public.' He then added, almost as much to himself as to DCI Stone. 'I know times are tough but why do people have to do this?'

'That's for our wonderful politicians to explain. Our job is simply to catch them and then present them to the courts,' Tom said quietly. 'You seem a bit angry. Is there a specific reason?'

'Not really, Sir. It's just these crimes seem so mindless. As I said, it's not just the theft of the lead but all of the additional costs, from the peripheral damage, that's often worse.'

Tom could see that Milner was still angry about these particular crimes. Although they had only worked together for a few months, this was the first time he had seen Milner become emotional.

'Just remember there is always some collateral damage, however seemingly trivial a crime might appear. And most of the damage is in human terms rather than simply financial.' He paused for a while to see whether or not Milner would respond. When he didn't he carried on. 'Is there anything to suggest there might be a link between the lead thefts and the other metal thefts? Could it be the same people who are doing this?'

'At this stage, it's too early to say, although I would be surprised if there was a link. The lead thefts are on a different scale entirely. The value of the stolen lead, on the black market, is likely to be in the thousands whilst the value of bronze plaques and manhole covers are only in the tens of pounds. As I said, it now seems to be happening everywhere.'

'I see what you mean,' answered Tom. 'But let's keep an open mind for the time being. You never know. And even if they are being carried out by different people they will still have to sell it to someone. Anyway, do we have anything to work on?'

'Not at the moment Sir, but we have asked for any CCTV from all of the nearby buildings. In the meantime we're visiting all of the local churches in our area to warn them of the dangers – although I suspect there's not a great deal they can do, other than to have a twenty-four-hour guard on site,' replied Milner, once again betraying his feelings.

Tom decided to move the conversation away specifically from churches. 'Have we visited our local scrap metal dealers yet? The metal must be going somewhere and scrap dealers would seem to be the most obvious place. After all, that is their business.'

'I've asked for a full list of all authorised dealers in our area but, of course, I'm sure there are many more unofficial ones who would be only too pleased to offer cash on a "no questions asked" basis.' He paused briefly. 'Did you know that even the authorised ones are only required, by law, to ask for a name and address when they buy any scrap metal? All the thieves have to do is to take the stolen metal to the scrap dealer and then give a false name and address. It's just so easy for them.'

'Okay,' said Tom. 'It seems like you have everything in hand. Is that all? Or is there anything else we need to discuss now?' Tom's tone left Milner in no doubt as what he was expected to say in reply.

Milner duly obliged. 'No, I think that's everything I wanted to update you on. The rest can wait until another time.'

Milner took his lead from this final comment, picked up all of his files and started to walk out of Tom's office. Before he left, however, Tom said, 'Actually, there is one thing you could do for me.' He picked up a piece of paper and handed it to Milner. 'Could you run a check for me on this person? Let me know if you find something.'

Milner looked at the details with a slightly puzzled expression and then said, 'Is it something to do with any of the ongoing cases?'

'No it isn't. I just need to check something.'

Milner thought about asking another follow-up question but, almost immediately, decided it was not his place to quiz his Detective Chief Inspector. If DCI Stone needed these details then there must be a good reason for it. He placed the piece of paper amongst all of the other papers.

Just as Milner was about to leave Tom's office he suddenly stopped and turned around. 'There was one other thing, Sir. I took a message from Superintendent Peters' PA earlier. He'd like to see you as soon possible.'

'I bet he would,' answered Tom, quietly under his breath. 'I bet he would.'

Chapter 3

A little while later Tom had made his way up to the fifth floor and was outside Superintendent Peters' office. When Peters had been promoted to his current position of Detective Superintendent, Tom had realised that he now had a boss who, for the very first time in his career, was actually younger than him. At first he had to admit that this milestone did worry him. Was this another sign, perhaps, that he was reaching the end of his own police career? Notwithstanding this, Tom had a lot of respect for Tony Peters and, until the fiasco of *Operation Torch*, he had undoubtedly been destined to go a lot higher in the Met.

'Superintendent Peters shouldn't be too long. He's just taking a call,' explained Janice, his PA. 'Can I get you something to drink while you're waiting?'

'That's very kind of you. Yes please. I'd love a cup of tea,' he replied.

'White with no sugar, isn't it? I seem to remember that you like your tea quite strong.'

'That's right. I'm impressed that you remember, particularly as it's not often that I receive an invitation to have tea and biscuits with the Station's Detective Superintendent.'

'I remembered from the last time you were here. Just after you'd helped to catch the multiple murderer, wasn't it? Anyway it's my job to remember what goes on in Superintendent Peters' office.'

As she said this the door to Peters' office opened. 'Tom, great to see you again,' said Superintendent Peters in, what seemed to Tom at least, was a surprisingly and genuinely welcoming tone. Still standing outside his office he said, 'You look well. Looks like you've caught a bit of sun. Did you go anywhere nice?'

'Yes, Sir. We went to the Canaries. It was a very nice break,' he answered, instantly regretting that he might have divulged too much information.

'You said "we." Do you want to tell me something?'

'Not really, Sir,' was all that Tom could think of in reply.

Superintendent Peters must have taken the hint that this was not something Tom wanted to discuss any further, because all he said in response to Tom's quite terse reply was, 'Let's go into my office.'

Peters led Tom inside and, following Peters' lead, he seated himself at the large table positioned at the far end of the room.

'Sorry about that, Tom. I shouldn't have asked about your personal circumstances, particularly in front of Janice. It's none of my business.' Peters waited momentarily for a reply but when none was forthcoming he carried on. 'Did Janice ask you if you wanted a drink?'

'Already sorted, Sir,' replied Tom. 'She seems very efficient and certainly has a very good memory. She even remembered how I took my tea.'

'I know. I'm not sure what I'd do now if she ever left.'

Almost on cue Janice entered the office carrying a large tray which held two cups, two spoons, a pot of tea, a pot of coffee, a jug of milk and a small bowl containing various sachets of white and brown sugar. There was also a plate overloaded with various types of biscuit.

Janice briefly glanced at Tom and smiled to him as she placed the tray on the table.

'Thank you Janice,' said Peters. 'Could you please hold all of my calls until DCI Stone and I have finished?'

'Certainly. Just buzz me if you need any more drinks,' she said, before leaving the office.

Peters waited until Janice had closed the door before speaking. 'Tom, I'm sure you know why I've asked to see you.'

He then placed an overloaded file immediately in front of him. Tom could see that the file had a large label on the front with the words *Operation Torch* clearly visible. Neither of them had yet picked up their drinks.

He continued. 'First of all I should tell you, whilst you have been away, I've had a number of meetings with Detective Chief Superintendent Small regarding the fallout from *Operation Torch*. As you can imagine he is not exactly sending out congratulatory letters to all of the officers involved in it. In fact, it's now gravitated up to Commander Jenkins. They are both extremely concerned about what this might do to the reputation of the Met. I don't need to tell you that another high-profile failed operation is the last thing the Met needs right now. At the moment only bits and pieces have got out but it's only a question of time before the full details start to leak out.' He looked directly at Tom. 'They have, therefore, instigated a major review and inquiry into all aspects of *Operation Torch*. The review will be carried out by an outside force. It's due to start in a few weeks' time.'

Tom waited for Superintendent Peters to continue speaking. When it became clear he wasn't about to, Tom said, 'You didn't mention my suspicions just then. Does that mean you didn't tell them?'

Superintendent Peters had anticipated this question. 'Tom, please just hear me out first. No, I didn't tell them about your informant theory. And for a very good reason. If I had, I know exactly what their response would have been.'

'And what would it have been?' asked Tom, his eyes now locked onto Superintendent Peters' face.

'Firstly, they would have thought we were looking for excuses or for things that just weren't there. And can you blame them? We have no real hard evidence that *Operation Torch* failed primarily because of an informant within our team. What evidence we do have is purely circumstantial. And secondly, it suits them better to believe it failed because of poor leadership and sloppy police work. They'd much rather have an incompetent copper than a corrupt one.'

Tom could feel himself starting to get agitated and there was real anger in his voice when he replied. 'Are you saying that the top brass would be happier if I just kept my concerns to myself and swept them under the carpet?' He paused momentarily. 'I don't think this is something that I'm happy to do. I'm not getting some sort of vicarious pleasure from voicing these suspicions, you know.'

Peters chose not to respond. Instead he started to pour coffee into his cup. After a while, when the initial anger had subsided, Tom said, 'I'm sorry about that little outburst, Sir. It's just I'd like to think that if I was a Chief Superintendent and my Superintendent had come to me and told me he suspected a major drug gang was obtaining information from a serving police officer then I would, at least, give it serious consideration.'

Peters gave a light laugh and then said, 'Perhaps that's why it's highly unlikely you'll ever make Chief Superintendent. Somehow I just can't see you playing the politics game at the expense of good, old-fashioned, investigative work. Did you know it's one of the unwritten laws of policing that the higher in the organisation you go the less you are encouraged to use those natural instincts and talents which got you there in the first place?' He paused before adding, by way of further explanation, 'This means sometimes it's easier to do nothing than to run the risk of rocking the boat. I took the view this would probably be one of those occasions.'

Peters' tone of voice became far more serious. 'Tom, please don't take this the wrong way but I have to ask you this. Are you sure that information relating to *Operation Torch* has been passed on to Fuller? I know some of the evidence is quite strong but, to be totally frank, as I said earlier, it's still largely circumstantial. I think even you would agree that, right now, we wouldn't get anywhere near a court of law with what we have.'

Tom took a sip from his cup. He had anticipated this question. In fact, he had thought of little else, even whilst he'd been away on holiday with Mary. Any anger had now completely disappeared from his voice as he answered. 'I can't think of any other explanation, Sir. Why would Fuller be so prepared when DCI Shaw and his team raided his house? It was almost as though he was waiting for it to happen. Now, why would that be? There's really only a couple of explanations. Either it was pure good fortune or he had been tipped off by someone who told him it was going to happen. Personally, I've never really subscribed to the good fortune theory, particularly having seen some of the video and CCTV footage Fuller's lawyers now, conveniently, have at their disposal. So, if they were tipped off then, of course, the key questions are, who did it and why? And there's something else which makes me very suspicious.'

'Oh. What's that?' asked Peters.

'I understand that Jimmy Ryan was murdered.' He paused momentarily before continuing. 'That's another convenient coincidence.'

'I understand that's what you might think. But, all of the evidence suggests it was carried out on the orders of James O'Driscoll.'

As Tom heard this he suddenly thought that he must congratulate Milner on his source of information within the station. If he needed to hear the latest station gossip he would now know where to go.

'What evidence do you have to substantiate that?' asked Tom.

There was a slight hesitation before Peters replied. 'At the moment, I admit, most of it is circumstantial, but the motive, at least, is very a very powerful one. Revenge.'

'With due respect, Sir, why is the circumstantial evidence on the killing any different from what I am proposing?'

There was a momentary tense silence. 'Tom. You might be right,' conceded Superintendent Peters. 'But, at the moment, we are pursuing this as our primary line of inquiry.'

Tom, clearly not entirely satisfied with Peters' explanation said, 'I also understand that DCI Shaw is leading the investigation. Can I ask why? As you know he, along with some of the other officers involved in *Operation Torch*, have to be suspects if my theory is correct. Is it wise therefore for him to be lead officer?'

Tom could sense that Superintendent Peters was uncomfortable with this question and this was quickly confirmed when Peters answered, his voice now rising. 'Tom. It was my decision to allow DCI Shaw to handle this. I'm sorry if you don't agree with that but, rightly or wrongly, that's what I'm paid to do. Make decisions.'

Tom decided not to pursue it. He would have to leave it for another occasion. Perhaps sensing he had too readily shown his anger Superintendent Peters was more like his usual calm self when he next spoke. 'Earlier, you said the key questions relating to *Operation Torch* were who did it and why? So, do you have your own thoughts as to what the answers might be? I'm sure you must have thought about this whilst you were away.'

'Well, yes, I did think about it a lot. After all, they are the key questions. The problem, however, is that every man and his dog seemed to know the bust was going to happen and, more importantly, when it was going to happen. Even Milner had been told by the duty sergeant something important was happening that night.'

'Yes, I remember how angry I was with you when you mentioned the fact that there were rumours swirling around about a big operation.' He paused for a while and then asked, 'So you also knew about *Operation Torch* then?' emphasising the word 'you'.

'No. Well, not the main details. I had heard something was about to happen, but initially I thought it was probably just the usual station gossip.' He hesitated slightly before adding, 'To be honest Sir, I was just fishing a bit to see how you would react and if you would reveal any details to me.' There was another brief pause. 'Sorry.' He then went on. 'If you remember it was at the time when I seemed to be deliberately excluded from any of the bigger operations.'

Superintendent Peters responded calmly and chose not to reply to Tom's final comment. Instead he just said, 'That's one of the disadvantages, I suppose, of getting to my exalted position. You start to think you know everything, and can control everything – even what's being gossiped about in the station canteen. Well, that's another lesson learned.'

'I wouldn't worry too much about it, Sir. It's something that has always gone on. If people don't know the full facts they like to fill in the gaps themselves by making up possible scenarios, however way off the mark,' replied Tom, trying to sound as understanding as possible. 'It makes them feel important.'

'So, on the basis that just about everyone knew what was going on, that surely makes the task of finding out who did it almost impossible,' suggested Peters.

'Well, not exactly, Sir. As I understand it, the final briefing, when the full details of the night's activities were revealed, took place at around ten o'clock, with the actual raid planned for 11.30pm. According to the file notes, and not counting those uniformed officers on standby, there were ten people in that meeting.'

Superintendent Peters interrupted. 'Does that include me?'

'Yes it does,' answered Tom, looking directly at Peters.

'So, I'm one of the suspects then?' asked Peters in as light-hearted a way as he could manage.

Tom hesitated before answering. 'I hope not, Sir.'

If Peters was less than impressed by Tom's answer he didn't show it as he said, 'Do you have a list of all of the officers at the meeting?'

Tom took out a sheet of A4 paper from his jacket pocket. 'This is the list of everyone who was there. I think it's important, Sir, that you examine the list, in order to check if this coincides with your own memory.'

'I'm not sure that's possible without speaking with some of the others who were there that night. After all it was quite a few weeks ago. But I'll do the best I can. Anyway, this will obviously be one of the key pieces of background information which the inquiry will ask to see. They've decided there will be a full comprehensive inquiry, with relevant officers called, to review all operational aspects of *Operation Torch*. I'm sure they will also want to know who did what and when.'

Tom's reply was not the one the Superintendent had anticipated. 'I'm not surprised. It's probably the least they would be expected to do, particularly given all of the publicity it's likely to generate. Better to be ahead of the game. It always helps if you can say that an investigation is already under way. At least it buys a bit of time. Fuller's lawyers must be rubbing their hands. With that footage they're are likely to have a field day. Anyway, you know how Senior Officers hate any bad publicity which is directed towards the Met. Their usual response is to work out how they can cover their own backsides, and setting up an inquiry is always a pretty good way to do that.'

'Well, thanks for the vote of confidence,' replied Peters, with a hint of a laugh. He then added, this time more seriously, 'Technically, of course, I'm also a Senior Officer. Or had you forgotten that?'

'Perhaps I should have said "very Senior Officers".'

'I'm not sure that makes me feel any better. Hopefully, though, we might be able to use this inquiry to our advantage.'

Tom placed his tea cup down on the table. 'I'm not sure I follow you, Sir. What do you mean?'

'I've been thinking about this whilst you were away. This official inquiry could give us the cover to carry out our own unofficial one. One which could run concurrently alongside the main one but under the radar.'

24

Tom was genuinely surprised by what he had just heard, and so it was with a genuine interest when he responded. 'But wouldn't that be against all of the normal rules which are applied when an investigation has been instigated? How can there be two inquiries running at the same time, one official and the other one unofficial?'

'Well, yes, I admit it's a bit unusual but I'm sure this would not be the first time this has happened,' replied Peters, rather intriguingly. Tom wondered if Superintendent Peters was about to reveal a few examples of when this might have occurred. 'As you just confirmed yourself, everyone will be expecting some form of inquiry and so all eyes are likely to be on that one. At the moment there's only two people – you and me – who are aware there might be an informant in the station. As far as everyone else is concerned the inquiry will focus mainly on the operational issues. It could offer us the perfect smokescreen. No one would suspect that anything, other than the official inquiry, was taking place.'

Superintendent Peters remained quiet for a while, allowing Tom time to absorb what was being suggested. Eventually Tom broke the silence. 'I see where you are coming from. But, presumably, we would still have to get the approval of Commander Jenkins and Chief Superintendent Small to do this. Do you really think they would agree to it?'

Superintendent Peters stood up, placed his hands together behind his back, and stared intently at a passing plane which was making its final descent into Heathrow. He remained silent, almost as though he was having difficulty finding the right words.

Tom, once again, adopted his 'silence-is-sometimes-the-best-tactic' approach.

After what seemed like an age Superintendent Peters, still with his back to Tom, finally spoke. 'I'm sure they wouldn't touch it with a barge pole. And frankly I wouldn't blame them either. As far as they are concerned the official inquiry is one inquiry too many. They have enough on their plate right now what with the ongoing hacking investigations and the other allegations regarding officers trading information for money with the press.' He then turned around to face Tom. 'But don't quote me on that.'

Tom was either still having problems fully understanding

what Superintendent Peters was suggesting or, more likely, simply couldn't quite believe what he was hearing.

'Sir, is that wise? I mean if they were to find out we were doing this, without their explicit approval, then we might both find ourselves back walking the beat. Or worse.' Both men remained silent, each deep in his own thoughts, as they considered the full implications.

Eventually Peters looked directly at Tom and said. 'I know – and that's why I have to ask you to do this alone.'

Suddenly Tom grasped what Peters had been suggesting, but he still needed absolute clarification. The questions came out exactly in the way he was thinking. 'Are you asking me to go native on this and run a one-man, clandestine undercover operation? And what happens if it all goes wrong? Are you saying it will just be me who would be responsible?'

Peters' eyes remained fixed on Tom. 'Yes, I suppose I am,' was all he said in reply.

Once again, silence filled the void, each man considering the various possible outcomes and the effect they might have on their own careers.

Peters then spoke. 'Tom, you don't have to do this. It's unfair.' He hesitated before adding, 'No, actually it's cruel of me to ask you to do it. But I've thought long and hard about this and, if I thought there was another way, I wouldn't be asking you to do it.'

If that was meant to make Tom feel any more comfortable or reassured then it failed. 'Why don't we just let the official inquiry handle it? We could still present whatever evidence we have and then let them decide whether or not to take it further,' suggested Tom. But even as he said this he realised it could never work.

It was Peters who articulated the reasons why this approach was unlikely to succeed. 'Tom, if that's what you want to do then I'll support you one hundred per cent. But you know as well as I do that the likelihood of anyone being charged is minimal. You said it yourself earlier. They would rather sacrifice a few police officers than admit there might be any corruption within the force. Also, any inquiry is likely to take quite a while to complete. By the time the final recommendations are made public it's likely it will be old news anyway. By then, some other crisis will, no doubt, have come along.' As he said this he continued to look at Tom. 'You know how the system works. How many times have we seen this happen over the years?'

Factually, Tom couldn't disagree with what Peters had just said. Nonetheless he was still very surprised to hear just how cynical Peters sounded. That was usually the preserve of less senior police officers, such as himself.

Tom suddenly realised he was confronted with having to make the biggest decision of his police career. He knew Fuller would eventually be arrested, tried and sent to prison. History was full of criminals who thought they were forever immune and above the law, only to eventually find out it was only a case of when, not if, they were finally brought to justice. What worried him though was how much more misery Fuller would, until that day arrived, continue to inflict on the people of London and the number of young lives which would be ruined due to his criminal activities. Perhaps here was a chance to do something about it. Knowing who the informant was would provide them with a much better chance of finally putting Fuller away. Set against this, however, was the likelihood that this clandestine inquiry would fail to identify that person, if indeed there was one at all. Worse still, if that happened, and Tom's involvement became known, then his long career with the police force would end in disgrace and humiliation.

'If I agree to do this then I would need to have total access to all operational files, both past and current, as well as access to officers' personal files and bank statements. And that's just for starters. I'm sure there will also be many other things, which I can't think of right now, which I'll also need to look at,' said Tom.

Once again Peters had anticipated Tom's request. 'Agreed. Although we would need to develop a fail-safe procedure whereby you see them at a time when they would be least likely to be missed. I also think it's very important you continue to function normally. In fact it's vital that you do this otherwise it might arouse suspicion, especially from our informant. And that's the last thing we need.'

'You really have thought this through, haven't you? And, if it's so important to carry on with my normal role, then when exactly am I expected to carry out my secret role?'

'Well, it will probably mean you'll just have to do this when you can or outside of your normal working hours. I know they are a bit unpredictable at times but you'll have to work around them. What about handing more of your casework over to young Milner?' Before Tom could answer, Peters continued. 'We'd also need to agree when and where we can meet. Too many regular meetings here, at least during normal working hours, would begin to look suspicious. So, where possible, we should only meet in the evening, when things are a little quieter. Even then we should always try and have a credible cover story for why we are meeting.'

Tom's head was in a spin. He had a thousand questions which he wanted to ask Superintendent Peters but now was probably not the best time. He needed to think calmly about this but, right now, calmness was something which was in short supply. And there was another thing. He knew that, by asking more questions, here and now, it would only drag him deeper and deeper into this crazy plan. If he wasn't careful his continual questioning of Superintendent Peters would imply he had all but agreed to it.

'Sir,' replied Tom, 'I need time to think about this. 'It's not every day you are asked to conduct an undercover operation against fellow police officers.'

'I totally understand. Why don't we meet again tomorrow evening, here, at say seven thirty? That will give both of us time to reflect on what we've just discussed.'

Tom thought Peters' use of the word 'reflect' was maybe the biggest understatement of all time.

Tom suddenly had another thought. 'Even if you provide me with all of the background information, ideally, I'd still need to be able to discuss various aspects of the operation with some of the key officers involved. How can I do that, without arousing their suspicions, or worse, simply duplicating what the main inquiry will want to do? They will smell something fishy straightaway.'

Peters was prepared for Tom's questions. 'Chief Superintendent Small has already asked me to provide some basic information, regarding *Operation Torch*, for the main inquiry, together with a few suggested procedural changes. I'll just say that I've delegated that task to you.'

Superintendent Peters' ready response somehow only seemd to add to Tom's sense of unease.

He headed back down to his own office on the second floor. Suddenly the stakes had been raised massively. What if he was wrong? What if he was looking for something that wasn't there? Was the *Operation Torch* fiasco simply the result of a massive cock-up?

One thing was for sure. This was not how he'd imagined his first day back at work to be.

Chapter 4

After his meeting with Superintendent Peters, Tom tried, not always successfully, to put to the back of his mind everything they'd discussed. So, he spent the remainder of the day working his way through the mass of paperwork which had accumulated whilst he had been away on holiday. He also took time to read through most of the crime reports which had been logged in that time.

Milner was certainly right when he had emphasised the sudden spate of metal thefts. In fact, they were fast approaching epidemic proportions. It seemed as though every type of metal, however small the individual piece, was now being targeted by criminals. By 5.30pm, though, he had read enough for one day and, as there was nothing new coming through, had decided to finish and head off home.

His brief conversation with Milner had provided him with a welcome distraction. But, he knew that's all it was – a brief respite. He suspected the next few hours, as he tried to take in everything Peters had suggested, would be some of the most difficult he had ever faced as a serving police officer. As he drove home he tried to make sense of everything.

Tom was the type of person who liked to compartmentalise different thoughts. It was his way of being able to cope with multiple priorities. On this occasion though, that ability seemed to have deserted him. On the one hand he couldn't help thinking he had been placed in an almost impossible position by Superintendent Peters. On the other, all throughout his career, he had despised police corruption. He still believed that a bent copper was the lowest of the low. If the public felt the police were outside the normal rules of law, then society truly was on the slippery path to chaos and anarchy.

Perhaps a bit too moralistic, but he had seen for himself how respect for the law fell every time there was a major police corruption scandal. Every time this happened it made their job of catching criminals even more difficult. Well, here was an opportunity for him to put into action all of those fine principles. Of course, he'd come across corruption, in all of its various forms, many times during his thirty plus years in the force. But never anything that was potentially on this scale and certainly nothing which involved one of London's most notorious criminals.

According to the clock in his car, the journey back home took longer than he'd anticipated, mainly because of the heavy rush hour traffic. He just wasn't used to leaving so early in the evening. But the strange thing was, he couldn't remember anything about the journey home. It was quite surreal and only confirmed – as if he needed any more confirmation – that his mind was elsewhere.

'Hi. I just thought I'd call to see how your first day back at work went. Were there any more murders waiting for you to solve?' asked Mary. Tom had only just returned home when his mobile had rung. Mary had realised early in their relationship that it was usually better to call his mobile as this gave her the best chance of actually getting through to him. Although it was only yesterday when they had last been together he was still happy to hear her voice.

'Just a couple. But I expect to have the murderers behind bars tomorrow,' replied Tom in a similarly flippant tone.

'It's nothing less than I would expect of the famous Detective Chief Inspector Stone. Have they struck a special medal for you yet?' asked Mary. 'I heard a couple of my customers discussing the murders. I so wanted to tell them it was my man who had solved them.'

Hearing her obvious pride in him, Tom felt a sudden and totally unexpected surge of feeling for Mary. Nonetheless, he felt he had to set the record straight. 'Thanks for those kind words but it wasn't just me involved in the case. I was just one man out of many in the team.'

'Yes. I know that but you're *my* man,' she answered with real feeling. There was a brief pause before she added, 'Seriously though, how was it? I expect it was a bit strange, after being away.'

'Well, yes, it was a bit. But, other than that, it was fairly routine,' answered Tom, just a little untruthfully.

'Probably the best way. That way you can gently ease yourself back in. So it's not too much of a shock to your system.'

If only she knew. He'd never, of course, mentioned to her his informant theory. After the failure of his marriage to Anne, and the second chance he had been given with Mary, he was determined to try and keep his personal life totally separate from his work life. He was also determined to devote more time to some of the other things which were now suddenly becoming important in his life. What was it the experts said everyone must have? A work-life balance? He'd never really given much thought to this previously.

In the past, particularly in the early days when he was forging his career within the Met, it was seen almost as a sign of virility to work long hours. The more hours you were seen to work, the higher your personal status seemed to climb, irrespective of whether those additional hours were productive or not. And the opposite was also certainly true. If you were spotted leaving early, even if you were on top of your case load, then this was chalked against you as a sign of weakness and lack of commitment to the job.

It was hardly surprising therefore that divorce, or marital problems, were seen as one of the many occupational hazards of being a police officer. Looking back from where he now was in his life, it was madness of course, and he had already paid the ultimate price with the failure of his marriage and the estrangement from his son. He'd recently started to regularly ask himself quite a fundamental question. If he had known then what he knew now, would he have done anything differently? But he'd usually conveniently rationalised that this was an impossible one to answer and, therefore, wouldn't worry himself unduly by even trying. Maybe, though, he was just frightened of the truth.

'Unfortunately it doesn't always work out that way,' replied Tom. 'Today we had a few more burglaries. That type of thing. There have also been a string of metal thefts whilst I've been away. Lead from church roofs. Bronze plaques stolen from war memorials. Cabling stolen from railway lines. It seems the region is being plagued by them at the moment.'

'I know. I was reading about them only today in the local

paper. How can anyone steal a bronze plaque that shows the names of local people who died giving their lives in world wars for their country? It's really despicable.'

'You sound just like Milner. He seemed to get quite upset when he was briefing me about them.'

'I'm not surprised. I think any sane person would get upset,' said Mary, suddenly becoming quite animated. 'Sorry, I'm sure you don't need to hear this. Me sounding off about things. I'll soon be asking you what you're going to do about it.' By now she had regained her normal composure. 'How was Milner, by the way? Was he glad to have you back?'

'Actually I think he was. I really must introduce you to him. You seem to have a lot in common.' There was a brief pause before Tom added, 'Anyway, thank you for calling. I always seem to feel so much better when I hear your voice.' He paused briefly and then said, 'It seems so strange, after the past couple of weeks, not to be with you.'

'Does that mean that you'd like me to come round tonight?'

'That would be nice but I've got an early start tomorrow and then a long day ahead of me. But, with a bit of luck, we should be able to get together later in the week. You'll just have to try and control your urges until then.'

'I'll try my best but I can't guarantee I won't be knocking on your door earlier than that,' she said with a light laugh.

'I'll give you a call when I know what's happening.'

As he said this he once again realised, despite his best intentions, just how much his job continued to impinge on his private life. In his more selfless moments he wondered whether it was fair on Mary to subject her to all of this. Despite her warm, seemingly understanding words, he knew she still didn't fully comprehend exactly what it meant to be in a relationship with a police officer. And why should she? They had only been together for a couple of months and both of them were still at that stage in the relationship where they were just pleased to get any opportunity to be together.

'Okay,' said Mary, 'but only if you're up to it.'

Now Tom started to laugh. 'I know that I'll soon be fifty-four but there's still a bit of life left in me.'

'I know,' said Mary, joining in the laughter. 'There certainly was whilst we were on holiday.'

'You see, that's what you've turned me into. I used to be a boring, middle-aged man. Now you think I'm God's gift to women.' He hesitated briefly before adding almost wistfully, 'If only.'

Mary, once again, began to laugh, 'And here's me thinking you are a one-woman man.'

'I am, but at least it will keep you on your toes,' he replied. There was a short pause before he asked, 'Anyway, how was your day?'

'Pretty quiet. As you know Monday is never really busy. But at least it gave me the chance to catch up on a few things.' Mary owned a small flower shop in Bagshot. She had bought the business after her husband had died a few years earlier. Although, as she often said, she was unlikely to ever make her fortune from the business, it paid the bills and she was doing something she really enjoyed. 'We have quite a large order, for a big wedding, which we have to get out tomorrow so that should keep me busy.' She hesitated briefly before speaking again, 'Is it anything exciting you're involved in tomorrow? You made it sound quite intriguing.'

Tom sometimes wished she wouldn't keep showing such a keen interest in his job. He knew her intentions were well-meaning but it just continued to highlight to him how his job was all-consuming. And he didn't like lying to her.

'Not really,' replied Tom, just a little too quickly. 'Just one of those boring regular meetings that seem to be the norm these days.' Although he knew he could completely trust Mary he saw little value in mentioning *Operation Torch*. He knew it would only make her worry even more about him.

'Everyone needs a bit of boredom occasionally. At our age I'm not sure that we could cope with continuous excitement anyway.'

'That's true,' answered Tom. 'Although it would be nice if we could choose when we wanted this to happen. But, in my experience, unfortunately, events are usually outside of our control.'

'More words of wisdom from the teachings of Detective Chief Inspector Tom Stone. You really should start to write all of these down you know.'

'I think I might just do that. That's something else I can do when I retire. That and playing golf.'

'Somehow I can't see you hitting a little white ball around. Anyway, what is the point of golf? It's hardly strenuous exercise. I suspect that retirement might be longer than you think,' added Mary, suddenly sounding a bit too serious for Tom's liking.

He decided not to continue with this particular line of conversation. He didn't like where it was heading. He settled on more mundane matters. 'What have you got planned for tonight? I thought Monday nights were rehearsal nights.'

Mary had been a member of the North West Surrey Players, a local amateur dramatics group, for the past ten years. 'Not tonight,' answered Mary. 'It's normally every other Monday and then more regularly when we're rehearsing.'

'Does that mean you missed last week's meeting, when we were on holiday?'

'The things I do for love.'

'I'm flattered. I must make it up to you at some point.'

Mary laughed. 'Is that a promise? I'll hold you to that when we next meet.'

'I'm not sure I can do that. Now I've got lots of female admirers, all wanting to spend time with me, you might just have to join the back of the queue. Sorry.'

Tom was relieved their conversation had ended on a less serious note. He always had mixed feelings when he spoke with Mary. He now found himself thinking about her constantly. He was sure he had fallen in love with her but was somehow reluctant to show his true feelings. Whenever he found himself getting close to doing so his default position was to use humour to try and make light of the situation. He guessed this was his way of protecting them both from any future disappointments. Although they had both agreed they would just let things develop and see where this led them he suspected that, for Mary at least, this was not a satisfactory solution and, sooner rather than later, she would want something a little more permanent.

He just hoped that he would be able to make the correct decision when that particular moment arrived.

Chapter 5

Next morning Tom arrived at the station just before eight o'clock. He had secretly hoped he would, for once, arrive at the station before Milner. He knew this was a bit childish but, nonetheless, it would still give him some sort of pleasure if he did.

So he was more than a little disappointed, as he made his way to his office on the second floor, when he was greeted by Milner.

'Good morning, Sir,' said Milner in what was, even by his usual enthusiastic standards, a particularly effusive tone.

'Milner,' replied Tom. 'What time did you get here today?'

Milner suddenly looked worried. 'Why, Sir? Has something happened I should have known about?'

Tom said quietly but firmly, 'Just the opposite. I know you are young and very keen but you really must pace yourself a bit better. Otherwise you'll start to burn yourself out.'

Milner, clearly relieved he hadn't missed anything, replied, 'It's just I don't want to let you down, Sir.'

This was not the reply Tom was expecting and he suddenly found himself getting a little embarrassed. And so it was with a fair degree of self-control that he said, in a way which tried not to betray this embarrassment, 'Milner. I know you don't want to let me down and I appreciate that, although I'm sure there will be times when it will happen. When it does though, I'll know there were valid reasons for it.'

Now it was Milner's turn to be embarrassed. Tom decided to move on to operational matters. 'We are seeing Anna Nowak this morning, aren't we?' he asked. 'What time do you think we should visit her?'

Milner was relieved that the conversation had quickly moved on to something he was more comfortable with. 'I thought we could get there at about nine o'clock. It's more likely she'll be in at that time.' Before Tom could comment,

Milner carried on. 'I spoke with the Landlord late yesterday afternoon. According to him they signed a twelve-month rental agreement and have, so far, lived there for about six months. I'm afraid that's all I could find out in the time available.'

'Well done, Milner. I think you've done more than enough in such a short time,' replied Tom, trying hard not to sound patronising. 'I've got a few things to do before then. Let's get together again at eight thirty. Challenor Road isn't that far away from here so we should be there by 9 o'clock.'

As Milner was preparing to leave his office, Tom suddenly said, 'By the way, have you had the chance yet to get the information on the woman we discussed yesterday?'

Milner wondered once again why Detective Chief Inspector Stone was showing so much interest in this woman. 'Not yet, Sir,' he answered. 'I'm still waiting for the report but I've been promised it for later today.' He looked closely at DCI Stone as he said this. He wanted to see how he reacted to what he had just told him. There was no obvious reaction however, and Tom simply said, 'Just let me know when you have it.'

Just after nine o'clock Tom and Milner were standing outside the flat at Challenor Road. Tom rang the bell. Almost immediately the door was opened by a slim, blonde-haired woman, who he estimated to be in her mid-twenties.

'Yes, can I help you?' asked the young lady, in slightly accented, although extremely pleasant, English.

Tom held up his identification card so she could easily see his details. 'I'm Detective Chief Inspector Stone. I believe that you have already met Detective Sergeant Milner,' he said looking towards Milner. Would it be okay if we came in? We'd like to talk to you about Maciej.'

Milner was pleasantly surprised to hear that DCI Stone had not used the word 'Acting' when introducing him. He quite liked that. It sounded good and suddenly, and quite unexpectedly, he felt more important.

The woman suddenly looked very anxious and when she next spoke, her voice betrayed her obvious anxiety. 'Why? Have you found him? Is he okay?'

'I'm afraid we haven't found him yet. We'd just like to try and get a bit more information about him. The more background information we have the better chance we will then have of finding him,' said Tom, by way of explanation.

'Please come in,' she answered politely.

She led them through a narrow hallway. They passed a tiny kitchen on the right-hand side. Opposite that was another room, which he could see was a bedroom, containing a bed and a single, old-fashioned wardrobe. They followed her along the hallway into the main living room. It was neat and tidy but sparsely furnished, with just a single armchair and a well-used two-seater sofa, between which was a small rectangular table. On the walls were prints of scenes from various places in Warsaw.

Anna sat down in the armchair.

'Do you mind if I sit down?' asked Tom.

'Please do,' she answered, gesturing towards the sofa. Milner decided that it was probably better if he positioned himself alongside DCI Stone, rather than try and squeeze onto the sofa next to him.

'There's just a bit of background information that we need to begin with. First of all, could you please confirm your name.'

'I'm Anna Nowak. Maciej's girlfriend.'

'Thank you. According to the landlord, you have both lived here for about six months. Is that correct?'

'Yes, that's correct,' answered Anna.

'Is that when you arrived from Poland?' he asked.

'Yes, it took us a few weeks to find somewhere to live. We rented this flat but would like to move somewhere better. But everything is so expensive here in the UK.'

'I understand that Maciej works at the Community Recycling Centre on Barton Street. Has he worked there long?'

'He got the job when we first arrived and so he's been there almost six months. But he was going to start looking for another job. Back home in Warsaw I was an English teacher and Maciej was a qualified car mechanic. We thought we might be able to get similar jobs here in the UK but there were no jobs available. So we had to take what we could find.'

Milner now spoke. 'So, he didn't enjoy working there?' he asked.

'It was a job,' she answered. 'Anyway, we were thinking of going back to Warsaw.'

'Oh. Any reason for that?' asked Tom.

'It's not so easy coming to a foreign country. Sometimes it's not as you expected it to be,' she explained.

'I'm sure that it's not. It must be very difficult,' replied Tom.

'As I said, everything costs so much more here. We have to work very hard just to pay the rent and buy food. I have a day job working in a bar and Maciej and I have another job, in the evening, cleaning offices.'

She continued with much more emotion. 'During the Second World War, Maciej's great-grandfather, Stanislaw, was a pilot, based not far from here with the Polish Fighter Squadron. His wife and young son never saw him again. He was killed in the Battle of Britain helping to defend your country from the Nazis. But no one seems to care any more. They just call us immigrants, who are taking all of their jobs.'

Tom looked at Anna and said, 'If it helps, I have to say I really admire what you and Maciej are trying to achieve.'

Milner took up the questioning. 'Miss Nowak, when was the last time you saw Maciej?'

Suddenly she started to get angry. 'Why are you asking me this again? I told you when I came to the Police Station. You should be trying to find Maciej, not asking me the same questions. Are you doing this just because we are foreigners?'

'Miss Nowak. We are simply trying to confirm when you last saw Maciej. We would ask the same question whoever had gone missing,' answered Tom.

Tom could see that Anna was upset and tears suddenly started to roll down her cheeks.

'Please take your time,' said Tom, taking a tissue from a box that was on the table and handing it to her.

'Thank you,' said Anna. 'I'm sorry about what I just said but I'm really worried about Maciej.' She wiped the tears from her face and continued. 'The last time I saw Maciej was on Wednesday morning. Just before he left for work.' There was a brief silence before she added, 'I haven't seen him since.' She started to cry once again. After a while she continued. 'He usually comes home just after six o'clock, because we start our cleaning job at seven. When he didn't come home I thought he must have been delayed and so I went to work myself. I was expecting him to be at home when I returned. I was angry with him because he hadn't phoned me.'

'And when he wasn't home, what did you do?' asked Tom.
'I tried calling him but there was no answer. I didn't know what to do after that. I couldn't call where he worked because they were closed. So, next morning I phoned them. They said that he left just after five thirty. It's only about fifteen minutes from here and so he should have been home in plenty of time.'

'Does Maciej have a car?'

'No. We couldn't afford one yet, so he always walked to work.'

'I know that you've already given us a description of what he was wearing but was there anything else he would have had with him?' asked Milner.

'He had a small black backpack. He always took his lunch in it.'

'What about keys, wallet, money? That sort of thing.'

'Yes. Of course he also took those with him.'

'How much money would he usually take?'

'About £20. Maybe a bit more.'

'I'm sorry about this but I have to ask you this question,' said Tom gently. 'Had you and Maciej had an argument? Were you happy together?'

Anna looked straight at Tom. 'I know what you are thinking. You think that Maciej might have left me for another woman. But that's not the case. We were planning to get married and start a family. Why would he leave me if we were going to do that?'

'That's true,' replied Tom reassuringly. 'Does Maciej have any close friends or even relatives here in the UK? It's possible that, for whatever reason, he might have decided to visit them.'

'That's not possible,' replied Anna firmly. 'Neither of us have any family here and Maciej did not have any friends.'

'What about at work?' asked Milner. 'He must have become friendly with some of his work colleagues.'

'If he did, he never mentioned it to me. In fact, he sometimes came home upset about how he was treated at work.'

'What do you mean?' asked Tom.

'He said that they used to make fun of him because he was Polish.'

They all remained silent for a while. Finally, Tom spoke.

40

'Thank you Miss Nowak. I know that it's upsetting but we both really appreciate you answering our questions.'

Tom stood up and handed her a card. 'If you remember anything else that you think we should know please call me on this number.'

Anna looked at the card and then said. 'Mr Stone. Please find Maciej.'

As Tom and Milner went out through the door they could hear Anna crying.

Chapter 6

Tom and Milner were back at the station by just after ten o'clock and were now both seated in Tom's office.

'I think you were right to be worried about Maciej,' said Tom. 'Like you I have a bad feeling about this. I don't think that Maciej has simply gone AWOL.'

There was a hint of relief in Milner's voice as he said. 'I'm glad you think so as well. What do you think we should do now?'

Tom looked thoughtful. 'Well, I think we should start by going to visit the Recycling Centre. I'd be interested to hear what they have to say about Maciej. In the meantime get his details out to everyone, particularly all of the local hospitals. It's possible he might have had an accident. It's happened before.'

'Anna seemed like a really nice lady. I'm not sure I'd take on as many jobs as they have. And in a foreign country.'

'You should never be influenced in your work by how much you personally like someone. Crime is crime, whoever is the victim.'

Milner looked a little crestfallen when he heard this, clearly taking it as a criticism. But, before he took it too personally, Tom added, 'Although on this one occasion I tend to agree with you. It's obvious they are a hard-working young couple who have taken jobs which our locals either aren't interested in or which don't pay enough.' He paused briefly and then added, although more to himself than to Milner, 'And that's why we are going to try our best to find Mr Sipowicz.'

Milner had rarely heard him speak in quite such a way. As far as Milner was concerned this constituted almost a spontaneous emotional outburst from DCI Stone, and he wondered whether he should try to respond in a similar way. He was beginning to realise though, that when dealing with DCI Stone, it was usually best to keep things on a business-like footing.

Anything else could take you into uncharted territory. So he simply said, 'I'll get onto it straight away.'

Tom had even surprised himself with his little outburst. Perhaps, finally, he really was mellowing. When he next spoke, though, he had regained his normal, default composure. 'Before you do that why don't you tell me what's the situation regarding the lead theft at St Augustine's Church?'

Tom was determined to keep as busy as possible for the remainder of the day. He wanted to minimise the amount of spare time he might have to think about other matters. That way he could forget, for a while at least, about tonight's meeting with Superintendent Peters.

'I've arranged to meet Father O'Connor, the priest at St Augustine's, at lunchtime,' replied Milner.

'Why are you meeting him?' asked Tom. 'Is there any particular reason?'

'Not really, Sir. Although I'd like to have another look round. There might just be something that uniform missed. And anyway ...' He seemed to hesitate, almost as though he was now having second thoughts about saying what he was thinking.

Tom made up his mind for him. 'Go on. Just say what you were about to say.'

'It's just that I did mention to Father O'Connor that I would keep him informed about our investigations and if there are any developments. He seemed very keen to know. I think it's the least I could do.'

'And what are the developments?' asked Tom.

'Well, not much, to be honest. We're still trying to get hold of all of the available CCTV footage. We have some but we're waiting for more to come in. Hopefully, there will be something on them which will give us a few leads to follow up on. But apart from that, nothing else, I'm afraid.'

'You don't have to apologise to me Milner,' offered Tom. 'Just try not to over-promise things to people that you can't deliver. It will make them and you unhappy. A colleague of mine, from way back, once said to me "It's always best to under-promise and over-deliver". It's a good principle to adopt. That way you have a much better chance of managing people's expectations.'

Milner liked these little homilies from DCI Stone. Even though sometimes they sounded a bit like how a father would speak to his son after he'd had a few beers.

'In future, I'll try and remember that, Sir,' said Milner.

Once again Tom wasn't quite sure if Milner was being sincere or not. So, he carried on. 'I think I should come along with you. What time are you leaving?' This time, and unlike earlier when he had appeared to ask for Milner's permission to accompany him to Challenor Road, Milner noticed that DCI Stone phrased this as a statement of intent rather than as a question.

'I was planning to leave here at about eleven thirty. Is that okay for you or should I change it?'

'No, that's fine. Come and meet me here at eleven thirty,' said Tom.

Chapter 7

After Milner left, Tom decided he really should start to think about his meeting with Superintendent Peters. As he had suspected he hadn't slept very well last night. He kept running through his mind all of the pros and cons of agreeing to what Peters had suggested. He also tried to think through all of the follow-up questions he would like to ask. When he did finally fall asleep he was still as undecided as ever.

What made it worse was the fact he was now even starting to doubt his own conclusions. Peters was right when he said all of the available information was purely circumstantial and that it wouldn't hold up for one minute in a court of law. If Milner had come to him with a similar scenario, and with the same quality of evidence, he would have sent him away and told him not to return until he had real evidence.

He was beginning to think it might be a personal thing with Detective Chief Inspector Shaw, the lead officer, and main driving force behind *Operation Torch*. He had even admitted to himself that he had never really liked Shaw. He was everything he wasn't. He was young – in fact, as a DCI he was one of the youngest in the Met. According to what he had heard on the grapevine Shaw's background was one of privilege and favour. He was also computer savvy and, undoubtedly, incredibly ambitious. In his experience, this degree of ambition often came hand in hand with a directly proportionate increase in risk-taking. The temptation to cut corners and take undue risks often correlated precisely with the level of personal ambition.

In his more mischievous moments he did wonder if it might be Shaw who was the officer passing on police operational information to Fuller. Or perhaps, deep down, he simply hoped this was the case. All of this was, of course, incredibly unfair on DCI Shaw. He might be everything Tom didn't like in a serving police officer but that didn't mean he was in the pocket of a major criminal.

What was clear though was that as soon as he had started to read the file on *Operation Torch*, the one thing which stood out, above everything else, was just how much credence Shaw had given to the information he was receiving from his own informant. Someone who claimed to be a close confidant of Tommy Fuller. He must be incredibly confident in his source. To Tom, though, this just didn't make any sense at all. He had come into contact with Jimmy Ryan, Shaw's informant, many times over the years. In fact the very first time he'd met him was when Ryan was just a low-level street dealer who sold drugs in order to pay for his own drug habit. Either Ryan's position within the Fuller organisation had risen dramatically since then or, more likely, at least in Tom's opinion, Ryan had been used. His recent murder only strengthened his opinion.

Tom thought about what he would have done if Ryan was his informant. The normal procedure would have been to corroborate the information coming from Ryan with another source. The vast majority of criminals usually become informants for a couple of reasons. It was either for money or because they had suddenly developed a grudge. Very occasionally it was due to a sudden change in principle or conscience. With Ryan, however, Tom found it impossible to believe that it had anything to do with any change in his moral compass. What's more, Ryan wasn't the brightest person he had ever met, and anyway, in his opinion, Ryan's conscience was conspicuous by its absence. So, if he was now a genuine informant it had to be one, or both, of those reasons.

As far as Tom could see, there was no reference at all to any other corroborative source in the file. What was fact, however, and undoubtedly strengthened Shaw's case that Ryan had been a high-grade informant, was that on a previous occasion he'd provided Shaw with other vital, detailed information. This had resulted in a great coup for the station when DCI Shaw had been successful in closing down a rival criminal gang within their area.

Ironically, the very success of this would have started to ring a few alarm bells in Tom's head. But not apparently in Shaw's. And now Ryan was dead. Very unfortunate for Ryan,

of course, but the reality was that a major source of information had suddenly, and if he was being totally cynical also
conveniently, been murdered. Tom also noticed, shortly after
this successful operation, how quickly Shaw had been
promoted to Detective Chief Inspector – making him one of
the Met's youngest ever DCIs.

Coincidentally, Tom might also have been involved in
Operation Sunlight, albeit only on the periphery. He had
heard, from a few trusted colleagues, however, that Shaw had
specifically refused to allow him to be involved in the main
operation. He didn't know if this was true or not – although
it wouldn't surprise him if it was. So perhaps DCI Shaw felt
just as strongly about him as he did about Shaw. It was
certainly true that DCI Shaw would go out of his way to
avoid him. This didn't particularly worry him because they
just didn't seem to have anything in common. Anyway, his
role in *Sunlight* would have simply been to provide reserve
back-up, should it have been required. In the event, he
wouldn't even have been needed for that, as the operation
went like clockwork, and the entire gang were swept up.

In his more rational moments, Tom knew it would be
almost impossible to prove, at least beyond question, that
there was a mole within the station. He might be able to
compile a list of possible suspects but, in truth, this would
potentially be even worse than no suspects at all, particularly
if there was no incontrovertible evidence to back up these
suspicions. If this ever became public knowledge then there
would forever be a cloud of suspicion hanging over these
officers who were, almost certainly, totally innocent. Tom
had seen careers destroyed for much less.

Was it worth risking the careers of honest police officers
just because he had this hair-brained theory? And there was
another, more practical, concern which was beginning to
worry him. How was he expected to keep this inquiry totally
secret? Tom considered himself to be a bit of an expert at
reading body language. Although most police officers had
received some training in this, it was his thirty-plus years of
experience of dealing with suspects, criminals and colleagues
as well as, he had to admit, some previous bosses, which had
really developed and fine-tuned this skill. Quite often it was
the subtle changes in behaviour or language which were the

most important giveaway signs: a sudden change to less direct eye contact when speaking; more formal, business-like dialogue than would normally be the case; an obvious reluctance to spend more time than was absolutely necessary with someone. He had even been guilty of this himself. Many years ago he and a fellow junior police officer were being considered for the same promotion to the position of Detective Sergeant. They were friends as well as colleagues. They had often entertained each other in their respective homes. Tom, however, had been told by his Detective Inspector that he would be offered the position.

He was told this even before any formal interviews had taken place. He could still remember how uncomfortable it made him feel whenever he came into contact with his friend. In fact he did everything he could to try and avoid contact with him until after they'd both been interviewed. Afterwards his colleague did mention to Tom how he had noticed that his behaviour towards him had changed significantly just before the interviews. He had initially put this down to the awkwardness of the situation they both found themselves in. Afterwards though he had asked him outright if he had already been offered the position before the interviews. He'd lied and said that he'd had no idea.

It wasn't something of which he was particularly proud. Nonetheless, he learnt from the experience and had, since then, tried his best to always maintain as normal a demeanour and behaviour as possible. If he did accept Peters' offer then he suspected he would have to make full use of all of his accumulated experience over the next few weeks.

Chapter 8

It was just after eleven fifteen when Milner arrived back at Tom's office. As usual he had a file in his hand.

Tom looked up. 'Just give me a couple of minutes,' he said as Milner came into his office. Milner could see DCI Stone had a single A4 sheet of paper in front of him. He had drawn a line drawn down the middle and there were a few words on either side of that line. But before he could make out anything written on it DCI Stone folded the paper and placed it inside his jacket pocket.

'Right,' said Tom, focusing his full attention on Milner. 'Is it time for church then?'

'I suppose it is,' replied Milner quietly. 'Are you sure you want to come along, Sir? As I told you earlier it's just a routine visit. I'm sure you've got lots of other things to do.' He found himself suddenly thinking about the piece of paper in DCI Stone's pocket.

'Thank you for your concern, Milner, but I think I'm old enough to decide what I should be doing with my time.'

'Sorry, Sir. It's just I thought, as this is only your second day back at work, you might have other more important things to do.'

Tom was beginning to get the distinct impression that Milner didn't really want him to come along. He wondered why that might be and was now even more determined to go.

'I haven't been to church for years. You never know, this might just be the inspiration I need to start attending again.' As he said this he watched Milner very closely. Almost instantly he could see that Milner had been affected by what he had just said. That same look of momentary anger, which he had witnessed yesterday, had reappeared on Milner's face. Tom suspected, for some reason, that he had upset Milner. He thought he should try and find out what it was.

'Milner. Have I said something out of turn? You look a little upset.'

'No, Sir. Nothing at all,' replied Milner, not very convincingly.

'Well, if I did, please accept my apologies. I shouldn't have been quite so flippant.' He paused, allowing space for Milner to respond. When it was clear he wasn't going to Tom simply said, 'It's Father O'Connor we will be seeing, isn't it?'

'Yes Sir, that's correct,' answered Milner. 'He's been the priest there for over twenty years and is well known in the local community.'

Tom wondered how Milner knew all this additional information but decided not to ask. Instead he stood up. 'Let's go then.'

'Sir, before we go, you might be interested in this?' suggested Milner, taking a sheet of paper out of the file which he was still holding. He passed it to Tom. 'It's the information you asked me to get for you on Pauline Jones. It turns out she is known to us. Did you expect that, Sir?'

'I'm not sure what I expected, Milner,' replied Tom, as he began to read what was on the sheet of paper. He then quickly folded it in half and put it inside his jacket pocket. Milner thought DCI Stone's inside jacket pocket now contained quite a few little mysteries.

A short time later they arrived at St Augustine's and entered the church. Tom was surprised to see that it was a hive of activity. He could instantly see that all of this activity was not due to a well-attended church service, but rather to the repair work being carried out inside the building.

Tom assumed that it was Father O'Connor whom he could see next to a man at the far end of the church. It struck him as quite an odd sight to see a Roman Catholic priest wearing a traditional black cassock, but with a brightly coloured yellow hard hat on his head. The other man was also wearing a hard hat but, unlike the others, who were wearing high viz, fluorescent jackets, he was smartly dressed in a dark blue suit with matching tie.

It wasn't long before Father O'Connor spotted them. He ended his conversation with the man in the suit and walked towards them.

'David,' he said, shaking Milner's hand quite vigorously.

'Lovely to see you again – although I wish it was in more pleasant circumstances.'

Father O'Connor was a tall, slim man, probably in his early sixties, with quite long and slightly unruly grey hair, which poked out randomly from under his hard hat.

Milner introduced Tom. 'Father O'Connor, this is Detective Chief Inspector Stone. He's my boss. He specifically asked if he could come along today and meet you.'

Tom smiled and said, 'Very pleased to meet you Father O'Connor. Although, as you say, it would have been better if we weren't here on official police business. I can see you're very busy today.'

'That's true. Although work has already begun on the repair work, we are still "negotiating" – I think that's the correct way of describing it – with our insurance company. In fact I was just speaking with their loss adjuster,' he said, gesturing towards the man in the suit.

'And do you think they will agree to pay for all of the repairs?' asked Tom, genuinely interested in his answer.

Father O'Connor simply smiled and then said, 'With God's help.'

For once Tom couldn't think of anything appropriate to say in response. So he made do with 'Do you know how much all of the repairs are likely to cost?'

'The latest estimate is about £150,000. The main cost is to repair all of the damage caused by the leaking roof . As you can see,' he said, pointing to a large hole just above the altar, 'there is a lot to repair.' He then looked directly at Milner, before adding, 'David can tell you just how much needs to be done.'

Milner flushed as Tom looked towards him waiting for a response. When he spoke it was, however, in a calm and measured way. 'I've already mentioned to Detective Chief Inspector Stone that it couldn't have happened in a worse position, or at a worse time due to the thunderstorm. The priority now is to get the roof fixed as soon as possible. What you can see is just temporary to keep the worst of the weather out. Once this is fixed permanently then work can get started on the repairs inside the church. At the moment most of the work being done is just clearing up and making the area safe.'

Tom continued to look at Milner and said, 'You seem to know a lot about it.'

It was Father O'Connor who, sensing Milner's slight embarrassment, answered. 'David has been coming to this church since he was a small boy. In fact, when he was just seven years old he made his first communion here.'

'First communion?' asked Tom.

Father O'Connor smiled. 'Can I take it that you are not a churchgoer, Detective Chief Inspector Stone?'

'Well, not really,' replied Tom. 'I never seemed to have any time for God.'

Once again Father O'Connor smiled. 'Just remember though God will always have time for you.' Fortunately for Tom he had no time to respond as Father O'Connor carried straight on. 'Taking communion is when you first make a promise to God. Although I have to say,' he added, now switching his attention towards Milner, 'David's attendance here has slipped a little over the past few years. In fact, since he joined the police force.'

Tom could see that Milner was starting to look uncomfortable and so he attempted to try and ease the situation. 'That's probably my fault, Father,' he said. 'Unfortunately criminals do not respect the Sabbath. They tend not to see Sunday as a day of rest.' He paused momentarily before adding, 'And anyway, Detective Sergeant Milner is one of our best officers. In fact, he may have told you he was recently promoted, partly as a result of his bravery when saving the life of a drowning man.'

Now both Tom and Father O'Connor were looking intently at Milner.

'No, he didn't mention it,' said Father O'Connor. 'Although I did read about it in one of the daily newspapers.'

To Milner's great relief, Tom then said, 'If you don't mind me saying, Father, you appear to be remarkably sanguine about what has happened. I'm not sure I would be quite so relaxed.'

'One of the first things that I learned as a priest, Detective Chief Inspector Stone, is that it's human life which is the most precious. I'm sure, whoever did this,' he said looking at the damage, 'had their reasons. As far as I know, no one has died. Just yesterday though I had to visit one of my congregation. Her son had just died from a drugs overdose. He was seventeen years old. Now that is a tragedy. In fact it's the second time this year we've lost a young person to drugs. It's a tragedy for everyone. For someone who is so young. For their family, who are left to grieve for their loss and, yes, even for whoever sold the drugs which killed them.' He paused for a while before adding, very quietly and more to himself than to anyone else, 'I wonder how many more young people are going to die, due to drugs, before this year is out?'

Tom could see that Father O'Connor was clearly moved by what he had just said. 'If it's any consolation,' said Tom, 'this is something the police force does have in common with the Church. Do you mind if we take a look around? Ideally I'd also like to see where the lead was taken from. Would that be possible?'

'I'm not sure,' replied Father O'Connor. 'The workmen have installed scaffolding but I don't know whether it's safe yet. You'd have to speak with their supervisor. He's just over there. The one wearing the white hat.'

Tom and Milner headed over to speak with the supervisor and introduced themselves.

'Would it be possible to take a look at the roof?' asked Tom.

'I don't see why not,' replied the supervisor. 'All of the scaffolding is now in place. In fact, I was going to contact the police anyway.'

'Why?' said Tom. 'Do you have some information?'

The supervisor took out a mobile phone from his pocket and handed it to Tom. ' No. Not information, just this. One of the scaffolding erectors found it in the guttering. It looks fairly new to me. Perhaps whoever did this left it up there by accident? Anyway, I hope it helps.'

'Thank you. You never know,' he answered, placing the phone carefully in a small plastic bag and then in his pocket.

Tom and Milner spent the next few minutes on a platform positioned at the side of the roof. From here they had a good view of the damage done to the roof. 'Whoever did this was either incredibly foolish or an expert climber with no fear of heights,' said Tom, as he looked down towards the ground.

After they had come down from the roof, Father O'Connor approached them. 'Did you find anything interesting up there?' he asked.

'It's always useful to visit the scene of the crime,' replied Tom, not answering Father O'Connor's question.

'Well, good luck,' said Father O'Connor. He shook Tom's hand and then offered his hand to Milner. As they were both walking towards the church door, Father O'Connor called out. 'Will we see you this Sunday, David?'

'I'm not sure, Father,' replied Milner, who then turned away, his eyes fixed firmly on the door directly in front of him.

They arrived back at the station just before three o'clock. Milner had, uncharacteristically, said very little on the way back. Tom suspected that he was perhaps embarrassed. Even though Tom now knew that St Augustine's was his local church, and that he had been attending services there ever since he was a small boy, there really was nothing for him to feel embarrassed about. He suspected though that Milner didn't quite see it that way.

Although he himself was, at best, agnostic, when it came to religion, this did not prevent him from respecting those people who were believers. Anything which legally gave comfort to people was something he had always encouraged. He would speak with Milner about this later as now was probably not the best time for him to raise the subject.

'Finding this mobile phone was a real stroke of good fortune,' said Tom as he handed the bag containing the phone over to Milner. 'Hopefully the lab boys will find something interesting on the SIM card. Also check any fingerprints on it against the national database. I know a few other people have now handled it, but you never know.'

'I'll get on to it right away, Sir,' replied Milner. He hesitated, before adding. 'I hope, Sir, you didn't think I was paying special attention to what happened at St Augustine's, simply because that's where I go.'

'Milner. I hope that's exactly what you are doing. If it was my church, then I would certainly be making sure I did everything possible to arrest whoever did this.' Now that Milner had raised the subject, Tom felt he could now legitimately discuss it.

'Father O'Connor obviously thinks very highly of you. I could also see he was proud of what you have achieved.' Milner remained silent and so Tom felt he would ask a question which Milner would have to answer. 'Do your parents also go there?'

'Well, my mother does. My father is more of a lapsed Catholic these days.'

'And how often do you go?'

'Well, as Father O'Connor said, not as much as perhaps I should. Sometimes I'm working, so I can't get there. Other times though I just find it difficult to attend as often as I used to.'

'Is there any particular reason for that?' asked Tom.

Milner hesitated. 'The truth, Sir, is that I've found it increasingly difficult to reconcile my police work with my religion.'

'Why?' asked Tom, clearly interested.

'No particular reason. It's just something which has built up slowly since I joined the force. Although what happened at St Augustine's just seemed to crystallise everything I've been feeling recently.' He was silent for a while before continuing. 'I know, as someone who has been involved with the Church for almost all of my life, I should forgive people for their weaknesses. But I can no longer do that any more. The more crime I see, the more I feel they are not just some minor weaknesses but more pure evil.' Looking directly at Tom, he said, 'You must feel the same, Sir.'

Tom could see there was a real danger that Milner might lose control of his emotions. 'Unfortunately, I don't think I'm the best qualified person to answer that question, but I do know someone who is. Why, don't you go and speak with Father O'Connor and tell him what you've just told me. I'm sure he's asked himself this many times before. He strikes me as being someone who is best qualified to reconcile matters of faith and conscience.'

Milner remained silent, trying to regain his composure. Eventually he said, 'Thank you, Sir. I think I will. I'll try not to let that happen again.'

'Milner. There is nothing for you to apologise for.'

This seemed like an appropriate time to end the conversation. When he had asked Milner about the church he never expected this outcome. There was still a lot he had to learn about Milner.

He returned the conversation to more conventional

matters. 'I don't think there is anything else we can do until we get the report back on the mobile phone. When you speak with them can you stress the urgency of this? I would have thought the thief has now realised that his phone is missing and is probably starting to wonder where he lost it. With a bit of luck he might also be starting to panic. When people panic they tend to make mistakes. Anyway, just tell them that we need it urgently.' As Milner was leaving Tom said, 'David. If you ever want to speak with anyone, I hope you feel you can come to me.'

'Thank you, Sir,' replied Milner, more surprised that DCI Stone had used his Christian name.

Afterwards, Tom's thoughts returned to the two pieces of paper in his pocket. He picked out the one relating to Pauline Jones first.

As he read it he found himself smiling. His antenna had clearly still been working well when they had met. He somehow knew she was not being entirely truthful about herself. She was not as young as she claimed to be. She was actually forty-nine years old, not the 'early 40s' which was written on her personal profile. Okay, he could live with that. But it was the fact she was known to the police which was the most important discrepancy. In the mid-90s she had been regularly cautioned for soliciting. Not only that but she had also been arrested, on more than one occasion, for possession of drugs, including cocaine. She had claimed they were for personal use but the quantity involved suggested she might have also been dealing them. That was probably the reason, he suspected, why she couldn't wait to get away from him once he had told her he was a Detective Chief Inspector.

During their meal he had noticed how she seemed to alternate between virtually non-stop talking and an almost sullen silence. In fact, as he thought back to that night, he remembered how she'd had to go to the toilet quite regularly. Perhaps she had done that so she could take something. It would certainly help to explain her sudden mood swings.

He gave a light laugh as he thought what Milner would have made of the fact that his Detective Chief Inspector had dated a known drug-taking prostitute and potential drugs dealer!

He replaced the paper in his pocket and took out the other

one. In just a few hours time he was due to have his follow-up meeting with Superintendent Peters. As he looked at the paper, and what he had written on it, he suddenly thought of Father O'Connor and what he had said to him regarding the death of the young boy.

He picked up the paper, screwed it up and threw it into the waste bin, just under his desk. He now knew what he had to do.

Chapter 9

Tom spent the remainder of the afternoon at his desk, once again working his way through all of the paperwork. He quickly flicked through the various reports and sheets of paper, making a decision as to the ones he judged required his immediate attention. He could see some had the word 'Urgent' printed in bold, capital letters on the front of the report or on top of the first sheet of paper. He pulled these out and put them to one side. He would deal with them first.

Most of the others were 'for information only'. He would read them if, and when, he had some free time. The rest, he quickly decided, did not really need any of his personal attention at all. Nonetheless, there might be something in them which he might need to know about. He would pass those over to Milner to sort through. It would be another step, for him on his long, and usually not very straight, career path, although, worryingly, Milner appeared to actually enjoy the paperwork part of being a police officer.

He then turned his attention to the most urgent reports. He was relieved to see that most, although they might have been urgent at some stage, were no longer so. Events had overtaken them and so they were no longer urgent. It was amazing, he thought, how often this happens. If you leave something long enough, eventually, as if by magic, it removes itself from the 'urgent' list.

There was, however, a brief, one-line note, which was almost hidden away in his work file, which caught his attention. It was from Detective Chief Inspector Shaw and referred to a discussion between himself and Jimmy Ryan. It simply stated that Shaw had met with Ryan, although he used his code name 'Justice', in order to protect his anonymity.

According to the date on the note, they had met not long after the botched raid on Fuller's house. 'That's not surprising,' Tom found himself saying out loud to himself. If he had been leading the operation, meeting with Ryan – his main informant – would also have been top of his 'to-do' list. Tom was intrigued to know what Ryan had to say at their meeting. At some stage Tom would have to ask Shaw about the meeting. It didn't take a mind reader to predict what his reaction would be! Shaw already knew that Superintendent Peters had asked Tom to carry out the initial review of *Operation Torch*. But, at the time, his terms of reference had been restricted to simply suggesting any recommendations or changes to future operational procedures, the main objective being to minimise the likelihood of this type of operational disaster ever happening again. He made a mental note to ask Superintendent Peters at their meeting if there was a copy of what had been discussed.

It was just after six o'clock when Milner appeared outside his office.

Tom looked up and said, 'Milner, I was just thinking about getting myself a drink. Can I get you one? It's coffee, no sugar isn't it?'

'Thank you, Sir. That would be nice,' he replied.

Tom made his way to the vending machine to get the drinks. He returned to his office and handed one of the cups to Milner.

'Do you know, Milner,' he said, 'we used to have a kettle in the office and we just made our own drinks. It worked perfectly fine. Then, a few years ago, health and safety carried out a risk assessment and decided we could no longer be trusted to do this ourselves. Apparently, even though most of us have been trained to handle lethal firearms, we are not trusted to be able to make a cup of tea without injuring ourselves.' He then added, more to himself than to Milner, 'Unbelievable really. Only a committee could come up with something like that. The outcome was that all kettles were banned and instead they installed a vending machine, which now also dispenses other fancy hot drinks which no one had asked for, and then started charging us for choosing them. The world has gone mad.' Tom was doing a good impression of a grumpy old man. Even then he wasn't finished. 'I wouldn't mind if the machine tea was any good but it tastes just like the proverbial lukewarm dishwater.'

'I know,' replied Milner, sounding like a young person

would sound when trying to humour an elderly one. He then added, as if to confirm he'd agreed with everything Tom had said, 'That's why I drink the coffee. It's slightly less awful.'

When Tom had returned to his office Milner was already seated at his desk with a selection of files in front of him. Tom's heart had sunk. He didn't want to dampen Milner's enthusiasm, particularly after his earlier emotional outburst, but he really wasn't in the right frame of mind for what, he suspected, Milner intended. If the number of files was anything to go by there was a danger he might be late for his meeting with Superintendent Peters.

Milner picked up his cup and sipped his coffee. He pulled a face. Detective Chief Inspector Stone had only ever bought him coffee twice before and on both occasions it had sugar in it. He suddenly wondered if this was DCI Stone's idea of fun and that he was now doing this deliberately. Before he arrived at a conclusion, on this important issue however, Tom asked, gesturing at the files, 'Is there anything in those which needs our immediate attention?' He made sure that he'd emphasised the word 'immediate'.

This wasn't lost on Milner. 'I was hoping to take you through a few more of the domestics and burglaries. But we could always do that another time.'

'Let's do that then,' answered Tom.

But Milner wasn't about to give in quite so easily. 'There was one other thing though.' He continued without allowing Tom the opportunity to ask what it was. 'I thought that I'd find out who else works at the Recycling Centre. It might be good background information when we go there. So, earlier, I asked for a list of people who work there. Although the Centre is owned by the Council it's run by a private company, National Waste Recycling and Disposal Services Ltd. They got back to me quickly, so I was able to run their names through the system.'

'What did you tell them about why you needed the names?' asked Tom.

Milner, shifting a little uncomfortably in his chair, said, 'Actually, Sir, I didn't phone them myself. I have a contact at the Council. They spoke to them and said they were updating all of their records and needed the very latest details.'

Tom was genuinely impressed. 'Good work, Milner. That's

just the sort of thing which councils would ask for.' He then carried on. 'And?'

Milner didn't exactly smile, but Tom could sense that he was pleased with himself. 'Very interesting actually. Two of the people who work there have criminal records. Gary Walker was found guilty of assault a few years ago and received a six-month custodial sentence. This was his second offence. After the first one he was given a suspended sentence. Then there's Darren Wood. He has a long history of petty thefts and burglaries and has served a few custodial sentences, first at young offenders' institutions and then prison.'

'Seems like your National Waste Company – or whatever it's called – takes quite a relaxed approach when it comes to employing ex-criminals. I'll look forward to speaking with Mr Walker and Mr Wood. Is there anything else? What about the mobile phone? Any news on that yet?'

'Nothing yet, Sir. I checked just before I came here. They told me it'll be tomorrow, at the earliest, before they have anything,' replied Milner. 'Is that all, Sir? It's just that Father O'Connor is trying to salvage whatever he can at the church, and I promised I would help him tonight.'

Tom was relieved that Milner was, once again, able to mention Father O'Connor and the church without any emotion.

Tom looked intently at Milner. 'I'm not sure how I could possibly refuse that request. And please, say thank you to Father O'Connor from me.'

Milner looked slightly puzzled as he said, 'Any particular reason for that, Sir?'

'There are lots, Milner but the main one is he reminded me why I became a policeman in the first place.'

By the time Milner left, Tom was becoming impatient to begin his meeting with Superintendent Peters. But he had agreed to meet Peters at seven thirty, so he carried on with his paperwork. In truth, though, he found it very difficult to concentrate and his mind kept wandering ahead to his upcoming meeting.

Eventually the clock ticked around to seven thirty and he made his way up to the fifth floor. As he entered Superintendent Peters' outer office he was surprised to see Janice still seated at her desk.

'Hello,' said a clearly surprised Janice. 'I was just thinking about leaving. I didn't have you in Superintendent Peters' diary.'

'No, you wouldn't. Superintendent Peters asked me to keep him updated on the metal thefts inquiries. Someone told me he was still here and so I came up on the off chance he could see me,' lied Tom.

Janice's reply confirmed to Tom she was far from convinced by his explanation. 'Isn't that something you could have more easily emailed to him?' she said, not unreasonably.

'You're probably right. Maybe that's what I'll do,' replied Tom, taking a chance.

It seemed to work as Janice then said, 'Well, now you're here you might as well see him. I'll just go and let him know you are here.'

Almost immediately she reappeared and said, smiling at him. 'You're in luck. He has a few other things to finish but will see you when he's done. Can I get you something to drink whilst you're waiting?' she asked helpfully.

Although he was tempted, especially as there was no sign of a hot drinks machine anywhere near Superintendent Peters' office, he wanted to get on with this as soon as possible. 'Thank you, but not at the moment. I think I've had my quota of tea for one day,' he replied.

Tom sat down and pretended to read one of the files which he had brought with him, whilst Janice was preparing to leave. Eventually she was ready. She buzzed through to Superintendent Peters. 'I was just about to leave, unless there's anything else you need from me tonight?' She paused. 'Okay. I'll see you tomorrow morning. Goodnight.'

She then placed a few things into one of the desk drawers, stood up, picked up her coat and bag and said, 'Good night Detective Chief Inspector Stone. I hope you don't have to wait too long. Can I suggest next time you phone through to make an appointment?'

With that final pithy comment she walked out of the office and headed towards the lift.

Almost immediately Superintendent Peters opened his office door and said, 'Sorry about that Tom. I forgot to mention to Janice that we had a meeting. Anyway, come on in.'

'She's one tough lady,' remarked Tom. 'I felt a bit like a naughty schoolboy who has been caught smoking behind the bike sheds and been sent to see the headmaster.' He laughed quietly.

'Maybe that's what you have done,' answered Peters, joining in the laughter.

After they were both seated Superintendent Peters spoke immediately. 'So, you've had a little time to think about what we discussed yesterday.' He hesitated briefly, before adding. 'Remember, what I told you. Whatever you decide you will continue to have my full support.'

Tom decided he should put Superintendent Peters out of his misery.

'I know that, Sir and I really appreciate it. And it was one of the reasons why I came to my decision to agree to do what you suggested.'

They were both silent – each, no doubt, deep in their own thoughts considering the implications of what Tom had just committed himself to.

Superintendent Peters stood up, shook Tom's hand and then spoke in a voice full of excitement. 'Tom. I was hoping that's what you would say. Tell me. What was the main factor which helped you to come to this decision?'

Tom thought for a moment and then said, 'It was a conversation I had today with a Catholic priest.'

Chapter 10

By the time he arrived back at home after his meeting with Superintendent Peters, Tom suddenly realised just how hungry he was. He did consider calling Mary to see if she wanted to come over but decided it was probably too late and, anyway, it would be unfair on her. He couldn't just call, and ask her to change everything she had planned, just because he needed her company.

So he made do with a pizza, which he found hidden at the back of his freezer. His culinary skills had always been fairly limited. He really envied those men who enjoyed cooking. But, in truth, this had never been something which had appealed to him, despite – or was it because of? – the number of cooking programmes on television. Perhaps the reason was the unsocial hours which he worked? More likely though was that it was just another example of his lack of motivation.

Superintendent Peters had provided him with another set of files, relating to *Operation Torch*, and so, as he ate, he started to read through them. He had his notebook close by just in case he needed to write anything down. He must have become engrossed in what he was doing because, when he next glanced at his watch, he realised that almost two hours had slipped by.

He was also starting to feel tired and so decided he had done enough for one night. He returned his notes to the file, stood up and went into his small study and placed it in one of the drawers there. Although he felt tired he suspected he might still find it very difficult to sleep. But it was now late and he felt he should, at least, try and get some rest.

Despite the fact that there were lots of different things swirling around in his head there was one particular thought which kept recurring. It was the thought that if he was wrong then he was about to embark on something which could only end one way – in personal and professional disaster.

Eventually though he must have given in and fallen into a fitful sleep, although it seemed like no time at all before his alarm started to ring. Despite now feeling very tired, he knew, from personal experience, that it would be much better for him if he was up and about, actually doing something, rather than just lying there thinking about doing something.

Milner, as ever, was waiting for him when he arrived at the station. This time though it was Tom who initiated the pleasantries. 'Did you manage to get much done last night?' he asked.

Milner, clearly misunderstanding Tom's question, replied, quite defensively, 'Not really, Sir. As I think I told you, we won't get the report on the phone until sometime today.'

Tom, resisting the urge to smile, simply said, 'Actually, Milner, I was asking about your clean-up work at St Augustine's.'

Milner flushed slightly. 'Sorry, Sir. I thought you were asking about the thefts.'

'We'll get on to those in a minute. I just wanted to know about the work at the church,' explained Tom.

This sudden, and unexpected, interest by Detective Chief Inspector Stone had clearly unsettled Milner. Nonetheless, he had regained his composure when he replied. 'There were a few of us there and so we managed to get quite a bit done. Although,' he added, 'as you saw for yourself yesterday, there's still so much more work to be done before the builders can start work on repairing the inside of the church.' His tone lightened a little as he carried on. 'There was some good news though. After we left, the insurance company called Father O'Connor to tell him they would pay for the work to repair the roof.'

Tom was genuinely pleased to hear this. 'That's great news. I hope the cost of the rest of the work is also approved by the insurance company.'

'So do I,' replied a suddenly anxious Milner.

'How long do they think it will take before the church can be reopened?'

'As they're still carrying out structural tests, they can't really say. But I think it will be at least a couple of months.'

'Well, however long it takes I'm sure it will be worth it. I'd appreciate it if you could keep me informed on the progress.'

Milner was still a little surprised by Tom's sudden interest in St Augustine's. 'I will, Sir,' he answered.

Tom could sense that Milner wanted to say something else. One of the things he had learned about Milner was how he had a habit of letting concerns fester away in his head rather than voicing them. It was something Tom would have to try and encourage him to change. He looked intently at Milner and said. 'Why don't you tell me what else you want to say. If we are to work together then we must be open with each other.'

Milner's immediate thought was that DCI Stone was a person who was among the least likely when it came to being open. Nonetheless, he could detect in his voice a genuine interest. Milner thought he should reciprocate in the same spirit. 'It's about yesterday, Sir. I'm sorry for involving you in my problems. It was very unprofessional of me. It won't happen again.'

As he heard this Tom felt a sudden and deep-seated affection for Milner. Perhaps it was his vulnerability which had touched him, or maybe just his honesty. Whatever the reason, Tom was, uncharacteristically, moved.

'Milner, there's nothing to apologise for. Let me tell you something. This might surprise you but even I occasionally have pangs of conscience. It comes with the job. As long as you continue to care you won't go far wrong.'

'Thank you Sir. I really appreciate that.' He then added, with a slight laugh, 'By the way, Father O'Connor asked me to tell you that you are always welcome at St Augustine's.'

As he said this, Milner thought back to his conversation, last night, with Father O'Connor. He had been embarrassed when DCI Stone had found out about his long involvement with St Augustine's and then even more so after his emotional outburst. He'd had to work really hard to stop himself from actually shedding some tears. He sensed it was this more than anything else which had forced him to evaluate whether he would ever be able to reconcile his faith with being a police officer. Deep down he had always known that, sooner or later, he would have to confront this. Maybe, in retrospect, it was best that it had happened at this early point in his career.

After he had arrived at the church, but before he'd started to help with the clean-up, Father O'Connor had sought him out and asked if he could speak with him. He did think, momentarily, that perhaps DCI Stone had, himself, spoken with Father O'Connor about their earlier conversation. Possibly, though, it was because, strange as it might seem, they both had similar moral compasses, but just used them in different ways.

What soon became clear, though, was how Father O'Connor appeared to sense the inner turmoil he was going through. He had asked him if his commitment to the Church had changed and whether or not this was troubling him. At first Milner had been reluctant to admit his concerns but this didn't last long because, before he realised, he was telling Father O'Connor everything. About how, for some time now, he had found himself questioning the beliefs that had been part of his life since he was a child. About how he increasingly felt that the Church was no longer relevant to the everyday lives of people. But particularly about how he was finding it almost impossible to reconcile the values of the Church with his own career as a police officer. Wasn't the Church about forgiveness? How though could he possibly apply this principle having seen what people could do to each other and the impact that their actions had on other, innocent, people's lives. Surely, any emotional investment should be directed at the victims of crime rather than the perpetrators?

Of course, he had expected Father O'Connor to be understanding. Most of his previous experiences had revolved around hearing him speak, either to his congregation collectively or individually. What he had not realised though, was just how good a listener he was. What was surprising was how, as soon as he had finished, it was as though a huge weight had been lifted and he now felt almost liberated. After listening to what he had to say Father O'Connor remained silent for a while. Eventually he asked him what had motivated him, in the first place, to join the police force. In reply Milner talked about doing his bit to protect the most vulnerable in society, as well as obtaining justice for those who had personally been affected by criminal activity. As he said this he noticed that Father O'Connor had started to smile.

'So, we are both doing the same thing,' said Father

O'Connor. 'It's simply that we have chosen different paths to achieve this. That's all they are. Different. But that doesn't mean, occasionally, they can't converge. In fact, often, the best work of the Church occurs when that happens. Your career as a policeman will, I'm certain, eventually strengthen your faith, not destroy it.' He paused momentarily. 'But, in the meantime, I'm relying on you to arrest whoever is responsible for all of this,' he said, pointing towards the mess in the far corner of the church.

'Milner, are you okay?' asked Tom. 'You look a little distracted.'

'Sorry Sir. I was just thinking back to a conversation I had with Father O'Connor last night.' There was a slight hesitation before he continued. 'I took your advice and spoke to him about what happened yesterday.'

'And was it a good conversation?'

'Actually Sir,' he answered, 'it was. Well, at least I felt a lot better after it.'

'Does that mean I've got to put up with you for a bit longer?' Tom asked, feigning concern.

'Unfortunately it does. Although I'm hoping that the criminal fraternity will, occasionally, allow me to attend church on Sundays.'

Whatever Father O'Connor had said to him it seemed to have resulted in Milner being in a far more comfortable frame of mind. Perhaps he would take up his offer to visit St Augustine's after all.

Chapter 11

'Have there been any other metal thefts reported since yesterday?' asked Tom, now returning the conversation to more conventional matters.

'Nothing that's come to our attention yet, although it's still a bit early,' replied Milner, himself now back into his normal business-like mode.

'Yes, I suppose it is,' said Tom. 'Anyway, let's hope it's been a quiet night.'

Just as he said this, Milner's mobile phone rang. After he had taken the call he said, with a hint of excitement in his voice, 'That was the lab boys, Sir. They've found something on the phone and felt that we would want to know about it straightaway.'

'Really?' answered Tom, a little quizzically. 'In my experience they usually won't release anything until they've completed their work. You obviously have some good contacts there.'

Milner ignored the compliment, partly because he was eager to tell DCI Stone what he'd just heard. 'Apparently it was like a gold mine,' he said, a huge smile suddenly appearing on his face. 'They've emailed it to me already. I'll just go and print it off.'

It wasn't long before he was back in Tom's office, holding a sheet of paper in his right hand. He passed it to Tom. 'You won't believe who the phone belongs to.'

'I see what you mean,' said Tom, quietly to himself, after he had read it. 'So, the phone belongs to our new friend Darren Wood.' He looked up, smiled and said, 'Milner, I think someone, on a higher level, might be helping us.' He then referred back to the sheet of paper. 'It looks as though Darren Wood likes to make lots of calls. In fact,' he suddenly said, looking even more closely at the list, 'there's one number on the list which keeps cropping up. I'd be interested to know whose number this is. See if you can find out who he has been calling so often.' He leant back in his chair. 'It certainly doesn't look good for Darren Wood. It seems like our luck might have suddenly changed for the better.'

Whilst Milner was away trying to obtain more information on Darren Wood, Tom looked through his emails. He could see immediately there was one from Superintendent Peters.

Its subject heading was 'Reporting'. This was the code word they had agreed for their inquiry. The thinking behind the chosen name was that, even if it was seen by anyone else, it would appear to be so potentially boring and mundane, that no one would be in the slightest bit interested in its content.

Tom opened the email and started to read its content. It was a summary of DCI Shaw's conversation with Jimmy Ryan, which had taken place not long after the raid. He was, however, only part way through this when a clearly excited Milner reappeared.

'Sir, I think you should see this.'

'Just give me a summary,' suggested Tom, closing down the email.

Milner took a deep breath and said. 'It's about Darren Wood, Sir.'

'What is it? Has he unexpectedly turned up at St Augustine's to help clean up the mess?'

'Not exactly, Sir. Not least because he's dead.'

'Dead?' repeated an almost unbelieving Tom, struggling to take in everything which had happened over the past few hours. 'Do we know how he died?'

Milner referred to his notes. 'His body was discovered at eight o'clock this morning, by a group of workmen who were planning to carry out engineering repairs on a railway line. It looks as though he was electrocuted, although we will have to wait for the post mortem for the final cause of death.' Milner looked up from his notes. 'The workmen did confirm however that the particular line, on which Wood's body was found, was live.'

'Live? Well that would explain your electrocution theory.' Tom remained quiet for a while and then said, 'Anything else? As though that wasn't enough.'

'Well, yes Sir, there is,' answered Milner. 'There were a

number of tools lying by the body. He still had a pair of industrial cutters in his hand. It looks as though he was trying to cut out some of the copper cabling.'

'So, he'd moved on from stealing lead from church roofs to stealing copper cables from live railway lines. As I said earlier, either incredibly brave or foolish. I think that we now have the answer. How do we know that it was Darren Wood?'

'Uniform were called to the scene, along with the paramedics. They seem very confident it was Darren Wood but, to be honest, I forgot to ask how they knew this.'

Just then, Milner's overworked mobile rang again. 'Excuse me Sir, while I take this.' Tom was still thinking about the circumstances of Wood's death and so paid little attention to the brief conversation Milner was having on his mobile.

'Sir, that was the lab boys again. They've really got the bit between their teeth with this one. They've started to trace the numbers on Wood's mobile. I'd asked them to first check up on the number which Wood had called most often and then call me back.'

Milner paused momentarily.

'Go on then,' said Tom, failing to hide his impatience.

'It belongs to Gary Walker. And we already know that he also works at the Recycling Centre,' said an even more excited Milner.

'Don't you think that's a bit unusual?' Tom asked. 'If they see each other every day at work why would they then need to speak so frequently on their phones outside of work?' He paused briefly. 'After all, we work together as well but we don't then spend the rest of our time phoning each other, do we?' Before Milner could confirm just how unlikely that possibility was, Tom then added, 'No, that's just very odd. Unless, of course, they are both up to something else outside of work. Everything comes back to the Recycling Centre. That's the common denominator.' He was now in full-on explanatory mode.

'First we had Maciej Sipowicz, who has gone missing. Then Darren Wood who is now dead, apparently in suspicious circumstances, and now this love-in with Gary Walker, all of whom work at the same place. One hell of a coincidence, wouldn't you say Milner?' Even then, and before Milner could reply, Tom continued. 'Personally though, as I may have told you before, I have never believed in coincidences. I think, Milner, it's high time you and I paid a visit to your famous Community Recycling Centre.'

Less than an hour later they were both standing in the Site Manager's office. The office was located immediately inside the property, just beside the main gate. Tom could see that a CCTV camera was fixed to one of the high walls surrounding the site. On the outside wall of the office was a sign proudly stating that seventy eight percent of all items had been recycled during the previous month. The office itself was very small, with barely enough standing room for the three of them. It contained a heavily scratched metal filing cabinet, on which were placed a kettle, a half empty bottle of milk, assorted mugs, a selection of different-sized spoons and an opened pack of sugar. Just below the window was a small desk and a single chair.

After Tom had introduced himself and Milner, he said, 'It's Mr McNulty, isn't it? Mr Gordon McNulty?'

'Yes, that's me. Is it about Darren? We heard this morning that he had died.'

'Yes, I'm afraid it is,' replied Tom. 'How did you find out he'd died?'

McNulty hesitated only slightly, but just enough for Tom to notice it. 'One of the lads told me,' he answered.

It was Milner who spoke next. 'Can you remember who that was?'

Once again McNulty hesitated before answering Milner's question. 'I can't. It's all been a bit of a blur since we found out.'

Milner decided to try and help him. 'Would it have been Gary Walker? I understand he also works here and was a very close friend of Darren's.'

The look of concern on McNulty's face was clear. 'It could have been, but as I told you, I can't really remember.'

'Had Darren worked here long?' asked Tom.

'About a year I think. Do you want me to check?'

'Yes. That would be very helpful.'

McNulty went to the filing cabinet, took out a file and began to flick through various pieces of paper. Whilst he was doing this Tom looked around outside. He could see three men, all wearing high viz safety jackets, on which were printed the name of the company. They were looking in the direction of the manager's office.

'Yes, as I thought,' said McNulty, 'Darren started working here in January. So that's almost a year ago.'

'What sort of worker was he?' asked Milner.

'What do you mean?' asked McNulty.

'Well,' replied Milner, 'was he a good worker? Was he punctual and reliable or was he prone to taking unexpected time off work?'

'Pretty normal really,' replied McNulty. 'He was young man so he liked to go out at night. Sometimes that meant he didn't make it to work the following day.' He said this in a way which made this behaviour sound perfectly normal.

'Have you any idea what he might have been doing on a dangerous railway line last night?' asked Tom.

'Not really. Perhaps he'd had a bit to drink and was taking a short cut.'

Tom offered his hand to McNulty. 'Thank you, Mr McNulty. You have been very helpful. Would you mind if we had a few words with his colleagues over there?' he asked, pointing directly towards the three men. For emphasis he then added, 'The ones who seem to be taking an interest in us.'

'No. I suppose not,' was all McNulty offered in reply.

As Tom was stepping out of the office he turned back to face McNulty. 'One other thing, Mr McNulty. I understand a Maciej Sipowicz used to work here. Do you have any idea where he might be?' asked Tom.

At the first mention of Sipowicz's name, McNulty's face started to lose its colour. 'I've no idea where he is,' he almost whispered. 'He just never returned to work.'

'When was the last time that you saw him?' asked Milner, notebook in hand.

'I think it was last Wednesday. Yes, that's right. Last Wednesday.'

'Was it normal for him to take unexpected time off?'

'Not really.'

Tom now joined the discussion. 'So, are you saying that it did happen sometimes?'

This time McNulty was more specific. 'No. In fact I can't ever remember him taking any time off – except, of course, for holidays.'

'Unlike Darren then,' said Milner, mainly to himself but just loud enough that McNulty heard it.

The three of them walked towards the other three men. McNulty spoke first. 'These two men are from the police. They want to know a few things about Darren.'

'I'm really sorry to hear about Darren. You must have been good friends of his?' asked Tom.

It was the tallest of the three, a man in his early thirties, who replied. 'I wouldn't say that. He just worked here.'

'Sorry. And you are?' replied a direct Milner.

'I'm Gary. Gary Walker,' he answered.

'So, you wouldn't consider yourself a close friend,' said Tom. 'Are you therefore saying that you didn't meet socially or keep in touch with one another outside of work?'

'We might go for a drink after work, but that's all,' he answered confidently.

'How long have you worked here, Mr Walker?' asked Tom.

'Since it opened about three years ago. I was one of the first here.'

'What about you two?' asked Tom, now turning his attention to the others.

The smaller and younger of the two men said, 'Nearly two years.'

'Could I take a note of your name as well please?' asked Milner, notebook at the ready.

'Why do you need my name? I ain't done nothing,' he replied defensively.

'I didn't say you had, Sir,' answered Milner in his most polite voice. It seemed to do the trick.

'It's Jason Lomas,' he finally volunteered.

'And what about you?' asked Milner turning his attention, and notebook, towards the final one.

'Pete Stevenson,' was all he said in reply.

'And how long have you worked here, Mr Stevenson?' asked Milner, determined to get answers to his questions.

'Only about six months,' he finally replied.

Now it was Tom's turn again to ask the questions. 'Did any of you see Darren last night, after work?'

There was an edgy silence. 'Does that mean you did or didn't?' asked Tom.

Once again, it was Walker who took it upon himself to answer on behalf of all three.

'The three of us went for a drink in the Grey Goose after

74

work. Darren said he had something else to do, and so he didn't come with us.'

'Did he say what that was?' asked Tom.

'All he said was what I just told you,' replied Walker.

Tom was silent for a while. He then turned his attention to Lomas. 'Mr Lomas. Do you have any idea why Darren was found with a pair of cable cutters in his hands?'

Lomas gave a light laugh as he said, 'Maybe he was trying to repair something.'

'So, you think it's funny to joke about your friend's death?' asked Tom in a slightly raised voice, making no effort to betray his disgust.

Lomas didn't respond. Tom continued, but this time in his previous level voice. 'Do you think he was trying to steal some of the copper cabling on the track?

No one answered. So Tom continued. 'It's just that we have reason to believe Darren was also involved in the theft of some lead, from the roof of a local church, a week or so ago.'

'How do you know that?' asked McNulty suddenly.

'Well, we found his mobile phone on the roof,' replied Tom, as dramatically as he could manage, whilst continuing to looking directly at them. He continued. 'I doubt very much he was up there for spiritual guidance. Do you?'

Once again, they all remained quiet. Tom went on. He was determined to make them feel as uncomfortable as possible. 'We're just checking all of his phone records. Who did he regularly call or text? Who called him and when? It's amazing what our technical people can do these days.'

'Just because he might have called us doesn't mean we had anything to do with it,' said Walker.

Tom chose not to reply. Instead, he turned towards McNulty and said, 'Mr McNulty, do you mind if we have a copy of Darren's file? It might help us with our inquiries.'

McNulty suddenly appeared to be only too happy to get away. 'I'll get you a copy right now,' he said, after which he walked back towards his office.

Tom turned his attention back to Walker, Lomas and Stevenson. 'One last thing. Have any of you been in contact with Maciej Sipowicz recently? I understand he also used to work here until a couple of weeks ago. We also need to speak to him about Darren.'

Once again it was Walker who replied. 'We haven't seen him for a few days. Maybe he's gone back to Poland.'

When he heard this Lomas started to snigger.

Tom stared at Lomas until he finally stopped laughing, although Tom did notice he still had a smirk on his face.

'Yes. I suppose that's exactly what he's done,' Tom answered eventually. 'Anyway, thank you. You've all been very helpful, although we might need to speak with you again as our inquiries develop.'

Tom and Milner left the three of them, standing together, and walked back towards the office. There they were met by McNulty, who handed them a couple of sheets of paper containing Darren Wood's employment details.

After they were back in their car, Milner said, 'I'd bet anything they are all up to their necks in this.'

'So why don't we find out then if you would have won your bet,' answered Tom.

Chapter 12

After they left the site they drove a short distance before stopping. They parked their car on the road which ran parallel with one side of the site, well away from the main entrance, and out of sight of anyone in the Recycling Centre. They both remained silent. Finally, Tom said, 'Let's drive round the site. I'd like to know if there's another way in.' As they did this, however, it became clear that it was a very secure site and the main entrance was the only way to enter or exit it, other than a small locked gate at the side of the main entrance.

They eventually arrived back at the main gate. As they passed it, Tom said, gesturing at the site, 'Do you know what Milner? I'm convinced the answer is in there somewhere.'

Milner, spotting the CCTV camera, pointed at it. 'Should I see if I can get hold of the footage? If anything was going on inside, then it should be on there.'

'That's something you definitely shouldn't bet on,' he replied.

'What do you mean, Sir?' answered a slightly puzzled Milner.

'Well, go ahead and check with their head office anyway but I suspect it might be one of those systems that can also be controlled from within the site. If that's the case then there won't be anything out of the ordinary on it,' explained Tom. 'But you could check with the bar staff at the Grey Goose. Get them to confirm if it was only the three of them there last night.'

'What do you think we should do now, Sir?' asked Milner.

'You tell me, Milner. I'd be interested to hear your thoughts first,' suggested Tom.

Milner paused whilst he formulated his thoughts. He then started to give his summary. 'Well, it was obvious Walker is the leader – if I can call him that – of the group. Even

McNulty, the site manager, seemed to defer to him. When we asked him anything, his answers were all very vague. He seemed to be trying hard not to give anything away. It was only when you mentioned we'd found the mobile phone that he started to show his true colours. That really shook them.'

Milner looked at Tom as if expecting a reaction. But 'Go on,' was all Tom said.

'As far as Lomas is concerned, he just doesn't seem to have any conscience at all. He made a joke about Darren Wood's death and just laughed when Sipowicz's name was mentioned. You certainly wouldn't want him as your friend. Why don't we follow them? If they're involved then it's only a question of time before they make mistakes and incriminate themselves.'

Milner looked at Tom for a response, but Tom simply continued to stare ahead.

Eventually, having evidently now made up his mind, he answered, 'Okay. This is what we'll do.'

By the time they arrived back at the station Tom's mind was starting to focus, once again, on his investigation into *Operation Torch*. He fired up his computer and opened the email from Superintendent Peters, the one he had started to read earlier in the day.

It was a summary of Shaw's meeting with Jimmy Ryan, his informant, immediately after the botched operation, and Tom was intrigued to know what Ryan had to say about it. As he read the report his anticipation soon proved to be fully justified. In one of the files given to him by Superintendent Peters, which he had read last night, DCI Shaw had acknowledged that Ryan wasn't his primary source of information. In fact, Ryan was simply being used as a conduit for information to be passed from an individual who was at the very heart of the criminal gang, through to DCI Shaw. A man who was a very close confidant of Tommy Fuller. That way, it was felt, the identity of the real informant would be more difficult to find out. Tom had to acknowledge that it was a clever way of adding an additional layer of protection and anonymity for the real informant.

Nonetheless, as he read this, his earlier nagging doubts still refused to go away. In his opinion the fact that Ryan had been involved at all in this level of subterfuge was difficult to understand. Okay, on the plus side, he had been correct in his initial assessment about Ryan. He had never bought into the idea he might have been the main informant. He was just too far down the food chain to have any real influence.

He had to admit, however, that this new information, about the higher level informant, added significantly more credibility to the integrity of *Operation Torch*. Tony Donovan, was very well known to the police and considered to be a very close friend of Tommy Fuller.

He had been given the code name 'Retribution' by DCI Shaw. Donovan had grown up on the same West London estate as the Fuller brothers, Tommy and his older brother Patrick. Like them, he had spent all of his adult life involved in various escalating criminal activities: petty theft, burglary, robberies, extortion, prostitution and latterly drug dealing. In the early days, as the eldest of the brothers, it was Patrick who was the head of their criminal enterprise. But about twelve years ago, he had been killed, shot dead by a police marksman, whilst taking part in a robbery on a betting shop.

Following a spate of similar robberies across the region, the police had launched a major operation to catch those responsible. They had pressurised all of their informants to provide information and eventually they had learnt about a plan to raid the betting shop. Based on this information the police had mounted a massive operation and committed significant resources. Although they had made arrests it had, nonetheless, caused a huge furore about the deployment of police firearms officers. The subsequent inquiry had confirmed that at the time Patrick Fuller had, in fact, been unarmed. Nonetheless, he had been shot dead and the police officers involved were completely exonerated. This was largely based on police statements that he had been pointing a gun, or what looked like a gun, directly at other police officers.

There were, however, independent eye witnesses who disputed this. They were certain he wasn't holding anything and, in fact, no gun was ever found. He had simply been pointing his hands at them. Afterwards there were press stories alleging that the police were operating a 'shoot first' policy and this had directly led to a marked increase in tension between the police and the known criminal community. Indeed, the popular press even went so far as to claim that criminals were now starting to acquire guns in order to protect themselves.

Tom had actually been involved in the police operation to try and put an end to the robberies. At the time, and along with most police officers, he had been in no doubt that it was the Fuller brothers who were behind them and subsequent events had proved them to be right. Nonetheless, he well remembered how the general consensus, even amongst those officers involved, was that the inquiry had been a whitewash. Whilst he had no definitive evidence that the police marksmen had been briefed to shoot there was little doubt they had been very trigger happy on that particular day.

Tom's own informants had also warned him to expect a serious escalation in criminal armed activity. Fortunately, apart from a few isolated incidents, this had not materialised. After the death of his older brother, Tommy Fuller assumed leadership of the gang, with Donovan becoming his right-hand man. As anyone who had ever met them would confirm, neither of them could be considered to be model citizens. But Donovan in particular was a nasty piece of work. He was the one who Fuller always turned to if he wanted any threats or violence to be meted out. But he did have one redeeming feature – if that's how it could be described. He was extremely loyal towards Fuller. In fact, rumour had it, about ten years ago he had willingly taken the rap for a crime in which Fuller had been the main suspect, and, as a result, had served three years in prison.

DCI Shaw's rationale for believing Donovan was now a genuine informant was based on the fact that Donovan, for some as yet unspecified reason, had recently developed a burning grievance against Fuller. He had apparently contacted DCI Shaw, via Ryan, and provided him with some valuable information. In return, Donovan had asked for immunity from any future possible prosecutions. Quite correctly, in Tom's view, Shaw had treated this offer with great scepticism and so had asked Donovan to prove his worth and demonstrate that his intentions were genuine.

It was after this that he started to pass information, via Ryan, through to Shaw on a fairly regular basis. The information from Donovan was even given a fancy cover name: *Nemesis*. Tom Googled the word to find out a bit more about its meaning. Apparently, in Greek mythology, *Nemesis* was the spirit of divine retribution. As he read this he found himself quietly chuckling to himself. *Retribution* was in effect both the code name for the informant as well as for the information he provided. As he read, he could easily imagine DCI Shaw suggesting all of this to Superintendent Peters. Did revenge and retribution hold a particular significance for DCI Shaw? Whatever his reasons it was still clever.

Simply by doing this, Shaw had, at a stroke, elevated his own importance as well as that of the information he was now receiving. The secrecy surrounding *Nemesis* had, however, been watertight. Tom, who had always prided himself on being able to notice if anything important was going on, had not even heard a whisper about *Nemesis*. It must, therefore, have been a very select group of officers who were in on this secret and obviously, he reluctantly admitted, he wasn't one of them.

To begin with this was fairly low-level stuff. The names of small-time drug dealers. Details relating to car thefts and domestic burglaries, that type of thing. But, about six months ago, the quality of the information suddenly increased dramatically.

The result was *Operation Sunlight* and the successful removal of another major criminal gang within their area. It was now obvious, from the information contained in the files, that this information was pivotal to the operation's success. But a key question remained unanswered. Why would Donovan be willing to do this?

Okay, Tom could just about buy into the possibility, put forward by DCI Shaw, that Donovan now held an all-consuming grudge against Fuller. This was certainly a possibility and was not unknown. What was undisputed, however, was how it had provided the Met with one of its most successful operations of recent years. One other thing, however, was also certain. It had also hugely increased Donovan's stock as a police informant, at least amongst those select officers in the know. They must have thought they now had access to a treasure trove of information. But what he still found difficult to understand, however, was why someone like Donovan should suddenly turn into a police informant.

Here was a man who, for almost his entire life, had been

involved in crime. People like him didn't just turn into a police informant. In fact, the reverse was often the case. It was hard-wired into their DNA to do everything possible to thwart the police at every opportunity. In their twisted code of honour, becoming a grass was deemed to be the worst of all crimes. If they had a grudge against a fellow criminal then the usual rule was to sort it out between themselves. Or at least this was the conventional thinking.

Notwithstanding his doubts, Tom was determined to try and retain an open mind. He couldn't help thinking though, that another significant consequence of this was the rapid ascendancy of DCI Shaw's profile within the force. It hadn't done any harm to Superintendent Peters' career either. Even Fuller came out of this ahead. The only exception, of course, was the now dead Ryan. The reality, though, was that Fuller now had the criminal field clear to himself, after the elimination of his main rival.

To Tom, however, this 'win-win-for-everyone' situation was just a little too good to be true. But right now Tom was interested in Ryan's explanation, and therefore presumably Donovan's, as to why *Operation Torch* had ended so disastrously.

According to DCI Shaw's report it was very simple. It was a straightforward cock-up. The information which Shaw had received, and the reason for *Operation Torch*, was that a significant delivery of drugs, estimated to have a street value of over £25million, was due to be delivered to Fuller. The information said approximately 100kg of cocaine was to be delivered to Fuller's own large residence in Denham. It would then be quickly distributed to his network of dealers throughout West London. If this was true then it was undoubtedly a major escalation in Fuller's drugs enterprise and, although this involved clear risks, it probably reflected his increasing confidence that he was now immune from the law. Tom's immediate thought was, if this was the case, then was it because he was being protected by someone in authority?

DCI Shaw was certainly correct when he said that it was a simple cock-up. In fact it was so simple it was almost farcical. The information they had received was that the drugs were to be delivered at around 11.30pm. A party had been arranged, as cover, at Fuller's house, ostensibly to celebrate his daughter's

30th birthday, and a band had been booked to perform. Unfortunately DCI Shaw had not been told about this part of the evening. The band had arrived at 11.15pm. A large number of police officers, led by Superintendent Peters and DCI Shaw, were staking out the house. They waited until the band were inside and then crashed into the house, assuming this was the drugs delivery and expecting to catch everyone red-handed. But, when they searched the boxes all they found, of course, were either musical instruments or equipment.

Apart from a small amount, found on a couple of the younger party guests, the house was absolutely clear of any significant quantity of drugs. As the police, in obvious and increasing desperation, searched for the drugs, or indeed any other incriminating evidence, they were being almost continually filmed by Fuller's guests, on camera phones and by a video camera.

Tom remembered what Pete Grey, the sergeant on station duty on the night of the operation, had told him about just how angry the team were when they arrived back at to the station. This had clearly not been a good day for West London police's finest. Tom found it hard not to let out a slight laugh. It would be comical if it wasn't so serious. So far the wider public had not really got hold of this part of the story. When they did, no doubt, they would have great fun at the police's expense.

Donovan, due to his closeness to Fuller, was furious that the operation had been botched. Understandably he was now fearful for his own safety and, not surprisingly, unwilling to provide Shaw with any more information. The subsequent murder of Jimmy Ryan would only add to that anxiety. And, as if things could not get any worse for Peters and Shaw, they had been informed that the drugs delivery had subsequently been diverted and was now, almost certainly, finding its way onto the streets of West London. This, in many ways, was the most serious outcome and, if made public, would have far-reaching implications for those officers involved. Whatever the outcome of the official police inquiry into *Operation Torch*, this would be nothing when compared with how the media, but particularly the tabloids, would report this story.

The police would be seen as a joke, at best, but more likely, simply incompetent.

Chapter 13

As Tom was digesting everything he had just read, Milner appeared outside his door. 'Is now a good time, Sir? You look as though you're fully engrossed in something,' he said pointing at Tom's computer.

Tom, his mind still largely on the contents of DCI Peters' email, looked up and said somewhat distractedly, 'No.'

Milner remained where he was and said. 'Sir? Is that a "no" this is not a good time or "no" I'm not fully engrossed?'

Milner's boldness had the desired effect. Tom answered. 'Milner, don't try and play a game of fancy semantics with me. You knew exactly what I meant. Just come in, sit down and tell me what you have.'

For once, Milner didn't feel as though this was another of DCI Stone's putdowns. In fact he felt quite good about himself that he had been able to play him at his own game. But even so, he couldn't fail to notice how DCI Stone immediately closed down whatever he had been reading as soon as he saw he was there.

Milner sat down and opened the omnipresent file. 'First of all, I checked with the manager of the Grey Goose. Your instincts were correct, Sir,' he said, waiting for a response. When none came he carried on. 'They were all there last night. Walker, Stevenson, Lomas *and* Darren Wood. According to the manager they arrived at about 5.45pm, had a few drinks and then all left together about thirty minutes later. Apparently it was quite usual for them to have an early drink. As you know, the Grey Goose is not too far away from the Recycling Centre. Interestingly though, it seems that Mr Sipowicz had never been a part of their little drinking group.'

Tom still didn't say anything and so Milner continued, now getting better at recognising Tom's body language. 'I've also checked with the company which manages the site where they all work. They gave me a contact number for the security company which installed the CCTV cameras. You were right again, Sir. The cameras *can* be operated from the Site Manager's office.'

Finally Tom spoke. 'Not bad, eh?' he said rhetorically.

Milner carried on. 'I know it's all circumstantial but, at least, it doesn't rule out that they weren't involved.'

'Exactly,' replied Tom, before adding. 'And by the way, Milner. That's always a good way to look at circumstantial information. First try and discredit anything that is circumstantial because if you don't then you might find that some hot-shot defence lawyer does.'

'I'll try and remember that, Sir,' replied Milner.

Tom looked up at Milner, as if he was about to say something further. But, in the event, he settled for, 'What about tonight's little operation? Is everything organised?'

'I think so, Sir,' replied Milner.

'You think so?' answered Tom, rather sharply. 'I was hoping to hear a straight "yes, Sir".'

'In that case, yes, Sir. Everything is organised.' After his earlier confidence, Milner had now gravitated back to feeling a little chastened.

'Good,' answered Tom. 'So tell me what the plan is.'

'The briefing has been arranged for four thirty. In total there will be ten officers involved, five of us and five uniform. One of the uniform officers will be responsible for ensuring everything is captured on film.' Milner hesitated, before asking, 'Do you think we will get them tonight, Sir?'

This time Tom did respond. 'I sincerely hope so. I think we really shook them when we met earlier. If there's anything still at the site which shouldn't be there, then they'll want to get it out as quickly as possible before we pay them another visit. With a bit of luck we'll have panicked them into moving it out. The really interesting thing, though, will be to see where they move it to.'

'I checked, and the site closes at five thirty. I wonder if they'll stick to their usual habit of going to the Grey Goose?' asked Milner.

'If they do then I'm sure we'll be on for tonight,' replied Tom. 'I've got a couple of other things to do between now and four thirty, and so I'll see you in the briefing room then.'

That was clearly the signal for Milner to leave. As he was

leaving Tom said, 'Incidentally, Milner. That was a good piece of work. You followed up on everything we had agreed, very efficiently. And there's another thing. I wouldn't have thought about asking if Sipowicz was in the habit of going to the pub with them. I think that's quite significant just in itself. Well done. I think tonight we might have a few more souls for Father O'Connor to save.' Milner winced as he heard this.

When Tom was sure Milner had left, he restarted his computer. Amongst the latest emails, which he had received whilst he'd had his short meeting with Milner, was one from Superintendent Peters. It was titled '*Reporting*'. Tom immediately clicked it open. It was very brief and simply stated that a new report form was now available for Tom to complete. It finished by saying that when Tom got the opportunity, perhaps he'd like to come up to the fifth floor and collect it himself. To anyone who might see this it was just the sort of bureaucratic, jobsworth nonsense which was the bane of most police officer's lives. That was the hope anyway.

By now it was mid-afternoon and, bearing in mind that he and Milner had their briefing in less than a couple of hours' time, he decided now would be a good time to collect the 'report'. A few minutes later he was standing in the area just outside Superintendent Peters' office.

'Hello again,' said a surprised Janice. 'Is Superintendent Peters expecting you?'

'Sort of,' replied Tom. 'He asked me to come up to collect something, whenever I got the chance. We have something on tonight, so I thought I'd come up now.'

'It's just that you seem to be making a habit of turning up without an appointment,' she replied pointedly, before immediately adding, 'Are you expecting anything exciting tonight?'

'I hope so,' was all Tom said in reply. Janice smiled at him.

Just then Superintendent Peters opened his office door. 'Hi Tom,' he said. 'Thanks for coming up. Here's the report form I want you to take a look at. I hope it's easy to understand. Anyway, let me know what you think when you've had the chance to look at it. If there's anything which you think could be changed to make it a bit simpler, then just add some comments at the end.'

Superintendent Peters was clearly taking this subterfuge between the two of them very seriously. 'I will, Sir,' was all

Tom could think to say in reply. Peters handed Tom a buff-coloured A4 file. Tom was pleased to see that it wasn't one of those transparent plastic folders. The ones which allowed any eagle-eyed interested observer to read parts of it.

Tom started to walk out of the office, but, before he'd left, Superintendent Peters said, 'Oh, by the way. Good luck with tonight's operation. I had to sign off the operational resource form which Milner sent up for my approval. He seems very efficient. I know you have high expectations of him. Anyway, I hope you get a result. I think it's despicable what those people are doing. Why don't you come up tomorrow and tell me all about it?'

'No pressure then, Sir?' answered Tom. 'Let's hope it's a success.'

Chapter 14

Tom and Milner were in the briefing room, together with the rest of the team. Tom walked to the front of the room and addressed the group. 'Thank you for all for getting here on time.' He then got straight to the point. 'Tonight we are going to round up a group of men who have been responsible for the theft of various metal items over the past few months. No doubt you've read about them. The papers have been full of these type of thefts for quite a while now. Our men have stolen lead from local church roofs and even brass plaques from war memorials.

Not surprisingly the general public are becoming seriously upset and are looking to us to catch the people responsible. Well, tonight we have the opportunity to do just that. Last night, things took a dramatic turn for the worse. We believe one of their gang died whilst trying to steal copper wire cabling from a railway line. Unfortunately for him, the line was still live. The others who were with him just left him there.' Tom paused for a while and then added, 'That's the type of people who have been committing these crimes. Well, after tonight, they will have the opportunity to get to know each other even better. As guests at one of her Majesty's prisons.'

One of the uniformed police officers then spoke. 'Sir, do we have any idea what they're doing with all of the metal they have stolen?'

'Good question,' replied Tom. 'They must be selling it to someone. My best guess is that they have a contact within the local scrap dealer community. Someone who doesn't ask too many questions about where it all comes from. Anyway, with a bit of luck, I'm hoping we'll soon have the answer to that one as well.'

'Are you expecting any rough stuff?' asked another officer.

'I think we have to plan for that possibility. One of them is already known to us and has already served time for assault. So, be careful and don't take any undue risks.'

The same officer asked a follow-up question. 'Will we have any back up available just in case it all kicks off?'

It was Milner who answered this particular question. 'I've already taken care of that.'

Tom and Milner spent the next ten minutes outlining, in detail, what each of the assembled officers' roles would be during tonight's operation. When they had finished Tom could sense a growing excitement amongst all of the officers involved. He got the distinct impression they were all really up for it. More than anything else, what seemed to really anger them was the theft of the bronze plaques from local war memorials. Perhaps it was because it could easily have been the name of their own relatives on one of those plaques. Whatever the reason, Tom knew he now had a fully committed group of officers on the team.

Just before 5.30pm they were all in place. Tom and Milner were in a car, parked within sight of the Grey Goose, whilst two other detectives had positioned themselves to get a clear view of the entrance to the Recycling Centre.

One other detective, DC Simmons, was already in the pub bar where Walker, Stevenson and Lomas regularly drank. He had been 'wired' so he could, hopefully, pick up some of their conversation. The uniformed police were all in a plain dark-coloured van, very close to where the other two detectives had parked. All they could do now was to wait and see how events developed.

They didn't have to wait long. Just after five thirty, when the last of the public had left, the gates to the Recycling Centre were closed. Within a couple of minutes, three men emerged from the side gate and started walking in the general direction of the pub.

One of the detectives outside the Recycling Centre spoke into his radio. 'Standby. Suspects on foot and on the move and heading in your direction.' Tom and Milner looked down the road, towards the Recycling Centre.

'Okay. I have them,' said Milner into his radio. Tom could see three men walking towards the pub. A short while later they were in the pub bar, each of them with a drink in hand.

Tom could just about pick up snippets of conversation

between them. DC Simmons had been briefed carefully not to risk compromising the operation by trying to get too close to them. It was the right decision, of course, but nonetheless, Tom hoped he would still try to get as close as possible without attracting attention.

As he was thinking this he heard Walker speaking, loud and clear. 'We'll have another drink and then go back and pick the stuff up.' After that a sudden increase in background noise drowned out what he said next. He hoped the microphone would have picked up all of this.

For the next half hour or so they were able to hear the odd word now and then. All they could do though was to remain patient and wait. Just after six fifteen they all emerged and started to walk back towards the Recycling Centre. 'Suspects heading back,' said Milner to all of the officers. 'Vehicles into position.'

Tom waited until DC Simmons, who had been in the pub, came out. He got into Tom's car. 'How did it go?' asked Tom impatiently. 'Do you think you managed to get a lot of it?'

'I hope so,' replied Simmons. 'It was a bit hairy at one point. Stevenson kept giving me the eye, so I had to back off. One other thing though. Walker and Lomas seemed to be knocking it back a bit. Stevenson just drank coke. Maybe he's their driver for the night.'

A voice came over the radio. 'Suspects back at base. One of them made a call on his mobile and almost immediately the side gate was opened for them.'

'Right. You start listening to the tape,' said Tom, looking at DC Simmons. 'Let me know if you hear anything about where they might be going tonight. Milner, let's get moving.' With that, they set off back to the Recycling Centre, parked the car and settled down to wait.

Just before seven o'clock the main gate opened and a white transit van drove out. The gate was then immediately closed. Tom spotted that it was Walker, not Stevenson, who was driving. 'Look, Sir,' said Milner. 'McNulty is closing the gate.'

'Did we get that on film?' asked Tom, speaking into the radio.

'Affirmative,' replied a voice.

'Good. Let's follow them,' said Tom. 'But, not too closely. We don't want them spotting us. So let's make sure we do this by the training manual.'

The two cars and van took turns to follow their suspects. After about fifteen minutes the van turned left into an unlit lane.

Tom's car was the one immediately behind. 'All units carry straight on and park up behind me,' he said, into his radio.

'Okay,' said Tom, once everyone was there. 'This is not exactly what we hoped for but we still have the advantage of surprise on our side. This could be the place where they are planning to offload the stuff. Milner and myself will drive down the lane first. I suggest the van comes next and then the other car. Make sure your headlights are off and, for God's sake, be careful not to stop suddenly or run into the vehicle in front.' He paused, before adding, more to himself than to the others. 'I've seen that happen before and compromise an operation. Trust me, it's not a good career move.'

Milner spoke. 'Sir, I've just checked on my phone's sat nav and it looks as though there's some sort of industrial unit about half a mile up the lane. That might be the place.'

Tom spoke again. 'You all know what your job is tonight. Everything by the book. Good luck and let's go and get them.' Turning to face Milner he added, 'I think now might be a good time to warn back-up.'

They both then got back into their car and Milner started the engine. He eased the car down the lane, with the others following at a safe distance. Very soon they were outside the industrial unit. They all parked up and switched off their engines. The unit had clearly seen better days. What looked like an old, battered, corrugated iron fence surrounded the property. What gave it quite a sinister look, however, was the barbed wire which had been, rather unprofessionally, stuck on top of it. The entrance was via a couple of large metal gates. Each side of the gate had an improvised sign on it, giving a warning to any unwelcome visitors that dogs were inside. Milner was the first to spot this. 'Sir,' he whispered, pointing to the gates. 'Look at that.'

When Tom saw what Milner was pointing to he suddenly felt quite anxious. 'Sod it. I didn't think about that,' he said. He turned to face the rest of the group and said quietly, 'Let's stick with the plan but be careful. We all know how unpredictable and dangerous dogs can be. Maybe, though, they're the type of dogs who roll over and let you tickle their tummy.'

If this was Tom's attempt to put them all at their ease then it was obvious that it had not worked as everyone remained totally silent. And it was a nervous silence, their thoughts focused on the possibility of vicious dogs running wild behind the gates.

Tom and Milner, backed up by four of the uniformed police officers, approached the gates. The others had taken up position at various locations around the site just in case anyone else, inside, tried to make a run for it There was a small gap between the two gates, which was secured by an impressive looking chain. Tom turned around and gestured to one of the uniformed officers to come forward. In his hand he held a large bolt cutter. Tom simply pointed at the chain and whispered, 'As quietly as possible.' The bolt cutter made surprisingly easy work of the chain.

Milner gently pushed one of the gates open, peered around it and then said as quietly as possible, 'Everything looks quiet. There's a small Portakabin half way down on the left. There's lights on and I could just make out some people in the cabin. Walker's white van is parked right outside it. The rear doors are wide open.'

'Any sign of the dogs?' asked Tom, unable to hide his concern.

'Not that I could see anyway,' answered Milner.

'Good. Let's hope they've been taken out for their evening walkies. Right. Here we go. Milner, let everyone know we are going in.'

Milner spoke quietly into his radio and then took up his position just behind DCI Stone.

Tom gently eased the gates open, just wide enough for them all to squeeze through. He then walked briskly towards the cabin, wherever possible making sure that he stayed in the shadows.

As he approached the Portakabin he could feel his heart rate increasing. He suddenly realised he was now getting a bit too old for all of this. In future, he promised himself, he would try and leave it to the younger officers.

But, just as he was thinking this, he began to pick out some voices. A few steps later and Walker's voice suddenly became clear. 'You promised us much more than that,' he heard him say, quite aggressively. 'Don't even think about trying to screw us.'

By now Tom and Milner, followed by the others, were right outside the door. 'We've got what you wanted. You've just seen it. Just give us our money.'

As Walker was speaking Tom turned to the others and gave a thumbs-up. This was the signal for them to burst into the cabin. As they did this one of the officers was giving the call sign to all of the others. 'Entry. Entry. Entry,' he almost shouted into his radio, before following the others into the cabin.

In addition to Walker, Stevenson and Lomas there was one other man there. He was a small man, probably in his early fifties. He was holding a bundle of £20 notes in his right hand. The cabin wasn't small, but now that there were more people in it, plus another officer blocking the door, it suddenly became very congested.

Tom had hoped that their entry would have caught them all off-guard. He was surprised however by just how quickly they reacted and it was Walker who was the first to show real aggression. He threw himself at Milner and managed to land a number of meaty blows on Milner's face before he was eventually overpowered by two of the officers.

Milner picked himself up and felt his face. Tom could see the area just above his left cheek bone was already starting to swell. He'd have an impressive bruise there later. Of more concern though was Lomas, who had suddenly pulled out a knife from his pocket and pressed a switch, revealing a fearsome looking serrated blade. He began to wave it in the direction of the other officers. 'Back off,' he shouted, 'or I'll stick you.'

As soon as he spotted the knife, Tom shouted, 'Call for back-up.' One of the officers immediately spoke into his radio. By now Walker was subdued. Stevenson and the other man didn't look as though they posed much of a threat. The same, though, could not be said of Lomas. What particularly worried Tom was that it looked as though he was almost enjoying this. In his experience these were often the most dangerous situations to be caught in. When he had first met Lomas he had quickly gained the impression that he was likely to be the most unpredictable. At this particular moment, with Lomas waving the knife at him, it was no consolation to find out that he had been correct in his assessment.

'Why don't you put that down, Mr Lomas,' was all that Tom could think of to say, as he continued to focus all of his attention on him.

Eventually, he started to gather his thoughts. 'We have policemen outside and more on the way. If you use that,' said Tom, pointing at the knife, 'then you will be spending the rest of your life in prison. Is that what you want?'

'I don't care,' he replied. 'It would be worth it to do one of you lot.'

Tom took a step forward, and holding out his hand said, 'Jason. It's not worth it. You'll regret this for the rest of your life. Trust me. Why don't you give the knife to me?'

'Why should I trust a copper?' replied Jason, clearly still very highly charged.

It was then that Stevenson, quite unexpectedly, spoke. 'Jason. He's right. Nicking a bit of metal is one thing but attacking a copper with a knife is something else. Put the knife down.'

But Lomas was unwilling or unable to heed this advice. Suddenly he lunged at Tom, making a slashing motion, almost as if he were holding a sword. Although Tom had the presence of mind to throw himself to one side his reactions were not quick enough, and he felt the knife make contact with the sleeve of his jacket. Before Lomas could do any more damage he was overpowered by Milner and one of the other officers and quickly handcuffed.

With both Walker and Lomas now restrained, Tom felt that the situation was fully under control.

'Sir? Are you okay?' asked Milner, focusing his attention on Tom's arm.

Tom looked at his arm and was surprised to see a large tear in his sleeve. 'I'm okay,' he answered, 'although my jacket looks as though its days are numbered.'

As Tom gingerly felt his arm he looked in the direction of the other man. 'I know everyone else here, except you. Perhaps you could tell me who you are?'

'I'm Willie Brady,' he answered. 'I own this place.'

'So, what were you doing tonight with Mr Walker, Mr Stevenson and Mr Lomas?' he asked.

'They said they had something I might be interested in and so I let them in. I had just taken a look at what they had when you lot arrived,' he replied, confidently. 'I get people here all of the time asking me to buy stuff.'

'And did they?' asked Tom.

'Did they what?'

'Did they have anything interesting?'

'Just the usual bits and pieces of metal. Nothing out of the ordinary.'

'And did you buy them? When we came in here you seemed to have a lot of money in your hand.'

Brady now seemed to be even more confident. 'They couldn't guarantee the stuff was kosher and so I told them I didn't want it. I run a legit business. These premises are authorised. It wouldn't be worth my while to take the risk.'

It was Milner who spoke next. 'Mr Brady. Are you saying you've never met these men before?'

Just momentarily Brady hesitated before, a little nervously, answering. 'This is the first time I've ever seen them.'

When he heard this Walker tried to struggle free from the grasp of the two police officers who were restraining him. 'You lying bastard!' he shouted. 'You've been taking stuff from us for months.'

The officers had by now, once again, restrained Walker before he could attack Brady. But this didn't prevent Walker from shouting, 'He's in it up to his neck. He takes stuff from everybody. Has done for years. Take a look around his yard. There's loads of nicked stuff he's bought.'

'Don't worry Mr Walker, we will,' answered Tom.

Just then three police cars came racing into the yard, sirens blaring and lights flashing.

'Looks like the cavalry have just arrived,' said Milner, before adding, 'Late as usual.'

Tom gave Milner a withering look before turning his attention back to Brady. 'Mr Brady. We are arresting you on suspicion of handling stolen goods. Officer, please read Mr Brady his rights.' After this had been completed Tom looked at Walker, Stevenson and Lomas. 'You three are to be charged with theft.'

Before he could finish, however, Walker said, 'All this just because we took a bit of metal?'

'In fact, there are so many things you will be charged with we couldn't remember them all and so I had to write them down.' Tom then quite theatrically took a notebook from his pocket and started to read from it.

'In addition to the thefts,' he glanced up and, looking directly at Walker, said, 'you'll have noticed I said "thefts", plural, because we believe there are many of them, there's also the mysterious death, last night, of Darren Wood. This, as I'm sure you can imagine, is an extremely serious charge. If it's proved that any of you were there with him then it will be for the courts to decide whether or not your illegal actions contributed to his death.'

Tom now had their full attention. 'To these we now have to add the assaults on DS Milner and myself. I have to tell you that our courts do not look too kindly on police officers being attacked, particularly where knives are concerned. I think the evidence speaks for itself.' As he said this he looked at Milner's face. If Milner could have seen his own face he could not have failed to notice the large, egg-sized bulge which had now appeared on his cheek. He then continued. 'Oh, and there's another one to add to the list.' Looking specifically at Walker, he said, 'I also have reason to believe that you have been drinking tonight. Officer. Could you please breathalyse Mr Walker?' He then turned back towards the three men. 'I think that's everything. Unless, that is, there's anything else you want to tell us about? For example, the whereabouts of Mr Sipowicz?'

Even Lomas had suddenly become quiet, as the full implications of what Tom had said started to sink in.

It was almost ten o'clock and Tom and Milner were back at the station, sitting in Tom's office, Tom drinking tea and Milner a cup of coffee. 'How's your face?' asked Tom, looking closely at Milner's bruises. 'You should get that looked at. You might have broken a cheek bone or something.'

'I'm sure it's okay,' answered Milner, gently feeling his face. 'It probably looks far worse than it actually is.'

'I'm not sure about that,' replied a doubtful Tom. 'When will you see the Police doctor?'

'He's not available at the moment.'

'You should go to the local hospital then and get it checked out. I'll come with you, if you want. I know it's late but it's not worth taking any chances.'

When Milner replied to Tom's offer it was with genuine

gratitude. 'That's very kind of you, Sir, but I'm sure I can manage that myself. Anyway, it's getting late and you know how long you can sometimes wait in A&E before you're eventually seen.'

'Okay, but at least promise me that you'll go.'

'I'll go on my way home,' answered Milner, before adding, 'I promise.'

'What about your arm, Sir? That could have been far more serious than a bruised face.'

'But it wasn't. That's the main thing,' he answered firmly.

Milner took the hint that Tom didn't want to discuss this particular part of the evening's events.

So Milner picked up his coffee cup, took a sip and then said, 'Sir. What do you think we should do next? Should we arrest McNulty?'

'We should certainly go and pay him a visit tomorrow morning. He'll be worried anyway when his three partners in crime don't show up for work.' Tom paused for a while and then added. 'Although I'd be surprised if he was actually involved in the thefts, he's certainly been involved when it came to getting rid of the stolen stuff. The other point, of course, is that he was allowing Walker, and the rest of them, to use the Recycling Centre to hide the stolen metal. Actually, just thinking about it, you have to give them some credit for that.'

'I don't understand, Sir. What do you mean?' asked a puzzled Milner. As far as he was concerned they were not worthy of any credit.

'Well. Can you think of a better place to hide stolen metal?' answered Tom. 'You said yourself they are recycling material all of the time. Who would be suspicious, therefore, if they saw pieces of metal there? They would just think the general public had brought it in to be recycled. Quite clever really. I wonder whose idea that was?' He then answered his own question. 'If I had to pick anyone my money would be on Stevenson. He struck me as being the one with the most brains.'

'I know what you mean,' replied Milner. 'And at least he did try to persuade Lomas to drop the knife.'

Despite his seeming ambivalence about the knife attack Tom had to admit, at least to himself, that he had been affected by it. In his younger days he would have welcomed the danger. In fact, it was almost considered a rite of passage for any young copper to be confronted by physical danger. You were not a proper copper until someone had threatened you with a knife or worse. But over the past few years, he had become more and more aware of the dangers and the possible dire outcome. Theses days, he was certainly less willing to take any undue risks. The reality was that he was very fortunate indeed not to have sustained any serious injury. When he was younger he would not have allowed Lomas to get anywhere near him. Yet another sign of getting older, he told himself.

Tom decided he should, however difficult it might be, try to put this thought to the back of his mind. Instead he said, 'I was more worried about the dogs. Do we know where they were?'

'Apparently Brady had locked them in one of the old cars that had been parked at the far end of the site,' replied Milner. 'Probably another clue that Brady had been expecting Walker and the rest to show up.'

'That reminds me,' said Tom quite suddenly. 'I'd like to know what was on the tape DC Simmons was carrying. Could you get on to that tomorrow? There might be something on it which further incriminates Brady. I suspect we'll need as much evidence as possible with him. At the moment, unless we find anything else, it's just the word of Walker and the rest versus his.'

He thought for a moment and then asked, 'We need to make sure everything is legit when we search his yard tomorrow. I don't want us cocking this up just because we've cut a few corners with the paperwork.'

'Don't worry, Sir,' replied Milner. 'I'll personally make sure that doesn't happen.'

'Good.' Even as Tom looked at Milner's face, he could see that, if anything, it had deteriorated even further whilst they had been at the station. 'Right. That's it for tonight. Get yourself off to the hospital. And that's an order.'

Milner drank the last of his coffee, stood up and headed towards the door. Just as he was walking out Tom spoke again. 'Oh, and incidentally, Milner. In future, if you have any derogatory comments to make about our rapid response colleagues could you please keep them to yourself. Or at least until the bad guys have been taken away. I can guarantee one day you will be thankful that they arrive at all.'

As he heard this Milner's face suddenly started to throb quite painfully. Detective Chief Inspector Stone, he thought, could sometimes have that effect on you.

Chapter 15

Even though he had not got home until after midnight Tom still hadn't felt tired. He was beginning to worry that his old problem, of not being able to sleep, might once again be returning. He had hoped, now that Mary had become a major part of his life, that he would be able to get some balance into his life. Part of the reason, he knew, was that he was still on a high after the operation at the scrap yard. Here, age didn't matter. He still got a buzz, along with a real sense of satisfaction, both professional and personal, from being involved in operations such as the one earlier that night.

He had always found it difficult to sleep after them, whether they had been a success or a failure. As he lay in bed after an operation, he would often run through all of the events, trying to identify what could have been done better. Of course, there were always things that everyone, not just him, could have done better. In all of his time as a police officer he still had not been part of *the* perfect operation.

Okay, the fact that a volatile, cornered, young man had threatened him with a vicious-looking knife was not something you could easily get out of your mind. But it's usually only afterwards when you begin to think about all of the possible scenarios. At the time it's usually best to rely your instincts and reactions. What concerned Tom, however, was that, whilst his instincts still appeared to be intact, his reactions were not as sharp as they once were.

But it wasn't only this which was worrying him. After Milner had left he had unlocked his bottom desk drawer and taken out the buff-coloured file which Superintendent Peters had given to him earlier that day. Although it was late he decided to lock his office door. This was not something he would normally do and he was aware he was in danger of breaking his own rule: the one about not changing your behaviour or the way you would normally operate. But on this occasion, he took the view that it would be worse if he was interrupted by one of the other officers still on duty.

When they had returned to the station he was surprised to see DCI Shaw still there. They had acknowledged each other's presence but that was about all. There had been an increased tension between them ever since Superintendent Peters had told Shaw that Tom would be carrying out a review of the planning and implementation relating to *Operation Torch*. No, the last thing he needed was for DCI Shaw to suddenly walk into his office whilst he was reading the file. That would be uncomfortable. For both of them.

He had asked Superintendent Peters to provide him with personal information relating to everyone who was at that final *Operation Torch* briefing. He wasn't sure how Peters had got hold of this without arousing any suspicions. He might ask him if he got the opportunity. He'd also asked for copies of bank statements for each of the people on the list. But, as Peters had said, obtaining these would be far more complicated and difficult to deliver and so he couldn't guarantee he could get them. Tom wasn't convinced by that argument. He would hear what Peters had to say about this when they next met. To him it was crucial information as the most likely motive, for whoever was doing this, was probably some sort of financial gain. Regular amounts of money deposited into their bank account would certainly be worth further investigation.

If this also coincided with a sudden change to a more ostentatious lifestyle then that would be another strong clue. But right now he didn't have that information and he was reliant upon Superintendent Peters to provide it. So he would just have to wait.

A thought suddenly struck Tom. He had the files of everyone who was there that night, except one. Superintendent Peters' own file. He would add this to the growing list of things he needed to discuss with Superintendent Peters.

Of the ten people who attended that final briefing, five were detectives: DCI Shaw, Detective Sergeant John Anderson and Detective Constables Jane Booker, William James and Gary Bennett. All of these were members of Shaw's team.

Then there were four uniformed police sergeants: Mark

Brown, Terry Evans, Mike Turton and Peter Gunn. And of course Superintendent Peters. Tom was convinced that the informant, or informants, was on this list.

Tom had already decided that the most likely suspects would be those people who had been involved in both *Operation Sunlight* and *Operation Torch*. In Tom's mind they were both inextricably linked.

He decided to start with the detectives who had attended the briefing. As he worked his way through their files, he was struck by just how ordinary most of them were. Not ordinary in terms of their competence or ability, but rather their background. They were all from working- or lower-middle-class families and had joined the force either straight from school or university.

The exception was DCI Shaw. His route to the police force had been far from ordinary and Tom became increasingly engrossed as he read his file. He'd clearly had a privileged upbringing and his family had considerable wealth. His father had been a very distinguished QC, specialising in prosecution cases, and had been involved in some of the most high-profile criminal court cases of the 80s, 90s and early 2000s.

According to Shaw's file, both his mother and father were no longer alive. At one stage it seemed as though Shaw had plans to follow his father and pursue the same legal career. After studying law at Cambridge University he had then, almost effortlessly, obtained a position at one of the top London law firms, where he spent the next few years building up his reputation as an aggressive and relentless prosecution lawyer.

But it was the fact that he had suddenly given all of this up and joined the police force which caught Tom's attention and then intrigued him. What impressed him even more though, was that Shaw could not be accused of taking the soft option. His degree and intellect had undoubtedly given him a head start on all of the others who joined at the same time. But from there on, it was his own personal ability and drive to achieve results which had brought him to the attention of senior officers. And *Operation Sunlight* must have appeared to have been just another stepping stone in his seemingly inevitable rise to the very top of the Met.

As he read this, Tom suddenly, and to his great surprise,

found himself developing a grudging respect for DCI Shaw. Okay, they would never be personal friends, but that didn't mean he couldn't respect and appreciate everything which Shaw had achieved. One thing was certain. It would have been financially far more lucrative, and probably less stressful, to have pursued a legal career rather than the one to which he had now committed himself. So it was highly unlikely he had made this sudden career change for the money, although Tom did notice that he lived in a very upmarket part of Chelsea. Not the sort of place where you would expect your average DCI to live.

There was also no mention of a wife or family in his file, so perhaps he was happy to live the eligible bachelor's life for now. He had always thought Detective Chief Inspector Richard Shaw to be a man in a great hurry and everything which he had just read about him seemed to confirm that. How much of a hurry though, only he knew.

Detective Sergeant John Anderson's file was also interesting. He was in his mid-thirties – so about the same age as his boss, DCI Shaw – and had been a police officer all of his working life. He had joined as soon as he was old enough, and made the switch from uniformed officer to detective about six years ago – never a particularly easy switch.

What was interesting, however, was that he had also been promoted to Detective Sergeant, at the same time as Shaw gained his promotion to DCI. And for the same reason. The success of *Operation Sunlight*. In Tom's experience, when this happened, the result was often an even greater bond and sense of loyalty developing between the subordinate and his boss. This was especially so on the part of the subordinate. It was almost as though, now conscious of just how much he owed to his boss, he had to somehow continue to demonstrate this.

Tom suspected this process had already begun with Milner, especially since Tom had recommended him for promotion to Acting Detective Sergeant. He had seen this a few times throughout his career. Usually, it was a very positive change but, very occasionally, it could be unhealthy, developing into a dangerous form of support, where objectivity and reasoning gave way to blind, unquestioning loyalty.

Anderson had married but about two years ago had

divorced. His two children lived with their mother, whilst he lived in a small flat close to Uxbridge. All of this, once again, reminded him of his own failed marriage. He wondered if Anderson had also devoted too much time to his career at the expense of his marriage.

Detective Constable Jane Booker was the youngest of all the detectives in Shaw's team. She was twenty-four years old – so about the same age as Milner. In fact, he now remembered that Milner had mentioned her by name a few times, and Tom had seen them together in the canteen. Perhaps they had struck up a friendship? Booker had transferred to the West London Regional Team just over a year ago and, as far as he could see, *Operation Torch* had been her first major case. She was single and still lived at home with her parents in Egham. She didn't immediately strike him as being the ideal candidate as an informant. She was young and, although she might not think so herself, still very inexperienced in police matters. But he made a mental note to discreetly ask Milner about DC Booker.

Tom knew Detective Constable Gary Bennett very well. Whilst he had never been part of Tom's team they had worked together a few times over the years, on various operations. In fact, Tom had specifically asked for DC Bennett to be seconded to his team for the earlier operation at the scrap yard, but, he'd been informed that Bennett was off sick.

Bennett was thirty-eight and, as such, one of the oldest members of Shaw's team. He was married with three teenage children and Tom had met his wife on a number of social occasions. Tom liked Bennett. Whilst he was not the most inspirational of detectives he was, however, detailed, committed and very dependable, as well as having a copper's innate extra sense when it came to criminals.

Not everyone could be a high-flyer and without men such as DC Bennett, those high-flyers could never be successful. He had been a Detective Constable for over ten years now. It had always surprised Tom that he had never been promoted to Detective Sergeant, especially as he too had been involved in *Sunlight*. Perhaps he was just happy to remain a Detective Constable. He thought it would be very helpful if he could speak with DC Bennett, and get his views as to what went wrong on that fateful night.

The other detective who had attended the final *Operation Torch* briefing was Detective Constable William James. He was another officer who had not been with the West London Regional force too long – in fact, in his case, just less than a year. Despite being relatively new he had still been a part of the team that ran *Sunlight*. His file said he had transferred from one of the Yorkshire Divisions at his own specific request. Tom wondered what his motivation was for doing that. Did he have relatives or a girlfriend down here? Or perhaps he simply felt the opportunities for promotion were greater in a London Regional Division.

Tom had seen him around the station. His Yorkshire accent, for a start, made him stand out from the rest of the team. He was physically a big man, with an equally large personality. Given the promotions that were handed out as a result of *Sunlight*, Tom wondered why James had not received one. As he read James's file, he suddenly remembered an old contact from the Yorkshire force. He smiled to himself. He would call him. It was always interesting to have a conversation with Dave Richards.

He now turned his attention to the uniformed officers who were at the briefing. He doubted if any of these officers were their man. Generally, it's CID who run major operations and they would normally only ask for uniformed support, or back-up, after the main planning had been completed. Nonetheless, and as he kept telling himself, if there was one fundamental rule of good detective work, it was never to assume anything and *always* check. So, he worked his way through these files as well. Applying the same cross-referencing criterion which he had applied to the list of detectives had identified just one uniformed officer who had been involved in both operations.

Sergeant Peter Gunn was another career policeman. He was now in his late forties, married with two children, in their late teens. Gunn was someone else who Tom knew very well and had worked with many times over the years. Despite this there were still things he didn't know about Gunn. Reading the file, Tom was surprised to see that he had, a few years previously, applied to join CID. For some unspecified reason the file simply said his application had not been successful. Could it have been this rejection which tempted Gunn to offer his services to Fuller? Yet another reason why he needed all of their financial details.

By the time he had read through all the files the events of the day had finally started to catch up with him. It was time to go home. As he locked the files in his drawer he suddenly thought of Mary. He'd promised to keep in touch with her but, to his great shame, had forgotten all about it. Initially he tried to rationalise this memory loss on the basis that he'd had an incredibly busy day and hadn't had the opportunity to call her. But even he didn't believe this.

What made it even worse was that when he switched on his mobile phone there were three missed calls – all from Mary.

Chapter 16

Tom was up, showered and shaved and on his way into the station by eight o'clock the following morning. As he was driving into work he called up Mary's number on his mobile and pressed the button. It had only rung once before it was answered. 'Hello stranger,' said Mary. 'I thought you'd lost my number.' Tom thought he could detect just a hint of annoyance in her voice. He couldn't blame her.

'I know. I'm really sorry,' replied Tom, as contritely as he could, without betraying the full extent of the guilt he was feeling.

'Is that all you can say?' she said, her voice now containing undisguised anger. 'When you didn't return any of my calls I started to worry that something might have happened to you.' She paused for a while and then said, although by this time her anger had disappeared, leaving just genuine concern, 'I was really worried about you.'

'Mary, I know you were. I should have called you last night. But by the time I switched on my phone again it was well after midnight. I didn't think you'd appreciate it if I called you while you were asleep.'

'Tom, you know that's not the case. I'd rather you call me at three o'clock in the morning than not at all. Well, maybe not at three o'clock, but you know what I mean.'

Tom didn't know what to say. Fortunately Mary carried on. 'What have you been up to that prevented you from calling me? Was it the metal thefts?'

'Well, that was certainly one of the things,' he replied, deliberately vaguely.

'Have you made any progress trying to catch the culprits?' she asked, clearly interested in developments.

'Hopefully,' replied Tom. 'Although there's a bit more to be done before we can say for certain.' Tom liked the fact that Mary took a genuine interest in his work – and his wellbeing

– but he was still reluctant to give her all of the details. It would just complicate things. He was still determined to try and distance Mary from his work.

'Well, remember just about everyone is on your side,' she answered in her best supporting voice. She then hesitated for a while before saying, this time with genuine distaste, 'I can't believe there are people who are willing to do things like that.'

Tom chose not to respond, hoping this would draw an end to this particular conversation.

But when Mary next spoke it was clear she still wanted to continue. 'I was speaking to one of my customers today about it. She couldn't believe that they are allowed to get away with it.'

Tom gave a light laugh. 'Is that a criticism of the police?'

'Well, I have to say, everyone is wondering what you are doing about it.'

Now it was Tom's turn to show some annoyance. 'You can tell your friends we are doing our best.'

This time there was an uneasy silence before Mary next spoke. 'Tom. I'm sorry. I know you are. You have enough pressure without me adding to it.'

The silence was still there, as both of them tried to think what to say next. Eventually, once again, it was Mary who spoke. 'Do you think we'll be able to get together at all this week?' before adding, this time with real feeling, 'I really miss you.'

Although Tom was relieved their conversation had moved on from the metal thefts he couldn't quite believe he'd much rather speak about his personal feelings than about his work. Yet again he found himself thinking just how much his life had changed since he'd first met Mary.

'I miss you as well, but I think it will be the weekend before I have some spare time.' He then added, but this time in a more light-hearted way, 'Do you think you will be able to wait that long or should I send you a photo of myself just to remind you what I look like?'

The earlier tension seemed to have now totally disappeared. 'I'd rather have the real thing. So, I suppose I'll just have to wait.'

'Correct answer. Why don't you come round on Saturday night?'

'Should I bring an overnight bag?'

'I should. Unless you want to use my stuff.'

'Don't be offended, but I think I'll bring my own bag,' she said, continuing their now light-hearted conversation.

'That's a date then. I've got a few things to get out of the way first, so why don't you get to my place at about seven o'clock?'

'Perfect,' she answered. 'That will give me time to close up the shop, collect a few things and then come over to you.'

'Don't work too hard. I don't want you falling asleep on me,' he said, before adding, this time with a light laugh, 'well, not straight away.'

Even the thought of seeing Mary again had disappeared by the time Tom was in his office. The first thing he did was to make a call. It was quickly answered by a man with an unmistakable Yorkshire accent. 'Detective Chief Inspector Richards.'

'Dave. It's Tom Stone. How are you?'

'Bloody hell. Not *the* Tom Stone? The recent hero of the hour. I'm surprised a person as famous as you can even be bothered nowadays to talk to someone like me.'

'The very same,' replied Tom. 'I thought I'd call you so you can then tell all of your friends that you've just had a call from Detective Chief Inspector Tom Stone. That's the sort of person I am. One who likes to share his fame with old colleagues. You can now bask in a bit of reflected glory.'

Tom and Dave Richards had worked together many years ago when they were both young Detective Constables. Tom had been seconded by the Yorkshire Regional Force to help out on a serial murder case. Initially, and understandably, his presence had not been particularly welcomed. In fact, there had been outright hostility towards him when he had first arrived from London.

Dave, in particular, made no attempt to hide his feelings, partly fuelled by his genetic antagonism towards everyone who had a southern accent. Eventually though, they had started to gain each other's respect. This had then developed into a genuine friendship, to such an extent that Tom had felt disappointed when, after the case, he'd had to move back to London. Indeed, at one stage, he had even thought seriously about applying for a permanent position within the Yorkshire

Force. He couldn't remember now why he hadn't followed this up. Perhaps it was because, at the time, he and Anne were going through one of their many difficult phases. Since that time he and Dave, whilst not being on each other's Christmas card lists, had tried to stay in contact.

'Much as it pains me to say this, you did a grand job on that multiple murder inquiry. I know you weren't the lead officer, but I heard you played a blinder.' Coming from Dave, this was praise indeed and Tom was genuinely appreciative, although, of course, he knew it would be bad form to take all of the praise.

'Well, it was DCI Jack Chapman and his team who did most of the work. I just helped out.'

'That's not exactly what I heard,' answered Dave, before adding. 'Any road, now we've done the pleasantries bit what can I do for you? We do have crime up here as well, you know.'

'You had a DC William James working for you. You probably know he's now working for us. I wonder if you could tell me what you know about him?'

'Bloody hell. Does he call himself William now? When he was up here he was plain Bill. I suppose that's what happens when you move down south. He'll be drinking cappuccinos next.' There was then a slight pause before Dave said, 'Can I ask why you want to know?'

Tom knew Dave well enough to know he would appreciate some plain speaking.

'You can ask but I'm not going to tell you.'

'Fair enough,' replied Dave, obviously happy with Tom's unequivocal reply. He carried on. 'Bill's a good copper and dead straight. He's also a bit of a whizz when it comes to all of that technical stuff, although I couldn't understand what he was talking about half of the time. I was really disappointed to lose him and tried my hardest to talk some sense into him. But he'd gone through a bit of a messy split from his long-time girlfriend. Apparently she'd met someone else. Anyway, as a result of this, he decided he needed a clean break, and to put some distance between them, so he applied for the position within the Met. Does that help?'

'Yes. Thanks. I was interested to know what his motivation had been to make the move south. After all, it's not often that a Yorkshire man decides, of his own free will, to swap God's county for the smoke, is it?'

'And if I had my way I would make it a hanging offence. It's worse than treachery,' answered Dave, only half jokingly. More seriously he then asked, 'How is he doing?'

'He's not in my team but, from what I've seen and heard, he's doing pretty well. Although he's still got that funny Yorkshire accent,' answered Tom.

'Thank God for that.'

Tom was still thinking about his conversation with DCI Richards when Milner appeared outside his office. When he saw his face, however, he quickly forgot all about Richards.

'Milner. You look as though one of those children's face painters has been practising on you.' Milner's face did look a bit of a mess. Although his left cheek was still very swollen it was his eye or, more specifically, the area immediately below it, which attracted Tom's attention. That part of his face, between his partly closed left eye and his swollen cheek bone, was an impressive rainbow of colours.

'Does it look that bad, Sir?' replied Milner.

'I'm surprised you're able to see out of that eye. What did they say at the hospital?'

'Well, fortunately, nothing is broken. It is a bit sore though,' Milner said in an understated way.

'I bet it is. Did they give you anything for it?'

'Just painkillers, Sir. They said the swelling should start to go down in a few days' time. In the meantime I just have to be careful.'

'So, until that happens, why don't you stay at home? I'm sure we can cope without you for a few days at least.'

'I did think about it, Sir, but I want to be there when we visit McNulty,' he replied, looking at Tom through his one good eye. 'Anyway, it's not going to get better any quicker, simply by me staying at home.'

Tom remained silent for a while before saying, 'Okay. But only if you promise not to get involved in any more fights. Or, if you do, at least this time try and get a blow in first.'

Tom thought he detected a thin smile appear on Milner's lips, followed immediately by a painful grimace. 'Please don't try and make me smile, Sir. It hurts every time.'

'I'll bear that in mind,' Tom replied, resisting the urge to smile himself. 'But the first thing I want you to do is to go and get your face photographed. A photo of a face like that,' he said, nodding in Milner's direction, 'will be worth a thousand words when it comes to the trial.'

As Milner left Tom's office, he said in such a quiet voice that no one else would hear. 'Glad that I can be of help.'

Chapter 17

Tom had only been at his desk for a few minutes when his mobile rang. He looked at the display to see if it was a number he recognised, but it just read 'Private number'. He pressed the answer button. 'DCI Stone here,' he said.

'Hello Tom. Remember me?' said the voice on the other end. He vaguely recognised the voice but, before he could remember who it was, the answer was provided to him. 'It's Pauline. Pauline Jones. I've been trying to get in touch with you for a while now. Did you get my letter? I came round to see you but you weren't in and so I wrote a note to you.'

Tom was genuinely shocked. She was the very last person who he expected to hear from. 'Are you still there?' she asked.

'Yes. I'm still here. Why are you calling me?' asked Tom, quite sharply.

Pauline either didn't recognise the slight hostility in Tom's voice or, if she did, chose to ignore it. 'We had that nice night out together a few weeks ago. We seemed to get on well and I could tell you liked me. I was hoping we could meet up again on another date.' Before he had time to respond she then said excitedly, 'You can tell me all about those murders which you were involved in. Your face was in all of the papers. You didn't tell me you were famous. I've told all of my friends about you.'

'Well, I don't think I was famous then,' he replied, concerned with what she had just said. The part about telling all her friends about him.

'You can tell me all about it when we next meet,' she said, before adding, 'I've never been out with a famous person before.'

Tom didn't like the way this conversation was going. 'I don't think that would be a good idea. A lot of things have happened since then and, anyway, I'm really busy at the moment,' he explained.

If he had hoped this would put her off he was mistaken and this was soon confirmed when she next spoke. 'That's all right. I don't mean tonight or anything. We could leave it until the weekend.' She then added, rather alarmingly, at least as far as Tom was concerned, 'I only live in West Drayton. So, we're not too far away from one another. I could come round to see you if you want now that I know where you live.'

'I don't want to sound rude,' Tom replied, 'but I really don't think it would be a good idea for us to meet again. Anyway, since then, I've met someone else. I don't think it would be fair on her if we were to see one another again.' He instantly regretted admitting that there was now someone else in his life.

Pauline didn't immediately respond to what Tom had just said. There was a brief silence before she did reply. 'Well, we could always meet just as friends. There's nothing wrong in that, is there? Just because a man and woman go out for a meal doesn't mean they are going to jump into bed straightaway,' she said ominously.

'As I said, I really don't have any spare time at all.' He was still trying to let her down as gently as he could.

When she next replied it was with sudden, unexpected aggression in her voice. 'When we first met, I could see the way you kept looking at me and that you fancied me. You're all the same, you coppers. Now that you've been in the papers and on telly, you think you're too good for someone like me, don't you?'

Tom had, by now, had enough of this bizarre conversation and so he simply said, 'I'm sorry you feel like that but there's nothing more I really have to say,' and he pressed the 'end call' button.

As he sat at his desk, looking vacantly towards some distant point, his mind was racing. The conversation had clearly disturbed him. There was something quite sinister in the way she had spoken, although he couldn't quite put his finger on what it was.

As he was sitting there, with these thoughts racing through his mind, he was distracted by a noise.

It was Milner, with a cup in each hand and a file tucked under his arm. All that was missing was a pair of glasses perched precariously on the top of his head. 'I thought you might want a cup of tea, Sir,' he said, placing both cups on Tom's desk. 'I wondered if we could go through the file before we go and see McNulty.'

For once Tom welcomed Milner disturbing him, even though he had that file with him. He was surprised how unsettling the phone call from Pauline had been and it took a while before he had regained, at least some, of his normal composure. 'Yes. Thank you, Milner. That's very thoughtful of you,' he finally said.

'Is everything okay, Sir?' asked Milner. 'You look a bit distracted.'

'Everything is fine,' he lied. 'So, what have you got?'

'The tape of the conversation in the pub. Do you remember? You asked me to get hold of it.'

'Of course I remember. I'm not completely senile yet,' answered Tom, instantly regretting the brusqueness of his answer.

Milner chose to ignore this not-so-veiled criticism. He simply carried on. 'Anyway, I've collected the tape from DC Simmons. I haven't had the chance to listen to it yet but DC Simmons says we'll be really pleased when we do.' He then took out a small tape recorder from his pocket and put the tape into the machine. 'Do you want to listen to it now?' he asked.

'In a minute,' replied Tom. 'I would like to hear what they have to say before we visit McNulty and Brady. But, first, is there anything else?'

'One other thing you might find interesting, Sir.'

'What's that?'

'Last night I ran a check on Brady, and guess what?'

'Let me guess,' replied Tom. 'He's also known to us?'

'Spot on,' replied Milner. 'About two years ago Brady was sentenced to six months, suspended for two years, for handling stolen goods.'

Tom was once again drawn to Milner's face. 'Did you get your face photographed? I'd like a visual record of all of those injuries.'

'Not yet, Sir. That's where I'm going when we've finished this briefing. One of the lab boys is going to do it,' he explained.

'Are you sure you are okay?' asked Tom, once again concerned about Milner's condition.

'I'm fine, Sir. And, anyway, even if I wasn't, I'd still want to come with you to visit McNulty and Brady. What time should we leave?'

'As soon as you've had your photograph taken and I've had a quick listen to the tape,' answered Tom. 'I think we should go and see McNulty first and then Brady. Come back here as soon as you've finished.'

As Milner left the office, Tom's thoughts returned to his earlier conversation with Pauline. He really didn't know what to make of it, although, somehow, he didn't think any of it was good news. Suddenly the phone rang. 'DCI Stone,' he said.

'Good morning, DCI Stone. This is Janice. Superintendent Peters' PA. He asked if, when you have the time, you could come up and brief him on last night's operation. What would be the best time for you?' she asked.

'It's a bit difficult to say at the moment. We have a couple of follow-up meetings to carry out first with some of the main suspects and I'm not sure when they'll finish,' explained Tom, as deliberately vague as possible, trying to keep all options open.

'Why don't you call me then when you're back,' suggested Janice helpfully, whilst simultaneously making it clear this was an instruction, not an invitation.

'Good idea. I'll do that,' replied Tom obediently.

Tom just had time to listen to part of the tape before Milner reappeared.

'Are you ready yet, Sir?' asked Milner, conscious that DCI Stone was not one to be rushed into doing things when he wasn't fully ready.

'Just about,' replied Tom. 'Did you get the photos taken?' he asked.

'All done, Sir. Although I don't think I'll be sending any of them to my family,' he replied, trying not to laugh.

'You're right there,' said Tom. 'More importantly it might put off all the ladies from fancying you as well.' As he said this he suddenly remembered Milner's friendship with Detective Constable Booker.

Chapter 18

Tom and Milner had parked just outside the Recycling Centre. 'I think I'm going to enjoy this,' said Tom, with uncharacteristic enthusiasm. 'It will be interesting to hear what Mr McNulty has to say for himself.'

They got out of the car and walked towards the entrance to the site. As they got closer they could see McNulty in his office. He was looking in their direction. His expression suggested it wasn't a visit he was particularly looking forward to.

By the time they had got there he had come out of the office to meet them. If anything he now had an even more nervous look on his face. 'Mr McNulty. We'd like to ask you a few more questions,' said Tom, dispensing with any introductory pleasantries.

'But I answered everything yesterday. I don't know what else I could tell you,' replied McNulty, surprisingly calmly.

It was Milner who replied. 'There's been a few developments since then.'

McNulty looked at Milner's face with genuine shock. 'What happened to you?' he asked.

'Well, that's one of the developments,' replied Milner. Tom could see even Milner was now enjoying this.

Tom decided they'd had their bit of fun at McNulty's expense. 'You probably noticed that three of your staff didn't turn in for work today,' he said, looking directly into McNulty's eyes. 'Well, we are a few short today,' explained McNulty, still desperately trying to keep calm.

It was Milner who delivered the *coup de grâce*. 'That's probably because Walker, Lomas and Stevenson are currently under arrest,' he helpfully explained.

'Why? What have they done?' he asked with seemingly genuine interest.

Tom nodded towards Milner. 'Detective Sergeant Milner. Why don't you list the charges.'

'It will be a pleasure, Sir,' replied Milner. Tom looked towards Milner with raised eyebrows.

Milner seemed to take the hint and, when he next spoke it was with his usual calmness. He took out his notebook and started to read from it.

'Mr Stevenson has been arrested on suspicion of theft, as well as handling stolen goods. Mr Lomas has also been arrested on suspicion of theft, handling stolen goods *and* assaulting a police officer with a dangerous weapon.' He paused as he turned a page in his notebook. 'In addition to the suspicion of theft, handling stolen goods, driving whilst over the legal limit, driving without any current tax or insurance charges, Mr Walker has also been arrested for assaulting a police officer.' As he listed this final charge he looked up and said, 'By the way, I was the officer he assaulted.'

Tom thought Milner's last comment was a bit unprofessional but, under the circumstances, he could hardly blame him.

McNulty looked shell-shocked. Tom then added to his condition when he asked, 'Mr McNulty, what were your movements after the Recycling Centre closed last night?'

'I went home straight away,' he replied nervously.

'Do you want to reconsider that?' suggested Tom. 'You see we have evidence you were still here at about seven o'clock.'

McNulty was now really worried and this was confirmed when, his voice breaking slightly, he said, 'What evidence is that?'

'For a start, there are a number of police officers who were positioned immediately outside here who are willing to testify to that effect. But, just in case the courts might take your word against all of theirs, we also have you on video. You are clearly seen opening the side gate to let them in, and then closing the main gates, after Walker, Lomas and Stevenson had driven their white van out of the site.'

When McNulty didn't respond Tom then said, 'Also we have an audio recording of Walker, Lomas and Stevenson where they clearly implicate you in the thefts.'

He looked at McNulty for any reaction. It wasn't too long before it came. McNulty covered his eyes with his right hand. No one spoke for a while. Tom was happy to maintain the silence.

Sure enough, it was McNulty who finally spoke. 'I told them not to do this but they wouldn't listen. To begin with it was just a few pieces but then it got more and more. They threatened me. They said they would hurt me if I stopped them from using the site. I didn't want to do it.' He then added, almost pleading with them, 'You have to believe me. I had no choice.'

Tom ignored his pleading and simply said, 'Mr McNulty, in a minute Detective Sergeant Milner will be charging you with theft and the handling of stolen goods. But you might be able to make it easier for yourself if you could provide us with more information about what has been going on here.'

'What do you mean?' asked McNulty, now a broken man and clearly willing to do everything he could to help.

This was the moment Tom had been waiting for. 'Well, you can start by telling us what you know about the disappearance of Mr Sipowicz.'

'I told you. I don't know where he is.'

'Why is it that I don't believe you?' answered Tom. 'Everything else seems to come back to this place. Why should his sudden disappearance be any different? If you know anything I suggest that you tell us now. Otherwise it will be far worse when it goes to court.'

This seemed to convince McNulty to tell them what he knew.

'He was upset because they had stolen a bronze plaque, which had the names of Polish war dead on it. He told them he was going to the police,' he said, before adding ominously, 'so they decided to teach him a lesson.'

'Teach him a lesson?' repeated Milner. 'What do you mean?'

'They beat him up,' replied McNulty in a matter-of-fact way.

'Who beat him up?'

'Walker and Lomas,' answered McNulty very quietly.

'Had he been involved in the thefts up to then?' asked Tom.

'No. I think he knew they were doing something illegal but he wasn't involved. It was only when he saw them with the plaque from the Polish War Memorial, that he suddenly got angry with them.'

'Did he mention it to you?' asked Milner.

McNulty was now ashen-faced and was clearly struggling with his emotions when he replied, 'He did.' Both Tom and Milner remained quiet. It wasn't long before McNulty spoke again. 'He came to see me to tell me what was going on. I told him to forget about it, keep away from them and just concentrate on his own job.' He was silent for a while before saying, 'But he didn't take my advice. And not long after that he was beaten up.'

'When was this?' asked Milner. 'Was it last Wednesday night?'

'Yes. After work.'

'Where is he now?' asked Tom.

'I don't know. They took him somewhere later that night.'

'Why didn't you go to the police? After all, you knew that a serious crime had been committed and Mr Sipowicz was an employee of yours.'

'I told you. They threatened me. I saw what they did to Sipowicz. I was scared that they'd do the same to me.' McNulty started to sob. After a while the sobbing stopped and he said. 'What will happen to me?'

It was Tom who answered. 'Mr McNulty. You are in very serious trouble. Not as serious as the others, if what you say is true. But still serious. Your only option now is to tell us everything that you know. I can't guarantee it, but this might help you if you fully cooperate with us.'

'Did you know who was buying the metal?' asked Milner.

'They've been selling it to a scrap metal dealer,' he volunteered quickly.

'Could you please give us his name,' suggested Milner, notebook and pencil now in hand. It was an instruction rather than a suggestion.

'His name is Brady. William Brady. I didn't like him. He seemed a nasty piece of work. He came here to the site once to have a look at some of the stuff. I didn't like that. I mentioned it to Walker but he just told me to keep my nose out.'

'Did you see him handing any money to Walker or any of the others?' asked Tom.

'No. As I said, when he was here, all he did was to take a look around.'

'So, you are saying you personally never received any

money from the sale of the stolen goods?' suggested Milner.

McNulty remained silent.

'Mr McNulty. Believe me, it's in your interests to tell the truth. We are bound to find out anyway. If you deny this and then we later find out you have been lying then your situation will be even worse,' explained Milner.

Finally, McNulty answered. 'I was offered a few pounds to begin with. I said I didn't want it but they insisted I take it. After that, I had no choice.' He then added quietly, 'If only I hadn't taken that money.'

'And what can you tell us about Darren Wood's death?' asked Tom.

'I wasn't there,' replied McNulty very defensively. 'That was nothing to do with me.'

'So, who was it to do with then?' asked Tom.

Again McNulty hesitated. 'Mr McNulty. If you don't tell us what you know we will have to work on the basis that you were there, and are deliberately holding something back.'

This seemed to do the trick. 'They – all four of them – had heard that there was some metal by the railway line. I heard it was Darren who started to cut away at some cabling that was nearby. It was then that … well, you know what happened. He was always the one who took all of the risks.'

'What? Like climbing onto church roofs?' suggested Milner.

'Yes. That was him as well. I kept telling them that, sooner or later, someone was going to get hurt. But all they were interested in was making easy money.'

'Thank you, Mr McNulty. For the time being I have one last question,' Tom said. 'Are there any stolen items left here on the site?'

'Yes, there are,' he replied. 'I checked this morning and there's still quite a bit of stuff they haven't been able to move yet.'

Tom turned to Milner. 'Get the team in here, as soon as possible, to catalogue everything. And make sure that, in the meantime, nothing is touched. Mr McNulty, I would like you to close the site. After you have done that you will be arrested for the theft and handling of stolen goods.' He then added, 'At least for now.'

Chapter 19

'Are you feeling better now we've been to see McNulty?' asked Tom. He and Milner were now back at the station.

'Actually, Sir. I do feel a bit better. Maybe it's psychological. I don't know. But it did feel good.'

'Well, you did look as though you were enjoying yourself,' replied Tom, laughing quietly. He continued, although this time more seriously, 'Despite what McNulty told us about Brady's involvement I still think it's going to be difficult for us to make anything stick.'

'But surely McNulty's testimony against Brady must carry some weight?' asked a slightly puzzled Milner.

'We'll see. I hope so, but I wouldn't bank on it. As far as I can see, unless we can find some stolen metal on his site, then it's just McNulty's word against that of Brady,' explained Tom.

This time Milner remained silent. Tom had seen this before with Milner. When he was concerned or worried about something he suddenly became very quiet.

'What is it?' asked Tom.

'Nothing, Sir,' replied Milner, just a little too quickly, confirming Tom's suspicion that indeed there was something amiss.

'Milner. We might not have worked together for many years yet but I think I know when something is bothering you. Is it what I just said about Brady?'

Milner nodded. 'It's just that without men like Brady, Walker and his gang wouldn't have a buyer for their stolen goods. If Brady walks away from this then, I'm sure in a few months' time he'll be tempted to start all over again. That can't be right.'

'As your career develops you'll quickly begin to realise that although eighty per cent is not as good as a hundred per cent, it's a lot better than nothing at all,' answered Tom, giving him the benefit of his own line of home-spun philosophy.

Just as Milner was trying to understand exactly what DCI Stone had meant by this, Tom then added, 'But on this particular occasion, you might be surprised to hear that I agree with you. I want to see him put away as well. All I'm saying is it's often advisable to set yourself realistic targets. That way you are less likely to be disappointed.'

Milner still wasn't quite sure what to say in response to this and so he settled on, 'Thank you, Sir.' Changing the subject he then said. 'What about Mr Sipowicz? What do you think has happened to him?'

Tom's earlier bonhomie appeared to desert him and he was suddenly very serious. 'I don't know. But I have to say I do fear the worst. He's been missing for about a week now, with no news at all. I just hope that it's not too late. But I suspect we'll soon find out when we interview Walker, Lomas and Stevenson. Why don't we go and get an early lunch? Then we can go and visit our Mr Brady?'

'Actually, Sir, I'd already agreed I would have lunch with DC Booker,' replied Milner, before adding, albeit without any great enthusiasm, 'but you're very welcome to join us.'

'Thank you for the invitation but I think I'd only cramp your style.' He then continued, nodding towards Milner's face, 'Mind you, with your face as it is, you might have your work cut out anyway.'

This seemed to lighten Milner's mood. 'I've always liked a challenge,' he said.

'Okay,' answered Tom. 'Could you at least bring me back a sandwich. Ham and cheese would do.'

As Milner was leaving, Tom called after him, 'And good luck.'

Tom switched on his computer, half expecting there to be another 'Reporting' email from Superintendent Peters. He was relieved when there was nothing there. He quickly scanned the headers of those emails he had received and opened the ones he felt needed his immediate attention. After about forty-five minutes, and judging that none of the others required any follow-up, he decided he would be better served by using his time to try and think through recent events.

He could not quite believe that less than a week ago he and Mary were enjoying the sunshine in the Canary Islands. So much had happened in such a short time.

Whilst he was happy to be involved with Milner in helping to resolve the metal thefts, he had to admit he had been unnerved when Lomas had lunged at him with the knife. Of course, he had been in more dangerous spots in the past but there was something about this particular situation that seemed different. Perhaps it was his age or maybe simply because Lomas was such an unpredictable person. He had always considered himself to be a cautious and fairly calculating person but, if anything, since he had met Mary, these traits seemed to have increased.

He was also very concerned about Maciej Sipowicz's wellbeing. This investigation had now taken a far more sinister turn and all of his instincts were telling him that any happy outcome was unlikely.

Then there was his conversation with Mary this morning. He couldn't really blame her for being angry with him, but he was determined to keep his work as separate as possible from his personal life. Only time would tell how Mary would react to this.

He also had another follow-up meeting with Superintendent Peters later today. Ostensibly this was to update him on last night's events at the scrap yard although, of course, the main reason was to review progress on 'Reporting'. Finally, there was the call from Pauline. He had detected something almost threatening in her voice. He couldn't rationalise this feeling but, nonetheless, those finely tuned instincts were once again in overdrive.

Milner's reappearance, paper bag in hand, brought him back to the here and now. 'They only had cheese. I brought you two. Is that okay?' he asked.

'Yes. That's fine. Thank you. Did you have a nice chat with DC Booker?' he asked, as he started to take the sandwiches out of the bag.

'Yes, thank you, Sir,' he answered, slightly concerned that DCI Stone had shown no sign, so far, of reimbursing him the cost of the two sandwiches.

'She seems a really nice young lady,' said Tom. 'Do you ever meet socially?'

Milner quickly realised where this conversation was heading. 'If you mean are we dating then the answer is no,' he replied. He then added as further explanation, 'We've had the occasional drink together, after work, but that's all. Anyway, she already has a boyfriend.'

Tom noticed the disappointment in his voice. 'That's a shame,' he said. 'Is he also a police officer?'

'No. He's a teacher,' replied Milner. Tom picked up one of the sandwiches and began to eat. After a couple of bites he said, 'Sorry. I didn't mean to be nosy but it's just that you don't say much about your personal life. I didn't, for example, know about your connection with St Augustine's until earlier this week.'

'Well, nor do you, Sir,' he answered. 'I don't even know if you're married or have a partner.'

Tom smiled and said, 'Good point.' He then added, this time a little more seriously. 'I made it a rule, many years ago, to try and keep my private life as separate as possible from my work life.' He didn't wait for any further response, clearly thinking that would be sufficient. 'What did DC Booker make of your facial injuries? Was she impressed?' he asked.

'I'm not sure that impressed is how I would describe it,' replied Milner, in a slightly disappointed tone of voice. 'More like she felt sorry for me.'

'Well. That can sometimes work in your favour as well,' Tom said as an encouragement. 'Did you tell her how you came by them?'

'I just said someone had a go at me last night. I didn't mention what we were doing. And anyway, she didn't ask,' he said, almost disappointedly.

Tom decided now was his best opportunity. 'I understand DC Booker was involved in *Operation Torch*. Has she ever mentioned it to you?'

Milner looked suspiciously at Tom and then said, 'Why would she do that, Sir? You know the rule about not discussing any operational issues.'

Tom could sense that Milner was treading very carefully. Perhaps she had discussed it but he was covering for her.

'I know that, Milner. I'm not asking you to drop her in it. I'm simply asking if she has mentioned it. After all, she must be a bit worried, especially as the official inquiry is not that far away.'

Milner seemed to hesitate as he considered how to respond to this. Eventually he conceded, 'Well, yes, she is worried. In fact, all of the officers involved in *Operation Torch* are worried.' Almost as an afterthought he then said 'And can you blame them?'

'What do you mean?' asked Tom.

'Well, from what little I know about it, the outcome was a total disaster. Despite the fact they had been planning it for weeks, and all of the station's top brass were involved.'

Milner suddenly realised what he had just said. 'I'm sorry, Sir,' he added. 'I mean *most* of the top brass were involved in it.'

'You don't have to apologise, Milner,' replied Tom. 'And anyway, I'm long past the time when I felt precious about these type of things. Go on Milner. I'm interested to hear your thoughts.' He took another bite from his sandwich.

'It's just that with so many senior officers involved you would have expected a far better result than the arrest of a couple of young users. We could all go out, any night of the week, and get the same result.'

'And does DC Booker share your view?'

Milner hesitated again. This conversation was still quite uncomfortable for him. But before he could answer Tom decided to ask a more direct question. 'Does she have any idea why it wasn't successful? After all, she had been involved in the operational planning.'

Tom thought that he detected a slight hesitation, or possibly even reluctance, to answer his question.

'Not really. As *Operation Sunlight* went so well, everyone involved thought, with the same information they had, *Operation Torch* would be just as successful. She told me there was a real buzz that night amongst all of the officers involved. That's why it was such a shock when it ended as it did.'

'Did she say where she thought they were getting their information from?' asked Tom.

'Just rumours really.'

Tom wasn't going to let this go just yet. 'And what were the rumours?' he asked.

He could see that this was a question which Milner didn't really want to answer and so decided to help him. 'Was the information coming from someone in Fuller's gang? Was that the rumour?'

'Yes, Sir,' answered Milner quietly. Suddenly, perhaps because it had been Tom who had suggested this, Milner seemed more willing to discuss it. 'Apparently DCI Shaw, in an earlier briefing on *Operation Sunlight*, had referred to the fact that they had a reliable source of information. As both DCI Shaw and Superintendent Peters seemed so confident, when *Torch* came around, they all just automatically assumed the information was equally reliable.'

Tom decided to press on. 'That's understandable, I suppose,' he said. 'But what about the raid itself? Did she mention who gave the "go" order?'

Milner looked quizzically at Tom before he answered. 'She said it couldn't have been DCI Shaw,' he answered. 'She was with him, and Superintendent Peters, at the side of the house. They took a call, saying that a van had pulled up outside the front door and boxes were being unloaded. She and DCI Shaw then hot-footed it there to see for themselves. She's certain that DCI Shaw didn't use his radio whilst they were running there. It was only when they all returned to the station, and DCI Shaw started to have a go at DC Bennett, that she assumed it must have been DC Bennett.'

'So did DC Booker tell you what happened when they all got back to the station after the raid? They must have discussed the possible reasons as to why it went wrong,' suggested Tom.

This time Milner's earlier quizzical expression had turned to one of suspicion. He voiced his increasing concern. 'Do you think we should be discussing this, Sir? These are all operational questions. Isn't that something which should be left to the inquiry?'

'Yes. You're probably right,' replied Tom, as ambivalently as he could manage. 'I was just interested to know what their thoughts were, that's all. As you say, it will all come out in the inquiry anyway.' Tom took another bite.

Milner's expression suggested he remained unconvinced. However, he eventually carried on. 'Well, as I mentioned, she did say it wasn't very pleasant. DCI Shaw was very angry, blaming the team for their lack of professionalism. In particular, apparently, he said DC Bennett had made a big mistake and it was this which had compromised the operation.' Milner once again hesitated before saying, 'He even apparently mentioned you and me.'

'Really? By name?' asked Tom, failing to hide his surprise. 'Yes. He said even we seemed to know a major operation was about to take place that night and that if we knew then God knows who else also knew.'

Tom remained quiet for a while, as he considered what Milner had just told him. Eventually he said, 'And what about Superintendent Peters? Did he also mention us?'

'I don't think so, Sir. According to DC Booker he didn't say anything. He left all of the talking – if that's how you could describe it – to DCI Shaw. In fact, she said, he – Superintendent Peters that is – was remarkably calm throughout the entire debrief.' He then said, but this time far more assertively, 'Why are you interested in all of this, Sir? I seem to remember you once telling me that I shouldn't listen to all of this station tittle-tattle.'

A very good put down, Tom thought, remembering exactly when he had said this. 'And I still stand by that. It's just that I can't help thinking how lucky we both were not to have been involved in the operation that night.' He then added, 'Anyway thank you, Milner. I hope you don't think I've compromised your relationship with DC Booker. Why don't we now go and see our friend Mr Brady. I have a little surprise for him.'

Chapter 20

A short time later they were driving into Brady's yard. As Tom and Milner got out of their car, Brady came out of his office to meet them.

'Good Morning, Mr Brady,' said Tom. 'We'd like to have another word with you, if that's okay?'

'Why? I told you everything I know last night.'

'Well, we have a few more questions we'd like to ask you, particularly concerning the accusations Mr Walker made about you,' answered Tom. 'Perhaps it would be better if we had this discussion in your office.'

'If that's what you want,' replied Brady. 'I've got nothing to hide.'

'That's good then,' replied Tom, not believing a word Brady had just said.

When they were all in the office Milner took out his notebook, turned to the relevant page and said, 'Mr Brady. Yesterday evening you said you'd never met Walker, Lomas or Stevenson before. Is that correct?'

'That's what I said, isn't it?' he answered.

'Yes, you did. But the problem is, Mr Brady, we have you on CCTV, meeting with them at the Waste Recycling Centre in Barton Street. Not only that, but the manager there,' said Milner, looking down at his notebook, 'a Mr McNulty, is willing to testify to that effect. So you can see we have a bit of a problem with your statement.'

'He's lying. I told you. I've never met any of them before,' Brady answered, still quite confidently.

Milner was now directly facing Brady. 'And what about the CCTV footage, which we now have in our possession, clearly showing you speaking with Walker. Are you saying that can't be you either?' asked Milner.

'It must be someone who looks like me,' replied Brady, still impressively maintaining his outward confidence.

'Is that your car out there?' asked Tom, pointing to a silver Mercedes, parked just in front of the office.

'Yes. Is it a crime to own a car now?' said Brady.

'I was just thinking what a very nice car it is. Very distinctive, wouldn't you say?'

'I suppose so,' replied a now increasingly wary Brady.

'It's just the CCTV also picked up footage of that very same car, and with that exact registration number, and here's the funny thing, at exactly the same time your doppelgänger was at the Recycling Centre talking to Walker and McNulty. Very strange that, wouldn't you agree, Mr Brady?'

'Strange things happen all the time,' replied Brady.

'So, just for the record, are you saying you've never met any of those four people before last night?' asked Tom.

'That's what I'm saying,' replied Brady.

'I'm sure, therefore, you wouldn't mind coming down to the station with us and signing a statement to that effect?' asked Tom. 'Just so that we have it on record.'

'Yes, I'd be willing to do that, but only if my lawyer is there with me,' answered Brady.

'That won't be a problem. I suggest you contact him now so that we can make the arrangements,' answered Tom.

'Now?' he replied, clearly shocked by the urgency of what Tom was suggesting. 'I've got too much to do here at the moment. I'll come down tomorrow.'

'Actually, Mr Brady, that's not possible,' Tom replied firmly. 'We are investigating the suspicious death of a person who, we believe, was also involved in these thefts. The person on the CCTV, who looks like you but, you say, isn't you, is seen talking to that person. A little while later he is found dead, lying by the side of a busy railway line. So, Mr Brady, this has moved on from being just about the handling of stolen metal to something far more serious.'

Tom waited for a response from Brady. When none came he played his last card. He took out a piece of paper from his pocket and handed it to Brady. 'Please take a look at this. It's a warrant to search your premises.' Before he could continue further though, Brady interrupted him. 'Search? For what? I've told you. This is a legit business. I don't buy dodgy stuff.'

It was Milner who answered. 'Mr Brady, that is not entirely true. According to police records you were sentenced to imprisonment, about two years ago, for handling stolen goods. Or was that the person who looks like you?'

Brady's confidence was now fast disappearing. 'That was a misunderstanding and, anyway, the prison sentence was suspended.'

'The courts didn't consider it was a misunderstanding,' replied Milner. 'You might not think that getting a suspended sentence is serious but, I can assure you, the courts certainly do. Particularly when the same person reoffends.'

'Okay, but that was then. I haven't touched anything since,' said Brady.

'In which case, Mr Brady, you have nothing to worry about,' answered Tom. He then turned to Milner and said. 'Detective Sergeant Milner could you please now call in the rest of the team and ask them to get over here as soon as possible, so that we can carry out the search.'

'Certainly, Sir,' was all Milner said in reply, taking out his mobile from his pocket.

'This warrant also gives us the authority to seize all of your records. So, we will be taking invoices for all the purchases you have made over the past two years, as well as your sales ledger,' explained Tom. 'Just to let you know that we will also be taking a very careful look at all of your phone records. This will tell us who you have called. Who called you. That sort of thing. It's amazing what you can find out from phone records.'

Brady now looked crestfallen. 'Okay. I admit that I did buy a few things from Walker but I swear I never knew they were hooky. They told me they had got them from a few house demolitions they had worked on. How was I to know they had been stolen?'

'Well. You could have asked to look at the paperwork for a start,' answered Tom. 'But my job is to catch criminals and recover any stolen goods. It will be up to the courts to decide if they believe you. But with your previous record, if I was you, I wouldn't be building up my hopes.'

Just then Milner reappeared. 'They're on their way, Sir. They will be here very shortly.'

'Good,' replied Tom, suddenly becoming quite concerned. 'Mr Brady. Where are your dogs today? Are they here?'

'No. My son has them, although he's due back here with them later today,' answered Brady. 'Why?'

Tom didn't reply, although Milner could see DCI Stone instantly looked very relieved.

Tom had been hoping Brady would have admitted his involvement and that the search team would not have been needed today. As a contingency though, he had asked if approval for the search warrant could be obtained as quickly as possible. Fortunately, it must have been a quiet day elsewhere and his request was approved.

Whilst they were waiting for the team to arrive, Tom left Milner with Brady and went for a wander around the site.

Like most scrap yards, at least in his limited experience, there didn't appear to be any logic in the way items were stored. To his eye it looked like everything had simply been dumped wherever there was any spare space. Crushed cars, parts from cars, burnt-out cars and relatively intact cars were all dumped together. In one part of the yard he could even see a well-established tree sapling emerging from the broken window of an old car. He thought that it must have been in that exact place for years for that to happen. In many ways it was the perfect place to hide things you didn't want other people to find.

Chapter 21

They had arrived back at the station at about seven o'clock and were both seated in Tom's office.

'I can't believe we found all of that stuff as quickly as we did,' said Milner, failing to hide his excitement. 'As soon as we found it Brady just seemed to give in.'

'We were lucky, Milner. It was because they had too much stuff, waiting to be melted down, or whatever they were planning to do with it, which was their downfall. That and their greed,' said Tom. 'It wouldn't surprise me if the search team find more of the stuff when they complete their search tomorrow. It had all the hallmarks of an Aladdin's cave to me.'

'Greed? What do you mean, Sir?' asked Milner.

'Well, after last night's raid they still had all day to move the stuff somewhere else. If I were them I would have dumped it as far away as possible. But they obviously thought – wrongly as it turned out – they still had time to melt it down before we showed up again,' explained Tom. 'It's impossible to prove anything if all of the stolen items have already been melted down. In many ways, it's a perfect crime.' He paused and then added, laughing. 'I suppose you could say that all of the evidence literally goes up in a puff of smoke.' He'd forgotten that some of that smoke might have come from the lead from the roof at St Augustine's.

Ignoring Tom's attempt at humour, Milner simply said, 'You keep saying *they*, Sir. Do you think Walker and his pals were helping to melt down the metal?'

'It's possible,' answered Tom. 'But it would surprise me if Brady's son wasn't also involved. After all, the sign outside the yard did say *William Brady and Son*. We should take a look at young Mr Brady.'

'So, what happens next, Sir?'

'We try and match what we found with what has gone

missing. That won't be easy with some of the lead and copper wiring, but all of the plaques should be reasonably straight-forward. We'll also check Brady's records. I'm sure he has many more items than he is showing in his paperwork,' explained Tom. 'Then there's his phone records. He's selling all of the melted metal to someone. Hopefully, his phone records will give us a clue as to who they are, although I suspect this will be the most difficult part – even if we do get some information. Apparently, a lot of the metal is sold on quite a few times before it reaches its final destination.'

'And where do you think that is?' asked Milner.

Tom looked at Milner and shrugged. 'It could be anywhere in the world. China is sometimes mentioned, but I really don't know. What I do know though is that there are many Bradys and Walkers out there who are also doing this. What we did last night is just a pinprick, in terms of trying to stop this, but all we can do, Milner, is to try and stop it happening on our patch.'

'And do you think we have done that now, Sir?' asked Milner.

'Probably for a few weeks at least. But I've got no doubts it will start again pretty soon. While there's a ready market for metals there will always be people willing to meet that demand, either legally or illegally,' he replied quietly.

'But what about our group? Do you think we have enough evidence to get a sentence?' asked Milner, clearly concerned by what Tom had just said.

'I gave up second guessing what the courts will decide long ago,' said Tom. 'But, with all of the evidence we have accu-mulated, and his previous record, I think we have a very strong case against Brady. As for the others, it would take a very forgiving court to let them off, given all of the evidence we have on them. Also, and I know that this shouldn't be the case, but there is a definite groundswell of public disgust against this type of crime.'

'But even if we do get a result against Brady, as you said, there are many more illegal scrap dealers out there willing to buy stolen metal,' said Milner.

'Milner. Try and look on the positive side about this. We've arrested five people so far in connection with these thefts. That sounds like a good couple of days' work to me.'

Milner still didn't seem convinced and this was confirmed when he said, 'But we still don't know where Mr Sipowicz is. Shouldn't we be questioning them, especially now that we have McNulty's statement about the attack?'

Tom could understand Milner's impatience. In many ways Sipowicz's disappearance was the most worrying aspect of all of this. But there was a time and place.

'We will. But I think that it will work more to our advantage if we let them stew for a while. Despite their outward bravado I'm sure that, right now, all of them ...' He paused. 'Well maybe not Lomas. Anyway, certainly the others will be starting to get really worried about what they've got themselves into. Let them ponder that a bit longer. Then we'll hit them with McNulty's evidence. Hopefully they will then see sense and start telling the truth.'

Tom could see that Milner remained far from convinced. 'Why don't you go home,' suggested Tom. 'It's been a long day and you still don't look too good. Anyway, there's nothing more that we can do tonight. We'll just have to be patient until the search has been completed.'

'I think I will, Sir.' Unless there's anything else you would like me to do.'

'Just go home, Milner and get some rest.'

Milner picked up his file and walked out of the office. Just as he was leaving he turned back to face Tom. 'Sir. Do you mind if I ask you a question?'

'Carry on,' replied Tom. 'Although I can't guarantee I will be able to answer it.'

'I saw you pick up something from the scrap yard and put it in the car boot. Can I ask you what it was?'

'Just a memento for someone we both know,' said Tom, rather mysteriously.

Milner shrugged his shoulders and resumed his walk out of the office.

As Tom watched him leave he suddenly felt genuine concern for him. His physical scars would soon heal but his bigger concern was more about the high standards he always seemed to set himself. There was nothing wrong with that, of course, but he did worry how Milner would react when most of the colleagues he would work with were happier to live and work by much lower standards.

Chapter 22

Just after Milner had left, Tom's phone rang. 'DCI Stone? It's Janice here. Superintendent Peters was wondering when you are likely to be able to see him. He has a engagement tonight and needs to get away soon.'

'Sorry. I've only just got back in. Tell him I'll come up right now,' replied Tom. He collected all his things, picked up his coat and took the lift to the fifth floor.

'Can I take your coat?' asked Janice, as helpfully as ever.

'Yes. Thanks. After my meeting with Superintendent Peters has finished I'm going straight home. It's been a long day,' said Tom, handing Janice his coat.

Superintendent Peters emerged from his office at that point and beckoned Tom to follow him back in.

'Can I get you both a drink?' asked Janice, having hung Tom's coat alongside her own.

'That would be very nice,' replied Peters. 'Tom? How about you?'

'Tea would be great,' he replied.

When Janice had left them, Superintendent Peters said, 'Tom. You look worn out. Busy day?'

'You could say that,' he replied a little wearily.

Tom began to update Superintendent Peters about the metal theft arrests and the connection with the Recycling Centre. Janice soon returned with their drinks. After placing them on the table she said, 'Don't forget that you have your engagement tonight.'

'I haven't forgotten. But thank you for reminding me, Janice,' he replied.

When she had left, Tom finished telling Superintendent Peters about the arrests.

'You've only been back a few days and already you've solved a series of crimes that have been plaguing us for months,' Peters said, laughing lightly. More seriously he then added, 'No wonder you look a bit tired.'

'We were lucky, Sir. If Darren Wood hadn't left his phone on the church roof then we'd still be trying to find them. It was just our lucky day.'

'Tom. I think that you are being far too modest. You know as well as I do, that in our job it's how you use that luck which is the most important thing. Didn't someone once say that "luck is when opportunity meets preparation?" Anyway, luck or not, well done and please pass on my thanks to young Milner.'

'Thanks, Sir. I will.'

'I heard he had taken a bit of a beating from one of the men you arrested. Will he be okay?' His concern was genuine.

'His face looks a mess, at the moment, but I think he'll be fine. In fact, I had to more or less order him to go home.'

'I also heard that you had a bit of excitement as well. Didn't one of them attack you with a knife?'

'Attack is a bit of an exaggeration. It was more a case of waving it at me. Anyway, it was all over pretty quickly.'

Superintendent Peters leaned back in his chair. 'That's not how it was described to me.'

He waited for a response. When none was forthcoming he then asked the question both of them knew was the real reason why Tom was there. 'Do you think you are making any progress with *Operation Torch?*'

Tom was ready for this. 'A little, although I wish I could say I have made more but, to be honest, it's proving to be difficult.'

'Didn't the files I sent to you help at all?'

'Well, yes they did. Having now read them I've reduced the number of potential suspects from ten to six.'

'Well, that's progress, isn't it?' asked Peters.

'I suppose so, but the real work starts now,' answered Tom.

'How did you decide on the six? I'm interested to know,' said Peters, picking up his cup and starting to drink from it.

Tom then explained his thinking. 'All of the six officers had been present at the final briefing and all six had also been deeply involved in both *Sunlight* and *Torch*.'

Superintendent Peters interrupted him. 'Do you see that as being important?'

'Yes, I do,' replied Tom, without hesitation. 'I believe *Operation Sunlight* was almost as important as *Torch*.'

'Why?'

'The whole basis of *Operation Torch* was predicated on the quality and reliability of the information provided by Tony Donovan. He established his own personal reputation, mainly as a result of the success of *Operation Sunlight*. His stock was so high after that success, that any other information he was able to provide would have to be accepted as gospel. After all, his information was deemed to be so important that you and DCI Shaw even gave it its own code name: *Nemesis*. To my mind, the two operations are inextricably linked. Without *Sunlight*, *Torch* could never have happened.'

Choosing to ignore Tom's comment about *Nemesis*, Peters simply said. 'So, who are the six?'

Tom took out a piece of paper from his pocket and started to read from it. 'There's DCI Shaw, DS Anderson, DS James, DC Bennett, Sergeant Gunn and, of course, yourself.' As Tom said the final name he handed the list to Superintendent Peters.

When he'd heard his own name mentioned Superintendent Peters had started to laugh. 'So, I'm on the list of suspects as well, am I?' he said, looking closely at the list of names on the paper.

'I'm afraid so,' replied Tom. There then followed an uneasy silence before Tom added, 'Actually, Sir. You didn't send me your own personal file. Was that an oversight?'

Peters, who now had stopped laughing, simply said, 'I'm not able to do that. It was tricky enough getting hold of all of the other files without attracting attention. My own personal file is held at Regional HQ. There's no way I could get access to it.'

'How did you get hold of the others?'

'I'd rather not say. Just accept even that wasn't easy.'

There was another silence between the two of them. It was eventually broken when Tom suddenly said, 'Who was it that gave the "go" order at Fuller's house?'

'What do you mean?' asked Peters, a little tetchily.

'Who gave the order to instigate the entry into Fuller's house? Presumably someone must have given it?' suggested Tom.

'I thought initially it must have been DCI Shaw. But it would appear it was DC Bennett. But it was all very confusing when the van arrived.'

'Confusing? What do you mean, Sir?' asked Tom.

'Just as we were all getting into position, a van suddenly arrived and parked up right in front of the main entrance. DCI Shaw, myself and a couple of other officers had taken our positions around the side of the house. We knew Fuller's house was quite large. DCI Shaw had already carried out a recce a week or so earlier and it was as a result of this that each officer had been assigned their own position around the house.

DCI Shaw's information was that the delivery would be made at a door around the right-hand side of the house. That made sense, of course. Who in their right mind would pull up right outside the main door, when all of the house lights and security lights were on, knock on the door and more or less, say "Drugs delivery for Mr Fuller"? From where we were, however, we couldn't see the front door, so we didn't know the van had pulled up there. We then got another message, over the radio, to say that four men had got out, unloaded various boxes and were now carrying them into the house, through the front door. So DCI Shaw and, I think, DC Booker immediately went to the front of the house to see for themselves.'

He paused for a while, almost as though it was too painful to recount what happened next. Finally, though, he carried on. 'But, by the time they got there, the signal to go had apparently been given. We then raced around to the front door and followed the other officers, who had already entered into the house, expecting to catch them red-handed, delivering drugs, but ... well, you know the rest.'

'Are you sure it was DC Bennett who gave the final "go" order?' asked Tom. 'After all it was DCI Shaw's operation. If I had been running it I'd want to be the one who made the final call.'

'As I said, it was all very confusing. I was still at the side of the house and didn't hear anything. And anyway, as I've told you already, I was there more as an observer,' he responded defensively.

'And how did Fuller react when you all stormed in? Did he seem surprised?' asked Tom.

'We quickly realised the boxes did not contain any drugs. It was then we started to get worried. Well, frankly, it was more like panic than worry. Fuller quickly appeared on the scene. Of course, he was very angry, although, at the time, I did think some of it was just a bit feigned.'

'What do you mean?'

'Difficult to explain really. What I do know though is that he seemed to be enjoying all of the camera phones that were filming us.'

'And what about Donovan? Was he there as well?'

'Yes. He was standing alongside Fuller. Although, of course, I was trying not to look in his direction too much. For obvious reasons.'

'But when you did, how did he seem?'

'As though he was about to explode,' replied Peters.

'How long did you stay in the house, carrying out the search?'

'It was probably about an hour from the time we went in to the time we called off the search. By then we had realised there was nothing interesting there. And anyway, all of Fuller's guests were really starting to enjoy our discomfort. There was a lot of mickey taking. You've probably seen some of it anyway.'

'Yes, I have,' admitted Tom. 'It didn't make for pleasant viewing. Well, not if you're a police officer anyway. But thank you, Sir. That couldn't have been easy.' He then added, moving away from what was clearly a difficult conversation for Superintendent Peters, 'Incidentally, I would still like to see the personal financial information,' he said.

'Including mine?' asked the Superintendent incredulously.

'Sir. You asked me to carry out this investigation. How can I do this if I'm denied vital information?'

'I'll see what I can do,' replied Peters, not very enthusiastically.

'Thanks. Can you remember what was said when you all got back to the station after the raid?'

'Well, as you can imagine, it was a bit tense. DCI Shaw was very angry. At the time I did think he went a bit over the top but, there again, I can understand why he felt that way.'

'Why? What did he say?' asked Tom.

'Basically, he was saying the operation failed because someone or some people hadn't done their jobs correctly.'

'Why? What specifically did he accuse them of getting wrong?'

'One of the things was that some of them were not in their agreed positions when they were supposed to be. But it was DC Bennett, in particular, who felt the brunt of DCI Shaw's anger. He was the officer assigned to cover the front door and it was he who was telling us about the delivery at the front of the house. DCI Shaw kept saying Bennett had totally misread what was happening there. It was based on what he was telling us that we all rushed in.'

He went on. 'To be fair to him, the information we had been given was that the delivery would be at the side of the house. When that van stopped at the front, and those four men began to unload boxes, which looked as though they could contain drugs, then Bennett had to make an immediate judgement as to what was in those boxes. In the event it looks as though he made the wrong decision.'

'I understand DC Bennett is currently on sick leave. Do you know if that's anything to do with the operation?' asked Tom.

'Well, it probably didn't help.' He looked at his watch. 'Look Tom, I'm afraid I've got to go to and it looks as though I'll be late. Could we carry on this conversation tomorrow?'

'Just one other thing, Sir,' said Tom. 'Have you interviewed O'Driscoll yet about Jimmy Ryan's murder?'

'I haven't personally, but DCI Shaw has.'

'And what did he say?' asked Tom.

'Well, of course, he denied he had anything to do with it. But, as they say, he would say that wouldn't he.'

'I suppose he would,' agreed Tom thoughtfully.

'Is it okay if I go now?' asked Peters. 'Or are you holding me for further questioning?'

'I think that's probably all for one night, Sir. But I really do need the financial details of *all* of the people on that list.'

For a brief moment it looked as though Superintendent Peters was about to get angry. If that was the case then it quickly disappeared when he replied, 'I'll do my best.'

'Thank you, Sir, and have a nice evening. Are you going anywhere special?' asked Tom.

'It's just a reception for someone who is leaving.'

Tom drank the remainder of his tea, stood up and, offering

his hand to Superintendent Peters, said, 'Goodnight, Sir. I'll let you know if I make any more progress.'

As he was leaving he glanced back. Superintendent Peters was in the process of folding up the piece of paper, which listed the main suspects, and placing it in his pocket.

'Take care of that, Sir. It might complicate things if it fell into the wrong hands,' he said.

Superintendent Peters didn't reply.

Chapter 23

Yet again it was quite late when he arrived home. As he opened the door and entered the hall he had a quick glance in the mirror on the wall, by the front door. Superintendent Peters had been correct when he'd mentioned earlier just how tired he looked. The dark circles under his eyes were testimony to this. He didn't put these down to the long hours he was working. That had never really bothered him. In fact, certainly in the past, he had positively thrived on long hours and some of his most successful cases had been resolved after long periods without sleep. Adrenalin can be a very powerful drug. But that was when he was younger. In a few weeks' time he would be fifty-four years old and, over the past few years, he had noticed how his energy levels were no longer what they used to be.

He could probably cope with this if he didn't also have to contend with the mentally tiring experience of trying to conduct this covert inquiry. Not that it was a surprise, but he was now beginning to realise exactly what he had committed himself to. Apart from Superintendent Peters he was not able to share the burden with anyone. And it was now even beginning to become increasingly difficult dealing with him.

Then there was the situation with Mary. He had to admit he was disappointed, after he had switched on his phone, to see there were no missed calls from her. Perhaps, after yesterday's conversation, she was deliberately trying not to put any undue pressure on him. He would call her shortly.

He didn't normally drink alone but he decided he had probably earned himself a drink tonight. So he poured himself a glass of red wine and sat at the kitchen table.

Just then his mobile rang. He looked at the number and was relieved to see it was Mary. For one horrible moment he feared it might have been Pauline again. He was definitely starting to get jumpy.

'Hello you,' said the voice on the phone.

'Hi,' replied Tom. 'I was just thinking about calling you. I've literally just arrived home and I'm now having a quiet drink by myself.'

'So, your first instinct was to have a drink by yourself rather than call me,' suggested Mary, with a slight laugh.

'Mary. You know that's not the case. Anyway, how are you? Did you manage to get that large order out?' he asked, suddenly remembering their conversation earlier in the week.

'I did,' she replied before adding, 'although that was a few days ago.'

There was a slight pause before Tom replied. 'Was it? Sorry. It's been one of those weeks.' Before she could respond Tom went on, this time in a far more positive tone of voice, 'By the way. You'll be pleased to know we have arrested five people in connection with those local metal thefts.'

'Tom, that's great news. When did this happen?' she asked, excitedly.

'We arrested three yesterday and the other two today.'

'Yesterday? Was that the reason why you didn't get the chance to call me?' she asked, her earlier excitement having now disappeared.

'Well, that was the main reason but, Mary, I should still have called you.' Mary didn't immediately answer. 'Are you still there?' asked Tom.

'Tom. I'm really sorry for what I said last night. You should have told me,' she said contritely.

When he answered it was in an equally conciliatory tone. 'You don't have to apologise for anything. I promised to call you and I should have, irrespective of what I'd been doing.'

Once again there was a brief silence. This time it was Mary who spoke first. 'I love you, Tom Stone,' she said with real feeling, and Tom was genuinely taken aback by the suddenness of this.

But he found himself being swept along with all of this emotion. 'I love you too. I hope you know that by now.' Slightly embarrassed by the speed at which he had responded he then added, almost belatedly trying to hide it, 'Will you tell me you love me every time I arrest someone?'

'Tom. I'm serious. I really mean it,' she answered.

'I know you do,' he replied. 'And you can't begin to understand how nice it is to hear you say it.'

'I'll try and say it more often. I promise. Are you able to tell me anything about the metal thefts?'

'Only that it looks as though they have been responsible for quite a lot of the recent thefts. One of them was also arrested for handling the stolen metal. He owned a local scrap yard.'

'Does that men there are unlikely to be any more thefts?'

'Unfortunately I doubt it,' replied Tom. 'Although, hopefully, they will be out of circulation for a while, there are many more out there who see this type of crime as a way to make easy money. Sorry.'

'Please don't apologise. I know you are doing everything possible.' She went on, although this time with just a hint of concern in her voice, 'Were the arrests straightforward or did they put up a struggle?'

'Fairly routine,' lied Tom, suddenly remembering the way Lomas had lunged at him with a knife. 'Although one of them did take a swing at Milner.'

'Did he connect?' she asked, now a little concerned.

'Actually he did. Milner's face isn't pretty at the moment, but fortunately there's no permanent damage and it will soon heal,' he replied.

'Tom, I do worry about you when you're working. You hear all the time about police officers being attacked.'

Tom tried to make light of this. 'That's why I leave it to youngsters, like Milner, to handle any rough stuff.' He decided that now might be a good time to change the subject. 'Are we still on for Saturday?'

'Of course. Just try and keep me away,' she answered, before adding, 'It seems such a long time since we last saw one another. I can't believe how slowly this week has gone.'

Tom wished he could have said the same. Instead he made do with, 'I thought absence makes the heart grow fonder.'

'Well, in my case, my heart couldn't be any fonder. You know how I feel about you,' she replied wistfully.

He was still finding it difficult to have this type of conversation. Telling someone that you loved them – even though you did – was not something which came easily to him. Maybe it was his natural defence mechanism kicking in to prevent any future disappointment.

Just then Tom's doorbell rang. Mary, hearing this, said, 'Sounds like there's someone at your door. It's a bit late for callers, isn't it? I'll let you go. Call me when you get the chance, otherwise I'll see you on Saturday. Love you.'

'I'll count down the hours,' replied Tom, although, in truth, part of his mind was wondering who was ringing his doorbell at this late time of night.

He opened his front door.

It was Pauline. 'Hello Tom. I'm sorry about what I said on the phone. I didn't mean it. I was just upset,' she said.

'Have you been waiting for me to come home?' he asked dispensing with any pleasantries.

'I saw you arrive about ten minutes ago. Aren't you going to invite me in?' she asked, slightly slurring her words, suggesting to Tom she had been drinking.

'I'm not. There's no point,' he answered bluntly. 'It's late. Why don't you just go home?'

'Can't we just talk? I don't bite, you know,' she said, now laughing slightly.

He tried a different, more reasonable tack. 'Pauline. I'm sure you are a very nice lady but, as I told you on the phone, I've now met someone. We are happy together. You and I only met once and that was only briefly. This is not a good idea. Can't you see that?'

Tom noticed Pauline was no longer laughing as she said, 'What's she got that I haven't? Anyway, who is she? Did you meet her through the dating agency?'

He tried to remain as calm as possible. 'I don't think it's relevant who she is or where I met her. The fact is all we did was to have dinner together. That's all. Nothing else. I certainly didn't give you any reason to think there might be anything between us. Why don't you just go home?'

Tom could see that his approach was not having the desired effect and Pauline was getting visibly agitated. With a raised voice she said, 'I don't believe you. You've just used me.' She started to walk away, stumbling slightly as she did, but suddenly stopped, turned around and shouted, 'You can't use me. You're not going to get away with this. You'll see.'

Chapter 24

However hard he tried, Tom couldn't get the events of last night out of his mind. Whichever way he looked at it he was now extremely worried. Pauline was obviously someone who was suffering from a serious case of delusion. He also could tell that she had been drinking. Although he was by no means an expert this seemed a dangerous combination.

He'd been involved in a few stalking cases over the years and so knew just how invasive, as well as frightening, they could be for the person being stalked. In the early days there had been a tendency by the police not to take these too seriously and simply treat them as harmless obsessions. But Tom had seen for himself the personal impact it could have on the victim. Little did he know though that one day he too would become a victim of stalking.

Except, in his case, it seemed to have taken quite a sinister turn. Pauline's departing words had chilled him. All of his instincts were telling him things were likely to get significantly worse. He had always prided himself on being able to decide on a course of action quickly and then stick to it. Of course, it had not always been the right course of action but, over the years, he liked to think he had got many more things right than wrong. What worried him most about this situation was that he really didn't know what to do. Should he speak with Pauline again and try and make her see sense? Should he report her for harassment? Or should he simply ignore it and hope she eventually got the message that there never was, and was never likely to be, anything between them? And what about Mary? Should he tell her about Pauline? Whatever he eventually decided to do he would have to do it quickly.

As he arrived at the station, he saw Superintendent Peters parking his car. 'Morning Tom,' said Peters, cheerily. 'Did you manage to get home at a reasonable time last night?'

'Yes. It wasn't too late,' answered Tom. He then asked, 'How about you? What time did you get away from your function?'

'The function? Oh, it wasn't too late. I think I left around midnight.'

Just then DCI Shaw also pulled in to the car park and parked his car. Tom could see that DCI Shaw had spotted both of them. He also noticed he had then parked his car as far away from Tom's as possible. Tom waited for DCI Shaw to get near to him. 'Morning Richard,' he said in as friendly a tone as he could manage, given his concerns about the situation with Pauline. DCI Shaw didn't reply. Tom continued, although this time, he lowered his voice, 'Could we meet up this morning? I'd like to discuss something with you.'

'I've been waiting for you to approach me,' replied Shaw, in a slightly refined accent, perfectly matching the expensive cut of his suit. 'I suppose it's in relation to *Operation Torch*. Superintendent Peters mentioned to me that he'd asked you to review some of the aspects of *my* case,' he said in a way which made it crystal clear what he actually thought about any such review.

'How do you feel about that?' asked Tom.

'What? About you reviewing my case? How do you think I feel?' he replied, his voice now suddenly rising.

'Look, Richard,' replied Tom, 'I understand you're going to be hacked off with this. I certainly would be if the roles were reversed, but it is what it is. Either we can work together – and by the way, that's what I would prefer – or I'll complete my review and recommend any procedural changes without your input. It's your choice. I'll leave it up to you. If you want to be involved then you know where I am. If not then I'll understand that as well. But whatever you decide, rest assured that no one else will know about it.' Tom hadn't meant to sound quite so aggressive but he was tired and still slightly distracted.

But it appeared to work as there was just the merest hint of possible agreement when Shaw replied, 'I'll think about it.' With those final few words on the subject DCI Shaw turned away and walked into the station.

Superintendent Peters approached Tom and said, 'What

was all that about? It seemed like you and DCI Shaw were having quite an intense discussion.'

'To be honest, Sir, that's probably the longest discussion we've had for weeks. I asked him if I could talk to him about *Torch*. As you can imagine he wasn't too happy about it,' explained Tom.

Superintendent Peters looked slightly concerned as he said, 'I thought you wanted to keep this as quiet as possible.' He now also lowered his voice. 'Don't forget he's on your list of suspects.'

Tom smiled. 'I know, Sir, but if I was not able to speak with everyone on the list I wouldn't be here talking to you.' Superintendent Peters' face made it perfectly clear he was not impressed with this attempt at humour.

This was becoming a day of firsts for Tom. He'd had quite a civil conversation with DCI Shaw and now he had made it to the station ahead of Milner. In fact, it was almost ten thirty before Milner arrived.

'Morning Milner,' said Tom, looking up from his computer screen. 'Overslept?' he asked, deliberately being mischievous.

'Yes. Sorry, Sir, but I forgot to tell you last night that I had a follow-up appointment back at the hospital first thing this morning,' he replied.

Tom's earlier jocularity had disappeared and he now tried to hide his embarrassment as he asked, 'And what did they say?'

'They seem to have become a bit worried about my cheekbone, so they want to see me again in a couple of days,' he explained, in a matter-of-fact way.

'Does it still hurt?' Tom asked, looking at Milner's still swollen cheek.

'A little bit. It's still a bit sore, particularly when I accidentally touch it,' he explained.

Tom could see that Milner, not surprisingly, was a little down at the moment. He needed cheering up.

'Why don't you take some time off?' said Tom. 'I think you've earned a few days off. You did a great job yesterday on the metal thefts.' Tom suddenly remembered last night's conversation. 'By the way, Superintendent Peters asked me to pass on his thanks and congratulations to you.'

If this cheered Milner up he certainly didn't show it. 'But it wasn't just me, Sir.'

Before Tom could reply his phone rang. He answered it. 'DCI Stone.' There then followed a period of silence before Tom next spoke. 'Are you sure that's what it is?' This was quickly followed by, 'Yes, sorry that was a bit of a stupid question. Anyway, thanks and let me know if you find anything else.'

Tom remained quiet for a while. When he did speak it was clearly with a sense of disbelief. 'That was someone from the search team calling to inform me that they've just found a body in one of the burnt-out cars.'

Chapter 25

About thirty minutes later they where both standing inside the Portakabin at the scrap yard, speaking with the lead officer of the search team.

Ironically it had been Brady's dogs which first alerted the search team to the dead body. Understandably, the team had insisted they should be placed into a secure, separately fenced-off area at the back of the site whilst they continued with their search. This area also contained a few burnt-out cars. As soon as the dogs were put in there they instantly made a beeline for one of them and started barking furiously at it. Initially the team thought that perhaps there were rats in it, but when after ten minutes they were still concentrating all of their aggressive attention towards the car, two members of the team decided to investigate and the dogs were carefully removed. It wasn't long before they had the answer as to why the dogs had been so interested in that particular car: it contained the badly burnt remains of what was clearly a human being. Search teams never liked finding unexpected bodies because, apart from complicating matters, it also caused considerable delays to their work. But, in such circumstances, there was a protocol to follow and that was when they made their call for forensics support. After that, the lead officer had called Tom.

Milner had insisted that he come along with Tom. His face might still have been hurting, but this was a development he didn't want to miss.

'How long do you think it will take before we have more information about the body?' asked Tom, directing his question at the one of the forensic team's members. 'Just knowing the age and sex of the deceased will be useful.'

'Why is it that you policemen always want information so quickly? Surely it's better to wait until we are absolutely certain rather than pressurising us to guess,' he answered. He then added, not too helpfully, 'We might have something tomorrow. But, there again, if there are complications, it might take longer.'

Failing to hide his impatience Tom simply said, 'Okay. But please call me as soon as you have anything. Will you, at least, promise me that?'

'Of course.'

'Is it okay if the team resume their search?' Tom was still clearly frustrated.

'By all means. But the cordoned-off area, where the body was found, is still off limits. If you'll excuse me I'll get back to work now. The sooner I do that the quicker you'll have your answers.'

After he had left Milner voiced the question both of them had been asking themselves. 'Do you think it might be Maciej's body?'

'I don't know,' answered Tom quietly. 'I hope not. Let's not speculate. Hopefully, despite what he just said, we'll have something soon. Even if it's just the sex and approximate age. I'm afraid we'll just have to be patient. What we can do, though, is go and talk to Brady and his son.'

Tom and Milner went out of the Portakabin and walked towards a group of people who were standing near to the cordoned-off area. 'Okay Phil, you can resume the search. Just don't go inside there,' Tom said, pointing at the quarantined area.

'Have you found anything?' asked Milner. 'Apart from the body, that is.'

'Yes, Quite a few things. We've marked everything that looks slightly dodgy. It's amazing what's in these places.'

'Like what?' asked Tom.

'Well, how about a large bell for example? It looks as though it's come from a church. Who would want to sell something like that to a scrap dealer, unless it had been nicked? There's quite a few manhole covers and what looks like copper wiring. There's even a statue. Bronze, I think. Although for the life of me I still can't make out what it's supposed to be. Probably modern. A bit like one of paintings where the subject has a square head and only one eye. Who wants to pay thousands of pounds just to look at something like that?' He then added, as his final comment on the subject, 'Probably got more money than sense.'

152

Tom laughed lightly. 'Thanks Phil. I'll remember not to get you any tickets for the Tate Modern.' He then asked more seriously, 'When do you think you'll be finished and be able to let me have the final inventory?'

'Should be tomorrow. Although the section with the body will have to wait until forensics have finished.'

'Let me have the list, and photos of the items, as soon as you can. Good work, Phil.' He turned to Milner. 'Right. Let's go and see what the Bradys know about this.'

They spent the next half hour with Brady and his son, James. Unsurprisingly they both denied knowing anything about how the body had come to be found in their scrap yard. They couldn't even remember when the car had been placed there.

As they were leaving the Portakabin Tom turned towards Milner. 'I don't believe a word of what they said. Well, certainly not James Brady. I'd stake my police pension on the fact that he knows far more about the body than he's making out. There will come a time, and hopefully it will be soon, when they won't be able to stonewall any more. Anyway, there's not much more we can do here. Let's go and get some lunch. I'll buy.'

Milner's voice betrayed his surprise. 'Thanks, Sir. That's a good idea.' He wanted to add ... particularly as you still haven't paid me for the sandwiches I bought you earlier in the week. In the event he simply smiled to himself.

Chapter 26

It was mid-afternoon and Tom was back in his office looking at his computer. As he was doing this he was interrupted by a knock on his door. He looked up, expecting to see Milner standing there. Instead he was surprised to see it was DCI Shaw. 'Is now a good time?' asked DCI Shaw, pleasantly.

'Yes, come in,' replied Tom. 'I was only catching up on my emails.'

DCI Shaw entered Tom's office, closed the door and seated himself opposite Tom.

'Incidentally, congratulations,' he said. 'I heard you had a good result with the metal theft enquiries. I've just been with the Super and he told me all about it. He also mentioned that you and Milner both sustained a few injuries.'

'Thankfully nothing too serious. Although we did have a bit of luck,' replied Tom, wondering if this was the same DCI Shaw he had met earlier. He also wondered if it was pure coincidence that, shortly after meeting with Superintendent Peters, Shaw was now knocking on his door. He couldn't remember the last time Shaw had even set foot in his office.

'That's not what Superintendent Peters told me,' replied Shaw.

Tom, a little unnerved by his uncharacteristically congratu-latory tone, asked, 'Can I get you a drink? Tea? Coffee?'

'No thanks. I've just had one. Where do you want to start?'

'Well, let me start by saying I didn't suggest I take on this review. Superintendent Peters asked me to do it. Although, frankly, I felt I had little choice.' Tom paused, before adding, 'But now I am involved I am going to do it to the best of my ability.' He wanted to add something along the lines of 'and if that means ruffling a few feathers along the way then so be it'. However, he decided to take his lead from DCI Shaw's sudden and uncharacteristic friendliness. So, instead, diplo-matically, he simply said, 'I know, as lead officer, this is difficult for you as well but I genuinely would like to hear your thoughts. Not only on why things went wrong but, more importantly, what you would suggest in terms of any future operational changes.'

DCI Shaw looked closely at Tom. 'Why don't you start by telling me what you already know about *Operation Torch*?'

'Only what the Super has told me, plus a few snippets picked up here and there. That's why I'm interested to hear your account.'

'So you know we have someone in Fuller's gang who has been regularly passing information through to me?'

'Yes, I do,' answered Tom. 'That will be – sorry, was – Jimmy Ryan and Tony Donovan, wouldn't it? I believe they were given the code names *Justice* and *Retribution*.'

Shaw was visibly shocked that Tom knew this level of detail and there was undisguised anger in his voice when he said, 'Was it Superintendent Peters who gave you those names?'

'It was. But only after I'd told him that, without their names, I wouldn't be able to do my job thoroughly,' he lied.

'You do understand that this is *extremely* classified information. God knows what would happen if this information was to leak out. There would probably be a bloodbath in the borough. It took me a long time to convince them their names would never get out.'

'But surely it's started anyway with the murder of Jimmy Ryan,' suggested Tom.

There was almost a tone of intimidation as Shaw replied, 'Even more reason, therefore, that Donovan's involvement should remain secret.'

Tom chose not to respond in similar fashion. Instead he said, 'Incidentally, how is the Ryan murder investigation progressing?'

DCI Shaw, clearly a bit put out by Tom's directness, said, 'I thought the terms of the brief you had been given had very well-defined parameters and any questions were limited to operational change recommendations. What has the status of the Ryan murder got to do with that?'

He was right, of course. As far as DCI Shaw was concerned the Ryan murder investigation was clearly outside of those guidelines.

'Technically, you are right,' admitted Tom. 'But as Ryan was such a key figure in *Operation Torch* you could argue that his sudden murder is material to my review.'

Before DCI Shaw could answer Tom offered an olive branch. 'Richard. If you don't feel you can go into any detail then I will totally understand.' As there was no immediate reply, Tom continued, 'But it would help me if you could.'

DCI Shaw seemed to be carefully considering Tom's request. Eventually he responded. 'As you seem to know most things anyway, it would be churlish of me not to fill in the gaps.'

Tom looked directly at DCI Shaw and, with a grateful nod of his head said, 'Richard. Thank you very much. I appreciate that.'

'To be honest, we've made little progress so far. O'Driscoll is clearly our prime suspect – after all he was the one who lost the most due to Ryan's information. Not him personally, as we have him in custody. We believe though that it was he who gave the order for the killing. But, so far, we have no hard evidence to link him with the murder.'

'What about forensics? Was there anything there?' asked Tom.

'No, there wasn't. This was a very professional job. It had all the hallmarks of an assassination rather than a murder. A single shot to the head. It was very professionally executed,' he explained, almost in admiration. 'No pun intended. Of course, we know the type of gun used, from the ballistics. It also looks like the killer used a silencer. But without the gun, any witnesses or any other firm evidence, it's all speculation.'

'Have you charged O'Driscoll?' asked Tom.

'No. As he denies having anything to do with it, and we don't have any evidence at all, other than a possible motive. We've reached stalemate.'

'Does Donovan have a view on this?' asked Tom, although he suspected he knew the answer to that already.

'Are you serious?' said DCI Shaw almost incredulously. 'What do you think his view is?' Before Tom could reply, DCI Shaw decided to answer his own questions. 'He's scared witless that he will be next. He's certain it was O'Driscoll, or at least, someone on the orders of O'Driscoll. He's refusing to meet with me as he thinks we leaked the information that Ryan was our informant.'

'So, what's likely to happen next?'

'Well, let me ask what *you* would do,' suggested a now tetchy DCI Shaw.

Tom hadn't expected this question but, nonetheless, felt he should, at least, try and respond constructively. 'Given what you've just said about the total lack of evidence, I would start by sweating all of my street contacts. Even if nothing comes from it everyone will, at least, know we are pursuing the investigation vigorously. I'd also increase the pressure on O'Driscoll's gang members. You have most of them already, as a result of *Sunlight*. Perhaps one of them might be open to a deal. They might know something and the thought of spending the next few years locked away might suddenly not be that attractive.'

DCI Shaw looked very pensive as he considered Tom's suggestions. 'We are already speaking with all of our informants but I like your idea about offering a deal.'

'It's your case, of course, but if you would like me to do anything, however routine, you only have to ask,' offered Tom.

'Thanks. I might just do that,' answered an apparently now genuinely appreciative DCI Shaw.

Tom still couldn't quite believe how, after such a frosty start, the conversation had now elevated to a far more friendly level. Whilst it would be beneficial if this more positive atmosphere continued, he knew he still had to ask some difficult questions. He decided that now was as a good a time as ever to ask the most difficult one of all.

'Why did someone like Tony Donovan, a man who has always been fiercely loyal to the Fullers, suddenly decide to become a supergrass?' Tom maintained eye contact with Shaw, hoping to get a clue as to what he was thinking. If their roles had been reversed, and Tom had been asked this question, then, right now, he would be asking himself if he could trust Shaw. This would be the key moment in their new, friendlier relationship.

'Tom. This is highly sensitive information.' Tom was encouraged that DCI Shaw had, for the first time, used his Christian name. 'Right now there are only three people who know the answer to your question. Myself, Superintendent Peters and, of course, Tony Donovan himself. If I were to tell you, then this, their names or even code names, must not be included anywhere in your report. Do you understand?'

'Totally. But what will you say when you are called to give evidence at the official inquiry? Surely they will ask the very same question.'

'Well. I certainly won't be volunteering any names or even clues as to who they are. Okay, this operation went bad but, eventually, we will get another chance to put Fuller away. I'm willing, in the meantime, to take any flak that comes my way, if that means we protect my source, because, when it does happen, I want to be the person who does it.'

Tom was taken aback by just how passionate DCI Shaw had suddenly become. This was the first time that he had seen this in Shaw. It made a pleasant change from the aloof, arrogant DCI Shaw who he'd come to know from their previous meetings.

'You make it sound as though it's become personal with Fuller. Is there a reason for that?' he asked, suddenly genuinely intrigued. He was certain he had detected a flash of anger in Shaw's eyes.

If there had been when he first answered, however, any anger had now gone. 'Not at all. It's just that people such as Fuller always believe they are above the law. It will send a powerful message to his like, when we put him away, that *no one*, not even Tommy Fuller, is above the law.'

'You seem sure you will put him away.'

'I am,' he answered quietly. 'It's only a question of when.'

After Shaw's unexpected passionate outburst, there was a brief silence, as Shaw considered whether or not to answer Tom's earlier question.

Finally, he continued. 'About a year ago I took a call from Jimmy Ryan. He said he had some information concerning the James O'Driscoll gang. Coincidentally, I'd just been asked by Superintendent Peters to head up a small team to see if there was anything that could be done to close them down. For some time I had been working on a plan targeting Fuller's operation.'

He continued. 'I'd already presented the details of my plan to Superintendent Peters but he felt we still weren't ready. Initially I didn't agree with him but eventually he convinced me. So instead I agreed to go for O'Driscoll. Although it wasn't as big as Fuller's operation, it would still be a great result if we could take them out. It would also give us the confidence, and additional resources, to then take on Fuller. So, the call from Ryan came at an opportune time.'

'How long was it from the time Superintendent Peters asked you to set up your team to the time when you got the call from Ryan?'

Shaw looked at Tom suspiciously. 'Does it really matter?'

'I'm just trying to get the right time frame in my mind. That's all.'

Tom could see Shaw was still far from convinced and it was with some obvious reluctance that he answered, 'Perhaps three or four weeks.'

'Thank you. What happened then?'

'The first thing I did was to make a few enquiries about Ryan. I'd come across his name a couple of times but I didn't really know much about him personally.'

'Who did you ask?'

'DS Anderson and DC Bennett. Both of them have spent most of their professional lives in the borough and would, for sure, have come across someone like Ryan. For the same reason I also spoke with Sergeant Gunn. There may have been others, but it was over a year ago and I can't be one hundred per cent certain.'

'I understand.'

Shaw took up from where he left off. 'After I'd made my enquiries I gradually built up a picture of Ryan. It was clear he had always been on the periphery of the local criminal frater-nity although, by then, he was dealing drugs and almost certainly working for Fuller. What surprised me though, was that everything I'd found out about him suggested he was very low down the organisation. As I said, just a street dealer really.'

'But you still decided to meet with him though,' said Tom.

'Yes. I thought there was nothing to lose, although I didn't have any real high hopes at the time.' He paused for a while and then asked, 'Had you come across Ryan before?'

'Quite a few times actually,' answered Tom. 'You should have asked me, although I get the impression that asking for my input was not, perhaps, top of your list at the time.'

Tom instantly regretted saying this but was surprised with Shaw's moderate response. 'I suppose, occasionally, we all do things which we regret. I had my reasons but perhaps they were wrong as well.'

Tom suspected it had taken quite an effort for Shaw to admit this. This contrite side of DCI Shaw was proving to be difficult to get used to. So, he decided not to ask what the 'reasons' were. 'We've all done that in our career,' said Tom, embracing this new-found mood of honesty. 'Where did you meet with Ryan?'

'I met him in a multi-storey car park. He wouldn't get in my car, so we sat in his. Even so he was clearly still very nervous and suspicious. He kept looking around to see if he had been followed or if we were being watched by other police officers. He's not the sharpest knife in the drawer and I must admit I wondered if I was being set up. It was also obvious he couldn't wait to get away, so I got straight to the point and asked him why he wanted to see me and what information he had. He didn't say anything. He just handed me a single piece of A4 paper.'

'Do you still have it?' asked Tom.

'It's probably in the file somewhere,' replied Shaw a little vaguely.

This was a crucial piece of information and Tom was sure DCI Shaw knew exactly where it was. He waited to see if Shaw would offer him the chance to see it. When it didn't come Tom just said, 'What did it say?'

'It had a list of names. According to Ryan they were all members of the O'Driscoll gang. There were fifteen names on the list. They ranged from street dealers to O'Driscoll's most trusted friends. Almost like the gang's order of battle. Most of them were known to us but there were a few new names we didn't know. If it was genuine then it was really valuable information.'

Tom couldn't hide his scepticism when he asked, 'Did he give a reason for providing you with all this information? After all, it's not every day that this much detailed information, about a major criminal gang, falls into your lap.'

'Exactly. He wouldn't tell me at first and so I thought I'd call his bluff. I said I didn't believe any of this and that it smelled of a stitch-up and I was seriously thinking of arresting him for wasting police time. A bit thin, I know, but I couldn't think of anything better at the time.'

'Did it work?' asked Tom.

'It must have, because then he told me about Donovan.'

'What? Just like that? Can you remember his exact words?'

DCI Shaw, not for the first time, looked suspiciously at Tom. 'Why do you want to know all this? I thought you were only interested in operational issues.'

Tom was ready for this. 'And this is an operational issue. As you know, determining the veracity of information received from police informants, is important but, ultimately, it's an issue of judgement by the lead officer. But there might be instances where the introduction of checks and balances might be appropriate.'

'And do you think that's the case here?' asked Shaw.

'I genuinely don't know. That's why I'm trying to obtain as much information as possible, factual as well as any relevant background information.'

It was now Shaw's turn to betray his own scepticism. 'If you say so.' Tom didn't respond. Shaw continued. 'I can't remember his exact words. But just the fact he mentioned Donovan suddenly took this to another level. Donovan, I did know about.

Prior to trying to convince Superintendent Peters to set up a covert team to remove Fuller and his henchmen, I did a lot of background research and Donovan's name kept cropping up. It looked as though, after the death of Patrick Fuller, they all shuffled up one place in the hierarchy. That was when Donovan became Tommy Fuller's right-hand man and undisputed number two in their organisation. So, you can imagine my surprise when Ryan told me Donovan wanted to meet with me.'

'So Ryan was just acting as the go-between,' suggested Tom.

'That's the impression I had,' replied Shaw. 'It would make sense. That way he could distance himself from it if anything went wrong. It would be Ryan who then took all of the blame. Ryan was not very bright. I suspect he was chosen either because he was loyal to Donovan or, more likely, he was just doing as he was told.'

'Or because he was expendable,' remarked Tom pointedly.

Shaw looked directly at Tom and said, 'What? You think it was Donovan who murdered Ryan?'

'I'm not saying that. But it does seems a little odd that someone like Ryan, a person you yourself described as not being the sharpest knife in the drawer, would be entrusted with something as confidential as this.'

'That's possible, I suppose,' replied Shaw in a way which made it clear that he didn't think it was a possibility. 'It's more likely Ryan was chosen because, according to our sources, he was in total awe of Donovan. Ryan would have done anything Donovan told him to do.'

'Anyway, what reason did he give for Donovan wanting to meet with you?' asked Tom.

'He said the information which he'd just given me about the O'Driscolls was just a starter. There was more information available, relating to a big drugs delivery which they were planning and that Donovan was willing to let me have it.' He paused for a while before continuing. 'As I said earlier, Ryan was not the smartest and it sounded to me as if he had been coached to say what he said. In fact, he recited the words almost parrot fashion.'

'Did he say what Donovan wanted in return?' asked Tom.

'Of course I asked him that, but he said he didn't know and Donovan would tell me himself when we met. Again he answered as if he had anticipated that particular question and had been coached to say it.'

'So, how did you leave it with Ryan?'

'I said I would need to consider it all first. I gave Ryan my mobile number and asked him to call me in a couple of days' time. That would also give me the opportunity to discuss it with Superintendent Peters. I then got back in my car and drove back to the station.'

As Tom had listened to what Shaw told him he found it even more incredible that he was suddenly willing to divulge so much information. Okay, Shaw knew Tom had been asked to review all operational issues relating to *Operation Torch*, but Shaw had told him far more than Tom had expected. So he decided he might as well press on.

'What was Superintendent Peters' reaction when you told him?' asked Tom.

'He was as astounded as I was. It took a while for it to sink in. It was only when he studied the list that he began to believe it might just be genuine. We decided that if Ryan called, we would agree to meet with Donovan. After all, we couldn't see what we had to lose, although we would treat everything which Donovan told us with scepticism. In the meantime we would run checks on all of the names on the list. Initially we were going to pull in a few of them in order to test the water. But we then decided to wait until after the meeting with Donovan, as we didn't want to unnecessarily alert O'Driscoll. As you can imagine I was a bit distracted over the next two days wondering if Ryan would call me.'

'What did he say when he did ring?' asked Tom.

'He just asked if I was willing to meet. When I said I was, he simply said I'd get a call. Then he rang off.'

'Was it Donovan himself who next rang?'

'No. It was Ryan again. He told me where the meet was and at what time. That was all he said.'

'So, when and where did you meet with Donovan?'

DCI Shaw's earlier hesitancy about sharing information with Tom now seemed to have disappeared completely. It even looked as though he was now enjoying telling the story.

'We met at an old disused factory in Iver. It was quite an isolated place. Quite rural really. The meet was set for 10.30pm but Donovan didn't show until after eleven. He suddenly appeared at the side of my car. I hadn't noticed his car arriving, so he must have arrived earlier and stayed out of sight, just in case things got a bit hairy. Anyway, I didn't ask him.'

'Or perhaps he had been checking to see if you were alone,' suggested Tom.

'Probably,' replied Shaw.

'And were you alone?' asked Tom.

'I was. Superintendent Peters and I had decided we wouldn't do anything which jeopardised the meeting.'

'So you weren't even wired?'

'No. I told you, we didn't want to give Donovan any reason to abort.'

'Was that wise? It could easily have been a set-up, with you as the target.'

'It did cross my mind but, as I said, the chance to meet with Donovan was just too good an opportunity to miss. Anyway, if anything did happen then I only had myself to blame.'

Tom was not so sure he would have been willing to put himself in such a potentially dangerous situation if it had been him who had taken that first call from Ryan. His sudden, new-found, respect for DCI Shaw had just increased by another few degrees.

Shaw continued with his description of his meeting with Donovan. 'He knocked on the passenger window and gestured me to get out of the car. He then told me to follow him and started walking towards a door at the side of the factory. He opened it and walked in. I followed him. The place was gloomy but Donovan seemed to know where he was going. Eventually, he entered what turned out to be the toilets and then turned around to look at me.'

'You said that it was gloomy. Were you able to see his face?' asked Tom.

'Do you mean was I sure it was Donovan?' suggested Shaw.

Tom nodded. 'Yes. I suppose that is what I was asking.'

'It was definitely Donovan,' he said, without any further explanation.

'I'm sorry. I just needed to double check.'

DCI Shaw chose not to respond to Tom's half apology. He went on. 'There were no pleasantries at all. He simply took out, from his inside pocket, a piece of paper and handed it to me. I quickly read it. Clearly laid out in typed letters were names, places, dates, even specific times, all apparently relating to the impending big drugs delivery. It was all there. According to this the delivery was due to take place the following week. The drugs were coming in from Spain by private plane, landing at a small airport in Surrey.

After I'd read it I asked him how I would know this was genuine and not some sort of set-up. It was then that he spoke for the first time. He said if that's what I thought then he wasn't going to waste any more time and started to walk away. So I called him back.'

'What did you say? Can you remember?'

'Not the exact words, no. I think I might have said something along the lines of not being used to receiving this quality of information and how would he react if the positions were reversed. It appeared to reassure him because he then explained how O'Driscoll had used this route a few times previously but this was, by far, the biggest delivery. He said the drugs had a street value of many millions. It was then I asked him why he was doing this.'

Tom looked thoughtful. Donovan's answer to DCI Shaw's question was clearly another vital piece in this complicated jigsaw. 'And what did he say?' asked Tom.

Now it was DCI Shaw's turn to remain silent, adding further to Tom's increased sense of expectancy. Shaw smiled. 'I bet this is what you've been waiting for. Am I right, Tom?'

Tom nodded and then said, 'Well, it is pretty pivotal to the entire operation. Wouldn't you agree?'

'I'm sure it is,' replied Shaw, suddenly relishing the sense of drama he had created.

This wasn't lost on Tom. 'Richard. For God's sake, either tell me or talk about something else.'

Shaw started to laugh. 'As it's never good to see a grown man begging, I suppose I'd better put you out of your misery.' When he carried on, it was in a more serious tone. 'He said he had a contact who was very close to O'Driscoll, and he'd been paying him to pass on information about the activities of the O'Driscoll gang. This allowed him to keep tabs on what they were up to.

Until then it had all been fairly low-level stuff but recently it seems O'Driscoll had started to get much loftier ambitions. And this involved encroaching into Fuller's territory. There had already been a bit of conflict between the two gangs, mainly over who owned the territory, within the borough, for their drug dealing activities. The information he was now receiving had suggested they were beginning to think about making a bigger move into Fuller's territory.

As Donovan said to me, they couldn't let this happen – or at least words to that effect. But, as they didn't want any sort of turf war, they decided to hand over all of the information to us and let us handle it.'

Tom interrupted. 'So, he'd obtained the details about the big drugs delivery from his own informant within the O'Driscoll gang. As an honest citizen he then thought it was his civic duty to pass it onto the police. They could then make sure they were there when the delivery was made and wrap up the entire gang in the act. The police could then claim a great result whilst, at the same time, and purely coincidentally, the Fullers' main rival has been eliminated. And everyone lives happily ever after.' Tom's voice was heavy with undisguised cynicism.

There followed a brief, tense silence, before Shaw spoke, although, surprisingly, without any of the emotion which Tom had just shown. 'Tom, I'm only telling you what Donovan told me. That's what you asked me to do. Remember? As I said earlier, I'm still not exactly sure why you need to know all of this. Do you want me to carry on or not?'

Tom was annoyed with himself for his earlier outburst. It was totally out of character for someone who always liked be in control of his emotions. He suddenly wondered if the stresses of the past few days were now starting to affect him.

'Richard. I'm sorry,' he said, not for the first time today. 'Please go on.'

'A bit of good, old-fashioned copper's cynicism is good for the soul sometimes,' said Shaw, smiling as he said it. 'As I was just about to say, I also raised the same points. His response was along the lines of, if we didn't sort it out then they would. He pointed out there hadn't been this type of outright gang rivalry, and conflict, in our borough for many years. He asked if that was what we really wanted.' Shaw waited for Tom to comment, although Tom remained silent and so he just carried on. 'Presented with that choice what would you have done?' asked Shaw rhetorically. 'Anyway, my judgement was that the last thing we needed was a violent drugs war on our streets.'

Tom finally broke his silence. 'So you accepted the list.'

'I did, although I'm not sure I thanked him,' he said. 'He then told me he was leaving and I was to stay where I was for another twenty minutes. I don't think he still entirely trusted me.'

'And that's when *Operation Sunlight* was planned,' suggested Tom.

'That's right. We didn't have a lot of time, but at least the detailed information which Donovan had given me meant there was no second guessing.'

'I can certainly see that,' answered Tom. What he didn't mention, however, was his big concern that all of this seemed to have been handed to him on a plate.

Chapter 27

DCI Shaw looked at his watch. 'Do you have to be somewhere else?' asked Tom.

'No. Not yet anyway. I've got a bit longer,' he answered.

'Thanks for all of that,' said Tom. 'It really is useful information. I appreciate you taking the time to fill me in.'

'Actually, I think I've probably told you far more than I intended,' replied Shaw, a slight smile appearing on his face.

Tom suddenly realised this was as good a time as any to try and clear the air between the two of them. 'Richard. I know we've had our disagreements in the past. You probably thought I was one of those detectives whose better days were behind them and so should have been pensioned off years before. Am I right?' asked Tom. Before he could answer though, Tom added, 'Richard. Let's at least be honest with each other. One of the advantages of getting older is that you tend to develop a thicker skin.'

'Do you know what my biggest problem was with you?' Shaw asked, looking Tom squarely in the eyes.

Now it was Tom's turn to smile. 'You mean there was more than one?'

'Quite a few actually. But the main one was your apparent lack of ambition. Not so much your personal ambition – although I tend to believe that the two are linked. No, it was more about your lack of professional ambition. The ambition that drives us to want to lock up people like Fuller and O'Driscoll. You seemed to be happy with just catching petty criminals. Like that pizza leaflet thief.'

This was a reference to a fairly recent case involving a petty thief who had been responsible for a number of opportunistic thefts. DCI Shaw was in full flow now and before Tom could respond he said, 'Then there was the multiple murder case. As we're now being honest with one another, I have to admit I did resent your involvement in it and all of the publicity you received. It wasn't even as though it was your case. So, whilst we were trying our best to put Fuller and all of his gang away, you had gone from catching a petty thief to stumbling into one of the biggest murder cases ever.'

'Wow,' said Tom, half laughing. 'I'm not sure now it was such a good idea to suggest this outbreak of honesty.'

'Do you want me to carry on?'

'You mean there's even more? Well, why not. Better out than in, as they say.'

'The talk in the station was that, recently, you'd become a bit of a loner. It was almost as though you didn't trust anyone any more. Not good if you are a Detective Chief Inspector,' suggested Shaw.

Tom had to admit, at least to himself, that there was more than a grain of truth in what DCI Shaw had said. His point about not trusting anyone probably referred to the time immediately prior to his involvement in the multiple murder investigation. It was about then, when he was seriously reviewing his life, personal as well as professional, that he had come to the conclusion that the best thing he could do would be to ask for early retirement.

DCI Shaw continued. 'Officers didn't want to be associated with you because you were seen as yesterday's man. Sorry.' Before Tom could respond Shaw said, 'So, now I've been honest with you, how about you saying what you thought about me.'

'Are you sure?' asked Tom.

'Why not? I think you might find it to be quite a cathartic experience. I certainly did.'

'To be absolutely frank, I don't know too much about you. In fact, I've probably learnt more about you today than I have in the previous couple of years.' Tom paused for a short while before continuing. 'But if you insist. I just felt you were typical of a new breed of young detectives in the Met, who always seemed to be in such a hurry to gain promotion. In my experience this normally means there is a great temptation to take undue risks and cut corners. And cutting corners usually results in sloppy police work. And sloppy police work almost always ends in disaster.'

'And is that what you think happened with *Operation Torch*?' asked Shaw.

'That was certainly my first impression but, until I have all of the facts, I won't really know.'

'Well, why don't I try and give you the facts. Or, at least, the facts as I see them,' offered Shaw.

'Before we move on to *Torch* is there anything else you think I should know about the actual wrap up of the O'Driscoll gang?'

'There's not too much to say. It was a text book operation. Everything which Donovan said would happen, did happen. Although there are probably one or two members of their gang still at large, I'm pretty sure we netted all of the main ones. We captured everything on video. The plane landing and even the packages being handed over. We then followed them back to where O'Driscoll himself was waiting. We even have him checking the quality of the drugs. That's when we went in. To say they were surprised would probably be the understatement of the year.'

He paused briefly and then continued. 'In addition to the arrests we also intercepted a large quantity of high-grade cocaine. We estimated it actually had a street value of about twenty-five million pounds. All in all it was good day's work.'

'So, afterwards, you were all feeling pretty good about yourselves I suppose?' suggested Tom.

'Well, yes. There was a bit of celebration afterwards. You know what it's like. It's a real adrenalin rush. Everyone was still on a high and a few drinks seemed to help. Anyway, sometimes it's good to celebrate successes.'

'I know. Believe it or not I have been involved in the occasional celebration.' He paused for a while and then said, 'Apart from the celebrations, weren't there also a couple of promotions for your team?'

'There's nothing wrong with that is there? Or are you saying we shouldn't reward success any more?' asked Shaw a little tetchily.

'Not at all. I'm just trying to find out who benefitted. That's all.'

Shaw was not convinced. 'Benefitted? You make it sound as though it's a crime.'

'Sorry. I didn't mean it to come over like that.' This contrition appeared to appease Shaw.

'I recommended DC Anderson for promotion and it was

endorsed by Superintendent Peters. He displayed great initiative during *Sunlight* and it was the least he deserved. In my opinion he has all of the moral resilience needed to put away people like O'Driscoll and Fuller. If I had the opportunity again I would do exactly the same thing,' he said very firmly.

'Moral resilience?' asked Tom. 'Do you think that's important in a detective?'

'I do,' answered Shaw. 'Without wanting to sound almost pious I believe that all of the best police officers, but particularly police detectives, need a strong moral compass. Dealing with the type of people we regularly come into contact with, inevitably means there will be many temptations and opportunities to profit personally. The strong officers – and I don't mean physically strong – will be the ones who are most likely to resist these temptations. These are the type of officers we need to identify and encourage if we are ever to take out Fuller and his like.'

'You make it sound as though we need a team of untouchables.'

'I suppose I do,' reflected Shaw. 'Although I wouldn't portray myself as Elliot Ness,' he added, with a slight laugh. 'Although he was successful, eventually, in getting a conviction against Al Capone.'

'If I remember correctly, Capone was finally convicted on tax fraud charges. And did Anderson fit the bill?'

'In my opinion DS Anderson is exactly the type of police officer we need.'

'Was Anderson the only person on the operation who you recommended for promotion?'

'He was, yes. DC James had really only just joined the team and, although he showed real promise, I thought it was too early for him.'

'But not DC Bennett,' suggested Tom.

Shaw now became visibly agitated. 'I know DC Bennett is an old friend of yours,' he said in a way which made it seem that in itself was a crime. 'But I simply didn't think he had the right qualities.' He hesitated slightly before adding. 'And the way he screwed up outside Fuller's house suggests I was right in my assessment.'

'Yes, I'd like to come on to that later, if you don't mind. But staying with the promotions for the time being, weren't you also promoted as a result of *Sunlight*?' asked Tom.

Tom had expected an aggressive reply and so he was quite surprised when Shaw said. 'I was, yes. Did you have a problem with that?'

'More surprised really. It's quite rare for someone with your limited experience to be promoted to DCI so quickly.'

'So, you think that any promotion should be based on length of service, do you?' asked Shaw, with just a hint of aggression in his voice.

After all of the earlier bonhomie their conversation was now in danger of gravitating back to their original position of undisguised hostility. This was not what Tom had intended.

'No I don't. In fact, believe it or not, I think, in the past, far too many officers have been promoted on the basis that they are considered to be the right age or, worse, because of who they know.'

There was a brief, tense silence before DCI Shaw spoke. 'Tom, I'd like to share something with you. It's up to you whether or not you want to believe it. Whatever you might think of me, personal glorification has never been my over-riding motivation. It's true that I am ambitious. But that ambition is for practical reasons. The higher and faster I can climb within the force, the more I will be able to achieve. You might think this is some form of almost religious fanaticism but for me I truly believe that I can be a force for change within the Met. The operations against O'Driscoll and Fuller are what we should be doing more of. In other words, taking the fight to these types of high-profile criminal operations. In my opinion we have, for too long, allowed them to take the initiative.'

'And you don't believe that we have?' asked Tom.

'No, I don't. After all we are a police *force*.' He then added, although this time more to himself than to Tom, 'I sometimes think that we've forgotten that.'

Tom was genuinely taken aback by the strength of Shaw's feelings. He had meant it when he had said earlier that he had learnt more about DCI Shaw in the past few minutes than in all of their time previously. DCI Shaw's latest comment simply reinforced that view.

Tom decided to change the subject before their new-found

friendship evaporated. He continued. 'What then happened to make you think you could now get Tommy Fuller? After all, O'Driscoll is one thing but Fuller – well, come to think of it, he's the one who should have the untouchable title.'

'Very good,' answered Shaw, in a far more relaxed way. 'But to answer your question. It was Donovan. After *Sunlight* I tried to get him to meet with me again.'

'Via Ryan?' asked Tom.

'Yes, via Ryan. But he didn't want to know. Then, one day, out of the blue, Ryan called me to say Donovan wanted to meet up. He gave me a time. Six o'clock. The place for the meet was the same as last time.'

'Did you have any idea what he might have wanted to discuss with you?'

'None at all,' answered Shaw. 'So, we met again. This time though, the atmosphere was totally different from the first time. Much more relaxed, with none of the tension or melodrama of our first meeting. When I got there he was already seated at a small table, which had mysteriously appeared, along with two chairs. And so I sat down opposite him. He came straight to the point. There was no preamble. He said that if I was interested in putting Tommy Fuller away then he could help me.

I tried not to show too much excitement but, I can tell you, my heart beat had gone into overdrive when I heard that. So, I replied that, of course, as a Detective Chief Inspector, I would be failing in my duty if I didn't respond positively.'

'How did he react to that?' asked Tom.

'He started to laugh and then said something quite strange. He said that quite a few Detective Chief Inspectors had tried and failed, over the years, to make anything stick on Tommy, and that included you.'

'*Me?*' answered Tom, his voice rising. 'Did he actually mention me by name?'

'Yes, he did. I asked him why he'd named you specifically. But all he said was that you were the only one left who had previously tried. All of the others had apparently retired or been transferred elsewhere.'

'Didn't that strike you as a bit strange?' suggested Tom. 'The fact he seemed to know about me and the others.'

'Not particularly at the time but, afterwards, I did think

that it was a bit odd. But I decided that it was him just showing off.'

'Did you think about mentioning this to me?' asked Tom, already knowing the answer.

'Absolutely not,' replied Shaw, unhesitatingly. 'It was my case, and anyway you know what I thought about you. Sorry.'

Tom smiled. 'Thanks for letting me down gently.' He then asked, more seriously. 'So, I guess the sixty-four thousand dollar question is … What was his motivation for suddenly making his offer?'

'At first he was very reluctant to tell me. He simply said he had his reasons and, anyway, did it really matter? I told him that *yes* it did really matter. It would be very difficult for me to sell the idea that he had suddenly turned informant, if he couldn't give me a credible reason.'

'So, you insisted,' replied Tom.

'I did, yes. I could see he still didn't want to tell me but, after I'd started to walk away, he suddenly asked me to sit down again. It was then he told me his reason.'

'And what was it?' asked Tom, his voice, once again, betraying his impatience.

'He said it was all to do with drugs. In the past he had been happy enough for them to deal certain drugs. But, generally, they were mostly lifestyle drugs, aimed at young people. The sort of drugs which kids were regularly taking anyway at parties, clubs, raves – that type of event. But recently Fuller had decided, now they had the field to themselves, that they should significantly expand their drugs operation, by supplying harder drugs, as that was where the really big money was. Donovan didn't agree with this, although he wouldn't say why. Perhaps he had a conscience after all. Who knows? Anyway, whatever his reason he couldn't buy into Fuller's new strategy. And that's why he was now passing me all of the information regarding the impending drugs delivery.'

'And did you believe him?' asked Tom.

'I didn't know what to believe. But his information about O'Driscoll had been spot on, so I had to at least hear what he had to say. Or do you think I should have just said thanks very much but I don't believe you?'

Tom didn't answer. He appeared lost, deep in his own thoughts.

Finally though he said, 'I'd heard he asked for some form of immunity from future prosecutions. Was that right? asked Tom.

'You seem to have been very well briefed,' replied Shaw, peeved that Tom clearly already knew about this.

'So, he did ask for it.'

'That's supposed to be ultra-confidential as well. But, hey, the more people who know the better,' answered Shaw in his most sarcastic tone.

Tom thought he should reassure DCI Shaw that things weren't quite as bad as he feared.

'Richard. It was Superintendent Peters who told me as part of this review. It's not as though it was common knowledge in the canteen.'

'Well, that's something I suppose,' said Shaw, having now regained his earlier equanimity.

'So, just for the record,' said Tom. 'Donovan offered to shop Tommy Fuller in return for immunity from any prosecution. Is that correct?'

'Yes. That and his aversion to Fuller's plan to sell hard drugs,' answered Shaw and then added, 'Just for the record.'

'Did you believe him about the drugs?' asked Tom.

'I've already told you. I neither believed nor disbelieved him. Although, when he then handed me full details of the drugs delivery, I did veer towards believing him. Just as with the O'Driscoll operation, it was all there. Dates, times, quantities, how it would be delivered and of, course, where it would be delivered.'

'I would imagine your eyes lit up when you saw all of that,' suggested Tom.

'Wouldn't yours?' asked Shaw, his voice rising slightly.

'Yes, I suppose they would,' replied Tom. Particularly if, he thought, but didn't say, I had invested so much personal time in formulating a plan to finally put Fuller away.

Shaw glanced at his watch again. 'Are you sure you don't have to get away? We could leave it there and meet again soon,' Tom suggested.

'No. I'm fine,' answered Shaw in a way which suggested that he wasn't fine.

'So, now you had this valuable information, what did you do with it?'

'I got back to the station at about seven thirty, and called

Superintendent Peters. He was still at the station but in a meeting, although I managed to persuade his PA to get a message to him, saying I urgently needed to see him. We met later that night, in his office, when it was quiet. I briefed him on what had happened and then showed him the details which Donovan had given me.'

Tom interrupted. 'What was Superintendent Peters' reaction?'

'Shock. Disbelief. Delight. You name it. Exactly what you would expect,' he answered, giving the clear impression it was not the most testing question he had ever been asked.

'I'm sure it was. But what about after his emotions had settled down?' asked Tom.

'We agreed there and then to mount *Operation Torch*,' Shaw replied, as if the answer was obvious. 'Sometimes it's better to seize the moment rather than try and psycho-analyse every single aspect of the information. You might think this was another example of me taking short cuts but, occasionally, you have to trust your judgement,' he added pointedly.

Or cloud your judgement, thought Tom. Once again an edge had returned to their discussion. Perhaps DCI Shaw had also recognised this danger because, when he next spoke, it was in a far more tolerant and reasonable manner. 'Of course, we both knew that was the easy part. Planning and then executing *Operation Torch* would be far more difficult, as well as riskier.'

'Risky? In any specific way?' asked Tom.

'For a start, we didn't have a lot of time. But the main risk, as far as I was concerned, was ensuring we prevented any of this from leaking out during the planning process.' He looked directly at Tom and said, 'You might remember, when we bumped into each other, outside the station on the night of the operation, how angry I became when you casually asked if there was a big operation planned for later that night.'

'I do remember,' admitted Tom. 'You did seem to be a bit fired up.' He gave a little laugh.

This seemed to ease the tension even further. 'Yes. I suppose I was,' Shaw said, joining in the laughter. 'But, surely, even you couldn't blame me for that.'

'Put like that, I think you're right. But, of course I didn't know then what I know now.'

Shaw shrugged and said, 'And that's true as well.'

This seemed like a good time to take a break. 'How about a drink? Let me buy you a cup of coffee,' offered Tom.

'Why not?' replied Shaw.

They both stood up and walked towards the nearby drinks machine. 'How do you take your coffee?' asked Tom.

'As it comes. Just black. I sometimes think it's only black coffee which keeps me going.'

'I used to be the same when I was your age. But you'll find when you're old as I am, that too much coffee just keeps you awake at night.'

'I'll try and remember that – when I'm as old as you,' Shaw answered, once again laughing.

Tom thought about how much his attitude towards DCI Shaw had changed in such a short time. Earlier today, they had almost had an argument in the station car park, in front of their superior officer. Now, a few short hours later, he was buying him coffee and swapping jokes.

'Richard,' said Tom. 'I don't even know if you're married or not.' Before Shaw could answer Tom added, 'Please tell me it's none of my business, if you like, I won't be offended.'

'It's not a problem. No, I'm not married. Although I came close a few years ago. Before I joined the force.'

Tom seized the opportunity this had presented. 'Could I ask what you did before this?'

'Actually, I was a lawyer. At the time I even had ambitions to become a barrister but, one day, I realised I would rather enforce the law rather than just practise it,' he explained.

'What? A sort of epiphany?' suggested Tom.

'I suppose it was in a way,' Shaw replied thoughtfully. 'Although I guess my reasons were more earthly than spiritual.'

'Wasn't your father also a lawyer?' asked Tom.

'Actually he was a QC, but that was quite a few years ago now.'

'He must have been very surprised then when you told him you were going to join the police.'

As Tom said this he could see that Shaw had suddenly become quite emotional. It clearly took a big effort on his part to regain his composure before he could reply.

'My father died before I joined the Met, so he never knew.'

But before Tom could follow up on this, Shaw continued,

'But that's enough about me for one day. Now it's my turn to ask the questions.'

Suddenly Tom realised he would now have to pay his own price for that insight into DCI Shaw's personal life. He nodded and said, 'Please feel free.'

By now they were back in Tom's office. 'What about you? Are you married?' asked Shaw.

'I was, many years ago, but I'm afraid to say my career came first and got in the way,' he answered.

'Any children?'

'Yes. A son. Paul. He and his mum emigrated to Australia, not long after we divorced. I haven't seen him for many years,' he answered, almost wistfully.

Shaw, sensing that Tom was far from comfortable with this, then said, surprisingly, sympathetically. 'That must be difficult for you. Is there a chance you and he might one day get together again?'

Tom shrugged a little and simply said, 'Who knows?'

DCI Shaw took his cue from the way Tom had answered that particular question about his son. 'So, there's no one special in your life at the moment?' he asked, more cheerfully.

Tom wondered whether or not to tell DCI Shaw about Mary. His natural instincts told him not to answer, or at least, to be as ambiguous as possible. But, suddenly and quite inexplicably, he found himself talking quite openly. 'Actually, yes there is. Her name is Mary. We met a couple of months ago.'

'Is it serious?' asked Shaw.

Tom smiled. 'It's still early days, of course, but I feel really positive about things.'

Now it was Shaw's turn to smile. 'I hope you've told her you are a detective. Well, good luck. I hope it works out for the two of you.'

'Thanks,' replied Tom, resisting the temptation to add that he'd let him know. Instead, he returned to the main subject. 'Do you mind now telling me what happened on the night of the operation?'

'As that's supposedly the main reason why you've been asked to conduct this review, I guess that I should,' replied Shaw. 'Although we seem to have covered far more territory than I had anticipated.' He began his explanation. 'The team met for the final briefing at about 10pm. Superintendent

Peters was there but, as it was my operation, I did the final briefing,' he said, making it crystal clear who was in charge.

'I had been to Fuller's house – covertly of course – in order to understand the layout of it. Using this information, every officer had been pre-allocated a position around the house. In addition, we also had additional uniformed officers, as well as some armed back-up available if needed.' Shaw looked at Tom and added as further explanation, 'Given Fuller's reputation, I didn't want to take any chances.'

'Wise move,' answered Tom, hoping that this didn't sound too patronising.

'Thank you,' replied Shaw in a way which suggested Tom had failed. He continued. 'We were all in position by about 11pm. The information from Donovan was that the delivery would be made at eleven fifteen, at the side door, on the right-hand side of the house. I even double checked with Donovan to confirm that he meant the right-hand side looking directly at the main entrance to the house. So myself, Superintendent Peters, DC Booker and a few others were all hidden close by the door. It was all a bit surreal really as the house was lit up like a Christmas tree and the whole place was rocking The drugs delivery was to coincide with a party which was being held there. It was Fuller's daughter's 30th birthday party and the party was clearly in full swing as we took up our positions. We could see people all over the house, looking as though they were enjoying themselves.'

'Very clever,' replied Tom, thoughtfully.

'That's exactly what I thought,' agreed Shaw. 'Although that was not exactly what I was thinking a little later, when they were all taking photographs and video footage of us on their phone cameras. Anyway, a little earlier than I had expected, I got a message that a van was approaching the house and another one very shortly afterwards saying it had pulled up right outside the main entrance.'

'What did you think when you heard this?' asked Tom.

'My immediate thought was to get more information. Remember, I was positioned around the side of the house, so I was reliant upon the information I was receiving from my team over the radio. So I asked for more information. Specifically, what, if anything, was being unloaded from the van?'

'Who were you speaking with? Who was positioned outside the front?' asked Tom, already knowing the answer.

'It was DC Bennett and a couple of uniformed officers,' replied Shaw, barely able to conceal his contempt. He continued. 'He told me that four men had emerged from the van and were now unloading boxes. I told him not to move until I had got there myself. Superintendent Peters remained at the side door whilst myself and DC Booker made our way to the front of the house as quickly as possible.'

'How long did it take you to get there?' asked Tom.

'It took us less than a minute. Probably about thirty seconds.'

'Were you or DC Booker on the radio at the time?'

'Are you joking?' replied Shaw clearly puzzled by Tom's line of questioning. 'Both of us were trying to get there as quickly as possible but without being seen. But by the time we got there all hell had broken loose.'

'What? The team had gone in or had been spotted?' asked Tom.

'The team had gone in,' answered a still angry Shaw. 'I told Bennett not to do anything until I got there but he took it upon himself to disobey my orders and charge in,' he said once again as if to reinforce the point that it had been DC Bennett's decision. 'All I could then do was to give the order for the rest of the team to go as well.'

'Why did DC Bennett not wait for you? What did he say?'

'He said he thought I'd given the order to go,' he answered. 'But I suspect he probably panicked or, more likely, was trying to get some personal glory,' he added rather bitterly.

'And did you give the order?'

This was the closest, during their conversation, that Shaw had come to really losing his temper. But, yet again, he impressively managed to control himself as he said, 'I've already told you I didn't.' There then followed another period of silence. 'I think you know the rest,' said Shaw eventually.

'Only what Superintendent Peters has told me. I'd still like to hear your version of it though.'

'My version of it? Why do you think it will be any different from Superintendent Peters'?' he asked suspiciously.

'I don't,' answered Tom. 'It's just that, in my experience, people's perceptions are sometimes slightly different, especially in such highly charged situations. Different people often see different things.'

'Hmm ...' said Shaw, clearly not entirely buying into Tom's theory. It looked as though he was about to add something to this effect but then instead thought better of it. '*My* recollection was one of absolute helplessness. When I entered the house I had a very strong feeling we wouldn't find anything. Fuller was there, of course, and he seemed to be thinking the same. Bennett and his team had started by opening the boxes which they had just seen being carried in. But all they contained were musical instruments. Some of the party guests were very kindly videoing this. In fact, if you want to see it I can let you have a copy of the footage. Although,' he added, now looking directly at Tom, 'I suspect you might have seen it already.'

'I'm afraid that I have,' Tom simply said.

'Some wit then suggested the band should sing something whilst the search was going on. Of course this was also filmed and then posted on the internet. Have you seen that as well?' asked Shaw.

Tom simply nodded.

Shaw, showing that even he could see the humour of the situation, said. 'Actually they were very good, even though they were just improvising. I'd definitely recommend them if you are ever considering having a party. I still have their details.' He then went on. 'We searched the house from top to bottom but found nothing of any significance. Absolutely nothing. By this time I could sense the team just wanted this to end so that they could get out of the house.' Once again, he looked directly at Tom and said, although this time with sudden honesty, 'Tom. If I said it was a disaster it wouldn't be doing justice to the word "disaster". In fact, I can't actually think of a word which adequately describes the situation.'

'And what was Donovan doing whilst all of this was going on?' asked Tom, interested to know if Shaw's recollection coincided with Superintendent Peters'.

'He was stood alongside Fuller. He gave the appearance of someone who was clearly enjoying our discomfort. But, if I had been in his position, I guess I would have done the same.'

'And what has he said since then?' asked Tom.

'I'm sure you don't need me to answer that question. But

just for the record, after he had gone through his entire repertoire of expletives, he told me, in no uncertain terms, that he would never again provide me with any more information. Of more concern was the fact that Fuller was now certain we had received information about the drugs delivery from someone close to the organisation and was conducting his own internal investigation – if that's the right way to describe it. When I spoke to him he seemed to be genuinely scared, so there's no way we're going to get any more information from him for a very long time – if at all.'

After a pause, Shaw said, 'Tom. I'm afraid I do have to go now. I have something arranged.'

'No problem. I'm just grateful you've been able to find the time to fill me in.'

'Look Tom. I'm still a bit unclear as to what your exact brief is. You seem to have been interested in a bit more than just operational details. But I suppose you have your reasons.'

DCI Shaw stood up and surprised Tom by offering him his hand. 'If there's anything else I can help you with just ask,' he said, before adding, mysteriously, 'although I can't guarantee I'll always be able to tell you what you want to hear.'

He then walked out of Tom's office and along the corridor, heading towards his own office.

A little while later Tom was still thinking about his meeting with DCI Shaw. He didn't know what had surprised him the most: the fact Shaw had actually come to see him or that he had been willing to provide him with so much detailed information. He had even, although admittedly only briefly, opened up a little about his own personal background. In many ways this was perhaps the most interesting part of their discussion. That, and his explanation concerning the moment when DC Bennett decided to enter Fuller's house. For Tom this was the pivotal part of the entire operation. It would help if he knew who really had given the order to go but, more importantly, why the order was given.

His thoughts then turned to the other issue which was concerning him. The situation with Pauline. Even during his intriguing discussion with DCI Shaw, his thoughts occasionally drifted back to his last conversation with Pauline. He had to try and resolve the situation one way or another. He would visit her on his way home to see if he could finally make her see sense. He didn't hold out any great hope. Pauline didn't seem to be the type of person who might respond to reason. But even knowing this, he felt he had to try.

Before he left the office, he turned on his computer to check his emails. He was hoping to find an email from Superintendent Peters, providing the financial details of those officers on his suspect list. There was nothing there, so he quickly checked the rest of his emails, decided there was nothing of any great importance, and switched off his computer.

Pauline lived in West Drayton, quite close to the bus station. He knocked on her door. Tom was surprised to see the door opened by a man, in his late twenties.

'Is Pauline in?' asked Tom.

'Who wants to know?' asked the man, making it obvious that Tom's unexpected presence wasn't welcome.

'Could you say Tom, Tom Stone would like to speak with her.'

'You're that copper, aren't you? The one who attacked mum,' he said, suddenly becoming worryingly aggressive.

'Did she tell you that?' asked Tom, now genuinely concerned with the way this conversation was heading.

Just then Pauline appeared. 'Tom, it's you. I was hoping you'd come and see me. This is my son Frankie. Why don't you come in?'

Tom ignored her invitation. 'Pauline, your son just said I'd attacked you. You know that's not true. Why did you tell him that?'

'Come in and have a drink. I've got a bottle open. We can talk about it indoors. Frankie will make himself scarce, won't you son?' she said looking towards him.

'I ain't going nowhere after what he did to you,' he answered menacingly.

'Pauline. What's this about me attacking you? What am I supposed to have done?'

'You know what you did. You tried to rape me,' she replied calmly.

'Rape you? What gave you that idea? All we did was have dinner together,' he said, clearly shocked by what she had just said.

'Come on in and we'll talk about it.'

'Pauline. You can't go around accusing people of trying to rape you,' Tom replied firmly.

Suddenly her earlier calmness disappeared and she began to shout at him. 'That's right. Accuse me of lying. Just because we had dinner together you thought you'd be able to have sex with me. Well, I'm not that easy you know,' she said, her words becoming increasingly slurred. 'You sort of men are all the same. Just because you're a copper you think you can just take what you want. Well, you're not getting away with it. I'm going to see to that.'

Frankie ushered his mum inside and then said, 'You're for it copper. You're finished,' and then closed the door leaving Tom standing alone on the pavement. He was stunned. What had possessed him to think he would be able to reason with her? The situation had now descended into seriously dangerous territory.

As he drove home he tried to make sense of it all. Why would she level this accusation at him? As far as he could see she was not trying to demand money from him. Not yet, anyway. He had earlier suspected she was quite neurotic, but accusing him of attempted rape was something else. It was now obvious he would have to report this to Superintendent Peters as soon as possible. He had hoped he could resolve the situation without having to do that, but now that events had taken a far more sinister turn, he had no choice.

And what about Mary? He owed it to her to let her know what was happening. It looked as though the romantic meal he and Mary had planned for tomorrow night might not be quite the enjoyable occasion he had hoped for.

Chapter 28

Tom was seated at his kitchen table, picking at his breakfast without any great enthusiasm.

It was almost impossible to think of anything except last night's conversation with Pauline. With everything else that was happening in his life right now, the last thing he needed was to be accused of such a serious crime by a clearly unbalanced woman. As far as he could remember, at no time had he given her the slightest indication that he wanted to see her again.

When she had contacted him she had mentioned something about him now being a famous person. Perhaps that's what it was? Maybe she was a woman who liked the kudos of being associated with someone who, however fleetingly, had been in the public spotlight. Whatever the reasons were, and however ludicrous the accusation, being accused of attempted rape was everyone's personal nightmare. He had left a message for Superintendent Peters to call him as soon as possible. The tone of his voice had, no doubt, reinforced the seriousness of the situation.

However difficult it would be he knew he had to do something to try and take his mind off last night's events, otherwise it would be a very long day indeed. Rather than hang around, waiting for Superintendent Peters to call him, he decided to use the time more constructively. So, later that morning he found himself standing outside DC Bennett's small terraced house in Feltham. He rang the bell. Before too long the door opened to reveal a petite, blonde-haired woman in her late thirties. She was wearing white trainers, black Lycra bottoms and a white sweatshirt.

'It's Julie, isn't it?' asked Tom.

'That's right. Do I know you?' she asked politely.

'Sorry. I'm Detective Chief Inspector Stone. I work at the same station as your husband. Is Gary in?'

'Oh, I remember now. I think you were at a few of the police dos we went to.'

'Yes, that's right. Although it was a few years ago.'

'Please come in,' she said, making way for him. 'As you can see I'm just on my way out. Saturday is my gym day. I'm sure Gary will be pleased to see you though. He's in the kitchen. Just go straight through. It's there, on the right.'

When Tom entered the kitchen he could see Gary was seated at the table, reading the paper, a mug of something in front of him.

'Someone to see you Gary,' said Julie.

DC Bennett looked up from his newspaper. 'DCI Stone,' he said with a surprised expression on his face. 'What are you doing here?' As he said this he stood up and offered his hand to Tom. He had clearly not expected any visitors. He was wearing an old pair of blue jeans and a slightly stained T-shirt. Tom knew he was also in his late thirties but, as he stood there in front of him, he looked as though he had aged considerably since he had last seen him.

Apart from his slightly shabby appearance he was also sporting a couple of days' worth of stubble, although, in his case, it was hardly of the designer type. But it was his eyes which shocked Tom. They appeared to be sunk deep into their sockets, and were surrounded by dark circles. He looked a mess.

'Are you here on official business?' he asked.

'Well, not official, official business, if you know what I mean. It's more me speaking with you off the record.' Before Bennett could reply Tom continued. 'Anyway. Before that, how are you? I understand you've been off sick for a few days.'

'Actually DCI Stone, Gary has been off now for almost two weeks,' interrupted Julie.

'Sorry. I should have known,' replied an embarrassed Tom. 'And by the way, it's Tom.'

'If you would excuse me, Tom, I have to collect my friend in a few minutes. Nice to meet you again,' she said, shaking Tom's hand. 'I hope you can talk some sense into Gary. If you can't do that at least persuade him to smarten himself up.'

'Julie, please leave it,' said Gary.

'Why? What do you mean?' asked Tom.

'He's got it into his head he's responsible for that big operation which went wrong. I keep telling him there was more than just him involved. But he won't have it. He's also worried about the inquiry. He thinks they'll blame him for everything.' As she said this she looked directly at her husband. 'Anyway, I'll leave you two to it.' Julie walked over to Gary and kissed him on the cheek. 'Don't forget to collect Karen,' she said before picking up a small sports bag and walking towards the front door.

After Julie had left, Gary said, 'I don't know how she's put up with me over these past few weeks. I don't deserve her.'

'Well, she's obviously concerned about you,' said Tom. He looked closely at Gary. 'And she has a point about smartening yourself up. Sorry.' He continued, although this time in a more considerate tone of voice. '*Are* you worried about the inquiry?'

'They'll have to blame someone. I'm sure DCI Shaw or Superintendent Peters won't be the ones and so that leaves me as the convenient scapegoat,' Gary said bitterly.

'But, as your wife said, a lot of officers were involved. It wasn't just you.'

'You know how these things work. The Met has always been good at covering its own backside.'

Tom couldn't really disagree with him, although he wasn't about to say that. Instead he said, 'Gary, why are you off sick? As far as I remember you're not the type of person who takes time off.'

'I know, and that's what's making it worse I suppose,' answered Gary. 'I just couldn't take any more of the comments and whispers about how I'd screwed up that operation. Getting a bollocking from DCI Shaw is one thing, as he's a bit of an odd bastard anyway, but hearing your so-called mates talking about you is another. I think it all got on top of me. I haven't been sleeping well since that night. I can't concentrate and I've started to take it out on Julie and the kids.' Tom remained silent. Gary then continued. 'To be honest, I'd been thinking about my career for a while now. I've been a DC for over ten years and I'll be forty in a couple of years' time. If I was going to make it in the force it would have happened by now. If my face didn't fit before all of this it certainly doesn't now.' Gary looked down at the table. He suddenly said, 'I suppose I could have made a mistake. Misheard him or something. The line was a bit crackly but, at the time, I was certain DCI Shaw had given the "go" call.'

'Was that the call to start the *Operation Torch* raid?' asked Tom.

'Yes. I know you weren't involved in it but you know what these operations are like. There's a lot of tension, nerves are on edge and the adrenalin is flowing. I've seen other people make mistakes, so I was trying to be especially alert that night.' Suddenly Gary looked up at Tom and became quite agitated. 'Why are you interested? Have you been sent to quiz me? Is that why you are here? It wasn't as though it was your case.' There was desperation in Gary's voice almost bordering on paranoia.

'Gary, I'm here because I heard you were off sick,' Tom said reassuringly. 'I wanted to see how you were. After all, we've known each other for a long time now.' He paused before continuing. 'But I'll be honest with you. I've been asked by Superintendent Peters to carry out a full review of all of the operational aspects of *Operation Torch* with a view to suggesting changes to prevent this type of thing ever happening again.'

'And you think you'll be able to do that, do you?' Before Tom could reply, Gary added, 'Whenever people are involved, cock-ups have always happened and always will happen. How can you write a procedure for that?'

'Yes. You're right,' admitted Tom. 'But there might be ways to at least minimise them. Gary. You said you thought you heard DCI Shaw give the "go" call. Surely, as it was over the radio, other people would also have heard it?'

'I thought so as well. But apparently no one else did. And the other strange thing is it wasn't recorded. Well, not so that it was clearly audible. Apparently there was a transmission glitch or something. The end result is my word against DCI Shaw's. So what chance do I have?'

'What exactly did you hear DCI Shaw say?' asked Tom, determined to fully understand what happened that night.

'I told you,' he replied, a bit sharply. 'He said, "Go, go". That's all. I've replayed that moment, in my mind, a thousand times now.' I'm *sure* that's what I heard.'

'And you are certain that it was DCI Shaw's voice?' asked Tom.

'Of course it was. I know it was only two words but I think I would recognise that plummy voice anywhere.'

'I know,' said Tom, 'but, as you said, the line was a bit dodgy.'

'It was DCI Shaw's voice,' Gary replied firmly.

'Did you ask for any confirmation before you went into the house?'

Gary looked crestfallen as he replied. 'No, I didn't. I know I should have done, particularly as we thought the delivery would be at the side of the house. But I didn't.' There was a brief silence before he spoke again. 'There seemed to be such an urgency in DCI Shaw's call that I just responded instinctively.'

'DCI Shaw says he asked you to hold off until he got to you,' said Tom.

Gary seemed genuinely shocked when he heard this and there was real anger in his voice as he said, 'Then he's lying. He might have done initially but it was him who told me to go in. If you ask me he's just covering his own arse because it was such a balls-up.'

Once again a brief silence returned.

'Did you see Superintendent Peters during the operation?' asked Tom.

'Only at the briefings and then in the house. Why do you want to know that?'

'I'm just trying to get clear where the senior officers were, that's all.'

'When we didn't find anything, I thought it must have been due to wrong information. It was only after we came out of the house that DCI Shaw started to have a go at me,' Gary volunteered. 'And then, of course, again, back at the station. And it didn't stop there,' he added mysteriously.

'What do you mean?' asked Tom.

Gary stood up and walked out of the kitchen. He soon returned, holding a letter in his right hand. 'Take a look at this,' he said, passing the letter to Tom. He opened it and could immediately see that it was headed, 'Disciplinary Hearing'. It was brief and to the point. The gist of it was that he had been 'invited' to attend a disciplinary panel hearing where he would be asked to explain his actions on the night of the raid on Fuller's house. The implication was clear. It was due to his actions that the raid had been unsuccessful. The hearing was due to take place in just over a couple of weeks' time. Tom passed the letter back to him.

'I know it looks bad but all you have to do is tell the truth.

Just tell them exactly what you just told me. Will you have any legal help at the hearing?'

'I'll have someone from the Union there but it's all a waste of time. You know that it'll be a whitewash.'

'Is there's anything I can do? Why don't I, at least, write a character reference for you?'

'Thanks, Tom. I know you mean well but what chance have I got? They've already made up their minds that it was all down to me,' he said, placing the letter on the kitchen table.

'When are you planning to return to work?' asked Tom.

'I don't know. As I said, I'm seriously thinking about jacking it all in. There's likely to be no future for me there anyway after the hearing.'

'Gary. I know it's easy for me to sit here and say this but I really do think you are being far too hard on yourself. You're a good detective. We've worked together over the years, so I know.'

'Well, that's obviously not what DCI Shaw thinks. Everyone else seemed to get either promotion or, at least, some credit, after *Operation Sunlight*. But not me,' he said. 'How do you think that made me feel?' he added bitterly.

'All I'm asking is that you don't make any rash decisions. Promise you'll at least call me before you make any final decision. Will you please do that?' asked Tom.

'Okay. I promise,' Gary replied, reluctantly.

Tom stood up and walked towards the front door, followed closely by Gary. They shook hands. 'Thanks for coming Tom. I really appreciate it. You're the only one who has bothered to come and see how I am. You would have thought, after all of the years I've worked for the Met, that at least a few would have visited.' There was sadness in his voice.

'Gary. Whatever happens remember you have a loving family supporting you. That's rare in the force – believe me.'

As Tom walked away back towards his car, he felt an overwhelming anger. Gary had been right when he'd said that the powers-that-be appeared to have already made up their minds to blame him for the *Operation Torch* fiasco. Gary Bennett was a decent, conscientious and loyal copper. Seeing Gary in this state reminded him just how brutal and unforgiving the force could be.

But little did he know just how brutal.

Chapter 29

As Tom drove back home he thought about what DC Bennett had said. Particularly the question as to whether or not DCI Shaw had given the final order. DC Bennett was sure it had been Shaw, although he did admit to now having a few doubts. But he thought that was understandable, given the huge pressure he was under. In his experience DC Bennett had always been a very reliable and detailed copper. What was it he had said? 'I'd recognise that plummy voice anywhere.'

On the other hand, DCI Shaw was equally adamant that he had definitely not given the go ahead. And one of Shaw's personal characteristics was that he was certainly not given to self-doubt. Clearly they couldn't both be correct. All of this confirmed, once again, how this question held the vital clue as to who was the informant. If he could only find the answer to this he was certain it would go a long way to solving the bigger question. But, right now, he admitted to himself, he couldn't think of a way to achieve it.

When he arrived home and checked his calls, he was not surprised to see there was a message from Superintendent Peters, returning his earlier call. There was a worrying urgency in Peters' voice which slightly unnerved him. He pressed the call back number. Almost immediately it was answered.

'Tom. I've been trying to get hold of you all morning,' said an obviously agitated Peters.

'Is it to return my earlier call?' he asked.

'No it's not,' he said definitely. 'Tom. I need to see you urgently. I'm at the station at the moment. When can you get here?'

'I can be with you in about thirty minutes.'

'Good. I'll see you then,' answered Peters.

As Tom parked his car he was surprised to see Milner's car was also in the car park. Tom shook his head slightly. No doubt this was Milner's way of catching up on a few things without him knowing. He didn't want to embarrass Milner and so he made his way immediately up to Superintendent Peters' office on the fifth floor.

When he entered the office, even though it was a Saturday, he could see Janice, seated at her desk.

'I'll let the Superintendent know you're here,' she said quite brusquely, without any of the usual pleasantries. He also noticed that the usual offer of a cup of tea was conspicuous by its absence.

Superintendent Peters came out of his office to meet him. 'Tom. I'm glad you were able to get here so quickly. Come in.' This was followed by, 'Janice. Please take my calls. I don't want to be disturbed.'

There was an edge to Peters' voice. The same edge Tom had noticed when they had spoken earlier on the phone. After they were both in his office, Peters said, 'Tom. I'll get straight to the point.' Peters had remained standing. 'Last night a complaint was made against you. A very serious complaint,' he added, with emphasis. 'A woman, named Pauline Jones, has accused you of trying to rape her,' he said, without any attempt to break the news gently. He looked at Tom for a response. When none came, Peters carried on. 'She claims you tried to rape her a few weeks ago, after you'd had dinner together.'

Tom spoke in a surprisingly calm voice. 'I know. That's why I was trying to get hold of you. To inform you about her allegation. As a matter of interest where does she claim this was supposed to have taken place?'

'At your house,' replied Peters. 'She said after you had dinner you invited her back to your house and then attacked her. It was only when she started screaming that you backed off.'

'And do you believe her?' asked Tom, not averting his eyes from Peters' face.

'Tom. This is a very serious allegation, involving one of my most senior officers,' he replied. Tom couldn't help noticing how he had, once again, avoided answering his direct question.

'What evidence is there to back up her claim? Or is it her word against mine?' asked Tom, an edge now starting to appear in his own voice.

'Are you denying it then?' asked Peters.

'Of course I'm denying it,' answered Tom, now raising his voice. He then added, although this time with his usual equanimity, 'Or at least I'm denying the attempted rape part. I did have dinner with her. That bit is true. But when we left the restaurant I had no intention of seeing her again. And I certainly didn't invite her back to my house. Pauline Jones is a very disturbed lady who seems to have developed some sort of fixation towards me. I believe it might be related to the media coverage I received after the multiple murder investigation. She seems to like the idea of being associated with someone who has been in the media.'

He went on. 'A few days ago I received a phone call from her asking if I'd like to meet again. I told her I wouldn't. She'd already personally posted a letter through my letter box, whilst I was away on holiday, asking to meet again. She also came to see me – she must have been waiting for me to arrive home – and the same thing happened. When I told her I didn't want to see her again she started threatening me. Nothing specific, just a general threat. "You can't do this. I'll get you." That type of thing.'

'Why didn't you report this straight away?' asked Peters.

Tom remained silent for a while. 'I should have done. But I thought I could resolve it myself, so last night I went to see her.'

'What, at her house?' asked Peters incredulously.

'I know. In retrospect it was a stupid thing to do. But I thought I could persuade her to, at least, stop contacting me. She was reasonable to begin with but as soon as I declined her offer to have a drink, in her house, she started shouting and threatening me. It was then, as I stood on the pavement outside her house, that she accused me of trying to rape her. It was after that I tried to contact you.'

'So, apart from yesterday, when you went to see her, you have not initiated any of the meetings with her?'

Tom hesitated just enough to catch Peters' attention. 'As I said, when I got home from holiday, there was the letter from her. After I read it I decided to find out if she had a record. I just had a feeling, when we met, that she might have. Her behaviour during the meal was very odd, so I asked Milner to run a check on her.'

'So you thought you'd involve a third party in your own

personal investigation, did you?' asked Peters, suddenly becoming very angry.

'Sir, I asked Milner to do this for me as I was busy at the time,' he said, looking directly at Superintendent Peters. 'I had my mind on other things if you remember. As far as I can remember I didn't tell him to do this secretively or to make sure no one found out he was doing it. I just suspected that she might have been known to us – and as it turned out, I was right. She has been convicted of soliciting, and being caught in possession of drugs. There was also a strong possibility, although it was not proven, that she was dealing drugs. I just wanted to find out. That's all.'

Superintendent Peters seemed to consider what Tom had just told him. He then said firmly, 'Tom. I'm afraid I have no choice but to suspend you until this allegation has been investigated. I'm sorry but I really don't have a choice.'

Tom looked totally stunned. 'Suspend me? What, from everything?' asked Tom, emphasising the last word.

'Everything,' replied Superintendent Peters, equally emphatically. 'I'd like you to hand over your day-to-day case work to Milner. Janice called him and asked him to come in. He's downstairs waiting for you.'

'And what am I supposed to tell him?' asked Tom.

'Just tell him that I've asked you to work on something else for the next couple of weeks. In a way, of course, it's true. Or at least was true.'

Tom was now finding it very difficult to control his temper. 'I'm also involved in a missing persons case. One that might have far more sinister implications. If you take me off this case then there's a possibility that we will lose momentum.'

'Tom. I know this has come as a shock to you, and right now you are angry, but, given the circumstances, I really have little choice.'

Tom then asked the question they both knew would have to be asked. 'What about *Reporting*? Am I now supposed to forget all about that as well?'

'For the time being, yes. It wouldn't make sense for you to be suspended from your official duties only for me to give you the green light to carry on with your unofficial ones.'

'I thought that was exactly what you had asked me to do,' replied a now bristling Tom.

'That was totally different. And you know it. You hadn't been accused of attempted rape then,' said Peters, equally indignantly. There was a brief, tense silence before Peters continued. 'Hopefully, all this will get sorted out quickly. If what you say about her is true, it won't take long to completely compromise her story.'

'Compromise? You make it sound as though my only hope is for us to focus on the part of her story which is the weakest. Once again, and for the record, the only part of her story which is true is the bit about us having dinner together.'

Superintendent Peters waited until he thought Tom had calmed down. 'Can I ask how you came to have dinner with her? She doesn't strike me as being a normal – if that's the correct expression – dinner date.'

'I met her through an agency. She wasn't exactly being truthful when she completed her personal profile. We had absolutely nothing in common and I couldn't wait for the dinner to finish so I could go home.' He then added for absolute clarity, 'Alone. In fact, it was such an unpleasant experience I even asked for my money back from the agency.'

'And did you?' asked Peters.

'Did I what?'

'Did you get your money back?'

'I didn't. The terms and conditions stated it was non-refundable.'

'So, you didn't use them again,' suggested Peters.

'Actually I did. And, as it turned out, I'm glad I did because that's how I met Mary.' He then added, as further explanation, 'We've been together for a few months now. Anyway, what has this to do with me being accused of attempted rape?'

'I'm sorry to have to ask but it's something you are likely to be questioned about as part of any investigation. If this is to go to court then you know as well as I do that the prosecution will make great play of the fact that you regularly use dating agencies.'

'Regularly use?' answered Tom, his anger returning. 'I've had two dates and used one agency. I don't think even the most fervent prosecution lawyer could claim that's being a serial user.'

'I know that,' replied Superintendent Peters. 'I'm only pointing out what's likely to be said.'

They both remained silent for a while. Superintendent Peters could sense Tom's discomfort and so, a little tactlessly given what he had just told Tom, changed the subject back to their own personal inquiry.

'As you just mentioned *Reporting*, does this mean you've made some progress since we last spoke?'

Even Tom was slightly taken aback by Peters' directness as his own thoughts were still focused on the rape allegations. It was with real effort that he replied, 'Yes. A bit of progress. I'm fairly confident I've been able to eliminate a few other officers from the suspects list but, there's a lot I'm still trying to find out.'

'And were you planning to tell me who you've eliminated from your list?'

'Not yet, Sir. As I said, there's still a lot to be done. I'd rather wait a bit longer. I don't see any value in just drip feeding you information,' he answered, less than convincingly. He then continued, although this time with undisguised sarcasm in his voice. 'Anyway, Sir, as you said earlier, I'm now suspended from all inquiries.'

Peters looked thoughtfully at Tom, clearly trying to decide whether or not to respond in kind. In the event he made do with, 'You can resume your inquiries when all this is over.' And, just in case there was any ambiguity, he added, 'You are to stop everything you are working on. And I mean everything. I also don't want to see you around the station. You are not to discuss this with anyone. I have already put this in writing.' As he said this he picked up a letter that was on his desk, and handed it to Tom. 'Go home. I will keep you informed about any developments. I would suggest, however, that you start to write up everything about your meetings with Pauline Jones. The initial dinner date, the letter, the phone call and all of the meetings which you had. Don't leave anything out, however potentially embarrassing.'

Tom continued to look closely at Superintendent Peters and didn't even bother to open the letter. He was sure he detected the merest hint of a smile. But, in his current state of mind, he could have been wrong.

He could see there was little to be gained by trying to persuade Superintendent Peters to allow him to continue working on Maciej Sipowicz's disappearance or indeed

Reporting. Deep down, in fact not even that deep, he knew Superintendent Peters had no choice. He would have done exactly the same if their roles had been reversed. Of course, it didn't make him feel any better. In fact, just the opposite, as he believed he had made some real progress over the past few days, particularly after his conversations with DCI Shaw and DC Bennett. But he wasn't going to admit that to Superintendent Peters.

Chapter 30

A little while later, Tom was in his own office together with Milner.

'I expect you're wondering why Superintendent Peters asked you to wait for me,' said Tom.

'Well yes. It was a bit of a strange request. Is it anything to do with me?' he asked nervously.

'No, it's not. You don't have anything to worry about,' Tom replied, although thinking "unlike me". He immediately continued. 'I've been asked by Superintendent Peters to work on another project for the next few weeks. This means that, in the meantime, you will be the lead officer.'

'Me?' exclaimed Milner. 'What, even the metal thefts case?'

'Yes you, Milner,' answered Tom. 'Do you have a problem with that?'

'Not really. It's just that I would have expected a more senior detective, say DCI Shaw, to have been assigned to it. Particularly with the Sipowicz connection.'

'You are more than capable of handling it. It might be worthwhile though if we took the remainder of the afternoon to review everything and decide what needs to be done next.'

Milner's response was instant, suggesting that he welcomed Tom's suggestion. 'I'd really appreciate it if we could do that, Sir.'

They spent the next hour or so reviewing all of the information that they had and, in particular, the evidence against all the people currently being held or still under investigation. As they did this it became clear that they were able to construct a compelling case, implicating Walker, Lomas, Stevenson and, of course the now deceased Wood, with the metal thefts. They also had additional charges, ranging from driving without insurance and whilst under the influence of alcohol, to assaulting police officers. Although the evidence against McNulty was not as extensive, and notwithstanding the information he had provided to the police, it was still almost certain that he too would not escape a custodial sentence. The charges against William Brady were not on the scale of Walker's and his gang, but, even here, Tom felt sure that they were strong enough to secure a conviction. But then there was Maciej Sipowicz's continued disappearance. It was this, more than anything else, which most worried him. They already had the witness statement from McNulty, confirming how Sipowicz had been beaten by Walker and the others. Afterwards he had been taken away by them. That much was clear. What wasn't clear though, was where he had been taken and what had happened next. The most sinister fact, however, was that Maciej Sipowicz had not been seen since. The recently found body in the scrap yard was just another deeply worrying development.

'So, do you now feel confident you can get these cases to court?' asked Tom.

'I'll feel more confident after we've conducted the next round of interviews and confronted them with the information and evidence which we now have. In particular, McNulty's evidence about the assault on Mr Sipowicz.'

'No doubt Walker, in particular, will deny everything, so just make sure you gradually apply pressure by confronting him with all of the evidence in a systematic way. If it was me I'd start with the less serious charges and then crank them up. I think though that your best chance of obtaining some sort of confession will be with Lomas. He's a very aggressive young man who, I think, almost glories in violence. He's also unpredictable, so make sure that he doesn't catch you unawares. You don't want to lose your good looks entirely.'

'Don't worry I will,' answered Milner, not for the first time gingerly touching his cheek, before adding. 'How do you think I should follow up on the body we found in the scrap yard?'

'You can't really do anything until you receive information back from forensics and then the full post mortem. Wait until you know the sex, likely age and approximate date of death, plus, of course the cause of death, and then start the formal investigation. Hopefully, you should have some of this very soon.'

'What if it's Sipowicz?' asked Milner.

'It pointless speculating. Who knows how long the body has been there? But, if it is, I'd like you to call me.'

'But I thought you said you'd been assigned another case?' he replied, a slightly puzzled expression on his face.

'That's correct but it doesn't mean that I'm not interested in Mr Sipowicz's whereabouts.'

'Is there anything else I can do for you?' asked Milner.

Tom thought about his earlier discussion with Superintendent Peters and his decision to stop him from pursuing his clandestine inquiry. It seemed as though suddenly something flashed across his mind. 'Actually there might be something,' he answered, rather cryptically.

Chapter 31

Tom arrived home just before five o'clock. He felt both physically and mentally exhausted. Physically, because the previous night he hadn't slept very well as he kept running his doorstep conversation with Pauline over and over again in his mind. And mentally because the events of the past couple of hours had left him numb.

Part of the problem was that the more he thought about Pauline's allegation the more helpless he felt. Events felt as though they were rapidly spinning out control. And that was something he had never been comfortable with. He knew, of course, he was innocent and was confident any inquiry would subsequently confirm this to be the case. But, he also knew there was some truth in the old saying about mud sticking.

There would be people amongst the general public who would prefer to believe Pauline's allegation. There were also a few people within the force who were unlikely to shed any tears for him either. Then there was Mary. He had to tell her, of course. Fortunately, she would be arriving soon, as they had planned to spend the evening together. It was probably best to tell her as soon as possible, but he could only guess at what her reaction might be. What was certain, however, was that it was likely to be a 'make or break' point in their relationship.

While all of this was going through his mind he also now had to try and make sense of his role in the covert *Operation Torch* investigation. Superintendent Peters could not have made it any clearer to him, that he was also to immediately suspend work on this investigation. But, as he had mentioned earlier to him, he did feel he had made some progress. The big decision now, of course, was to decide whether or not to put all of this on hold, as indeed Superintendent Peters had ordered, or to continue with his own private investigation.

The latter option, he knew, had always been full of risks,

personal and professional. If he was to continue then he might have to add criminal to that list. The logical decision would be to stop any follow-up work until after the rape allegations had been resolved. But the more he considered this option, the more he realised that even if he was completely exonerated by any inquiry, his reputation and standing within the force would be compromised or, at the very least, tarnished. He had absolutely no doubt he would, once again, be sidelined and then quietly pensioned off.

Major investigations – successful ones at least – always seemed to gain a character of their own. If he now had to suspend work on this then there was a real possibility that any momentum, which he felt was just starting to develop, would be lost. Perhaps forever.

What was also noticeable was how much Superintendent Peters' early enthusiasm for their investigation had recently begun to cool. His reluctance to provide him with any personal financial information had become obvious. And, when they had spoken earlier, in private, he had the distinct impression that he was now almost relieved that their search for the possible mole within the station was now also suspended. There was a real danger that it might even be abandoned completely.

Ironically, it was this thought which finally helped him to make up his mind. There were huge risks, and so he would have to tread very carefully, but he would carry on with his investigation. Although his 'reassignment' was the cover, he was realistic enough to know it would soon be public knowledge – at least within the station – that the real reason was that he had been suspended from all duties. There wasn't one chance in a thousand of keeping that quiet.

Simply the fact that he was not allowed to even visit the station during his suspension would raise many awkward questions. Not having access to his computer files would, however, represent a real practical problem. Fortunately, he'd had the foresight to bring with him all of the hard copy files he had been working on. He was surprised Superintendent Peters hadn't already asked for these to be returned to him. He suspected though that it was only a matter of time before he would. In the meantime he would copy them himself before Peters asked for them.

Tom just had time for a quick shower and change of clothes before Mary arrived. They hadn't seen each other for almost a week and this separation was reflected in the warmth of their embrace. Tom pulled her close to him and kissed her with real passion.

She pulled away from him slightly. 'You're eager,' she said, with a light laugh. 'I know we haven't seen each other for a week but I hadn't expected you to ravish me on the doorstep. At least wait until I've taken my coat off,' she added, still laughing.

Mary's use of the word 'ravish' immediately made Tom remember Pauline's allegation. But he suddenly found himself carried away with the excitement of the moment and he once again pulled her to him and began kissing her again. This time though she responded. 'Okay,' she said, taking hold of his hand. 'You've persuaded me.'

Later, as they lay in Tom's bed, Mary with her head resting on his chest, she said, 'That was wonderful. You were so . . .'

'So, what?'

'Well. So . . . enthusiastic,' she replied, sitting up to look at him. 'Not that I'm complaining, of course. It's just that you took me a little by surprise, that's all. I thought we'd at least have dinner first.' She then kissed him gently on the forehead.

'I'm glad you're not complaining,' he answered. 'I wouldn't want my best work to go unappreciated.'

'How about me appreciating your best work again?' replied Mary reaching for him.

It was quite late before they sat down to eat. Tom hadn't had the time to prepare anything special. The events of the day and the past hour or so had put paid to that and so they settled for pasta and a bottle of red wine. After Tom had opened the wine and filled their glasses Tom said. 'Mary. There's something I need to tell you.'

'Is it to do with your work?' she asked, with a hint of concern in her voice.

'Well, yes it is,' he answered. 'How did you know?'

'I guess it's because I'm getting to know you better all the time,' she answered. Although she could have said, it's because you always have a distinctive tone to your voice when you are discussing your work. 'Anyway, what is it you have to tell me?'

'Do you remember I told you about the experience of my first date? The one just before I met you,' he said seriously.

'How could I forget? It nearly put you off dating for life, didn't it?' replied Mary with a slight laugh.

Tom didn't answer Mary's question. Instead he said. 'Her name is Pauline Jones. She's been contacting me since we got back from holiday. I've received a letter from her. Delivered personally here,' he added. 'Then a couple of phone calls and, a couple of nights ago, she came here to see me.'

Mary, sensing Tom's discomfort, was no longer laughing. 'What here? What did she want?'

'Yes, here,' he answered. 'To begin with she wanted us to have dinner together again. For some reason she seemed to think that there was something between us. When I told her that wasn't the case she suddenly started to get very angry. Eventually, as the week progressed, that anger turned into something far more sinister.'

'Sinister? I don't understand,' answered Mary, suddenly worried by Tom's use of that particular word.

Tom appeared to take a deep breath before looking directly at Mary and saying, 'She has accused me of attempting to rape her.'

'What?' said Mary, her voice rising. 'Rape? When did this supposedly happen?'

'After we'd had dinner together. After that first date. She claims we came back here together and it was then I attacked her.'

'Here?' she repeated. 'That's absurd,' she added, now clearly angry. 'What evidence does she have?'

'None of course. It's just her word against mine. Last night I went to see her to try and finally persuade her that there wasn't anything between us. In retrospect it was a stupid thing to do, as that only made her even more irrational. It was then she accused me of trying to rape her.' He then added, almost matter-of-factly, 'But that's not all. After I'd seen her last night she made a formal complaint. The result was that, earlier today, I was called to the station by Superintendent Peters. I've been suspended with immediate effect.'

'Suspended? But why has he done that?' she asked, now suddenly realising the full seriousness of the situation.

'It's normal procedure. But how long it lasts all depends upon if, and when, it goes to court.'

203

There was a hint of anger in her voice when she said. 'Why didn't you tell me that she had been contacting you since we got back from holiday?'

'I didn't want to involve you. I thought that I could sort it out by myself.'

After a brief silence Mary looked at Tom, tears starting to appear in her eyes. 'I'm so sorry. You must be shell-shocked.'

'That's certainly one way of describing it.'

Mary took hold of Tom and pulled him close to her. They didn't say anything, just continued to hold each other close. It was Tom who eventually pulled away. He held both her hands and, looking straight at her, said, 'Any investigation is likely to take quite a while. In my opinion she is clearly unbalanced and delusional and so, I think, we have to be prepared for even more lurid allegations.' Just to reinforce his point he then added, 'It's bound to get nasty. It's even possible that you will also get sucked into it. Of course, I'll do everything I can to keep your name out of it but, I have to tell you, it is likely that your name will get mentioned.'

'Tom, I don't care,' Mary replied firmly. 'Do you really think I'm going to give you anything less than one hundred per cent support? All that matters is that this allegation is proved to be false. I don't care how long it takes, or whether or not my name is mentioned, I'll stand by you. I hope you know that?'

'I was hoping that's what you would say. I just wanted you to know that things are likely to get very dirty. That's all.'

Mary kissed him. 'In fact, I hope my name *is* mentioned because, that way, I can show just how ridiculous her accusation is.' For a moment they both remained silent before Mary spoke again. 'Tom? Why is she doing this?'

'I really don't know,' he answered. 'But I don't think it's a coincidence that she contacted me again after my name had appeared in the papers and on television. In fact, she even mentioned something about never having been out with anyone famous before. Anyway, that's really for the professionals to find out.' Tom handed her the letter Pauline had left for him. 'Take a look for yourself at what she wrote.'

After Mary had read it, she put the letter down and said, 'Anyone who reads this will know instantly she is unbalanced.'

'I hope so,' replied Tom, none too confidently.

'Is there anything you can do?' she asked.

'Not really. Suspended means exactly what it implies. I'm not allowed to do anything that is related to the case. In fact,' he added, 'I'm not allowed to do anything related to any of my current cases.'

'So, you're expected to sit at home and wait until they contact you. Is that it?' she asked, quite angrily.

'That's what suspended means,' he replied as confirmation.

'So how are you supposed to defend yourself against this accusation?'

'I haven't thought about that yet,' he answered. 'But I'd better think of something fast, otherwise I might soon be the disgraced Detective Chief Inspector Stone.'

'Tom, please don't joke about things like that. You worry me when you say things like that.'

'Sorry. I didn't mean to worry you. In fact it was a stupid attempt to do exactly the opposite.'

Unsurprisingly, Tom and Mary were both very subdued for the remainder of the evening.

Next morning, as Mary made breakfast, Tom made a call.

The number kept ringing and Tom was just about to press the 'end call' button, when a breathless Milner answered. 'Morning, Sir. Sorry about that but I've just been for a run and I heard the phone ringing as I was opening the front door.'

'That's very commendable of you,' replied a genuinely impressed Tom. 'I didn't know you liked running.'

'Well, I don't really, Sir,' he said. 'It's just I've realised I'm not as fit as I should be. Maybe if I had been a bit faster I might have dodged that attack on me at the scrap yard.'

'Maybe,' replied an unconvinced Tom. 'But I think the fact you were the nearest to him was the crucial factor. Anyway, I'm sure it can't do any harm.' He paused. 'Milner, yesterday you asked if there was anything you could do. Do you remember?'

'Of course I remember, Sir' replied Milner, genuinely pleased that he might be able to help. There was even a slight excitement in his voice as he asked. 'What is it you'd like me to do?'

He simply said, 'It's nothing to do with any of the cases we've been working on. I'd just like you to find out something. It's a bit too technical for me, so I'd like you to contact someone who's likely to know the answer.'

'That's no problem, Sir. Who is it?' answered a now intrigued Milner.

'His name is Derek Johnson. Although he's a civvy he works in the communications section at Regional HQ. I've worked with him quite a few times over the years. There's nothing he doesn't know about telecommunications.'

'Telecommunications?' answered a slightly puzzled Milner.

'Yes. Telecommunications. But, for the time being, this is just between the two of us. Here's what I would like you to ask him ...'

Chapter 32

After they had eaten breakfast Mary suggested they go for a walk. Tom immediately agreed. It was beginning to become a bit claustrophobic in the house. The situation regarding Pauline Jones's accusation was overhanging everything. However hard they tried to discuss other things it was clear the accusation was always there, at the forefront of their minds.

'What will you do while you're off?' asked Mary. But before Tom could answer she added suddenly, as an idea came to her, 'Perhaps we could go away on holiday again. It might help to completely get away.'

'I might just take you up on that,' replied Tom. Going away on holiday again was probably the last thing he wanted to do right now, but he didn't want to knock down Mary's idea. 'But to answer your first question, I'm not too sure what I will do. I know what I can't do. That's the easy bit. This is the first time I've ever been suspended and so it's all a new experience for me.'

As they continued to walk, arm in arm, Mary, without looking at Tom, said. 'Surely there must be something that you can find out about her. From what you've told me, and having read her letter, she seems to be really unhinged.' She suddenly stopped and turned to face Tom. 'Perhaps she's done this sort of thing before. You said she had a police record. Maybe there's something else in her file like this.'

'Well she definitely has an interesting past. As I said she had previously been arrested for prostitution and possession of drugs. She was also charged with drug dealing but that was later dropped due to lack of hard evidence.'

'Well, that's good news isn't it?' Mary's voice betrayed her excitement.

'It obviously would have been better for her if she wasn't known to the police but, if it does go to court, this might not be deemed to be admissible anyway.'

Mary suddenly looked distraught. 'But surely the fact she has a record is very relevant,' she said, almost pleadingly.

'Unfortunately, I don't think the law has caught up with what you are suggesting yet.'

Suddenly a thought came to her. 'You said you checked up on her earlier in the week. I thought you said she only made the accusation last night.'

'You'd make a good detective,' said Tom, as light-heartedly as he could manage. But he was far more serious when he then said, 'What I did wasn't my finest hour.' Before Mary could interrupt, Tom quickly continued. 'After I received her letter my curiosity got the better of me I'm afraid. From the first moment I met her I just had a feeling there was more to her than she was telling me and the letter seemed to confirm that. So, on Monday I asked Milner to run a check on her.'

Mary could immediately sense this probably wasn't normal procedure. As ever she got straight to the heart of the matter. 'Why did you ask Milner to do it? I can understand your interest but was it wise to involve Milner?'

'No, it wasn't and that's something I now regret,' he said honestly. 'But I can't change that now.' They both remained quiet as they continued their walk. Finally Tom spoke. 'Mary. I don't think you still fully understand what lies ahead. I think you should really consider staying away from me until all of this has been settled.'

Mary's anger became clear when she replied, 'That's ridiculous. What sort of person do you think I am? You need me now more than ever. I'm here and I'm here to stay. Whatever happens.'

Later that night, after Mary had left, Tom poured himself a glass of wine and sat down at his kitchen table. He was trying desperately to remember everything which had happened that night at the restaurant. Perhaps it was the wine or, more likely, the skill he had developed, over the years, for retaining as much information and detail, as possible, but whatever the reason, the full events of that evening were now starting to come back. They had met for dinner at a restaurant in Egham. He had booked a table for eight o'clock, and, even though the restaurant was less than a couple of miles away from where he lived, he had decided to take a taxi and had booked the same taxi company to take him home afterwards.

When he arrived Pauline was already there and, he'd noticed, had already made good progress in working her way through a bottle of white wine. She had driven to the restaurant and, as the evening progressed and she continued to drink, he had become concerned about her increasingly irrational behaviour. In fact, having seen the amount she had drunk during the meal, he had insisted she leave her car where it was and take a taxi home.

What's more, he had booked the taxi for her himself. Her allegation, of course, was that he had attacked her in *his* house. He was tempted to call the taxi company himself, right now, to request information about both of their separate taxi journeys. But they would only release any customer information if it was an official police request. And, as he was officially suspended, he would have to be patient. Jumping in himself might only further compromise his situation. He would call Superintendent Peters first thing in the morning to pass on this information and ask him to follow up, with the taxi company, through official channels.

Although he now felt a bit more positive about the events relating to Pauline's accusation, he knew it was never advisable to get too far ahead of yourself. With someone as unpredictable as Pauline there was always the chance she would suddenly start making further allegations. Now she had opened her own Pandora's box she would find it difficult to close the lid. His own personal mantra had always been to hope for the best whilst, at the same time, planning for the worst. This was one such occasion when that philosophy was definitely worth adopting.

His ongoing inquiries into *Operation Torch* had also reached a crucial point. The fact he was prevented from pursuing his inquiry any further, was, of course, a major problem. But he couldn't just press a switch and stop thinking about the investigation. He would have found this difficult to do anyway, but as he now felt he was on the verge of a breakthrough, it would be almost impossible. It really depended on what Milner came back with, after his conversation with Derek.

If the message came back that there was nothing there then he would have to re-evaluate his involvement in the case. If, though, his suspicions were confirmed, then it would take the inquiry on to a new level entirely.

Finally, there was his conversation with Mary concerning Pauline's accusation. He had detected, as the day had worn on, that the full realisation and implications of these allegations had finally begun to affect Mary. Of course, she had said all of the right things about always being there to support him. In fact, having now got to know Mary's forceful personality, it would have been a surprise if she hadn't shown such support.

Notwithstanding this, he could sense she was more fearful of how all of this would affect their relationship than she was willing to admit. The next few days, he knew, would, on many different levels, be hugely important in determining his and their immediate futures.

Chapter 33

Even though he was suspended, and therefore not allowed to go anywhere near the station, Tom had still risen at his 'normal' working day time. Until his case had been decided he was determined to keep to as normal a routine as possible.

He quickly realised, though, that this would be more difficult than he'd imagined. The getting up bit was the easy part. It was how he would fill the rest of the day which, he suspected, would be more difficult and frustrating.

Before he got to that situation though, he had a few calls to make, and the first one was to Superintendent Peters. He called Peters' number at the station and almost immediately it was answered by his PA. 'This is Detective Chief Inspector Stone, Janice. Can I to speak with Superintendent Peters?' said Tom, in his most formal voice.

There was a brief pause before she answered in a distinctly cooler and slightly unfriendly tone, 'I'll see if he is available.' A short while later she came back and simply said, 'I'm putting you through.'

'Tom, I was going to call you yesterday to see how you were but decided you probably needed a bit of time by yourself. Anyway, how are you?'

'I've certainly had better weekends,' was Tom's succinct reply.

'Yes. I can imagine you have,' answered Peters. He then added, almost too apologetically, 'I hope you realise that I don't, for one minute, believe a word of what she is saying. I'm sure we'll soon find something which confirms that.'

'That's exactly why I called you,' answered Tom.

'Really?' replied Peters, with undisguised surprise in his voice. 'What have you got?'

'Well, it was so obvious. It was staring me in the face all the time.'

Tom could sense he now had Superintendent Peters' undivided attention.

'I hope you're right. So, what is it?'

'After I left the restaurant I took a taxi home. As she'd had a few too many drinks I also booked a taxi to take her home and so she left her car in the car park all night. I'm sure if you check with the taxi company they'll be able to let you have the addresses where they dropped us. In her case, to her house in West Drayton and in mine to my house in Staines.'

He paused briefly, until he was sure Peters had fully grasped the significance, and then continued. 'The restaurant should also have CCTV. If you obtain the footage for that night, I'm certain you'll see her car was there all night.'

Once again he paused, allowing Superintendent Peters the opportunity to comment or ask any follow-up question. When he didn't Tom himself asked the all-important question. 'Didn't she claim we'd both immediately gone back to my house, where the attack was supposed to have taken place?'

'That's what she said,' answered Superintendent Peters, just a little too unenthusiastically as far as Tom was concerned.

To further reinforce his point Tom said, 'Well, the facts will soon prove conclusively we couldn't have.'

'Yes. You're right, of course,' said Peters. 'That's great news. I'll get someone to contact the taxi company and restaurant immediately,' he added, although this time with the level of enthusiasm Tom had been expecting earlier.

'I think there's something else you could do,' suggested Tom.

'What is that?' asked Peters.

'I think it would be useful to dig a bit deeper into her background. The check which Milner ran was fairly superficial. If we look a bit further back then there might be some more relevant information about her.'

'On that one, at least, I'm ahead of you,' replied Peters. 'I've already started doing that. I'll let you know if we turn up anything interesting.'

'Thank you, Sir,' answered Tom, taking his cue from Peters that their conversation was coming to an end.

'I'll call you when I get the report back. In the meantime, if there is anything else, you think I can do, don't hesitate to contact me.'

After his conversation with Superintendent Peters, Tom

spent the rest of the morning and early afternoon reviewing all of the *Torch* files. He didn't necessarily think he had missed anything important, but he often found it useful to approach these things again with a fresh mind. Just as he was finishing, his mobile rang. It was Milner.

'Good afternoon, Sir,' he said in a tone which was enthusiastic and friendly even by his own high standards.

'Good afternoon, Milner. Did you speak with Derek?'

'I did, Sir. Yes.' He then added, almost as an afterthought, 'He sends his regards by the way.'

'Where are you? Are you at the station?' asked Tom, suddenly sounding concerned.

'Yes, I am, Sir,' he replied, instinctively lowering his voice.

'Why don't you come round to my house? That way we won't be disturbed.'

'You make it sound as though I shouldn't be heard speaking with you,' said Milner, with a light laugh.

If you only knew, thought Tom. He quickly explained. 'I just think it would be better if you told me what he said outside of the station, that's all.'

Tom didn't like putting any more pressure on Milner, particularly after asking him to check up on Pauline. But he knew how these situations could be interpreted. If Milner was seen and heard whispering down the phone then that would be bound to arouse suspicions. Better to remove that possibility entirely.

'Okay, Sir,' replied Milner. 'I've just got some things to clear up first. Would five o'clock be a good time?'

'Five o'clock is perfect,' answered Tom, making clear his own gratitude.

Milner arrived on time, at five o'clock precisely.

Tom led him into his kitchen. 'Can I get you a cup of coffee? I was going to have something myself,' said Tom.

'Coffee would be great, Sir,' replied Milner.

Tom filled the kettle and switched it on. 'Seems to be getting better,' said Tom, pointing at Milner's face. 'I can now see both of your eyes.'

'Yes. I think it's getting better every day,' he replied, automatically putting his hand to his face. 'But I've got another appointment with my GP later in the week. Hopefully, he'll tell me everything is fine now.'

213

'I wouldn't build up your hopes too soon,' said Tom. 'I suspect it will be a while yet before you've regained all of your natural good looks. Walker did a good job on you.'

Unfortunately, despite his best intentions, all Tom's words did were to remind Milner about the attack. 'Yes. I suppose he did,' replied Milner, unable to resist touching his face once again.

By now the kettle had boiled and Tom poured the hot water into a mug. 'Milk and two sugars, isn't it?' he asked.

'Actually, Sir, it's just milk. No sugar thank you.'

'When did you give up sugar?' asked Tom. 'I suppose it's all to do with this healthy lifestyle you've now adopted. Incidentally, how is the running coming along?'

'Fine, Sir,' was all that Milner could bring himself to say as he checked to see if DCI Stone had still reached for the sugar.

By now they were seated at Tom's kitchen table. 'So, what did Derek say?' asked Tom.

'I explained to him exactly the scenario you had described and then asked if it was technically possible.'

'And what did he say?' asked Tom, sipping at his tea, trying to appear as ambivalent as possible.

'To be honest, Sir, I didn't understand half of what he was saying. It was far too technical for me.'

'I know what you mean. But now you can see why I asked you to do it rather asking him myself,' said Tom. 'But he does know his stuff.'

'After he had finished I asked him to summarise so I could explain it to you. Anyway, that seemed to do the trick.'

'And what was that?' asked Tom.

'Basically, he said that it is possible for someone to interrupt a radio transmission undetected. But it would require good knowledge of the radio frequencies.'

Tom looked thoughtful before asking, 'Has he any experience of this happening before?'

'Only unsuccessful attempts which failed due to human error or technical incompetence. What he doesn't know, however, is if it has ever worked successfully.'

'Did you ask him how he would be able tell if the radio transmissions had been intercepted?' asked Tom.

'I asked him everything you told me to,' replied a slightly indignant Milner. 'He said he would need to have a recording of the full transmission. If he had that he could then run various tests on it. He did explain what they were but it wasn't long before he had lost me again. The basic point though, is that he would need the original transmission.'

'Thank you, Milner. You did a good job there.'

'Could I ask why you want to know all of this, Sir?' asked Milner, clearly interested.

Under normal circumstances Tom would probably not even have acknowledged Milner's question but, in truth, he was still feeling guilty about asking him to check up on Pauline.

'I'm sorry, but I can't tell you right now. But I promise I will as soon as possible,' he answered uncharacteristically politely, before adding, 'I think that's the least I owe you.'

Milner was tempted to ask DCI Stone why he felt he was owed anything. Instead he simply said. 'Is there anything else I can do, Sir?'

'Not at the moment. I think you've done enough for me already. But rest assured, if there is anything else, you'll be the first to know.'

Chapter 34

As soon as Tom thought Derek would be at work he called him. 'Morning Derek. It's Tom. Tom Stone.'

Overnight, he had decided not to involve Milner in any further follow-up conversations with Derek. There was a risk that Milner's curiosity would get the better of him and he would eventually start to ask difficult questions. It would be better for him if he knew as little as possible about this.

'Tom. How are you? I had that young DS of yours here yesterday asking me lots of questions about radio transmissions,' he said, before muttering, as much to himself as to Tom, 'What was his name?'

Tom helped him. 'Milner. Detective Sergeant Milner.'

'Milner. That's right. A bit young for a DS, if you don't mind me saying so. Also quite a serious young man, although he looked a bit fearsome with all of that bruising on his face. How did it happen?'

'All in the line of duty. He was attacked whilst making an arrest.'

'That's the problem these days. Villains don't have any respect for the law any more,' Derek replied with uncharacteristic humour.

'You're right there,' answered Tom, hoping his reply would prevent any further discussions about the past morality of criminals. Either it worked or, more likely, Derek was impatient to get back to his work.

'How can I help you? I assume you need something from me and that's why you've called me. Am I right?'

'Right, as usual,' replied Tom, trying not to sound patronising.

'You detectives are all the same,' said Derek, with a little laugh. 'You get all the glory whilst we do all of the real smart work.'

This seemed like a good moment for Tom to mention the reason for his call. 'And that's why I'm calling you, Derek. DS

Milner passed on your comments about what would be involved in intercepting police radio messages.'

'So, if he's passed on my comments already, there must be something else you need from me,' suggested Derek. 'What is it you want? Nothing time-consuming I hope because I'm up to my eyes in it right now.'

Tom knew Derek was the type of person who was always up to his eyes in it. In fact, he positively thrived on being up to his eyes in it. Anyway, he had always subscribed to the principle that if you needed anything to be done quickly you should always try and delegate to someone who was already busy.

Tom decided there was little value to be gained in skirting around the issue. And besides, Derek was the type of person who also appreciated clear direction. He definitely wasn't the type who responded to subtle nuances of speech.

'I'd like you to get hold of a recent operational radio transmission and run some tests, or whatever you have to do, to see if it has been interfered with.'

'Interfered with? Do you mean blocked or changed?' asked Derek, his questions now betraying his sudden increased interest.

'Either of those,' replied Tom. 'Or even possibly both of them. I'd like you to find out if, at any time, and however briefly, the transmission was hijacked.'

'That part should be relatively straightforward, although it might take some time. But the more difficult part will be to get hold of the tapes in the first place. You mentioned it relates to an operation. Do you have the tapes?'

'No I don't,' he answered.

'So how recent was the operation?'

'It happened a few weeks ago. I'm sure though you have ways of getting hold of the tape. You must do this all the time.'

Derek's voice suddenly reflected a growing concern. 'Is this an official request?'

'No,' replied Tom, before quickly adding, 'well, not at this stage anyway. But it is urgent. I know you're always incredibly busy but I'd really appreciate it if you could find time to work on this.'

'So, it's not official then,' suggested Derek, seemingly more concerned with the first part of Tom's answer.

Tom hesitated slightly before replying. 'Look Derek. I'm asking if you can do this for me as an old friend. It's not official, but you've known me long enough to know I wouldn't ask you to do this if it wasn't very important. You also need to know, at this stage, it's just between the two of us.'

'I have to keep this secret as well. So, it's unofficial and secret? Is that what you're telling me?' replied Derek, clearly now enjoying making Tom work hard for his help.

'It is, I'm afraid,' answered Tom.

'Okay,' answered Derek without any hesitation. 'As you say, we've known each other long enough for me to sense when something is important. What is it you'd like me to do?'

So Tom told him.

Tom and Mary had arranged to have lunch together at the same pub bistro where they had first met.

It was Mary's idea. She felt that it might, temporarily at least, help to take their minds off what was happening. As Tom waited for Mary to arrive his mind, yet again, focused on the situation he was now confronted with. The one positive in all of this, though, was his feelings for Mary, and he was sure she felt the same.

His inbuilt antenna, however, was beginning to pick up strong signals indicating that, if he wasn't careful, even this relationship was at risk. There was nothing specific that he could point to, just his well-used additional sense. It definitely wasn't what he wanted but he knew that, sometimes, events spun out of control, leaving you almost powerless to control them. He could feel this might be one of those occasions.

He was so engrossed in his own thoughts that he didn't notice Mary approaching. 'Hello,' she said. 'Is this seat taken?'

Tom looked up and smiled. 'Actually it is. I'm saving it for someone who means a lot to me. But I suppose you can have it until she arrives.'

Mary leaned forward and kissed him. 'It's good to hear you've still got a sense of humour,' she said, smiling 'How have you been?' she went on with a more serious edge to her voice. 'I've been really worried about you.'

'I have to admit,' replied Tom, 'I'm finding all of this free time quite difficult to handle. I guess I'm just not used to sitting around, without anything specific to do. And, so far, it's only been a couple of days.'

'I suspected as much. I know it's pointless me telling you to try and keep yourself occupied but, nonetheless, I'm sure it's the right thing to do.'

'I'm trying to but all it does is confirm to me that, outside of the force, I have very few interests,' Tom said, a little too honestly.

'But you have me – or don't I count as one of your outside interests?' asked Mary, maintaining her more upbeat tone.

Tom took hold of both her hands, and looking into her eyes said, 'You, Mary Parker, are my number one interest. Inside or outside.'

Mary, once again, leaned forward and kissed him. 'Do you know,' she said, becoming quite emotional, 'that's one of the nicest things anyone has ever said to me.'

The next hour went far too quickly for Tom. Although they both tried desperately to try and maintain a more upbeat tone of conversation it was obvious the situation regarding the rape allegation was never too far away from their thoughts. Tom, sensing this, eventually said, 'I spoke with Superintendent Peters yesterday. I think we might have something which will help to disprove Pauline Jones's allegation.'

'That's wonderful,' said a clearly delighted Mary. 'Are you able to tell me what it is?'

'I don't see why not,' answered Tom. He then told her about the taxis and Pauline leaving her car in the pub car park. After he had finished she said, although this time less excitedly than previously, 'So that's good news, isn't it?'

'Yes it is but, unfortunately, all it proves is that we didn't go back to my house together. She might claim she arrived later,' he explained. 'But it certainly doesn't do any harm.'

'So, what happens next?' asked Mary.

'I would imagine she will be confronted with this information and, in light of it, offered the opportunity to withdraw her allegation,' he suggested, although without any great enthusiasm.

Mary picked up on this. 'You don't sound very confident. Do you think she'll still stick to her story?'

'I really don't know. Maybe I'm just trying to protect

myself by assuming the worst. What I do know though is that Pauline Jones is a highly charged and very irrational woman. So it's probably best not to get ahead of ourselves.'

Mary decided to change the subject. 'What are you doing for the rest of the day?' Before Tom could answer she continued, 'Why don't you stay with me tonight? I don't like the thought of you being all alone.'

Tom immediately thought about all of the *Reporting* files he had planned to finish reviewing. But the thought of spending more time with Mary was suddenly a far more attractive proposition. 'That would be nice. Why don't I go home and collect a few things. What time will you have finished work at the shop?'

'I should be home by about 6 o'clock.'

It was just after 2.30 when Tom arrived back home. He had barely got in the door when his mobile started to ring. He could see it was Superintendent Peters. 'Tom. I'm glad I was able to get hold of you. I have some good news.'

Tom tried not to get too excited, as he didn't want to betray his hopes. 'Is it about the taxis?' he asked, successfully keeping his excitement under control.

'Exactly. The taxi company has checked its records and spoken to the drivers. They both confirm what you said about booking separate taxis. In fact the taxi driver who took Pauline Jones home also remembered just how drunk she was. She eventually fell asleep in the taxi and he had to wake her when they arrived at her house.'

'And what about her car? Is there any CCTV footage in the pub car park?' asked Tom.

'That's the other good news. It's clearly visible in the car park all night.'

'Has she been told about all of this yet?'

'No. Not yet. We've only just had the confirmation from the taxi company. I thought you would like to know straight away.'

'Thank you very much, Sir. I appreciate that but, as both of us know, these type of allegations are very unpredictable in terms of the eventual outcome.'

'Well I know. But it's a good start nonetheless,' replied Peters, echoing Tom's earlier comment to Mary. 'I'll let you know how she reacts when we present this to her.'

After he had ended his conversation with Superintendent Peters, Tom saw he had a missed call. It was from Milner. Tom could detect more than a hint of concern in Milner's voice as he listened to the message asking him to call him as soon as possible.

'Sorry to call you Sir,' said Milner, after Tom had returned his call. 'But you did ask me to contact you when we received the initial report from the pathology people.'

'I did,' answered Tom. 'I'm assuming from the tone of your voice that it's not particularly good news.'

'Not exactly. They have been able to confirm that the body was that of a man, aged between twenty-five and thirty-five. They also confirm that the man died recently. Their best estimate is within the past few weeks. But the really worrying thing is that the most likely cause of death is some kind of head trauma. And that's not all,' he added. 'I've also now received full details relating to the death of Darren Wood. The PM confirms that he suffered a massive cardiac arrest, almost certainly brought on by exposure to the live rail on the railway, although that simply confirms what we suspected anyway. But it was what was found in his wallet that is the most interesting.'

'Go on then,' said Tom rather impatiently after Milner had paused for what seemed like dramatic effect.

'They found a credit card belonging to Maciej Sipowicz.'

Tom remained silent as he tried to take in these latest developments.

'Are you still there, Sir?' asked Milner.

'Yes, I'm still here Milner.' He then went on, although as much for his own benefit as Milner's, 'The evidence is now so compelling. First the argument with him. Then the beating, followed by his mysterious disappearance. And now the discovery of his credit card on the person of one of the suspected assailants. Finally, and perhaps the most worrying, the discovery of an unidentified body at a location known to all of the suspects. Even the most fervent believer in coincidences might have difficulty in explaining this series of events.'

'What do you suggest we do now, Sir?'

'Milner, it's your case now. What would *you* suggest?'

'I think we should start to get heavy with Walker and the

others. The time for pussyfooting around has come and gone. This is now potentially a murder investigation.'

Tom was a little surprised by Milner's aggressive tone, although quietly pleased that he now seemed to really have the bit between his teeth.

'I agree,' he simply replied. 'It looks like you might now be handling your very own murder case.'

Chapter 35

Tom and Mary had spent a wonderful night together. Whatever the reason, they both knew that this was a brief, albeit enjoyable, distraction from what lay ahead. Next morning Tom had gently turned down Mary's suggestion to stay with her for the next couple of days. He felt, now he'd committed himself to progressing the *Torch* investigation, that he had to focus all of his energies on it. He was also wanted, if possible, to keep in touch with the Maciej Sipowicz situation. The more he thought about this the angrier he became about his suspension. Although he had every confidence in Milner, there was still a part of him which wanted to ensure that he got this right. He had to admit, however, that there was another reason, relating to his own professional and personal satisfaction, of wanting to be involved in a potential murder inquiry. But that was now not possible.

Instead he needed to ensure that all his free time was used as constructively as possible in trying to resolve the secret informant investigation. On his way back home he began to realise just how much his ability to conduct this investigation had been seriously restricted by his suspension. Perhaps he had been fooling himself to think he could carry on with it under the current circumstances. It was quite a depressing thought and his mood wasn't helped when he took a call from Superintendent Peters.

'Tom. It's Superintendent Peters. I have some news for you. Well, actually – as the old saying goes – some good news and some bad news. I thought you would want to know about it as soon as possible.'

'How about giving me the bad news first. That way, at least, I'll have something to look forward to,' answered Tom.

'Well, the bad news relates to Pauline Jones's reaction when we presented that evidence to her.'

'How did she respond?'

'Initially she claimed we had rigged the evidence about the taxis. But when we presented her with the taxi company's records she started to change tack. She then said she must have got the place wrong. Although I'm not quite sure how you can get confused about the place where you were attacked. Anyway, she now claims you came over to her house later that evening and that's where the attack took place.'

'As you say, an easy mistake to make.'

Superintendent Peters continued. 'According to her you arrived at her place sometime after midnight. She let you in. You both had a few more drinks. She passed out and when she woke you were ... well that's when she said you were attacking her. She started to scream. You panicked and then left. That's my potted version, of course, but you get the gist.'

For a moment nothing was said. Eventually when Tom next spoke it was obvious he was finding it difficult to control his emotions. 'And do you believe that fairy story?'

'Tom. I can understand your anger but it doesn't help getting angry with me. I'm only recounting what she said.'

The silence returned, allowing Tom time to regain his composure. 'I apologise, Sir, for that outburst. It was totally uncalled for. I know you're only trying to help.'

'But now let me tell you about the good news.'

Tom could feel his heart suddenly begin to beat faster as he waited for Superintendent Peters to continue.

'We went back over her police record and found something very interesting. The reason we originally missed it was because she was known as Pauline Cheswick then. She later changed her surname to Jones,' explained Superintendent Peters. He carried straight on. 'She tried to blackmail a man who she claimed had sex with her. He was a quite a well-known businessman, who had received a lot of local media coverage relating to a messy divorce. She contacted him and threatened that, unless he paid her £5,000, she would go to the newspapers and tell them that he had tried to rape her. She claimed that the attack took place on a specific date. Fortunately for him and unfortunately for her, on that particular date he was out of the country on a golfing holiday with three friends. It was then that he went to the police.'

'So, she has form when it comes to making this type of allegation,' suggested Tom, the tone of his voice betraying his relief.

'Exactly,' replied Superintendent Peters. 'It also looks as though there might be something in your theory that she likes to be associated with men who have been in the news.'

'Did she receive a sentence?' asked Tom, without any reference to what Peters had just said.

'No. The businessman didn't want to pursue the case, so it was dropped. Fortunately though, it was entered onto her file.'

'Does she know that we know about this?'

'Not yet. We've only just had it confirmed. As I said, I wanted you to know first.'

'Thank you, Sir. I really appreciate that.'

Briefly they both remained silent.

Finally Superintendent Peters said, 'Even when she is confronted with this latest evidence it's possible she will still want to pursue the allegation. And if she does, and finds herself a good lawyer, then I'm afraid it might still mean a court case.'

'I know,' answered Tom. 'I just have to hope she sees sense. Or something unexpected crops up that convinces her to change her mind.'

Chapter 36

It was a call he took from Derek which finally removed any doubt Tom might have had about pursuing his covert investigation.

'Hello Derek. I wasn't expecting to hear back from you so soon. I hope you aren't about to tell me you can't find anything.'

'Just the opposite actually.'

'Really? So, what have you found?' asked Tom, his voice rising in anticipation.

'Patience. Patience,' answered Derek. 'You detectives are all the same. All you want to know is the result. You're never interested in how it was achieved. I bet you're the type of person who usually goes straight to the back of the book to read the ending.'

'Okay, you win,' replied Tom with a sigh. 'Go ahead and tell me how you did it.'

'That's better. You see – you can do it if you really want to.' Derek remained silent, almost as though he was intentionally building the tension. Tom was just about to tell him to get on with it when Derek spoke again. 'First of all, it wasn't easy getting hold of the radio tape. You can't believe the amount of red tape you have to get through before they'll release them. And even then they don't just release them to anyone.' For one agonising moment Tom thought Derek was about to talk him through the entire bureaucratic process. Fortunately his fears didn't materialise. Instead, and almost reading Tom's mind, Derek then said, 'But I won't bore you with what I had to do to get hold of it. Suffice to say that I had to call in quite a few favours, as well as having to tell one or two small white lies.' He paused, no doubt hoping that Tom would recognise what he'd had to do.

Tom didn't disappoint him. 'Derek. I can't begin to guess what you had to do. I'm sure it can't have been easy. All I can say is that I'm really grateful to you.' He hoped that would be sufficiently effusive.

It seemed as though it was, as Derek said, albeit with clear pride in his voice, 'That's all right. Occasionally I even surprise myself.'

Tom thought the danger now was that, as Derek was only just warming to his task of having a little fun at his expense, there was probably more of the same to follow. He decided, however, that a little assertiveness was now needed. 'Derek' he said, 'I know you are enjoying this but could you please tell me what you've found, otherwise, in future, I'll take my custom elsewhere.'

It seemed to do the trick. 'Well, your theory about the tape being tampered with was spot-on. Incidentally, you must tell me what it was which led you to believe that. But I suppose that can wait for later.' There was a momentary pause before he continued. 'Anyway, where was I? Oh yes, the tape. As I told, you the radio comms were definitely intercepted but the really interesting thing was what happened next.'

'And what did happen next?' asked Tom, confident he already knew the answer, although that didn't prevent his heartrate suddenly increasing.

'Actually, now that I think about it, perhaps intercepted is the wrong word,' mused Derek, perhaps intentionally increasing the tension even further. Tom resisted the temptation to say anything and, instead, waited for Derek to continue. Sure enough, once Derek realised Tom was not going to ask the obvious question, he tried once again to provoke Tom into making a comment. 'Yes,' said Derek. 'Intercepted is definitely the wrong word.'

Tom decided that unless he played Derek's game, he would never find out. 'Derek. I'm desperate to find out what the correct word is. Please put me out of my misery.'

Tom could imagine the smile of victory appearing on Derek's face and this was confirmed when he said, 'I knew you'd crack first.' Now Tom had finally acknowledged his victory, Derek began his explanation. 'I should have said hijacked. That's because additional, pre-recorded, words were, for a very brief period, dovetailed into the radio transmission and then deleted.' Before Tom could respond Derek continued. 'Well. When I say deleted, what I should have said was that someone tried to delete them. But they made a mistake,' he said, almost triumphantly.

'What mistake?' asked a slightly hesitant Tom, torn between wanting to know but not wanting a complicated technical answer. Fortunately, Derek resisted the second option.

'As I said, they tried to delete that part of the transmission but, frankly, it wasn't done very well. Perhaps they were in a hurry or interrupted,' he suggested. 'Or maybe they weren't as clever as they thought they were. Whatever the reason, they must not have realised that it could be recovered by the use of some very clever software that I just happen to have.'

Tom, whilst suspecting that the radio comms held the answer to the night's events, did not anticipate this. 'You said pre-recorded. Do you mean words had already been recorded and then inserted?'

'Isn't that what pre-recorded means?' asked Derek, barely able to conceal his contempt at Tom's apparent inability to understand his own native language.

'How can you tell that they were pre-recorded and not said live?' he asked, genuinely intrigued.

'Well. Once I started to look for that possibility it was quite easy. It was just a case of analysing all of the transmission data. Do you want me to explain it to you?' asked Derek, an increased level of excitement in his voice.

'I would definitely like to know. But can we leave it for later?' he asked diplomatically, before adding, 'What were the words which were added? Were they "Go, go"?'

'They were, but I suspect you might have known that all along,' Derek said, not trying to hide his admiration. 'But to continue. Once I got my hands on the tape, it didn't take me long to spot the gap in the transmission. What is really interesting though was that the words were spoken by the same man who was on the transmission earlier. In total it was only a matter of a couple of seconds. Very clever really.' He then added, so as not to leave Tom in any doubt, 'But, however, not as clever as me.'

'One more question,' said Tom. 'I'm assuming, whoever did this would have needed to have full access to the correct radio frequency. Is that right?'

'It is. But it's over to you now to find out who did this.'

228

'Thanks Derek. You're a real star. I can't begin to tell you just how important it is what you've been able to do. But could I ask you to do one other thing for me?'

'Why not?' answered Derek. 'You will anyway.'

'Could you write all of this up for me? The technical stuff, the data analysis, the timings. Everything. And, Derek. At this stage it's still just between the two of us.'

'So that's actually two more things you would like me to do. Put all of this is a report and don't tell anyone what I've been doing.'

'And I forgot to say,' added Tom. 'I need your report tomorrow.'

Tom now found himself with a real dilemma. There was no doubt that the information provided by Derek had elevated his investigation to a seriously higher level. The problem now, though, was what to do with that information.

The logical next step would be to inform Superintendent Peters. But there was one minor problem. He was suspended from carrying out any police work. It would be bad enough flaunting that restriction with any official work but, with unofficial work, the consequences would potentially be even more serious for him.

He decided he would sleep on it.

Chapter 37

'Good morning, Sir. It's Tom Stone.'

In the end the decision had been fairly straightforward. The new information about the radio transmissions was the deciding factor. This was the first real hard evidence, rather than just merely circumstantial, that someone within the West London Regional Force had sabotaged, or at least helped to sabotage, *Operation Torch*. Despite all of the personal and professional risks to his career, Tom couldn't just ignore what he now knew.

'Hello Tom,' answered Superintendent Peters. 'If you're calling to find out about Pauline Jones then, unfortunately, there's nothing new to report.'

'Actually, Sir, that's not the reason for my call. Although, of course, as you can imagine, I'm eager to get that resolved as quickly as possible.'

'So, if it's not that then what is it?' asked a curious Peters.

Tom dispensed with any preamble. 'I've just received some new information relating to *Operation Torch*, which, in my opinion, absolutely confirms the informant theory.'

Momentarily nothing was said. When the silence was broken Tom was surprised by Peters' question. Rather than asking what the information was he just said. 'How did you come across this information?'

There was little value in trying to sugar-coat his reply. 'It came from an old contact of mine. There's nothing he can't do with radio transmissions. I'd asked him to try and get hold of the comms tape for the night of the operation. He did some complicated analysis of it and came up with a surprising result.'

'When did you ask him to do this?' asked Peters. Tom noticed he still hadn't asked about the actual information.

'A couple of days ago,' replied Tom.

There was undisguised anger in Peters' voice as he said. 'A

couple of days ago, if you remember, you were suspended. Suspended from *all* duties. I made that absolutely clear at the time. But you still chose to deliberately ignore my order. I can't begin to tell you how angry I am. You do realise that you have now placed me in an impossible situation, don't you?'

'I realise that, Sir, but I did this off my own bat. I also understand the potential consequences but it was something which I just had to do.'

Superintendent Peters' anger had still not subsided. 'Something *you* had to do? Can I remind you that I'm still your superior officer. Whilst you are flagrantly disobeying my orders, in order to go off on your wild goose chase, I'm expected to pat you on the back and say well done, am I? Do I need to remind you why I suspended you in the first place?'

It took all of Tom's self-control not to respond in kind. Instead he simply said, 'I understand all of that, Sir. But at least give me the opportunity to tell you what I've found out. After that, I will accept any additional disciplinary action you think is appropriate.'

Another tense silence followed. Superintendent Peters finally responded. 'Come and see me this evening at seven o'clock. Come straight up to my office. The fewer people who see you the better.' The Superintendent still had not asked what information was so important that Tom was willing to risk his career in order to obtain it.

Tom arrived outside Superintendent Peters' office at seven o'clock precisely. In his hand he held a buff-coloured file which contained Derek's report. Peters' PA, Janice, was still there and personally escorted Tom into his office.

After the door had been closed Superintendent Peters spoke. 'Tom. I make no apology for the way I spoke with you earlier. What you did was totally unacceptable. I have to tell you that I am giving serious consideration to further disciplinary action.'

'That's your prerogative, Sir,' replied Tom.

'Yes, it is,' answered Peters. 'So, what is it you have found out?' He sounded slightly disinterested.

Tom told him about the gap in the radio transmission and the addition of the extra words. 'You'll remember DCI Shaw was adamant he had not given the "go" call whilst DC Bennett was certain that he had heard DCI Shaw say it. In fact, it turns out that they were both correct and this proves it,' he said, pointing at Derek's report.

'That's just incredible. Are you absolutely certain?' asked Peters, his earlier anger now gone.

'I am,' replied Tom.

Superintendent Peters picked up the file and quickly scanned the report. After he'd read it he placed it on the table. 'So, we now know how it was done but this still doesn't tell us who did it.'

'That's true. But it's a hell of a clue though. In my opinion, we can now focus in on who had access to the radio comms that night. It won't be easy, but at least we can now eliminate a few more of the people on our list.'

'For example who?' asked Peters.

'Well, DC Bennett and DCI Shaw for starters. If Bennett was the informant then he's paid a huge personal price. He's an absolute wreck at the moment. His health is suffering, and probably his marriage is as well. And as far as DCI Shaw is concerned then it would take the most ardent conspiracy theorist to argue that he would take the risk of intercepting the transmission and then substituting his own pre-recorded voice.'

'Unless he had an accomplice, of course,' replied Peters, now showing interest in Tom's theory.

'Yes. That's always possible,' admitted Tom. 'And I did consider that, but immediately discounted it.'

'Why?' asked Peters, his face showing surprise.

'The only time he could have done it was when he left you and ran around to the front with DC Booker. That took them less than a minute. DC Booker has already confirmed that they got there as quickly as possible and at no stage did DCI Shaw use his radio. Similarly, he has confirmed the same regarding Booker. And anyway, she's not on our list and, frankly, even if she was I just don't believe she would be involved.'

'So, who does that leave?' asked Superintendent Peters.

'DS Anderson, DC James, Sergeant Gunn and yourself,' Tom answered without any hesitation.

'Tom. You seem determined to continue with your little

game of having me on the list. Frankly, the joke is starting to wear a bit thin now. And anyway, don't you think this is all a bit odd?' asked Peters.

'I don't understand, Sir.'

'The fact that I'm still on your list of suspects and you're still on my list of suspended officers.'

'I see what you mean,' replied Tom. 'That's got to be a first.'

For a moment it seemed Superintendent Peters was about to say something else relating to his inclusion on the suspect list. But when he spoke he simply said. 'So, what do you propose next?'

'That really depends on the status of my suspension,' Tom answered, speculatively.

'Tom. I can see how this latest information has moved the investigation on significantly but the fact remains that you are suspended until the Pauline Jones case has been resolved. You should be in no doubt about that. On this occasion I'm willing to make an exception, but let me be clear.' He looked directly at Tom. 'If you continue to pursue this whilst you are suspended, I will have no choice but to instigate further disciplinary actions. Do you understand that?'

'I understand,' answered Tom in a resigned tone.

'Good. I'm glad we are both agreed on that because I would hate to be the one who ends your police career. In the meantime stay away from this, or any other, case. I will contact you as and when the Pauline Jones situation develops.'

'What will you do with the report?' asked Tom, pointing at the file.

'I need to think about that,' replied Superintendent Peters, picking it up and placing it in one of his drawers. 'In the meantime it's better if it stays here with me.'

As he drove home after his meeting with Superintendent Peters, Tom could perhaps be forgiven for thinking he had been offered and accepted a poisoned chalice when Peters had persuaded him to take on the investigation. But he only had himself to blame. It wasn't as if he had gone into this with his eyes closed.

In fact, all of his instincts had told him the odds were that it would end disastrously. Well, at least if it all ended with him being thrown out of the force, or worse, he could always console himself knowing they were still working. What he hadn't expected though was just how much he had been on his own during this inquiry.

Although Superintendent Peters had hinted at this it had still come as a huge frustration to him. What was the expression? Working with one hand tied behind your back. At times it felt as though he was in a straightjacket.

And that was before his suspension. Despite those promises of support at the early stages of the investigation, he had felt, at least latterly, that Superintendent Peters' enthusiasm had seriously waned. In fact, almost to the point where he now had the distinct impression that Peters wished he had never sanctioned this investigation in the first place.

The list of possible suspects had now been whittled down to four. The personal information provided by Peters had helped, but it was largely due to good detective work, and a healthy dose of luck, that he'd been able to do this. He couldn't keep relying on Lady Luck. From now on it would be hard information which would provide the final answers. And obtaining that hard information would now appear to be almost impossible.

Certainly Superintendent Peters was unlikely to provide it. Almost every request made by him had been met with either, at best, delays, or, more worryingly, refusals. Okay, Superintendent Peters had never point blank refused to provide him with information but, in practical terms, the result was the same. He could just about buy into the reasons why Peters wouldn't or couldn't let him have his own personal file. But, despite many requests, he was still waiting for the financial information on each of the suspects. Right from the start he had stressed just how important this was to the outcome of the investigation.

Given the current circumstances there now seemed even less chance of getting it. But despite all of these obstacles he wasn't about to give up. Any lingering doubts he might have had concerning his informant theory had been blown away by Derek's work on the radio transmissions. This had also now given him the additional motivation to continue.

What he needed, though, was another breakthrough. Another vital piece of information which would allow him to home in even closer. But, as he drove home, he couldn't think where that was likely to come from.

But all of his instincts told him that something needed to happen. And happen quickly.

Chapter 38

It was the early morning phone call from Milner which woke him. Over the past few months Tom had almost developed an extra intuitive sense when speaking with him. He was convinced that Milner would never make a good poker player. He tended to wear his heart on his sleeve or, more precisely, if it was possible, in his voice. Whilst that was not always the best thing, if you were a policeman regularly dealing with criminals, he couldn't help thinking that this was one of Milner's more endearing features. Tom could usually instantly tell whether he was about to impart good news or bad news. On this particular occasion his guess was that that it was good news. He was right, at least to begin with. Milner could hardly get his words out quickly enough. Walker, Lomas and Stevenson had all now been separately and formally interviewed. Not surprisingly they had all denied having any knowledge of or involvement in Maciej Sipowicz's disappearance. They had also denied beating him up. Even after they had each been confronted with McNulty's witness statement they all defiantly and rather impressively stuck to their story. They hadn't seen anything and they didn't know anything. It was only after Milner had presented the details relating to the discovery of the body, and the fact that this was now being treated as a murder investigation, that the first cracks in their story started to appear. It was Stevenson who realised the seriousness of the situation and finally admitted what had happened.

He confirmed what McNulty had witnessed. That there had been an argument with Sipowicz about one of the metal items that they'd stolen. It then developed into a fight and, according to Stevenson, Walker had held him whilst Lomas and Darren Wood had punched him. After Walker released his hold on Sipowicz he fell and hit his head quite hard on the floor. Initially they thought that he was just play-acting to protect himself, and it was then that Darren Wood gave him a kick just for good measure. After a few minutes, when Maciej had still not moved, they began to think that perhaps he had not been play-acting after all and, after checking him, they realised that he was, in fact, dead. They began to panic and, rather than call the emergency services, decided to hatch a plan to dispose of the dead body. Eventually someone came up with the gruesome idea of putting the body in one of the old cars at the scrap yard and then torching it, hoping that all evidence would be destroyed. After Milner heard this it immediately prompted another key question. Someone at the scrap yard must therefore have either known about this or been more intimately involved. It didn't take long to confirm that, in fact, it was the latter. Unbeknown to even his father, Walker and the others were separately also supplying William Brady's son with stolen metal. It was he who agreed to let them put Maciej's body in one of the scrap cars and so, as a result of this new information, James Brady was now also in police custody. All that was now missing was for DNA evidence to confirm that the body in the car was indeed that of Maciej Sipowicz. Unfortunately there was little doubt that was the case.

As Milner recounted the story Tom had real mixed emotions. There was a degree of professional satisfaction that this gang of criminals, and their associates, had now been charged. He had little doubt that it was never their intention to murder Maciej but the callous way in which they had disposed of the body was unlikely to be ignored by any jury. They deserved everything that was coming their way. But he also felt real sadness that an innocent person, Maciej Sipowicz, had been tragically caught up in all of this. He knew that Milner also felt the same and this much was obvious when he mentioned that he was planning to go and visit Maciej's girlfriend Anna. Tom had suggested that he go along with him but Milner, to his credit, had insisted that he wanted to do it.

Tom was now sitting at the table in his kitchen. He was staring intently at a sheet of A4 plain paper immediately in front of him. It contained four names: Superintendent Tony Peters, DS John Anderson, DC William James and Sergeant Peter Gunn.

Alongside each man he had written a few words. He had found, over the years, that whenever his mind seemed overloaded or confused it helped if he wrote down a few things. Unfortunately, he wasn't one of those gifted people who could think in a multi-dimensional way. His brain worked best the old-fashioned way, by writing everything down and then systematically distilling all of the information until he was left with just a few key words. As he viewed his work there was a sudden realisation just how much he still didn't know about those four men.

At the top of his list was Superintendent Peters. Although he had worked with him for less than a year, and despite his recent suspension, Tom still held him in high regard. He didn't even mind the fact that Peters was significantly younger than him. In the past he had always been honest and straightforward in all of their dealings. Even if that involved bad news.

But, as he had got sucked deeper and deeper into the *Operation Torch* investigation, he had begun to see a different side. Whereas in the pre-*Torch* period he had been decisive, Tom had noticed just how evasive Peters had become recently. This change in behaviour simply reinforced Tom's natural instinct not to believe in coincidences. There must be a reason for this change in behaviour. The little he already knew about Peters suggested he was a career cop, destined for the very highest echelons of the Met. He had all of the necessary qualities. He was young, ambitious and clearly very talented. He also had that natural disarming charm which allowed a person to say or do almost anything without offending.

There was also, when required, a streak of ruthlessness in his character. But that was almost mandatory if you had ambitions to get to the very top. His personal life, though, was a bit of a mystery. He knew he was married. Well, at least, that was what he had assumed from the family photograph which took pride of place in his office. Himself, his wife and two young children. Despite the tensions of the past few days he really liked Superintendent Peters. He sincerely hoped he wasn't the informant. And, anyway, what would he have to gain?

Although all of the other names had even fewer words

alongside them, his eye did keep coming back to DC James's name and two of the words he had written: Techie expert. As he read this he recalled his conversation with Dave Richards. Tom knew that any compliment, however backhanded, from Dave constituted a ringing endorsement, particularly as he was not known for his use of lavish praise. But, despite this Tom still couldn't take him off the list until he knew more about Detective Constable James and, in particular, why he had upped sticks and moved south.

Sergeant Gunn was another person on his list whom he had known for many years and they had worked together on numerous cases during that time. Like DC Bennett, Tom knew him as a dedicated and hard-working officer who didn't appear to be particularly driven by ambition and seemed to be happy with his current position within the force. That was why he had been surprised when he read that he had, unsuccessfully, applied to switch from uniform into the CID.

Once again, Tom had discreetly sounded out a few of his colleagues, who worked with Gunn, to find out what sort of person he was. The most revealing conversation had been with Tom's long-time colleague Sergeant Pete Grey. Of course, he couldn't tell Pete the real reason for his questions. Even so he was sure Pete suspected there was more to it than just a few inoffensive questions about a mutual colleague. If Pete had any suspicions concerning Tom's motives then he kept them to himself. In the event, Pete had been able to fill in some of the background information which, up to then, had been missing.

According to Pete, he had been turned down on health grounds. He'd got through the initial interview but his regular health check had picked up a heart murmur. Nothing life-threatening, but enough to spook the selection panel. Tom had then asked Pete how Sergeant Gunn had reacted to his non-selection. As far as Tom was concerned this was the crucial factor and, as he often described it, all about shoulders. Was he the type of man who would metaphorically shrug his shoulders and carry on with his current police career or one who would grow a chip on it, blaming the force for wrecking his career aspirations?

Pete couldn't have been any clearer. Peter Gunn fell into the first category and, he confirmed, he personally had never heard him either feel sorry for himself or blame the Met for his situation. Whilst Tom valued Pete's opinion, he had learned through bitter experience that it was always advisable to obtain corroborative information. Once again details of his financial affairs could provide the answer. But in their absence he would just need to dig a bit deeper.

That only left DS John Anderson on his list. In many ways Anderson was, perhaps, the most interesting of all of the suspects and reminded him of himself early in his police career.

He was clearly ambitious – successfully switching into CID was testament to that. He had also gained rapid promotion to his current position of DS, albeit partly due to DCI Shaw's patronage. Certainly Shaw saw something exceptional in him. Perhaps it was the same drive and single-minded approach which he himself brought to his crime fighting.

But Tom saw that there had been a heavy price to pay for all of this full-on commitment. Just as in his own life there had been a failed marriage. Maybe it was a price he had been willing to pay. From what he had heard Anderson almost hero- worshipped DCI Shaw. Would such a person deliberately ruin the career of a person whom he idolised? He personally found it difficult to believe but, there again, his judgement, of late, was somewhat tarnished. The current situation with Pauline proved that.

Apart from helping to clear his mind a little he had to accept that, if the informant was one of the four names on the list, he was no nearer to finding him. So he decided he would make himself a cup of tea. He'd found in the past that the simple task of doing this occasionally helped him to think through various problems. He liked to think that it was due to some, as yet undiscovered, magical property in tea.

More likely it was due to the action of walking away from the problem momentarily. Loading the dishwasher was probably just as effective, although not nearly as pleasant. After he'd made the tea and resumed his seat at the kitchen table he had decided what he needed to do. Okay, it was not like some biblical revelation, but at least he now felt he was doing something rather than sitting around worrying why he was not doing anything.

So he spent the rest of the day going back and reviewing all of the information available to him, listing every person whose name had cropped up in his investigation, however seemingly unrelated, and then cross-referencing them in order to confirm their relationship and, more importantly, to see if any pattern emerged. He had found some old flip chart paper and, sticking a few sheets together, had used this to include all of the names.

By the time he had finished it looked as though a novice spider had unsuccessfully tried to spin its very first web. As Tom stood back to view it he felt a real sense of satisfaction. To anyone else it looked totally impenetrable but to him it was almost like a work of art – albeit from the abstract school. That was the good news.

The bad news was that he couldn't, as yet, recognise any pattern. Still, he would leave it in a visible place and hope that at some time he would spot something in it. In the past he'd found that the closer he looked at these connection maps the more confusing they appeared. Sometimes any pattern only became clear after a quick sideways glance. Anyway, that was the hope.

As he was surveying his handiwork his phone rang. It was Mary.

'Hello. I thought I'd call to see how you are and what you've been up to,' she said.

'Not a great deal, to be honest. Although I have now had the chance to tie up a few loose ends,' he said looking directly at the flip chart paper. 'Actually I have some good news regarding Pauline Jones.' He told her about the previous rape allegations.

'That's fantastic news,' she said. 'Surely that means she'll now have to withdraw her accusation against you.'

Tom, clearly sensing her excitement, attempted to let her down as gently as possible. 'No. Well, not yet anyway. I think it would be wise to assume that, despite this new evidence, she will continue with her claim. As I told you previously, she's the type of person who appears to enjoy notoriety. It seems to give her a real thrill to be in the spotlight. She's probably not willing to give up on that just yet.'

'But it must, at the very least, seriously weaken her case against you,' replied Mary hopefully.

'Only if it is thought to be admissible. The likelihood though, is that we wouldn't be able to use it.'

'But how can that be?' asked Mary, now starting to get angry. 'This proves that the woman is a fantasist and a liar. Surely that's relevant.'

'Mary, I agree, but unfortunately I don't have any influence over this. We'll just have to wait and see.'

Mary remained silent for a while. When she did speak she had regained her normal composure. 'I'm so sorry, Tom. The last thing you need is for me to get upset again when I should be supporting you.'

'You are supporting me. Trust me,' he answered and then, changing the subject, asked, 'Anyway how did your rehearsal go? It's *Macbeth* isn't it?' he asked.

'It's still early days, so it's still all a bit chaotic. In fact we still haven't finally decided on the parts yet. But it's always like that at the beginning. Anyway, we have a few months yet.'

Mary had been part of the North West Surrey Players amateur dramatic society for a number of years. Tom knew how much this meant to her and wanted to do everything possible to support her. 'When is it? After your last amazing performance in *King Lear* I can't wait to see you again.'

'Thanks for your support but, as you very well know, I only had one of the minor parts. But to answer your question, it's some time in March. I don't think the exact date has been finalised yet.'

Now it was her turn to change the subject. 'But what about this weekend? Should I get to you at the same time as last Saturday?' she asked and then added, with a light laugh, 'or bearing in mind what happened last time, should I arrive a bit earlier?'

'Good idea,' he replied, now laughing himself. 'At least that would allow us, this time, to have dinner at a reasonable time.'

But as they discussed the coming weekend, little did either of them realise just how much their world was about to change. And not for the better.

Chapter 39

Tom had spent most of Friday working on his cross-referencing chart and, where possible, obtaining more background information on some of the individuals, mainly via Google and Wikipedia. For those less-well-known people, his intention was to try and use his many contacts to fill in the background gaps. Although he had not yet achieved the breakthrough he had hoped for, the time he had invested had thrown up some tantalising clues for him to follow up on, particularly with regard to DCI Shaw.

But it was now Saturday morning and Mary was due later in the day. So he thought he would call in and see how DC Gary Bennett was coping. He timed his arrival, hoping that Julie, his wife, would already have left for her usual Saturday morning gym class. He felt Gary was more likely to open up to him if she wasn't there.

He knocked on the door and almost immediately it was opened by Gary. Tom was encouraged to see that he had made an effort to smarten himself up. He was clean-shaven and wearing beige chinos and a blue polo shirt rather than the grubby jeans and tee shirt he was wearing when they last met. 'DCI Stone. Twice in a week. I am honoured,' he said jokingly. 'Come in. I could do with a bit of company. All the kids are out and Julie has just left for the gym.'

Tom followed Gary into the kitchen. 'Cup of tea?' asked Gary.

'Yes, please,' replied Tom enthusiastically. 'Milk. No sugar if you don't mind. I have to say you look a lot better than you did this time last week. I was beginning to get really worried about you.'

'Well that's largely down to you. I realised I was behaving like a prat, by feeling sorry for myself. The strange thing was I knew I was taking it out on Julie and the kids but I just couldn't stop doing it.'

'Well, as I mentioned to you last week, you are a very fortunate man to have a wife like Julie.'

'I know. Well, I know now anyway. It's crazy really. If I had carried on acting as I did I could have lost Julie and the kids. I now realise they are the most important thing to me. Certainly more important than the Met. That's for sure.'

'Speaking as someone who lost his wife and son to the Met many years ago I wish I had realised that then.' Tom surprised himself by revealing so much personal information to Gary.

Gary handed Tom a mug of tea and they both sat at the kitchen table. 'How do you feel about the disciplinary meeting?' asked Tom. 'I bet you'll be glad when it's out of the way.'

'Funnily enough I'm not stressed about it anymore,' he answered. 'All I can do is tell it as I saw it. If I'm sacked then, to be honest, it will come as a relief. My only regret is that DCI Shaw is likely to get away it.'

'What do you mean?' asked Tom, taking another sip from his mug.

Gary hesitated briefly before he answered. 'I know he's a colleague of yours but it's like I told you last week. He's using me as the scapegoat. It'll be me that gets disciplined. Not him. At worst he'll probably just get his knuckles rapped. But, at some point, they'll find out he's not as smart as he thinks he is. It will be just a shame that I'm not there when it happens.'

Tom declined to respond to Gary's comments. 'Do you mind if I ask you about some of the other officers' roles on that night?'

If Gary had any suspicions about Tom's motives for wanting to return to the raid on Fuller's house he didn't show them.

Instead he simply said, 'Fire away.'

Tom picked his words very carefully. 'As I understand it, DS Anderson and DC James were also there that night. Can you remember what their specific roles were?'

'If I remember correctly DC James had been positioned around the back of the house with one of the uniformed officers. I think it might have been Peter Gunn. Yes, I'm sure it was Pete. Anyway, their role was to keep an eye on the back of the house and stop anyone from leaving after we went in. After we had all got into position the next time I saw them was when we were in the house and had started the search.'

'How did they seem?'

'Like everyone else,' he replied. 'They were shocked and then angry. Shocked when it became clear that the information had been so wrong. And then angry as we were all subjected to a lot of verbals from Fuller's guests. What made it worse was that we all knew then we wouldn't find anything, but we still had to go through the motions of looking.'

'Did any of the officers respond to those verbals?'

'DS Anderson started to have a go back but Shaw told him to be quiet.'

'What did Anderson say?' asked an intrigued Tom.

'I can't remember exactly what he said but it was something along the lines of they might have got away with it this time but eventually they'll be arrested. I was surprised just how angry, and if I'm being honest, unprofessional Anderson was, even though he was just saying what all of us were thinking.'

'Where had he been positioned?' asked Tom.

'At the left-hand side of the house. There was another side door there and, although it wasn't the one where we thought the delivery would be made, Shaw wanted to cover every possibility. Everyone knew that DS Anderson was Shaw's favourite officer and I think Anderson felt pretty much the same about Shaw. Presumably, as Shaw personally was on station outside the main target door, he must have wanted his most trusted officer on the other side door.'

'How did that make you feel?' asked Tom.

'About what?' asked a slightly puzzled Gary.

'About Anderson being Shaw's favourite.'

'Personally I didn't have a problem with Anderson. Actually, much as I hate to admit it he was quite a good guy. As I said, my problem was with DCI Shaw.'

'One last question,' said Tom. 'Was everyone radioed up that night?'

'Well, yes,' replied Gary, clearly puzzled by his question. 'As you know it's standard procedure during this type of operation. Good communication is vital in order to get the coordination right.'

'But didn't you say there was a problem with the comms?'

'There was. Well, at least, there was with my radio. There was intermittent interruption in transmitting and receiving. Looking back I think it was one of the reasons why the operation got screwed up.' He then added quietly, but more to himself than to Tom, 'Probably if the comms had been working properly I wouldn't be where I am now.'

Tom had to fight hard not to tell Gary what really happened that night. Here was a loyal and dedicated police officer who had become another innocent victim of the informant's treachery. But, of course, he couldn't say anything. Not yet anyway.

He just had to hope that somehow he could get to the bottom of this before Gary was cast onto the scrapheap.

It was early afternoon when Tom arrived back home after his visit to see DC Bennett. The first thing he noticed was a car parked immediately outside his house. Sitting in the car was Superintendent Peters. As soon as Tom pulled up on his drive Superintendent Peters got out of his own car. There were no formalities. 'Tom. I have some rather bad news for you,' he said, in his most serious voice.

'You'd better come inside then,' replied Tom.

His immediate thought was that Pauline had not been persuaded to drop the charges. This would not come as a surprise to him and he had, mentally, prepared himself for this eventuality. 'I suppose you're going to tell me she still wants to press charges against me.'

'Not quite,' he answered. 'Not least because she's dead. That's why I wanted to tell you myself, face to face, rather than over the phone.'

'Dead?' replied Tom, with genuine shock. 'When did that happen?'

'Our best guess is sometime between 10pm last night and 2am this morning. Although the post mortem will be able to give a more definite time of death.'

'How did she die?' he asked.

Tom noticed Peters' slight hesitation. 'I'm not sure that I should be telling you this, but we believe it was an accidental overdose. She was lying on the settee surrounded by an empty bottle of vodka and the usual drug user's paraphernalia when she was found by her son. He arrived back home just after 3am and found her lying there.'

'Why shouldn't you be telling me?' Tom asked, clearly puzzled by Peters' earlier comment.

Briefly Superintendent Peters remained silent before adding. 'Tom. I have to tell you that Pauline's son is accusing you of murdering her.'

'Me?' said Tom, with a disbelieving laugh. 'Why would he think that?'

'He's claiming that it was because of the rape allegation. This was your way of making sure that it never got to court.'

'Well, at least that will be easy to disprove,' answered Tom.

'Tom. Please don't take this the wrong way but you know I have to ask you. Where were you last night?'

'I was here all night,' he replied.

'Alone?'

'Yes, I was alone. I watched a bit of television and went to bed just after eleven. I read for a while and then put the light out just after eleven thirty. I woke up at about six thirty this morning and then got up at seven. Does her son have a theory as to how I was supposed to have done all of this?'

'Actually he does,' answered Superintendent Peters. 'He thinks his mum let you in. You plied her with alcohol until she passed out and then injected her.'

'Well it certainly adds a new dimension to all of this fantasy,' Tom replied. 'And what about the fact that there isn't one shred of evidence to back up his claim? Does he have a view on that as well?'

Superintendent Peters didn't reply to Tom's question. He simply said. 'Tom. This has now moved on from a rape allegation to a murder allegation. I know everything is circumstantial, but I'm afraid it's still going to look very bad for you. I think, in view of this, it would be better if we now formally interviewed you.'

Tom was now suddenly angry. 'Better for who? The Met or me? And by the way she had accused me of *attempted* rape, not actual rape.'

Once again Superintendent Peters chose not to respond. 'Apparently Pauline's son is threatening to go the press with this. In light of her earlier accusation against you I think it would be in your best interests to voluntarily attend for interview.'

Tom's anger had now momentarily disappeared as he said, 'Who's leading this investigation?'

When he replied there was no disguising the irony in Superintendent Peters' voice. 'Well it can't be Milner and so I've asked DCI Shaw.'

'DCI Shaw?' Tom said with a laugh. 'Don't you think there's something a bit ironic about that?' Before Peters could reply though, Tom provided his own explanation. 'I'm about to be interviewed by a person who is one of the prime suspects on my list of possible informants. It should be an interesting meeting.'

The more he thought about this situation the more he realised just how surreal it had now become. He had been genuinely shocked when he had heard about Pauline's death. He could only believe that it had been a terrible accident. His judgement on Pauline was that, despite her obvious character defects, she still loved life. She was an attention-seeker. That much was certain and that's why he couldn't buy into any theory that she might have deliberately taken her life. So that left two alternatives. Either her death was accidental or she had been murdered. The problem, however, was that if she had been murdered then he was the obvious suspect.

Chapter 40

'Mary. It's me,' said Tom.

He and Superintendent Peters had agreed that he should come to the station as soon as possible. There was little value to be gained in delaying his interview. And anyway, he felt, it was always better to be seen volunteering than being forced to do something. The interview had therefore been arranged for 5pm that evening.

'Is everything okay?' she replied, a little hesitantly, having recognised a hint of concern in his voice.

'I wish I could say that it was,' he answered. 'But I'd be lying.' He told her about his latest conversation with Superintendent Peters. 'So, I'm afraid our romantic dinner will have to wait for another day.'

'Tom. How can you sound so calm when you've been accused of attempted rape and now murder?'

'Well. Believe me I'm not that calm inside but there's nothing to be gained by getting angry. As I said, the interview is voluntary. It's not as though I've been arrested. And anyway, there is absolutely no evidence. Despite what you might have heard even the police can't arrest someone purely on the basis that a spurious allegation has been made. If that was the case then we would need to build hundreds more prisons.'

'Why don't I come round anyway. I can wait until you get back.' She then added, her voice now full of concern, 'You will be coming back tonight, won't you?'

'I hope so,' he replied, with a slightly forced laugh. 'Otherwise I really am in trouble.'

'Tom. Please don't joke about this. I'm sure this is largely for my benefit. If I stay at home I'll only worry about you. I'd much rather worry at your place than mine,' she said, not unreasonably.

'You're right,' he answered. 'You've got a key. Just let yourself in. I'll be back with you as soon as I can.'

After his conversation Tom had showered and changed into one of his better suits and then left for the station. If he was going to be formally interviewed he might as well look smart. Under normal circumstances he might have quite appreciated the challenge of being interviewed by DCI Shaw. It would, at least, be interesting to experience, at first hand, his interviewing technique. But, these were far from normal circumstances and he couldn't help thinking that perhaps he was clutching at straws a little.

The first person he saw as he entered the station was Milner.

'Sir? I wasn't expecting to see you here. Has something happened?' he asked with genuine concern.

Tom felt there was no point in trying to keep this from him. It would be common knowledge soon enough anyway. Better to hear it from him than from someone later in the canteen.

'Actually something serious has happened. You might remember that I asked you to check up on Pauline Jones.' Before Milner could reply, Tom continued. 'She was found dead early this morning. It looks like she overdosed on drugs and alcohol. But her son has it in his head that I murdered her. In light of her earlier allegation, it's appropriate that I make myself available for interview.'

'What earlier allegation?' asked Milner.

So Tom briefly told him about how he'd met Pauline, the subsequent rape allegation and now her death, and finished with, 'Her son is now accusing me of killing her.'

There was a look of shock on Milner's face as he took in what Tom had just said. 'Are you saying you've been accused of murder?'

'Fortunately, only as far as her son is concerned,' answered Tom.

'That's ridiculous.'

'I think so as well. Let's hope DCI Shaw also thinks that way.'

'Is DCI Shaw interviewing you?' asked Milner with undisguised astonishment. 'But you and he ...'

Before he could finish what he was about to say, Tom interrupted him. 'Myself and DCI Shaw have not always seen eye to eye. Is that what you were about to say?'

'Well, yes,' replied Milner.

'I'm sure DCI Shaw will want to conduct this as professionally as possible.'

They both remained silent for a while. Eventually Milner said, 'Is there anything I can do?'

'Thanks for the offer. Hopefully, though, I won't need to take you up on it.'

Tom made his way to the agreed interview room. He was met by DCI Shaw and DS Anderson.

'Sorry about this Tom,' said Shaw, surprising him by holding out his hand. 'Superintendent Peters has filled me in on the allegation which Pauline Jones made against you. He also told me how you had originally met,' he added, relieving Tom of one potential source of embarrassment. 'I've also read her file so I'm aware she has form when it comes to this type of allegation. I'm also sure the evidence will prove her death to be accidental but, you know as well as I do – actually probably better – what's involved in these interviews. Why don't we get this over with as quickly as possible.'

Tom spent the next forty-five minutes answering all of their questions. He confirmed how they had met, explained the letter, subsequent phone calls and visit from Pauline, and finally told them about his visit to try and persuade her not to keep contacting him. He had anticipated that this would be embarrassing and uncomfortable. In the event it was neither, largely due to Shaw and Anderson's professional but sensitive questioning. After the formal interview had ended Tom said, 'Am I allowed to ask where you are with this investigation?'

'I don't see why not,' replied DCI Shaw. 'You can probably guess anyway. It's early days, of course, but we've already started the forensics. As you know it's standard procedure in situations such as this but we are not expecting to find anything which might suggest foul play. Hopefully, this part of it is being completed right now. I'm expecting an interim report later today. After that it's just a case of waiting for the PM results.' He then added, 'Tom. I know it's been a tough day already but would you mind staying a bit longer? There's a couple of things I'd like to discuss with you.'

After they had entered his office, DCI Shaw closed the door and said, 'Thanks for doing this. I'm sure the last thing you need is for me to be asking you questions about your private life.'

'I don't think I can be precious about that given the situation I'm in,' Tom replied with a tight smile.

'I suppose not,' answered DCI Shaw. 'Anyway, all I wanted to say was, rest assured, I will do everything possible to get this resolved as quickly as possible. In my opinion the allegations won't stand up to any close scrutiny and will soon be proved to be what they are – trumped-up charges brought by an opportunist.'

'Thanks for that, Richard.' He laughed slightly. 'There's a real irony here don't you think?

'What do you mean?'

'Just the fact that a week ago we both found it difficult to give each other even the time of day. Now I'm being accused of murder and here you are, potentially the investigating officer, trying your utmost to defend me.'

'I see what you mean,' Shaw answered, now also laughing. 'And they say a week is a long time in politics.'

Momentarily Tom almost forgot why he was at the station. Almost, but not quite.

'If there's anything I can do I hope you now feel that you can ask me,' offered DCI Shaw. Just as Tom was leaving, he said, 'Tom. Just one final thing. Last Friday, when we had out little heart to heart, you must have also been thinking about what was going on with this woman. I have to say you never gave the impression that you were anything less than one hundred per cent focused on our discussion. If it's any consolation I think that was very impressive.'

'Thanks, but perhaps if I hadn't been so focused I might have thought a bit more carefully about my decision to go and visit her.'

He arrived home earlier than he had anticipated. As he pulled onto his drive he could see Mary's car already there. She must have seen him arrive because, before he could put his key in the lock, the door opened. Mary threw her arms around him. Eventually she pulled herself away from him. 'I wasn't expecting you back so soon. How did it go?' she asked nervously.

'Better than I feared, although this is just the start of it,' he answered. After he had filled her in on his conversation with DCI Shaw, they had dinner. Both of them realised that, due to the circumstances, this was never going to be one of their most relaxing times together. Tom was beginning to think that maybe it wasn't such a good idea after all.

Perhaps sensing this, Mary said, 'Tom. I hope you know that I'll always be here for you. Whatever the outcome.'

It was her final words which concerned him. The final outcome was now outside his control.

After a leisurely Sunday morning, and then lunch, any hope of this relative normality lasting for the remainder of the day was abruptly shattered when Tom's doorbell sounded.

Tom opened the door and was confronted by a worryingly official-looking DCI Shaw, supported by DS Anderson and two other uniformed officers.

As Tom was still taking all of this in DCI Shaw said. 'Tom. I'm afraid this is not a social visit. I'm going to have to ask you to come down to the station with us.'

'Are you arresting me?' asked Tom.

'No,' answered DCI Shaw, before adding rather ominously. 'Not yet, anyway.'

Chapter 41

They were back in the same interview room where DCI Shaw had held yesterday's interview with Tom.

'Do you own a brown overcoat?' asked DS Anderson.

'Yes, I do,' answered Tom, who regularly wore it when the weather was cold. In fact he knew that both DS Anderson and DCI Shaw already knew this.

'Could you tell me where you were between 9pm Friday night and 5am Saturday morning?' asked DS Anderson.

'I was at home,' replied Tom calmly and without any emotion. 'Alone,' he then added.

'What if I was to tell you that a person fitting your description, and wearing a brown overcoat, similar to the one which you own, was seen close to Pauline Jones's house at around midnight?' asked Anderson.

'Then I would say exactly the same thing. It was not me. I was at home in bed,' answered Tom.

'Have you ever been to her house?'

'Yes. Once. Just over a week ago. But I didn't go into the house. I had a discussion with her on her doorstep.'

'When we spoke yesterday you said you went there to persuade her to stop contacting you. You felt that she was becoming almost fixated with you. Is that correct?'

'That's correct. For some reason she thought that I was romantically interested in her. Pauline Jones had repeatedly contacted me. First by letter. Then by phone and finally in person. She was under the misguided impression that I felt some sort of affection for her. She wanted us to arrange to have dinner, or go out for a drink, together. I had tried to let her down as gently as possible but when this failed, and she started to increasingly make threats towards me, I decided I should visit her and try and convince her that what she was doing was futile.'

'And did you?' asked Anderson.

'No. In fact it was then she accused me of attempting to rape her on the day we first met.'

'And how did you meet?'

'We met via a dating agency a few months ago. It was obvious – to me at least – that we were not compatible. At the end of our dinner I could see she was the worse for drink and so I arranged for a taxi to take her home. I thought that would be the last time we saw one another but it is now clear she thought differently.'

'So why do you think she wanted to rekindle the relationship?'

'I don't know for certain, of course, but I suspect it had something to do with the fact that, very briefly, my face and name were in the media due to a high-profile case I had been involved in. I think she is – sorry, was – the type of person who liked being associated with such people. But, as I'm not an expert in psychology it's probably better if you ask someone who is.'

DCI Shaw then spoke. 'Were you worried that her allegations – whether true or false – would have a bad effect on your career?'

'Well, yes, I was. Even though I knew that what she was alleging was untrue I'm also realistic enough to know that, often, mud sticks in such situations.'

'Particularly if she was insisting her allegations were true and she was determined to progress them through the courts,' added DCI Shaw.

'That wouldn't help, of course,' answered Tom. 'But it's still a big jump from thinking this to then murdering her.'

'Could I take you back to when you visited Pauline Jones? Are you certain that you never went into her house?'

'Absolutely one hundred per cent certain,' answered Tom. 'Why do you ask?' he added, suspecting a leading question by DCI Shaw.

There was a period of silence before Shaw spoke. 'We have your DNA in Pauline's front room close to where her body was found.'

'My DNA?' replied Tom, clearly shocked by this worrying and unexpected development.

'The forensic boys found a few strands of hair. When they ran the tests the DNA matched yours. There's no doubt about it, they are your hairs. Then there's the sighting of someone resembling you close to her house.' He waited until the full implications of all of these revelations had sunk in before continuing. 'How do you think that might have happened?'

'I have absolutely no idea. But, once again and for the record, I have never been inside Pauline Jones's house.'

Tom's mind was now in overdrive. What started as infatuation had, within a very short period of time, escalated into stalking, a rape accusation and now an allegation of murder. Things could hardly get any worse.

Shaw then summarised the case against him. 'You stand to benefit from Pauline's death as she can no longer pursue the rape allegation. We have a witness who saw someone, fitting your description and wearing a coat similar to the one you own, close to her house at about the time of her death. And finally, despite your strong denials that you've never been inside her house, we have your DNA alongside her body. I have to tell you that things are not looking good for you.'

Tom found himself smiling. 'Well. Put like that I don't think even I could argue with you.' After a moment's silence Tom continued. 'So, what happens now? Are you formally charging me?'

'No. We have a few other things to do first,' answered DCI Shaw. He then handed Tom a piece of paper. 'I'm afraid one of those will be to search your house.' Tom had a quick glance at the search warrant. He noticed one of the signatories was Superintendent Peters.

'When are you planning to carry this out?'

'As soon as we can. I assume you will want to be there when we do it.'

'Can I ask what, specifically, you are looking for?' asked Tom.

'Your overcoat would be a start. We'll need to take that away for further examination. After that, frankly, I'm not too sure. I don't really expect to find a quantity of the drugs that killed her but ... well, let's see.'

Tom made his way out of the interview room and towards the reception area where he knew Mary would be waiting for him. As he did this he almost bumped into Superintendent Peters. Worryingly, Peters didn't even acknowledge him and just continued walking towards DCI Shaw.

When Tom was out of sight Superintendent Peters spoke to DCI Shaw. 'How did it go?'

'Well, he was clearly shocked when I mentioned the DNA evidence but, other than that, he held himself together very well.' He hesitated briefly and then said, 'I know everything is there. The motive, opportunity and the means but I still cannot believe that Tom did this. If he did then he must have known that the finger of suspicion would, eventually, point towards him. He would have had to be stupid to do it – and DCI Stone is not stupid.'

'Perhaps that was his failing,' answered Peters.

'What do you mean?'

'Maybe he thought he was too clever for us. But it looks as though he made a mistake. After all, the DNA evidence is indisputable.' Now it was Peters' turn to hesitate. Finally he said. 'Look Richard. I know Tom is a colleague of ours and so I understand your desire to give him the benefit of the doubt. But you should do this by the book. I don't want to see him receiving any special favours. All hell will break loose when this becomes common knowledge. It was only a few weeks ago that Tom was making the headlines for the right reasons. Can you imagine what the media will make of this when they find out? They'll have an absolute field day. So I don't want them accusing us of going easy on him. Have I made myself clear?'

'Crystal,' answered DCI Shaw.

Chapter 42

Tom and Mary were alone in his kitchen whilst the officers were searching his house.

'What are they looking for?' asked Mary. Earlier, on their way back home, she had become very upset. But now she was just angry. 'Are they always like this?'

'Well, they're just doing their job,' answered Tom.

'But must they do it with such obvious relish? It's almost as though they are getting some sort of pleasure from going through all of your things.'

'I'm sure they are as uncomfortable about this as I am. Probably more so,' he added.

'Well they certainly don't look it to me.' As she said this Tom could see she was beginning to get tearful again. He pulled her towards him. As they silently embraced Tom could feel her body trembling in time with her increasingly loud sobs.

As they continued to hold each other Tom could sense that they were no longer alone. He pulled away from Mary and immediately saw DCI Shaw standing by the kitchen door.

'Tom. I think we've just about finished. Just to let you know there are a few things we're taking away for analysis. Your overcoat for example, and a few other items of clothing. We will also need to take possession of your car.'

'I understand,' replied Tom in a matter-of-fact manner.

'What happens next?' asked a still angry Mary. 'Are you going to handcuff him and haul him away for more questioning?'

'No, because we have not arrested DCI Stone,' Shaw answered calmly. 'And whether or not we do will depend on us completing our investigations. In the meantime you are free to carry on as normal.'

'Carry on as normal?' said Mary now raising her voice. 'How are we to do that when this ludicrous accusation is hanging over us? Why don't you spend your time investigating Pauline Jones's background rather than trying to ruin Tom's career?'

'Mary. DCI Shaw is only doing what any other police officer – including me – would do in similar circumstances,' said Tom, hoping his words would help to calm the situation. When Mary spoke, however, it was clear that he had failed. 'I can't believe that,' she said, her sobs once again returning, before adding, 'Doesn't loyalty mean anything any more?'

'I'm afraid, where murder is possibly involved, loyalty has to take second place,' answered DCI Shaw. Then, turning his attention to Tom, he said. 'But you both have my word that I will do everything possible to get this resolved, one way or another, as quickly as possible. If it's any consolation, and despite the available evidence, I don't believe you murdered Pauline Jones.'

Mary looked at DCI Shaw. She had stopped crying. 'Really?' she said in her most withering voice.

It was late Sunday evening by the time DCI Shaw and the rest of the officers had left. Tom and Mary were back in his kitchen.

'I can't believe you were so reasonable with that detective,' said Mary, an obvious edge in her voice. 'I thought he was supposed to be a colleague of yours.'

'I can understand you feeling this way, Mary but, as I told you, he was only doing his job. Given the evidence they have I thought he went very easy.'

'Really? It didn't seem like that to me,' she answered. 'He looked as though he was enjoying the situation.'

'Maybe,' replied Tom.

Mary's anger had now been replaced by real concern when she next spoke. 'Tom, what do you think will happen?'

'I really don't know. It all depends on how strong they think the evidence is against me. I suspect at the moment it's not conclusive enough. But they might decide to arrest me anyway.'

'Why would they do that?'

'Probably because they don't want to be accused of showing me any favours. The police looking after their own. That type of thing. Anyway, we'll soon find out one way or another.'

Mary looked at Tom and said, 'You seem extremely relaxed about all of this.'

Tom simply shrugged. He couldn't admit to Mary that she wasn't too far wrong in her assessment. In a strange sort of way he now felt much better about things because now, at least, he knew what he had to do.

Mary had insisted she stay with Tom for the night. She said she didn't like the idea of him being alone, particularly after everything that had happened. Tom suspected though that it was as much for her benefit as his. Under normal circumstances he would have welcomed her offer but, of course, these were far from normal circumstances. Next morning he had reassured her that he would be okay and that he would call her if anything happened. The real reason, though, why he didn't want her to stay was that he had decided on a course of action that would raise the stakes even higher.

After she had left, Tom immediately called Milner. 'Morning, Sir,' said Milner in his most cheerful voice, before adding, this time with a little more anxiety. 'How are you?'

'I'm fine, thank you, although I have to admit that weekends are turning out to be not the most pleasurable parts of the week.' He continued, 'I expect you have heard that, although I have not been charged, there appears to be quite a bit of evidence implicating me. Or has the rumour mill not started yet?'

'I'm afraid to say that it's the talk of the station right now.'

'I bet it is,' answered Tom quietly.

'Sir. I want you to know that I don't believe it,' said Milner forcefully.

'Thank you for that. But, just for the record, I would like to confirm that I had nothing to do with her death.'

'You don't need to say that to me, Sir.'

'Well, I've said it now anyway. Although things don't look too good for me right now.' He hesitated briefly. 'And that's why I need your help.'

Milner seemed genuinely uplifted by Tom's request. 'What do you want me to do? You know I'll do anything to help.'

'Thanks. But I wouldn't be too hasty with your offer. You haven't heard what I'm asking you to do yet.'

Tom then explained exactly what he wanted Milner to do.

After he had finished there was a uneasy silence before Milner spoke.

'Are you sure that's advisable, Sir? It might not look too good if it ever got out.'

'That's true, of course, but I wouldn't ask you to do this if I didn't have my reasons. Plus, of course, given my current situation it's not something I could do myself.'

Their earlier silence returned. Finally Milner said. 'Of course I'll do it. As you say, you must have a good reason. When do you want me to start?'

'Well. How about tonight?'

After their conversation Tom suddenly felt guilty that he had asked Milner to do this on his behalf. Milner was right when he warned of the implications if it ever became public. What was creating his guilt, though, was not what might happen to his career but what might happen to Milner's. All he could do now was to wait and see if his suspicions were justified.

Chapter 43

The past couple of days had been some of the most frustrating Tom had ever experienced. The feeling of helplessness was overwhelming. He was not used to this inactivity, much preferring to keep himself busy. What made it worse, of course, was that he was now reliant upon the actions of someone else. Although he tried to keep himself occupied he found it almost impossible to forget about what he'd asked Milner to do.

On more than one occasion he had almost called Milner to tell him to stop doing what he'd asked. But he had always resisted doing it, mainly because he knew this was his best way of proving his innocence, even though he felt guilty about involving Milner.

DCI Shaw had called him to keep him informed about the status of their investigations. It was unofficial and, by doing this, Tom realised that, like Milner, DCI Shaw was taking risks with his career. Not that what he had to say was good news. In fact just the opposite as there was now a real possibility that formal murder charges would shortly be brought against him. They now had a witness statement from the person who had seen someone fitting Tom's description, which confirmed that, although it was dark, the overcoat worn by that person was similar to Tom's.

His mobile phone suddenly rang. As it was still only 7 am he knew it was probably one of three callers. Mary to see how he was. Milner to update him on what, if anything, he had found or DCI Shaw to say that they would soon be arresting him. He was relieved to see that it was Milner.

'Sir,' he said in that excited way of his when he had some important news to impart. 'I think we need to meet.'

Less than thirty minutes later Milner was standing in Tom's kitchen.

'Are you sure?' asked an almost disbelieving Tom.

'Sir, I was there all night. I know what I saw.'

Tom was silent for a while. Of all the possible scenarios he had played around with this was definitely not something he had even imagined possible. As he stood there, facing Milner, his mind was trying to understand all of the possible implications that would result from this dramatic information.

Right now though, he couldn't see how this latest turn of events was relevant to the Pauline Jones situation. Nonetheless, in his experience, one unexpected event often led to another and so he was not about to give up just yet.

'What do you want me to do now, Sir?' asked Milner, breaking the silence.

Tom still didn't immediately respond. Milner had worked with DCI Stone long enough now to know that in situations such as this, it was advisable to allow him thinking time.

Finally, Tom answered. 'Are you certain that you would like to carry on with this?'

'Absolutely, Sir,' he replied surprisingly enthusiastically, considering he had not slept the previous night.

'Okay. Here's what I would like you to do. You know this anyway but it's worth emphasising again. It's vital that no one else finds out what you are doing. Are you clear on that?'

As Milner didn't feel as though he needed to answer this he simply nodded instead.

For the rest of the day Tom continued working on his flip chart, although the first thing he did was to add the new contact line. As he surveyed this his concentration was broken when his mobile began to ring. It was Milner again.

'Sir? I don't know how you do it but I did what you suggested and guess what?' said Milner teasingly.

'I try not to guess if I can possibly avoid it. Please just tell me what you've found.'

And so Milner told him. Even Tom, who thought he had seen most things during his career, was stunned by Milner's information.

'I know it's been a long night and day for you already, but could you come round here again?'

'Just try stopping me,' replied Milner.

Even after his conversation with Milner had ended Tom's heart was still beating rapidly.

As he glanced once more at his flip chart he could see how

this latest information allowed him to now make sense of the almost labyrinthine web in front of him. The novice spider had suddenly become an expert. The more immediate question now, however, was what to do next. He decided a cup of tea would help. Yet again it had the desired effect, because he quickly made up his mind what he now had to do.

But whether or not it was the right decision only time would tell.

'Tom. You know I shouldn't be here. There's a real danger that my position on the case will be compromised,' said DCI Shaw, looking suspiciously at Milner. 'This had better be good.'

Tom, more than anyone, fully understood the risk which DCI Shaw had taken by being there. He had thought long and hard about calling him but, ultimately, he felt he had little choice. He needed help if he was to get to the bottom of this. And DCI Richard Shaw was the person who could give him that help.

'I suggest we all sit down before I tell you why I've asked you here.' When they were all seated at Tom's kitchen table he began his explanation.

'First of all let me say how much I appreciate you both coming here tonight. I realise this is – to say the least – all a bit unofficial but, hopefully, after what I have to tell you, you will see that I didn't have any choice.'

Tom then proceeded to tell them about how he had confided in Superintendent Peters his suspicions about an informant being responsible for the failure of *Operation Torch*. DCI Shaw started to interrupt by asking a question, but Tom simply asked if he could hear him out fully first.

He then moved onto what they had agreed with respect to the clandestine investigation. It was at this stage that DCI Shaw could contain himself no longer. 'So, the reason for our pleasant little chat at the station, was really because you suspected me of being your informant.'

'I'm afraid so. Well, the initial reason at least. If it's any consolation I removed you from my list afterwards,' he answered without any obvious embarrassment.

'I'm not sure it is,' answered DCI Shaw.

'Although I have to say, a secondary reason was to try and get to know you a bit more. Find out what motivated you.

But especially what prompted you to give up a lucrative legal career to join the police. You must admit that could be seen as a bit of a mystery.'

'And were you able to solve the mystery?' asked DCI Shaw, imperceptibly leaning closer to Tom.

'I think so. I believe it had to do with your father's death. I understand he was a member of the prosecuting team in a trial where Tommy Fuller was the defendant. Your father suddenly and quite unexpectedly withdrew from the case and Fuller was subsequently cleared of all charges. It wasn't too long after afterwards that your father died. I'm really sorry to have to awaken this memory for you.'

DCI Shaw was suddenly quite moved and, when he spoke, it was clear he was struggling to control his emotions. 'If you must know, Fuller, or at least one of Fuller's team, informed my father they had evidence of an affair my father was conducting. They let it be known that if he didn't withdraw from the case then it was likely mother would find out. She was quite ill at the time and so father clearly decided that he couldn't take that risk. Not because it might be detrimental to his career – which it subsequently was – but because he didn't want to make things worse for her. In the event both of them died not long afterwards.'

'Richard. I appreciate you sharing that. Was that the reason you joined the force? Was it to try and track down Fuller?'

DCI Shaw had now regained his normal confident manner. 'It was, yes. Not the most principled motive, I know. But that's why, of course, I was so focused on putting Fuller away. And by the way, that determination is as strong today as it as ever been. One day – before too long – Tommy Fuller will find himself serving a long, uncomfortable prison sentence.'

'Hopefully, you might be able to achieve your objective a bit sooner than you think,' said Tom. Before DCI Shaw could respond Tom held up his hand and said. 'Richard. I know you have a thousand questions but let me finish first.'

He then briefly told them why he thought there was an informant and how the earlier *Sunlight* operation had been so crucial in establishing Donovan's credibility. Finally, because he knew it was almost impossible to prevent any questions, he told them about the reason why there had been the confusion about who exactly gave the order to enter Fuller's house.

'For me,' said Tom, 'this was the final proof someone had deliberately intercepted the radio comms that night and interjected with the "go" order. It was your voice Richard. There's no doubt about that. But it had been pre-recorded.'

'How could that happen though?' asked DCI Shaw.

'For someone who had quite regular access to you, it was just a case of setting the recorder and waiting until you used a word or words that would mean "enter". In the event it was even easier than that as you must have said the word "go" at some point during the planning process with Superintendent Peters.'

This was the very first time Tom has mentioned Peters' name. It had the desired effect on DCI Shaw, although Milner, who had more information, didn't show any surprise.

'Superintendent Peters?' he said with a high degree of incredulity. 'You mean it's Superintendent Peters who is responsible for all of this?'

'That's what I thought – although it wasn't something that particularly delighted me. All of the evidence kept pointing to him. Initially it was mainly circumstantial but then, little by little, more hard evidence emerged. And then there was the situation with Pauline Jones.'

'What has that got to do with *Operation Torch*?' asked a puzzled DCI Shaw.

'I'm sure it didn't have anything to do with it, but it provided a perfect opportunity to discredit me. First there was the attempted rape allegation and suspension, after which I was ordered by Superintendent Peters to immediately stop working on our investigation. But I carried on and after I briefed him about the radio comms intercept, well, that's when things took a real turn for the worse. A few days later, I was your prime suspect for the murder of Pauline Jones.'

'I just can't believe this. Are you seriously saying that Superintendent Peters killed Pauline Jones because of what you had found out about *Operation Torch*?'

Before Tom could respond, DCI Shaw continued. 'And anyway, if Superintendent Peters was some sort of latter-day Moriarty, why was he doing all of this? I can't see what he would have to gain from it.' He then began to list everything which Peters had going for him. 'He's a senior police officer, clearly destined for higher office. Although, as far as I know, he's not wealthy, his salary must provide him and his family with a comfortable lifestyle. Certainly he never struck me as being overly materialistic. He's also a dedicated family man with a wife he loves and two beautiful children. What possible reason would he have to sell his soul to Fuller?'

'I'm not sure he was responsible for Pauline Jones's death. Well, not directly anyway.' Tom looked towards Milner. 'Why don't you tell DCI Shaw about the events of the past two days?' And so Milner did.

'That's incredible,' said a visibly stunned DCI Shaw, after Milner had finished. He then added just a single word. 'Unbelievable.'

'Well I agree with you on the first one,' answered Tom.

'What do you suggest we do next?' asked DCI Shaw. 'After all you've had the advantage of being aware of this for a little longer than I have.'

'I do have an idea but I will need help from both of you if it's to work.'

'Okay,' answered DCI Shaw. 'Let's hear what it is.'

Chapter 44

DCI Shaw was standing outside Superintendent Peters' office.
'What's this about?' asked Janice.

'Could you please inform Superintendent Peters that I have some important information relating to DCI Stone and the Pauline Jones case.'

DCI Shaw remained in the outer office whilst Janice spoke with Superintendent Peters. It wasn't long before she returned. 'Superintendent Peters will see you now.' She then added, making sure DCI Shaw was aware of the disruptive impact that his unannounced visit was having on today's diary, 'But he needs to leave for another meeting in ten minutes' time.'

'What I have to tell him won't take long,' explained DCI Shaw.

As Shaw entered the office, Superintendent Peters looked up from his desk. 'Janice said you have some information about the Pauline Jones murder. I'm assuming it couldn't wait until tomorrow.'

'Not really, Sir. In fact, you might decide to change your schedule after you've heard what I have to say.'

Superintendent Peters leaned forward slightly and said, 'Richard. You make it sound quite sinister.'

'I guess, in a way, it is. I just took a call from DCI Stone. To be honest he sounded quite odd. I thought at first he might have been drinking. Whatever the reason, he sounded very strange. He told me he had some information which concerned the security of this station and that it's linked to the death of Pauline Jones. In fact, he admitted that he was responsible for her death.'

'He admitted to murdering her?' asked Superintendent Peters.

'Well, no, not exactly. He just said he was responsible for her death. Anyway, he then said something about all of this getting too much for him. I assume he means the situation with Pauline.'

'And you said he also mentioned something about the security of the station. Did he provide any details?' asked Superintendent Peters.

'It was all a bit cloak and dagger really. He mentioned that he now had clear evidence that there was an informant within the station and that he wanted to tell me who it was. But to be honest it was all a bit garbled. Anyway, he asked if I could meet him tomorrow at his house and he'd explain everything and also hand over his evidence to me. He said it had all become too much for him.'

'And did you agree?'

'Well, yes. I didn't think I had any choice really. As I said, he sounded very strange. Almost as though he was at the end of his tether. So I've arranged to see him at ten o'clock tomorrow morning.'

Superintendent Peters remained silent as he absorbed the full implications of what DCI Shaw had just told him. Finally he spoke. 'I now see why you wanted to see me so urgently. Although I've only known Tom for a relatively short time, this behaviour seems totally out of character. Perhaps the pressure he has been under, first with the rape accusation and then Pauline Jones's death, has finally started to affect his mental health.' He hesitated briefly before adding, 'Call me immediately after you've seen him.'

As soon as DCI Shaw was back in his office he made a call. 'Tom. It's Richard. Were in play.'

By 7pm they were all once again assembled in Tom's kitchen. 'What time do you think things are likely to kick off?' asked Milner.

'My best guess would be some time after midnight. So, we all have a bit of a wait.'

'And what happens if, well, nothing happens?

'I'd be surprised if nothing happens,' answered Tom. 'They now think that you're seeing me tomorrow. So that only gives them a small window to act. Anyway, all we can do now is be patient. But it's important that you all remain out of sight.' He then looked towards DCI Shaw. 'Richard. I know we've gone through the plan a few times already but I'd feel happier if we did it one last time.'

'Okay. If you insist,' replied DCI Shaw, his voice reflecting that if it was up to him there was no need for yet another briefing. 'DS Anderson will be positioned outside, where he has a good view of the approaches to your house. DS Milner and myself will be here inside. Milner will also ensure that all of the tapes and videos are working.'

Earlier in the day Tom had spoken with Derek Johnson to ask if he could set up a number of small cameras, as well as a voice activated recording system, throughout the house. Derek was initially puzzled as to why this was happening in Tom's own home but, eventually accepted Tom's explanation that it was all part of an operation against a local drugs criminal.

DCI Shaw continued. 'I also have back-up on standby. Although let's hope we don't need it. The important thing is for us to get everything on tape.' He then added, accompanied by a slight laugh, 'And also, of course, to make sure that DCI Stone is not killed.'

'So, which of those two is your main priority?' asked Tom.

'Well, if you were in my position which one would you choose?'

'Good answer,' replied Tom, joining in the laughter.

The next few hours seemed to last forever as the evening turned into night. They had decided that Tom would turn off his lights and appear to go to bed just after midnight. By 2.30am they were beginning to think that nothing was going to happen. Then their radios sprang into life. 'We have company,' said DS Anderson. 'Looks like two people. One tall. One quite a bit shorter.' Then Tom's landline phone rang. He let it ring a few times and then answered and simply said, 'Hello.'

'I have something that you might be interested to hear,' said a male voice.

'Who is this?' asked Tom.

'That doesn't matter. I have information about one of your officers who is selling information to Tommy Fuller. Are you interested?'

'Of course I am. But how do I know this information is genuine?'

'You will when you see it,' answered the voice.

'When can I see it?' asked Tom.

'Right now if you want. I'm outside your house.'

'Wait there until I get dressed and I'll let you in.'

'Right this is it,' said DCI Shaw. 'Let's all stay relaxed. No panic. We go on my order.'

Tom waited for a few minutes and then opened his front door. He didn't have to wait long before the two figures appeared. Tom couldn't make out who they were. Both were wearing full overcoats and hats which had been pulled down to cover the upper part of their faces. Ominously they were also wearing gloves.

When they got to where Tom was standing the taller of the two said quietly, 'Inside would be better – unless you want the whole street to hear what we have to say.'

Tom led them both into his front room. He still couldn't make out their faces.

'You might as well sit down now that you're here,' suggested Tom.

'We'll stand. What we have to say won't take long,' said the taller one.

'So. What's so important that you get me out of bed at this time of the night?' asked Tom.

'It's this,' said the tall one, taking off his hat and then suddenly pulling out a gun and pointing it directly at him. It was Tony Donovan.

Tom's face betrayed his surprise and then real fear as he focused his attention on the gun. 'What do you want?'

'Your file on the informant for starters,' he replied. 'And then your silence.'

'How do you know about that?' asked Tom.

'We know everything you do.' He then continued, even more menacingly. 'Just give us the file or we'll have to find it ourselves.'

'And what if I don't?'

It was the other person who replied, removing their hat. 'Then we will just have to persuade you.'

Tom turned to look directly towards the speaker and saw that it was Janice, Superintendent Peters' PA.

Chapter 45

'You?' said Tom. 'What have you got to do with all of this?'
'You really don't know, do you?' she replied angrily. 'Well, let me tell you. You might know me as Janice Clarke. I changed my name to Clarke by deed poll a few years ago. But my maiden name is Fuller. Does that help to explain things?'

'Fuller?' repeated Tom. 'You mean you're related to Tommy Fuller?'

'Tommy's my uncle. My father was Patrick Fuller. Remember him? He was gunned down in cold blood by the Met.' Worryingly she was now starting to get very angry. 'He was shot like a dog. He wasn't carrying anything. He wasn't even given any warning. Just murdered in broad daylight, on the streets of London. And guess what? No one in the Met was even reprimanded, let alone prosecuted. What sort of justice is that?'

She paused to regain some composure. 'I swore then that I would do everything possible to avenge the murder of my father.' She was now in full flow, almost as though she had waited a long time to unload all of her pent-up emotions. 'To begin with I just wanted to kill those people who were responsible, but there were too many. So I decided a much better way would be to destroy the Met from the inside. That's why I joined and then worked hard to get to the position I have today. PA to a Detective Superintendent within the West London Region. It was only a question of time before we would work our way to even higher positions. Then I could really damage the Met.'

'We? Does that mean Superintendent Peters is also involved in all of this?'

'Of course not,' replied an indignant Janice. 'He doesn't know anything about it. I just used his position to get access to all of the reports and information.'

'So why are you doing this now?'

'It was that slimeball Shaw. I knew why he had joined the

Met. It was to put Uncle Tommy away for good. When he came to Superintendent Peters with his plan to do it, we knew that it was time to act. So we devised our little plan to draw him in and then totally discredit him. He was so smug after *Operation Sunlight* that we could have told him anything and he would have believed us.'

'Are you saying that *Sunlight* and the arrest of O'Driscoll was all a set-up?

'Of course it was. But it was Shaw who was set up. Set up to do our dirty work and close down O'Driscoll's operation so that we could move in. Two birds with one stone. It worked perfectly. After that, we knew it was only a matter of time before Shaw would go for us, so we decided we would encourage him a bit. That way we would control the agenda and timetable. And finally the ending.'

'So you also knew about *Operation Torch*?' asked Tom.

'Knew about it? It was me who thought of the idea of getting Tony to play Shaw's supergrass.' As she said this she started to laugh. Still laughing, she carried on. 'And he fell for it hook, line and sinker. How stupid he was to think that Tony would sell out Uncle Tommy. They grew up together for God's sake. The footage of the raid that night is priceless. The Met were made to look so foolish and incompetent. After that Tommy's operation was almost untouchable.'

When Tom heard this he laughed inwardly, thinking back to his conversation with DCI Shaw and their own references to Elliot Ness and his untouchables.

'And what about Jimmy Ryan?' asked Tom, judging this to be a good opportunity to try and obtain the truth about his murder.

Suddenly Janice became serious again. 'Jimmy Ryan was a loose cannon. He was stupid as well as a junkie. We should not have used him to contact Shaw. That was a mistake. We received word that he was starting to get above himself, bragging to his mates about his role in the sting. We couldn't take the risk.'

'So you killed him?'

'Not me personally. It's Tony who's the expert,' she said, looking directly at Donovan. She continued. 'He had to go. And anyway, suspicion for his murder was bound to fall on O'Driscoll.'

'And did Pauline Jones have to go as well?' asked Tom, asking, at least as far as he was concerned, the most important question of all.

'Her death was your fault,' she said with real conviction. 'She would still be alive if you hadn't gone to Superintendent Peters with your informant theory. After I found out she had accused you of attempted rape it gave us the perfect opportunity to use her to turn the situation against you.'

Now it was Tom's turn to become angry. 'But why did you have to murder her? She had nothing to do with any of this,' he said, his voice rising.

'But she knew you,' answered Janice. 'It was too good an opportunity to miss.' She then started to laugh again. 'The famous Detective Chief Inspector Stone dating a known prostitute and drug user. I can't wait for that to make the papers.'

Tom didn't respond to her comments, although he understood only too well what it would do to his reputation as well as that of the Met. 'So it was you who placed those hairs alongside Pauline?'

'Very good. Did you work that out all by yourself?' she said sarcastically. 'I took them from your overcoat when you came to see Superintendent Peters.'

'And then you killed her?' asked Tom.

'She was just a drunk and a druggie who would have killed herself soon anyway. We just helped her on her way.'

Tom was genuinely shocked by her callousness but suddenly their two-way conversation was interrupted by Donovan. 'Janice. We don't have much time. Let's get this over with. The sooner we get out of here the better.'

'Get what over with?' asked Tom, with a sudden sense of foreboding.

Janice answered. 'We'd like you to give us everything you have on your investigation, and then write a brief suicide note for us. After that Tony is going to kill you.'

Tom was surprisingly calm as he said, 'If you're going to kill me anyway, why would I do anything for you?'

'Because if you don't we'll also make sure that your precious girlfriend ends up like Pauline.'

Tom's earlier anger now resurfaced. 'Mary has absolutely nothing to do with this. She would be a totally innocent victim.'

'So was my father,' answered Janice calmly.

It was at that moment that DCI Shaw decided to act and suddenly the room was filled with noise as Shaw, Milner and Anderson burst into the room.

'Stay where you are!' Shaw shouted. Milner and Anderson immediately went for Donovan, who, although taken by surprise, was still holding the gun in his right hand. As Anderson tried to grab it, Donovan lashed out with his other hand catching Milner a glancing blow on his cheek, who immediately let out a cry of pain.

Donovan was momentarily distracted by Milner's shout and this distraction gave Tom the opportunity to grab the gun. By now Milner had rejoined the struggle to overpower Donovan and, between the three of them, they finally managed to restrain and then handcuff him.

DCI Shaw took hold of Janice, who started to struggle as he held her, and only stopped her resistance after he had managed to get handcuffs on her as well. By the time the back-up arrived both Donovan and Janice no longer presented any physical danger, although Janice remained verbally aggressive.

'You knew, didn't you?' she shouted at Tom. Then, directing her attention towards DCI Shaw, she said, 'You set us up.'

'Now you know how it feels,' he replied.

Chapter 46

Tom and DCI Shaw were in Superintendent Peters' office. ' I can't believe it. Janice?' But why?'

DCI Shaw briefly explained her connection to Patrick and Tommy Fuller and finished by adding, 'She saw it as her mission in life to seek retribution for the death of her father.'

'And she was willing to have two people killed just to achieve her objective?' Peters asked rhetorically.

After a brief pause DCI Shaw said, 'Don't forget that she also came to Tom's house with the intention of killing him as well.'

As he said this Superintendent Peters looked at Tom. 'I really don't know what to say to you, Tom. Other than I am so, so sorry that I doubted you.'

'Well I suppose, from your standpoint, the evidence was mainly circumstantial. If I was looking at this dispassionately I would have to say it was pure genius,' replied Tom. 'A brilliant plan which, if it had worked, would have meant that Fuller would be able to control the streets of West London with impunity.' He then added. 'And Janice would have achieved her ambition.'

Superintendent Peters then asked the question which Tom and DCI Shaw knew would be the most difficult to answer. 'How did you find out it was Janice?'

It was Tom who answered. 'At one stage I thought it might be you, Sir.'

'Me? What possible reason would you have to think it might be me?'

'I had a few actually, Sir but the main one was that every time I came to you with evidence, things seemed to happen almost immediately afterwards. And usually at my expense. It was just too coincidental. And so I had you followed one night.'

'Followed?' repeated Peters incredulously.

'I'm afraid so. I felt I just had to find out one way or another.' He paused before carrying on. 'That was how we found out about your affair with Janice. You were seen going into Janice's house a couple of nights ago, and not leaving until the following morning.' He added, 'There's also photos of you both together ... if you want to see them.'

Peters' right hand covered his face. For one moment he looked as though he was about to break down. 'Photos? Oh my God.' Eventually he removed his hand and said. 'Of course I knew it was wrong, personally as well as profession-ally, but I just couldn't help myself. It was almost as though I was being swept along, helplessly, by a huge tidal wave.'

Tom then continued. 'After we found about you and Janice we did a bit of digging into her background. It wasn't long before we found her family link to the Fullers. Once we knew that, everything else just fell into place.' As he said this he thought back to his spider's web chart. 'God knows how her family connection to Patrick Fuller was missed. Perhaps they bribed or threatened someone in the records department to remove any reference to Fuller. Anyway, that's for another day.'

DCI Shaw took up the story. 'Tom then contacted me and explained everything. We decided we needed to flush her out. That's why I came to see you yesterday to tell you about Tom's phone call. Although, of course, there hadn't been a phone call. It was Tom's idea,' he said, looking at Tom. 'He guessed that if I came to see you, and told you about the vital information he was going to hand over to me, then that would prompt a reaction. At least that's what Tom called it. I would call it attempted murder.'

'Why didn't you bring me into this?' asked Superintendent Peters. Before either of them could answer he added, 'You used me instead.'

'We really didn't have a choice,' answered Tom. 'For all we knew you and Janice could have been planning this together.'

Superintendent Peters now became angry. 'And what possible motive could I have that necessitated two murders?'

'Your affair with Janice,' replied Tom. 'Illicit sex can do strange things to a man – particularly a married man.'

For one moment it looked as though Superintendent Peters was about to respond even more angrily to Tom's comment.

But he clearly thought better of it and simply said softly, 'So, what happens next?'

'Janice and Donovan were arrested last night – or rather this morning – and DCI Shaw arrested Tommy Fuller just over an hour ago.' As he mentioned the last name he looked at DCI Shaw. His face betrayed no emotion. 'They have all been charged with murder. I'm confident that we will also be able to put away a few of the others as well, once we start digging a bit deeper.'

'And what do you propose to do about me?'

'Well, we're not planning to arrest you, if that's what you mean,' answered Tom. 'I don't think it's a criminal offence yet to have an affair. Although your wife might feel differently.' Tom instantly regretted saying that. 'I'm sorry, Sir. That was unnecessary.' He carried on. 'But, of course, we will have to include your relationship with Janice in our report as it was that which allowed Janice to obtain the information she needed to make her plan work. I'm afraid you will also have to vacate your office for a while. We have a team outside who want to do a sweep of these offices. We believe that Janice bugged them to hear all of your conversations. After that, it will be up to Detective Chief Superintendent Small and the other top brass.'

'I can't believe she called me a slimeball,' said DCI Shaw. He started to laugh. 'A bit harsh, wouldn't you say?'

They were all in Tom's office. 'I've heard you called worse,' answered Tom, after which they all joined in the laughter.

'What do you think will happen to Superintendent Peters?' asked Milner, repeating almost word for word the very same question which Peters himself had asked earlier.

'That will be for those in higher positions than us to decide,' Tom answered. 'Fortunately. But it certainly will not enhance his career prospects. And that's a real shame because Superintendent Peters is a top cop. As far as his marriage is concerned,' he added with some understatement, 'I can only imagine he's in for a very difficult time.'

'Milner. I meant to congratulate you for tackling Donovan. That was a very brave of you, especially as he had that gun in his hand,' said DCI Shaw.

'Or foolish,' added Tom, looking directly at Milner.

Milner chose not to respond to either of the comments,

although, once again, he instinctively touched his cheek. Tom sensed it was only now that the full implications of what they had done were starting to sink in.

'That reminds me,' said DCI Shaw. 'Donovan's gun has been sent over to ballistics. Hopefully, they will be able to confirm that it was the same gun used in the shooting of Jimmy Ryan.'

'Let's hope so,' answered Tom. 'I'd just like to personally thank every one of you for doing this. I know just how much a risk it would have been to your careers if it had all gone wrong. Anyway, thanks for believing in me.'

'It was your evidence. It was just so compelling. Anyone would have acted on it,' explained DCI Shaw.

'Maybe,' replied Tom, not entirely convinced.

A smile suddenly appeared on DCI Shaw's face. 'Anyway, what about a drink later? It's not every day that our station has such a result.' He looked towards Tom. 'Remember our little conversation about celebrating success? I think this falls into that category. In fact, I might even buy them myself.'

As they all got up to leave his office, Tom said to DCI Shaw, 'Richard. There's something else I'd like to discuss with you.'

'Oh no,' he replied with a slight laugh. 'You haven't got another conspiracy theory have you? I think we've had enough excitement for one day.'

'Fortunately not. It's about DC Bennett.'

Suddenly DCI Shaw stopped laughing. 'DC Bennett? What is it you want to discuss?'

A short while later they were both standing outside DC Bennett's house in Feltham. Tom rang the bell and the door was opened almost immediately. 'DCI Stone? Was Gary expecting you?' asked Julie.

'Not really. But I have some news for him which I'm sure he will be interested to hear.'

'Good news?' asked Julie with an obvious nervousness in her voice.

'I think so,' answered Tom. 'By the way, this is DCI Shaw.'

The mention of Richard's name only added to her general concern. She looked warily at DCI Shaw. 'I'm not sure Gary will be happy to see you. He is not your number one fan.'

'I understand that,' answered DCI Shaw. 'And frankly I

don't blame him. I'm here because I'd like to apologise to him in person.'

'Really?' replied Julie, in a tone which suggested she couldn't quite believe what she had just heard. They followed her into the kitchen. 'Gary. You have some visitors.'

When Gary saw DCI Shaw his face suddenly betrayed his anger. 'You've got some nerve coming to my house. Have you come to deliver another disciplinary letter in person?'

Tom was tempted to interrupt but decided it would be better if DCI Shaw handled this himself.

'Gary. I'm here to apologise to you,' said DCI Shaw.

'Apologise? You?' replied a still disbelieving Gary.

'Believe it or not I can do apologies. Well, occasionally anyway.' Before Gary could respond, Shaw continued. 'I was wrong about your role in *Operation Torch*. And I was definitely wrong to instigate disciplinary proceedings. That was inexcusable. I'm sure you could find some rather stronger language to describe my behaviour, although, I have to tell you that I was called a slimeball earlier today.'

Gary ignored Shaw's attempt at humour. 'What's all this about?' he asked, still in the dark as to why DCI Shaw was saying this.

'I think DCI Stone is best qualified to answer that.'

Tom briefly explained the day's events and especially the problem with the radio comms.

After he had finished Gary looked directly at DCI Shaw. 'So, where does that leave me with the disciplinary hearing?'

'I've already stopped that. I've also formally written to the panel to inform them that there are no grounds for progressing this, that you are totally innocent of the allegations and that I take personal responsibility for wasting their time.' He paused briefly before adding, 'And I would like to invite you back onto the team as soon as you feel you're ready to return. Take your time though. Your job will be there waiting for you when you decide to come back. I really would like you back on the team.'

Chapter 47

Tom and Mary were once again together at Tom's house. Before going to the pub with the rest of the team the previous evening, he had called her and explained what had happened. Of course she was overjoyed to hear what he had to say and wanted to come round immediately to see him. But as it would be late by the time he returned from the pub, Mary had reluctantly agreed with Tom's suggestion to delay their reunion until Saturday afternoon.

Before then Tom had something else he needed to do. It was just before ten o'clock and he and Milner were standing outside Anna's front door. Tom had a rectangular parcel in his hands. Milner rang the bell and shortly afterwards the door was opened by Anna. Tom could immediately see from her appearance that the past few days, since the confirmation of Maciej's death, had taken their toll on her. She had dark circles under her eyes and her face had an almost ghostly complexion. It took a while before she recognised them.

'Would it be possible to come in?' asked Tom. 'We have something that we'd like to give to you. Something that Maciej would have been proud of.'

As she led them into the main room they passed a few half-filled suitcases and bags.

'Are you leaving?' asked Tom.

'There's nothing to keep me here any more, so I'm going back to Warsaw,' she replied, more than a hint of sadness in her voice.

'I'm truly sorry to hear about Maciej.' He paused briefly as Anna started to cry. 'I just wanted to tell you that Detective Sergeant Milner has arrested the people who were responsible. Maciej's death was a tragedy, I wanted to tell you that he died defending the honour of his great-grandfather *and* his country.'

Anna looked up. 'What do you mean?'

So Tom told her about the metal thefts and then about the one from the Polish memorial. He finally told her about why Maciej had confronted Walker and the others. After he had finished he reached down to pick up the rectangular parcel and started to unwrap it. It was a bronze plaque which listed the names of some of the Poles who had died in Britain during the Second World War. He had found it during their first search of the scrap yard. After he had unwrapped it he held it up. 'You can see there,' he said, pointing at it, 'a name you might recognise.'

As she looked at the memorial, Anna could immediately see that it listed the names of Polish fighter pilots who had died during the Battle of Britain. Just over halfway down the list she did indeed see a familiar name. It simply read:

Stanislaw Sipowicz, killed in action, 15th September 1940.

At the very bottom there was another legend which offered further explanation.

Members of 303 Polish Squadron who all died in the defence of liberty.

Tom handed it to Anna. 'I think Maciej would have been very proud of this.'

Later, back at home, Tom and Mary were holding each other although Mary was crying, her tears a mixture of relief and joy.

Eventually she pulled away from him. 'Tom Stone. Don't ever do that to me again. I really thought I was going to lose you.'

'I don't suppose it's any consolation but the thought did occasionally cross my mind as well.'

'Why didn't you tell me about what you were doing?'

'It would only have worried you.'

'So you think I wasn't worried when they arrested you?' she answered, suddenly quite angry.

'Well, technically at least, they didn't *actually* arrest me but I agree that it wasn't looking too clever for me.' Before she could respond he continued. 'Mary. You've every reason to be angry with me. But I took the view that the less you knew about it the better. I know you shrugged it off, but once Janice knew about me and you, she had something else to use against me. Trust me. She wouldn't have hesitated to hurt you. Anyway, it all worked out well in the end.'

'Worked out well in the end? Aren't you forgetting the fact that you were accused of attempted rape and then murder? And as if that wasn't enough you then had a gun pointed at you by a gangster who was just about to kill you.'

'I see what you mean,' said Tom, grateful that he hadn't also told her about Lomas threatening him with a knife. 'Put like that I suppose I have had better times.'

'Why do you joke about it? You could have been shot.'

'I have to admit that was a bit of a scary moment. Fortunately, though, Milner came to my rescue.'

'There you go again,' she said.

A brief uneasy silence followed before Mary spoke again.

'Tom. I'm sorry. I suppose we all handle things differently. I get angry when I think how I could have lost you. Please promise me that you won't do anything like this again.'

Tom didn't answer. Instead he pulled her towards him and hoped, for the time being at least, that they could both forget that he was a policeman.

Lightning Source UK Ltd.
Milton Keynes UK
UKOW041551250912

199592UK00001B/10/P